D0485684

PRAISE F...
DEIRDRE MARTIN

Total Rush

"*Total Rush* is just that—a total rush, an absolute delight. Deirdre Martin is the reason I read romance novels. This contemporary romance is so well-written, [it] has a hero to-die-for and a romance that turns you into a puddle. It fills your heart to overflowing with love, acceptance, and the beauty of uniqueness. I laughed, I cried, I celebrated. It's more than a read, it is a re-read. Brava, Ms. Martin, you're the greatest!"   —*The Best Reviews*

"The book is well-written and makes you want to keep turning the pages to see what happens next."
                                        —*The Columbia (SC) State*

"Martin's inventive take on opposites attracting is funny and poignant."   —*Booklist*

"A heartwarming story of passion, acceptance, and most importantly, love, this book is definitely a *Total Rush*."
                                        —*Romance Reviews Today*

"Fast-paced, sexy, fun yet tender, the pages of *Total Rush* practically turn themselves. This is Deirdre Martin's third novel and is as sensational as the first two. It's now Gemma Dante's turn to find love, and the attraction between her and Sean is dynamite. *Total Rush* is a definite winner."   —*Romance Junkies*

continued . . .

Fair Play

"Martin depicts the worlds of both professional hockey and ethnic Brooklyn with deftness and smart detail. She has an unerring eye for humorous family dynamics [and] sweet buoyancy."
— *Publishers Weekly*

"Fast-paced, wisecracking, and an enjoyable story . . . Makes you feel like you're flying."
— *Rendezvous*

"A fun and witty story . . . The depth of characterizations and the unexpectedly moving passages make this an exceptional romance and a must-read for all fans of the genre."
— *Booklist*

"A fine sports romance that will score big-time . . . Martin has provided a winner."
— *Midwest Book Review*

"Sure to delight both fans of professional ice hockey and those who enjoy a good romance."
— *Affaire de Coeur*

Body Check

"Heartwarming."   —*Booklist*

"Combines sports and romance in a way that reminded me of Susan Elizabeth Phillips's *It Had To Be You*, but Deirdre Martin has her own style and voice. *Body Check* is one of the best first novels I have read in a long time."
                        —*All About Romance* (Desert Island Keeper)

"Deirdre Martin aims for the net and scores with *Body Check*."   —*The Romance Reader* (Four Hearts)

"You don't have to be a hockey fan to cheer for *Body Check*. Deirdre Martin brings readers a story that scores."
                                        —*The Word On Romance*

"Fun, fast-paced, and sexy, *Body Check* is a dazzling debut."   —Millie Criswell, *USA Today* bestselling author of *No Strings Attached*

"Fun, delightful, emotional, and sexy, *Body Check* is an utterly enthralling, fast-paced novel. This is one author I eagerly look forward to reading more from."
                                        —*Romance Reviews Today*

"An engaging romance that scores a hat trick [with] a fine supporting cast."   —*The Best Reviews*

THE PENALTY BOX

Deirdre Martin

Northern Plains Public Library
Ault Colorado

BERKLEY SENSATION, NEW YORK

THE BERKLEY PUBLISHING GROUP
Published by the Penguin Group
Penguin Group (USA) Inc.
375 Hudson Street, New York, New York 10014, USA
Penguin Group (Canada), 90 Eglinton Avenue East, Suite 700, Toronto, Ontario M4P 2Y3, Canada
(a division of Pearson Penguin Canada Inc.)
Penguin Books Ltd., 80 Strand, London WC2R 0RL, England
Penguin Group Ireland, 25 St. Stephen's Green, Dublin 2, Ireland (a division of Penguin Books Ltd.)
Penguin Group (Australia), 250 Camberwell Road, Camberwell, Victoria 3124, Australia
(a division of Pearson Australia Group Pty. Ltd.)
Penguin Books India Pvt. Ltd., 11 Community Centre, Panchsheel Park, New Delhi—110 017, India
Penguin Group (NZ), Cnr. Airborne and Rosedale Roads, Albany, Auckland 1310, New Zealand
(a division of Pearson New Zealand Ltd.)
Penguin Books (South Africa) (Pty.) Ltd., 24 Sturdee Avenue, Rosebank, Johannesburg 2196, South Africa

Penguin Books Ltd., Registered Offices: 80 Strand, London WC2R 0RL, England

This is a work of fiction. Names, characters, places, and incidents either are the product of the author's imagination or are used fictitiously, and any resemblance to actual persons, living or dead, business establishments, events, or locales is entirely coincidental. The publisher does not have any control over and does not assume any responsibility for author or third-party websites or their content.

THE PENALTY BOX

A Berkley Sensation Book / published by arrangement with the author

PRINTING HISTORY
Berkley Sensation mass-market edition / March 2006

Copyright © 2006 by Deirdre Martin.
Cover art by Monica Lind.
Cover design by Lesley Worrell.
Hand lettering by Ron Zinn.
Interior text design by Kristin del Rosario.

All rights reserved.
No part of this book may be reproduced, scanned, or distributed in any printed or electronic form without permission. Please do not participate in or encourage piracy of copyrighted materials in violation of the author's rights. Purchase only authorized editions.
For information address: The Berkley Publishing Group,
a division of Penguin Group (USA) Inc.,
375 Hudson Street, New York, New York 10014.

ISBN: 0-425-20890-7

BERKLEY® SENSATION
Berkley Sensation Books are published by The Berkley Publishing Group,
a division of Penguin Group (USA) Inc.,
375 Hudson Street, New York, New York 10014.
BERKLEY SENSATION and the "B" design are trademarks belonging to Penguin Group (USA) Inc.

PRINTED IN THE UNITED STATES OF AMERICA

10 9 8 7 6 5 4 3 2 1

If you purchased this book without a cover, you should be aware that this book is stolen property. It was reported as "unsold and destroyed" to the publisher, and neither the author nor the publisher has received any payment for this "stripped book."

For my brother,
Bill,
who daily proves F. Scott Fitzgerald wrong

Acknowledgments

Thanks to:

Jon and JoAnn Epps, Mike and Jacquie Powers, Nancy Herkness, and anyone else I might have missed who shared their youth hockey stories with me.

My husband, Mark, for his patience and good humor.

Elaine English and Allison McCabe.

Mom, Dad, Bill, Allison, Beth, Jane, Dave, Tom, and the "lads" for continually reminding me what's important.

CHAPTER

01

According to Katie Fisher, there were two types of people in the world: those who attended high school reunions, and those who did not. She herself definitely fell into the latter category, which is why she almost passed Diet Coke through her nose when her mother casually informed her she'd taken the liberty of RSVPing the invitation to Katie's tenth high school reunion, saying she would attend.

"You did WHAT?" Katie gasped, inhaling an ice cube.

"I thought it would be fun," her mother replied gaily, transferring a chicken casserole from the oven to the counter. She glanced over her shoulder at Katie with concern. "Are you all right, dear?"

"Fine," Katie rasped. "Nothing like a good choke to end the day with."

"Oh, you." Her mother, a small, cheerful, doughy woman, clucked her tongue. She'd never quite gotten Katie's sense of humor.

Having narrowly avoided death by ice cube, Katie filled with dread at the thought of revisiting Didsbury High's class of '96. She wasn't a curmudgeon, or antisocial, or uppity. Nor had she contracted an unsavory social disease the way Lulu Davenport had, farted in the middle of chemistry class like Magnus Pane, or ruined the school's annual production of "The Nutcracker Suite" by crashing into a cardboard Christmas tree onstage like Bridget Devlin. Katie's sin had been unpopularity. High school had been painful.

She'd grown up poor, the result of her father having died young, forcing her mother to support the family on a factory worker's wages. It shouldn't have made a difference—tiny Didsbury, Connecticut, prided itself on being a mixed community with rich and poor alike—but it did. In the status-driven world of high school, to be rich was to be "in," to be poor "out." Katie had been a girl in clean but unfashionable clothing who came from the wrong part of town. A girl who hadn't had a home PC or a cell phone, who'd used public transportation because her mother hadn't had a car she could toodle around in on the weekends. Not that she'd had anyone to toodle around with.

Katie had also been brainy. Super-scary-knows-the-answer-to-every-question-the-teacher-asks brainy. To be a teenage brainiac was completely uncool, especially for a girl. It scared people. Especially guys. Especially jocks.

Last but not least, Katie had also been fat, which in high school was the equivalent of being an untouchable. She was the girl whose pants size exceeded her age. Boys had walked behind her in the hall making oinking noises. Girls had slammed her into lockers or invited her to phantom social events.

Nerdy, poor, and dumpy. Three strikes and you're out. The story of Katie Fisher's adolescent life.

Just thinking about it got her annoyed at her mother all over again.

"I can't believe you did that to me." She cringed as her mother deftly sprinkled Day-Glo orange Velveeta on top of the casserole and slid it back into the oven. "No *way* am I going."

Her mother clucked her tongue again. "Did what to you? You'll have fun. You'll get to see all your old friends."

"And who would that be? Ronald McDonald?"

"I don't know why you're so hard on yourself, Katie. You're a beautiful girl. You're a successful professor of sociology."

"*Now*," Katie corrected. "I wasn't *then*."

"All the more reason to attend the reunion."

So that was why her mother wanted her to go. She wanted her former loser of a daughter to go forth and gloat.

Maybe her mom was on to something here. Maybe it would be fun to walk into the reunion in her now svelte body and ramp up the va-va-voom, just to watch their jaws drop. Or to casually mention in conversation that she was now teaching at prestigious Fallowfield College in Vermont. Katie Fisher, the class of '96's biggest loser, back in town in a big way. Vengeance is mine, sayeth Katie. But that wasn't who she was. Nor was it why she was back in Didsbury.

She was on a yearlong paid sabbatical, working on a book about sports and male identity. She could have stayed in Fallowfield to write the book; most of her research and interviews were done. But there was her nephew.

"Where's Tuck?" she asked her mother, who was now humming to herself as she set the table for dinner.

Her mother frowned. "Upstairs on that computer you bought him."

"Mom, he needs the computer for school. Believe me."

"His eyes are going to go bad, playing all those crazy

games. He sits up there for *hours*." Her mother shot her a
look of mild disapproval. "It's not good, Katie."

Katie knew that look. Tuck was behaving the way Katie
once had, hiding away in his room. Though Tuck was only
nine, Katie knew he viewed his bedroom as his refuge, the
one place where he could escape and not have to face the
fact that his mother preferred a drink to him, and that no one
knew who his father *was*, his mother included. Katie knew
firsthand how painful being fatherless could be. She'd filled
the void by turning to food, while her sister, Mina, had em-
braced booze and bad behavior instead. Katie wanted to
make sure Tuck didn't follow in her sister's footsteps.

She almost said something to her mother about Mina
screwing up Tuck but held her tongue, knowing it would
only upset her. Plus, she had to give credit where it was due.
Mina *was* trying to get her act together. She had entered a
residential rehab facility six weeks before. And Mina did
have the presence of mind to ask their mother to take in
Tuck while she was away. Tuck loved his grandmother, and
she loved him. But that didn't mean she had the energy or
the means to care for a moody little boy who had seen and
heard things he shouldn't have. Katie decided to spend her
sabbatical year in Didsbury to help her mother take care of
Tuck. She wanted Tuck to know there was another adult in
his life, apart from his grandmother, upon whom he could
always count.

Taking the last plate from her mother, Katie set it down
on the table. "I'll talk to Tuck if you want. Tell him to get
out more, maybe join the Knights of Columbus or start playing golf."

Her mother shot her another look, albeit an affectionate
one. "Thank you, Miss Wiseacre. He loves you, you know.
Thinks you're the bee's knees."

"I think the same of him. And please don't use expres-

sions like 'Bee's knees'. It makes you sound like you're an-
cient, which you're *not*."

"Tell that to my joints." She gave Katie's arm a quick
squeeze before hustling back to the stove to check on the
broccoli. "So, you're going, then?"

"To talk to Tuck? I just said I was."

"No, to the reunion."

"Mom—"

"Promise me you'll at least think about it, Katie."

"Why is this so important to you?"

"It's not. I just think it'll be good for you, that's all."

"Mom, I *hated* high school. You *know* that. I would rather
watch C-Span than deal with any of those people again."

"But you're different now, and I bet they are, too. Or
some of them. Go."

"I'll think about it. But I'm not promising anything."

"You'll go," her mother trilled confidently.

Katie just rolled her eyes.

"*I hate when* she's right," Katie muttered to herself as she
slumped behind the steering wheel of her Neon at the far end
of the parking lot, the better to spy on former classmates entering Tivoli Gardens. The Tiv was a faux Bavarian catering
house that served overcooked Wiener schnitzel and soggy
tortes. Management made the male waitstaff dress in leder-
hosen and occasionally yodel, while Tiv waitresses sported
the "lusty serving wench clutching a beer stein" look. It was
the only space in town large enough to accommodate an
event like a reunion.

Katie had pretty much made up her mind not to go. But
then she started thinking about what her mother had said.
She *was* different. She had changed a lot in ten years. Didn't
it stand to reason that some of her former classmates had

changed, too? The more she thought about it, the more curious she became. Who was different and who was the same? Who was divorced, married, successful, single, gay, unemployed, a parent, incommunicado, dead? Who'd stayed in town and who'd left?

Besides, she was a *sociologist*. It was her job to analyze the collective behavior of organized groups of human beings. Going to the reunion would be like doing research.

That wasn't why she was going, though.

To be honest, she was there because she had something to prove. She wanted to see everyone's eyes bug out when they realized who she was. She knew it was petty to turn up with a not-so-hidden agenda that screamed, "Ha! You all thought I was a big fat loser, and look at me now!" but she couldn't help it. She was human and wanted, if not revenge, then satisfaction. She wanted to see the "Wow, that's Katie Fisher!" in their eyes.

So here she was, dressed to the teeth and wearing more makeup than a drag queen at Mardi Gras. At least, that's how it felt. Normally, Katie dressed casual but conservative: tweed blazers, turtlenecks, chinos, and practical shoes for running across campus. Rarely did she wear her long blond hair up, or even loose; she usually pulled it back in a ponytail. But not tonight. Tonight it was up, soft golden tendrils falling around her oval face. She'd poured herself into the tightest little black dress she could find, showing off every firm curve of the body she killed herself to maintain. When Tuck had said, "Wow, Aunt Katie, you look *hot*!" she'd blushed furiously because it was true: She *did* look hot.

Eyeing the dashboard, Katie checked the time. Eight thirty. A few people were still arriving, but most had to be inside by now. She could picture them standing in small clusters laughing, the ice in their drinks tinkling as their lips moved nonstop: *Remember this, remember that?* Panic

seized her. Maybe she shouldn't have come. She popped an
Altoid in her mouth and took a deep breath. *The cruelties of
the past can't hurt me now. Sticks and stones can break my
bones, but names can lead to years of therapy. No! Think
positive! You can do this. You're attractive and successful.
Remember: you're here as a sociologist observing group behavior.*

Head held high, Katie slid out of the car and headed for
Tivoli Gardens.

The minute Katie spotted the pert hostess in the red peas-
ant skirt and green velvet bodice standing outside the banquet room, she wanted to bolt. But Katie wasn't a quitter:
She made herself put one foot in front of the other until she
and Heidi were face-to-face.

"Guten Tag!" the woman said brightly. "Here for the reunion?"

Katie nodded.

"And you are—?"

Katie cleared her throat. "Katie Fisher."

The woman skimmed her list of attendees. "Ja, here you
are." She handed Katie a name tag. "Would you like to fill
out the 'All About Me!' form?"

"Form?"

"Just to tell people a little about yourself and what you're
up to now. At the end of the night, awards are given out. You
know: 'Least Changed,' 'Most Children,' things like that."

Katie discreetly backed away from the woman. "No,
thank you."

Heidi pointed to the door behind her. "The reunion is
being held right here in the Rhineland Banquet Room." She
flashed Katie a retina-burning smile. "Have a *great* time!"

"I'll try," Katie mumbled, affixing the name tag to her

dress. She toyed with the idea of not wearing it just to be rebellious, but that seemed kind of dumb. Besides, how rebellious could you be in a place named the Rhineland Banquet Room?

The pounding undercurrent of a bass guitar coming from within made the ground beneath her feet shake as her hand lingered on the door. *Do I really want to do this?*

Steeling herself, Katie slipped inside. Her eardrums were immediately assaulted by a DJ blasting Toni Braxton's "Unbreak My Heart," a song that had been popular the year she graduated. The evening would be filled with all the songs of 1996, good and bad. A banner hung from the far end of the banquet room proclaiming, "Welcome Back Didsbury High School Class of '96! I Believe I Can Fly!", the latter line a reference to the R. Kelly song that had been her graduating class's anthem. Katie had always thought the Beatles's "Free As a Bird," also a hit that year, would have been more apropos. At least, that was how *she'd* felt on graduation day.

She had to hand it to the reunion committee: The tables ringing the room looked great. Each had burning crimson tapers and a centerpiece of red roses and white carnations — their school colors. She could have done without the tacky napkins and glasses with "I Believe I Can Fly!" printed on them, though. A small dance floor had been set up in front of the DJ. Cocktail hour was in full swing. Just as she'd imagined, her former classmates stood in small groups, talking and laughing. Her stomach wobbled as she realized she would have to *join* one of these groups if she wanted to talk to anyone. She needed a drink.

She walked carefully to the bar, teetering in her too-high heels. It was stupid to have bought them, considering she'd probably never wear them again. But she had to admit they did make her feel sexy. Maybe there was life beyond Easy Spirit.

"A sea breeze, please," she told the bartender, who winked in response and began mixing her drink. Katie watched him work, finding it easier to face the bar. A tap on her shoulder made her turn. Behind her stood a large, smiling woman wearing so much perfume Katie's eyes started to burn.

"Hi, I'm Denise Coogan! And you are"—she squinted at Katie's bosom—"Katie Fisher! Ohmigodyoulookfantasticgoodforyou!"

"Thank you." Katie wracked her brain. Denise Coogan. Denise Coogan. She was drawing a blank. She smiled apologetically at the heavily made up woman. "I'm so sorry, but I don't remember you. I remember your brother, though. Dennis?"

The woman chortled. "Honey, I *am* Dennis! Or I was. Now I'm Denise. Grab that sissy drink of yours and I'll tell you all about it."

For the next ten minutes, Katie listened to Denise/Dennis outline the horrors of being a woman trapped in a man's body. "I can empathize," said Katie. "For years I was Jennifer Aniston trapped in the body of Marlon Brando." Denise howled her appreciation.

Hovering on the periphery, Katie noticed Alexis van Pelt motioning to Katie to join her. Katie hesitated; although Alexis was one of the few people ever to be nice to her in high school, she was standing among a small group of former cheerleaders. The mere sight of these women filled Katie with apprehension; still, she made herself approach them. The increasingly baffled expression on Alexis's face as Katie came closer told Katie that Alexis thought she was someone else. She gasped audibly when she read Katie's name tag.

"Oh my God! Is that really you, Katie?"

"It's really me."

"Wow!"

The other women in the group—Tanya Donnelly, Marsha Debenham, and Hannah Beck, all of whom had worked hard to make Katie miserable in high school—also looked shocked. Marsha, once suspected of having an eating disorder, had put on some weight, and Hannah had obviously spent the last ten years out in the sun: there were the beginnings of crow's feet around her small green eyes. Tanya still looked like a brunette stork.

"You really look great, Katie," said Marsha in a voice quivering with admiration.

Katie blushed. It felt odd, receiving praise from these women. But it also felt good. Maybe her mother was right; perhaps she wasn't the only one who had changed.

"How did you do it?" Marsha wanted to know.

"Had my jaw wired shut."

The women chuckled appreciatively.

Tanya Donnelly, who had once thrown Hershey bars at Katie in the cafeteria, touched her arm. "We were just talking about what stuck-up bitches we were in high school."

Katie felt the nervous flutter return to the pit of her stomach. "Oh?"

"I'm really sorry about the way I treated you," Hanna Beck murmured, looking uncomfortable. "I have a baby daughter, and the thought of anyone being as awful to her in school as we were to you . . ." She shuddered.

Heat flashed up Katie's face. "Thank you. It means a lot to hear that."

"Let's face it: Being a teenager sucks!" Alexis declared, gulping her drink.

"I'll raise my glass to that!" Marsha echoed.

Katie was in a daze as she listened to the friendly cross chatter of female voices. The last thing she'd expected from these women was an apology or being treated warmly. Yet here they all were, gabbing away about their lives, asking about hers and seeming genuinely interested in what she had to say. Maybe the past was just where it belonged: in the past.

Then Liz Flaherty showed up.

Of all the rich, perfectly dressed rah-rah girls who'd given Katie a hard time in high school, Liz topped the list. Once, over a long period of weeks, she pretended to be Katie's friend, eventually inviting her to a party at the house of Jesse Steadwell, one of the most popular guys in school. Katie was so excited she could barely contain herself. Invited to a party! Finally! But when she rang the Steadwells' doorbell, no one was home. It was only when she was walking back down the driveway that Liz and her friends popped out of the bushes, laughing at her and calling her a loser. By the time Katie arrived at school the following Monday, the story had made the rounds. Complete strangers were coming up to her jeering, "How was Jesse's party?"

"Hi, everyone!" Liz squealed. She looked almost the same as she had in high school: thin, tan, with long, caramel colored hair and big green eyes. Her makeup was impeccable. She wore a killer red sheath dress. She continued her girlish squealing as she hugged each woman in turn. But when she came to Katie, she froze.

"It can't be." Her face contorted in disbelief.

Katie made herself smile warmly. "How have you been, Liz?"

"Fine." Her laugh was mirthless. "Well, I guess miracles really *can* happen."

"No miracle," said Katie. "Just years of hard work."

The atmosphere, so congenial mere seconds before, began crackling with tension. Liz looked Katie up and down with a coolly appraising eye.

"I'm surprised to see you here, Katie."

"Why's that?"

"Well"—Liz glanced at the other women for confirmation—"because you were such a fat loser in high school."

The other women glanced away.

Katie met the challenge head-on. "People change. Or, at least, some people do."

"Meaning?"

"You're *exactly* the same as you were in high school."

Liz smiled as she sipped daintily from her champagne flute. "I'll take that as a compliment."

"Katie was telling us about the book she's writing," Hannah Beck said tentatively.

Liz sucked in her cheeks, bored. "That's nice. Katie, remember that time Paul van Dorn pasted a sign on your back that said 'Built like a mac truck'?" She laughed as if it were the funniest thing in the world.

Katie said nothing. *Paul van Dorn* . . . there was a name she hadn't heard in a while. Paul had been the boy every girl in school had a crush on, Katie included. He'd been Liz's boyfriend, of course. They were the golden couple: captain of the hockey team and head cheerleader. When he was apart from his friends and Liz, Paul had always been nice to Katie. But the minute he hooked up with his crew, he teased her mercilessly like everyone else.

To Katie's chagrin, Liz Flaherty continued goose stepping down memory lane. "Remember in gym class, when Mr. Nelson made us do the five hundred yard dash, and Katie collapsed because she was so fat and out of shape?" No one answered as all eyes dropped to the ground. "Oh, come on, I know you guys remember!"

"Can it, Liz," Alexis said under her breath.

"What?" Liz batted her eyes. "All I'm doing is reminiscing! That's why we're all here, right? To remember?" Another sip of champagne slid down her throat. "I was thinking about the prom on the way over here. I went with Paul." Her gaze glittered with malice. "But I can't seem to recall who *you* went with, Katie."

Katie smiled brightly. "Actually, I had two dates to the prom: Ben and Jerry. Can you excuse me a moment?"

She said her good-byes to the other women and quickly extricated herself from the group, quivering so hard inside she thought she might break. She'd always used humor and self-deprecation to deflect criticism and pain. It sprang from a determination never to let her tormentors see they'd gotten to her. That she'd just been forced to use two of the old weapons in her arsenal made her sad.

It had been a mistake to come.

No, that wasn't true. The mistake had been thinking Liz Flaherty could ever be anything but a bitch. Katie had meant what she said, though Liz had failed to see the irony: Liz *was* the same person she'd been in high school. Clearly the woman was insecure as hell. Katie knew she could have called her on it, but it seemed pointless. Draining the remains of her glass, she returned it to the bartender, hustling as fast as she could toward the banquet room door and the promise of blessed release. Her heart was hammering in her chest, her mind was a kaleidoscope of painful memories she'd been foolish to think she could avoid. She was walking so fast in her heels that when she hit a wet spot, she went flying. Were it not for the lightning fast reflexes of the man who reached out to grab her, she would have wound up spread eagle on the floor. Mortified, Katie slowly looked up into her savior's face to thank him.

It was Paul van Dorn.

CHAPTER

02

"Katie? Katie Fisher?"

"The one and only," Katie replied, smoothing the front of her dress. She couldn't believe how close she'd come to complete humiliation. Nor could she believe how little the man before her, who still had a protective grip on her forearm, had changed. Same killer body, same ice-blue laser beam eyes piercing her soul. His hair was different: buzzed as opposed to the stick-straight blond she remembered. But everything else was pure Paul van Dorn, right down to the brash confidence he exuded.

His eyes were wide as saucers as he continued staring at Katie. "Holy sh—" He caught himself, releasing her from his grasp. "Are you okay?"

"Yes, thanks to you." Her gaze shot back to Liz Flaherty, who thankfully seemed oblivious to Katie's near tumble.

"I . . ." Paul was at a total loss for words. Slack-jawed.

Katie laughed. "Yes?"

"I . . ." His eyes remained riveted to her body. "I cannot believe how *great* you look!"

"Thank you," Katie murmured. "So do you."

"Me?" Her statement seemed to catch him by surprise. "Nah, I'm just the same."

I hope not, Katie thought.

He put his hands on his hips, slowly shaking his head in disbelief. "This is unreal. Never in a million years would I have guessed it was you. If it wasn't for the name tag . . . damn! You're leaving already?"

"Yes. I'm not feeling well."

Paul's eyes made another slow tour of her body. "You look pretty healthy to me." His blatant appreciation made Katie feel like a specimen under the microscope. Uncomfortable, she turned away.

"I'm sorry," Paul apologized. "I can't help it. You just look so . . ."

"Hot?" Katie supplied hopefully, turning back around.

Paul laughed. "Yeah, hot. How long you in town for?"

"For the year. I'm on sabbatical, writing a book."

"You're a writer?"

"I'm a sociologist. Mainly. I teach at Fallowfield College. In Vermont?"

Paul nodded. "Soc 101 with Professor Katie Fisher. Maybe I'll take your class sometime."

"I thought you went to Cornell, Paul."

"Yeah, but I never graduated. Most of my time was spent at Lynah Rink."

"Ah."

"What's your book about?" he asked.

The desire to extricate herself from this conversation was strong. She was sure it was only a matter of time before he, like Liz Flaherty, reminded her of his past superiority to her. Yet Paul was easy on the eyes; part of her wanted to keep chatting. And, insane as it sounded, she sensed he was interested. "Sports and male identity."

"Really." Paul raised a skeptical eyebrow. "Want to fill me in?"

"Like I said, I'm a sociologist. I mainly study athletes, and I thought it would be interesting to explore the role sports plays in defining the masculinity of American men."

"I see."

"Society today lacks the initiation rituals that were part and parcel of tribal societies. The result has been that men are confused about being men."

Paul's gaze turned unexpectedly seductive. "I'm not."

Flustered, Katie continued, "My book is about how sports offers young men a way to experience masculine relationships, rituals, and values—things they would have received in a tribal setting. I also want to show that there's a relationship between the construct of male identity and sports as a social institution, that is, one which is regulated by—"

Paul held up a hand. "Gotcha."

"I'm sorry." Katie clasped her now clammy hands together. "I have a tendency to get carried away when I'm enthusiastic about something."

Paul looked amused. "I can see that." He rubbed his chin thoughtfully. "Hmm. Maybe I can help you out."

"Really? Would you be willing to be interviewed?"

"Sure."

"That would be great, especially since I'm trying to understand not only boys and men who are currently involved in sports and how it affects them, but ex-athletes as well."

Annoyance flickered across the handsome face. "Just because my career is over doesn't mean I'm an 'ex-athlete.'"

Katie blinked. "Right. Of course. Well, let's think about

setting up an interview sometime. How long are *you* in town for?"

"The rest of my life, Katie."

Knowing her mother would squawk if she came home too early, Katie left Tivoli Gardens and drove directly to the Barnes and Noble two towns over. Didsbury had yet to join the twenty-first century: There were no big box bookstores, no Starbucks, no multiplexes. Katie appreciated the quaintness, but she'd grown used to life in a vibrant college town where music, dance, lectures, indie films, ethnic restaurants, and, most important of all, skim-milk lattes, were readily available. Coming back to Didsbury was like stepping back in time.

She ordered a skim-milk latte and sat browsing through a big stack of magazines until enough time had passed for her mother to believe she'd been whooping it up at the reunion. Now, walking through the front door of her mother's house, she was greeted by the familiar sight of her mother sitting on the couch, absorbed in her needlepoint, occasionally lifting her head at the sound of something blowing up on the TV.

"Katie!" Her mother looked up. "How was the reunion? Tell me all about it!"

"It was nice," Katie said, joining her mother on the couch.

Her mother frowned. "Specifics, I want specifics."

"Well, there was someone there who used to be a man but is now a woman."

Her mother coughed nervously. "What else?"

"A couple of the guys I graduated with died in Iraq a few years ago."

"I'd heard that," her mother murmured. She put aside her

needlework and looked at Katie hopefully. "Were your old friends there?"

Yup, Katie longed to say, *Mickey D was there, and so was Little Debbie and the Frito Bandito*. Who were these mythical "old friends" her mother kept referring to? Her refusal to deal with the reality of Katie's life in high school was incredible. But it had always been that way. Katie would come home from school, her mother would ask how her day was, Katie would tell her some girls had started calling her Miss Piggy, and her mother would dismiss it with, "Oh, they didn't mean it." Or "Oh, you must be exaggerating." Her mother simply couldn't deal with the fact that her oldest child was a misfit. Her penchant for denial had been even stronger when it came to Mina, who started sneaking out at night to meet her druggy friends right after their father died. "Mina would never do that," her mother insisted. It wasn't until Mina dropped out of high school and then got pregnant with Tuck that her mother reluctantly admitted that her younger daughter was troubled.

Not wanting to burst her mother's bubble, Katie took the easy way out: she fibbed. "Yes, all my old friends were there. It was great to see them."

Her mother nodded knowingly. "I told you it would be fun."

"It was until Liz Flaherty showed up."

"Oohh, that little bitch."

"Mom!" Katie was genuinely shocked. Her mother rarely spoke ill of anyone.

"Well, it's true," her mother sniffed. "Everyone in that family has their nose so high in the air you can see the back of their throats! You'd think with all the money they have they'd give more to the Sunday collection plate at church, but no. They're cheap as a Woolworth's suit." Her mother paused a moment to watch a police shootout on TV. "She's back in town to stay, you know. Divorce," she said distractedly.

"Who, Liz?"

"Yes." She turned her full attention back to Katie. "Married some older man for his money—as if she didn't have enough!—had a child the first year they were married, and then took him for all he was worth. She's a bad seed, that one."

"Mom? Can I ask you a personal question?"

Alarm sprang into her mother's eyes. "As long as it doesn't have to do with s-e-x."

"How do you *know* these things?"

"It's a small town, Katie. People talk. A lot of dirt gets dished over coffee and cake after church."

Katie leaned forward to take off her high heels. "So, have you church ladies heard anything about Paul van Dorn?" she asked casually, wiggling her toes.

"Oh, that poor boy."

"What?" Katie was surprised. He looked pretty darn okay at the reunion. She wondered what could make him a "poor boy". A beautiful wife who died tragically young? Mazarati in the shop for repairs? Manhattan penthouse not big enough?

"You know he was a hockey star. In New York."

"Yes, Mom, I knew that," Katie said patiently. For a while, it was all anyone had been able to talk about in Didsbury: how Paul van Dorn went straight from Cornell to the NHL. Katie half expected the Chamber of Commerce to erect a statue of him in the town square.

"Well, he was forced to retire early. Three bad concussions in a row. The doctors told him if he kept playing he risked severe brain damage. His mother said he still gets dizzy spells. She makes a wonderful apple crisp, you know."

Forced to retire early. So that's why Paul's face had registered such naked pain when she'd asked him how long he was in town for. His hockey career was over at twenty-eight. *Poor boy is right,* Katie thought with genuine sympathy. She tried to imagine not being able to do the one thing you love best, but couldn't. It had to be awful.

"Remember Cuffy's Place on Main Street?"

Katie knew about it, though she had never set foot inside. Everyone knew Cuffy's; it was Didsbury's favorite tavern. It was also a dive.

"Please don't tell me he's working there."

"Working! He owns it!"

Katie's mouth fell open. "Paul van Dorn owns *Cuffy's*?"

"Well, it's not Cuffy's *anymore*. Cuffy wanted to retire and Paul bought it. Now it's called the Penalty Box. He redid the whole interior. Their curly fries are supposed to be terrific."

Katie wasn't surprised Paul had come back to Didsbury, scene of his earliest glory days. All the research she'd done indicated that men who primarily identify themselves as professional athletes have a hard time figuring out what to do once their careers are over. It wasn't uncommon for them to open bars or restaurants, since it was a way to continue receiving public adulation. She wondered how Paul was dealing with the Icarus-like plunge from fame to mere mortality. She supposed she'd find out, since he'd agreed to be interviewed. God, she loved being a sociologist. The whole world was her laboratory.

"Was Paul at the reunion?" her mother asked.

Katie nodded. "I talked to him for about five minutes." She bit nervously at the inside of her mouth. "He wasn't one of my favorite people in high school, to be honest."

Her mother looked amused. "Then why all the questions about him?"

"Just curious." Katie rose, stretching. "I'm beat. I think

I'm going to head upstairs to bed. Night, Mom." She kissed her mother's cheek before gathering up her shoes and heading toward the stairs.

"I'm so glad you went to the reunion," her mother called after her. "I told you it would be fun."

Katie wasn't sure *fun* was the word she would have chosen to describe her evening. But it had sure been interesting.

"*No more drinks,* people, or one of you will have to carry me home!"

Paul laughed, turning down the latest beer someone at the reunion tried to ply him with. As he'd expected, he was the center of attention. Old friends and barely remembered acquaintances alike pressed drinks on him, all paying homage to Didsbury's hockey hero. Holding court at his table, he regaled his former classmates with tales from life in the NHL and encouraged them to come down for a drink at the Penalty Box, which he knew they would.

Answering questions about particular games or particular players never bothered him. But whenever someone expressed sympathy for what had happened to him, Paul had to fight against the knee-jerk response to get up and walk away. He saw pity in their eyes, and if there was one thing he didn't want, it was pity. He had enough of his own.

He could still remember losing a midget hockey game because of a bad call by the ref. He'd railed against the injustice of it, and what had his father's response been? "No one ever said life was fair, kiddo." If anyone knew that now, it was him.

For five years, he'd been the New York Blades' wunderkind, the boy with the magic hockey stick who could do no wrong. Though he'd started out on the third line, within a year and a half he'd moved up to the second. By the end of his second year on the team he was on the first line, out skating and outscoring even the most seasoned opponents.

And then Trevor Malvy of Detroit caught him coming across center ice with his head down, and his world began to crumble.

Malvy fractured Paul's skull. An X ray showed it was minor stuff: basilar, not uncommon when you fall and hit the back of your head. There were some small concussive signs—nausea, and for a few days, Paul's eyes didn't seem to focus too well—but he hadn't become disoriented or lost consciousness on the ice, and that worked in his favor. Within three weeks, he was back on the first line, tougher than ever.

The following season, he was carrying the puck into Tampa's defensive zone when bam! Next thing he knew he was kissing the ice courtesy of defenseman Wally Marzullo. Even Paul had to admit that one was bad. He was seriously concussed: dizzy, nauseous, temporary amnesia, the whole nine yards. But he was a good boy and did what he was told by the doctors and trainers, taking it easy even though every game he missed was like a knife in his heart.

Triumphant, he returned to the ice. Six months later he was seriously concussed again by Ottawa's Ulf Torkelson, and Paul knew his career was over.

Just thinking about it made Paul feel like someone had slipped a bag over his head and he couldn't breathe. The six months following the final hit were the worst of his life. He got blinding headaches, couldn't remember things, jumbled words, lost his balance. Just walking up a flight of stairs left him exhausted. The Blades' trainers told him to be patient and give himself time to heal, but all Paul could think was: For what? Everyone knew he was finished, even if no one had the guts to say so. In the end, the only one with the balls to speak the truth was the neurologist, who said, "Get hit

again and you're going to wind up with shit for brains, son."
It didn't get any blunter than that.

And so, begrudgingly, he retired. Better to bow out at the
top of his game than hang on and risk being a vegetable,
right? At least that's what he told himself. But deep down,
he remained furious that his body had betrayed him.

"You sure you don't want another Heineken, lamby?"

The purr of Liz Flaherty's voice brought him out of his
reverie. She'd been hanging over him all night, blabbing
about how it was "fate" they were both back in town. Paul
wasn't so sure. Yeah, she was still hot, but she was also a
hellcat. Once she got her claws into him, he'd need a sur-
geon to remove them. Paul waved the beer away. "I'm fine,
Liz, thanks."

She brushed her nose seductively against his cheek.
"Want to dance again?"

"I'm too drunk."

"That never stopped you from dancing—or doing other
things—before," she whispered in his ear.

Irritated to find himself aroused, Paul ignored her. Why
couldn't it be Katie Fisher murmuring suggestively in his
ear?

It was incredible that Katie had become a drop-dead gorgeous woman. Writing about jocks, too. What was that
about? Maybe it was a form of revenge, studying the people
who had been absolute and total pricks to her. In his younger
years he'd been a prick to lots of people, including other athletes. He chuckled, recalling the way he'd busted on former
teammate Michael Dante when he had first joined the
Blades. What an arrogant little twerp he'd been. Now
Michael was one of his closest friends, one of the few ex-
teammates who kept in touch. He took a long sip of water,
hoping to quell the nausea burbling in his stomach. He'd
definitely had too much to drink.

"Penny for your thoughts." Having been unable to lure him back out onto the dance floor, Liz stayed glued to his side at the table.

"Actually, I was thinking about Katie Fisher."

Liz snorted. "What about her?"

"Did you *see* her? She looks like an entirely different person."

"I don't think that was really Katie. I think she hired someone to come here and play her. The real Katie is at home on a reinforced couch inhaling Oreos."

Paul frowned. "Why are you such a bitch?"

"Oh, excuse me! If I remember correctly, *you* were the one who thought it would be funny to nominate her for homecoming queen. And—"

"Point taken," Paul snapped. He'd forgotten about that. No wonder Katie looked so wary when he was talking to her; she probably thought he was going to play some joke on her that would result in her humiliation. Part of him always liked Katie Fisher. People would call her names and make fun of her, but Katie always held her head high. She was like an athlete in that way: She took the abuse and showed no fear and in the end, she earned respect. He respected Katie for not giving her tormentors the satisfaction of seeing her pain. But in retrospect, he hated himself for having caused so much of it. Maybe that's why his career ended early. Bad karma. What goes around comes around. He decided he'd make it up to her. If she remembered she'd asked him, he'd definitely talk to her for her jock book.

Liz was standing behind him now, massaging his shoulders. "You're very, very tense, Paul."

Closing his eyes, he let his head loll forward. "I'm also very, very drunk."

"Do you want me to drive you home?"

Let Liz drive him home. Now there was a thought. A bad one.

"Nah. I'll take a cab, thanks."

Liz playfully smacked his shoulder. "Oh, don't be such a martyr! I do know how to drive, Paul." Her mouth dipped down to his ear again, her hot breath teasing his senses. "As you may recall, I know how to do *lots* of things."

He was tired. He was drunk. He was lonely.

"Fine," he murmured, fumbling in his pocket for his car keys, too weary to fight her off any longer. "Drive me home."

"Aunt Katie?"

Katie had just turned out the light and slipped between the covers of her old bed when Tuck appeared in the doorway. It was strange, being back in her old room. Everything looked the same as it did when she'd departed for college: same nicked desk, same narrow bed, same lace curtains. The only thing different was she.

"C'mon on in, Tuck." She sat up and turned on the light, watching her nephew shuffle shyly into the room. He was clearly Mina's son; he had his mother's delicate features and enviably long eyelashes, as well as his mother's wiry body. Sometimes, when Katie looked at him, she found herself running down a mental checklist of all the men in Didsbury, trying to figure out who his father was. It was a futile exercise. Tuck looked like Mina, period.

"What's up, pal? Couldn't sleep?"

Tuck shook his head. Her mother had told Katie that Tuck frequently had trouble getting to sleep, and would sometimes come to sleep with her for comfort, wrapping his arms tight around his grandmother's neck.

"What's buggin' ya?" Katie continued.

"I dunno." Tuck shrugged. He hopped up on the end of her bed, legs swinging. "How long are you going to be here again?"

"A year, Tuck. Remember I told you that?"

Tuck picked at the bedspread, not looking at her. "But then you go away again?"

Katie felt her heart wrench. "Yes," she said quietly. "I go back to Vermont. But that's not for a long, long time. We've got months together, you and I."

Tuck raised his head, smiling. "Wanna play Motorcross Madness?"

"Right now?"

Tuck glanced furtively at the bedroom door and nodded.

"Honey, it's almost midnight. Aunt Katie is old. She's tired. Besides, *you* should be fast asleep. If Nana catches you awake, she'll paddle your beee-hind."

Tuck snorted with glee. "You're funny, Aunt Katie."

"It runs in the family. I bet you're funny, too."

"My *mom's* not funny."

Katie leaned forward, brushing the hair out of his eyes. "Still pretty mad at her, huh?"

Tuck jerked away.

"I know she's made some mistakes, but I also know she loves you. And as soon as we're allowed to go see her, you and I—"

"I don't want to see her." Tuck jumped off the bed. "I want to stay here with you and Nana. I never want to see her again!"

"Yesterday you said Nana was old and boring."

"She is."

Katie feigned being insulted. "Well, I guess that means I'm boring, too."

Tuck bounced back onto the bed. "You could never be boring!"

"You know what? Neither could you. C'mere." She coaxed Tuck into sitting in the crook of her arm. "I know it's hard living here with Nana. She gets crabby, and she doesn't always know what you're talking about, and she's really cheap with your allowance, and sometimes she makes the most *disgusting* vegetables, right?"

Tuck smiled knowingly.

"So, let's make a deal. From now on, I'll give you your allowance. And anytime you feel mad at your mom, or if Nana doesn't understand what you're saying, you come talk to me, all right?"

"Mom says Nana is a psycho."

Katie sighed. "Sometimes, when grownups are upset, they say mean things." Her voice was calm, but inwardly she was fuming. How *dare* Mina say that when their mother had made a career out of bailing her out time and time again? What an ungrateful—Katie stopped herself. Her sister had taken the step to go into rehab. She was trying to turn her life around. That's what Katie needed to focus on.

She gave Tuck a quick kiss on the top of the head. "So, you'll come to me when things are bugging you? Deal?"

Tuck stuck out his hand for Katie to shake. "Deal."

"Good man."

"Aunt Katie?" Tuck asked again as he clambered off her bed and headed toward the hall.

"Yes?"

He paused in the doorway. "If I was grown up," he mumbled quickly, "I'd want to be your boyfriend because you're so nice." With that he disappeared back to his own room.

Katie turned out the light and slid back down beneath the covers.

Well, at least *someone* wanted to be her boyfriend.

CHAPTER

03

Someone was staring at him. Hard. Paul could *feel* steady waves of pulsating energy being beamed his way. He made himself look. Standing not two inches away from the bed was a little boy with a pinched face and a surly expression.

"Shoot!" Paul grabbed the silk sheets, scrambling to cover his naked torso. He hated silk sheets. Slick, shiny—it was like sleeping on vaseline. "Uh . . . hi?"

The child scowled. "Are you Mom's new boyfriend?"

"Uh . . ."

"What happened to Gustav?"

Panicking, Paul reached over to the other side of the bed to shake Liz awake. She murmured something unintelligible before turning away from him, taking all the covers with her.

"Shit!" Paul grabbed back some covers to cover his nakedness. "Sorry," he said to the boy, who looked unfazed. Paul shook Liz harder. "Rise and shine. C'mon."

Moaning, Liz rolled onto her back, but her eyes remained resolutely shut. Clearly she was not a morning person.

"We've got company, *dear*," Paul hissed in her ear. Beneath the covers he gave her a sharp poke in ribs.

"Ouch!" Liz yelped, eyes springing open. Turning to Paul, she smiled like the cat who'd eaten the canary, sighing deeply, contentedly. It seemed to take her a few seconds before she realized her son was standing by the bed.

"Gary." There was displeasure in Liz's voice as she stifled a small yawn. "What are you doing here, sweetie?"

"I'm hungry," he whined.

"Well, go tell Laurie to fix you some cereal. Could you also be a doll and tell Laurie to make Mumma some nice, strong coffee?" She blew him an air kiss. "Oh, and close the door on your way out, will you, honey? Thanks."

Gary glared at Paul resentfully before stomping out of the bedroom, slamming the door behind him.

"Gary can be melodramatic sometimes," Liz murmured as she gave a big stretch.

"Jesus, Liz! Why didn't you tell me you had a kid?"

"I thought you knew."

"How the hell would I know?"

"Everyone knows." She nuzzled against him. "Everyone knows I'm a poor, single woman back in Didsbury after my horrible, painful divorce."

"I can see the experience really scarred you," Paul replied, gingerly moving away from her. "By the way, who's Gustav?"

"Gustav?" Liz frowned, as if trying to remember someone from long ago. "Oh, he was Gary's archery instructor. Why?"

"Gary seemed perturbed to find me here instead of him."

"Gary was very fond of Gustav. I never had the heart to

tell him Gustav had to go back to Austria to take over his father's hosiery factory."

"What a considerate mother you are." Paul rubbed sleep from his eyes. "And Laurie? Who's she? The nanny?"

"The maid. Lane is the nanny."

"Yeah, you're a poor single mom, all right. My heart bleeds for you."

Paul closed his eyes for a moment, trying to take this all in. He shouldn't have come here. Not only was he feeling like a fleet of limos had run him over, but his head was pounding and his mouth tasted like bilge water. Worst of all, he'd let his dick do his thinking. The glowering boy by the bedside was the icing on the cake. All of it was just plain *wrong*.

"Why are you being so mean?" Liz's bottom lip jutted out like a pouty little girl's. "Especially after all the fun we had last night." She was on him again, an anaconda coiling herself around him in a death grip. "You were good," she purred. "Even better than you were in high school."

Paul snorted, affronted. *I sure as hell hope so.*

"Liz?" He tried wriggling free but movement made his head pound so he lay back, marshaling his energy. "Don't you care that your son saw you in bed with a strange man? Or that he saw my, you know?"

"Your *what?* Your willy?" Liz guffawed. "Your ding dong? Your johnson? Little Elvis? Can't you even say the *word*, Paul?"

"It's not funny, Liz. Your kid walking in here is totally inappropriate—"

"So spank me." She bit down softly on his shoulder. "I've been a bad, bad girl."

Paul much preferred to muzzle her. He took a deep breath, and in one strong, swift motion tried to peel her off him. She was tenacious, sticking to him like a barnacle, but he was stronger. He broke free and in a swift move that sent his pounding head spinning, he leapt out of bed and snatched up his briefs, nearly falling over as he struggled to put them on. He hadn't been hung over this badly in *years*.

Liz frowned, watching him from the bed. "What's the rush? The maid is making Gary breakfast. We have more than enough time for another—"

"No, thanks. I've got places to go, people to see."

"Like who?"

"The Didsbury Youth Hockey Board. I find out today who I'm coaching."

"Gary's trying out for hockey," Liz said brightly. "Maybe you'll wind up being his coach." She rolled over on her stomach, inching over to where Paul now sat. "You know," she said, trailing her perfectly manicured nails along his thigh, "I'd be willing to pay you to give Gary some private tutoring on the ice."

"I don't think so." He calmly removed her hand as he stood to put his trousers on. "I don't really have time."

"Not even as a favor to his mother, whose brains you were happy to fuck out last night?"

Paul sighed, sinking back down on the bed. He'd been hoping to get out without having this conversation, but he knew now he was going to have to lay it on the line.

"Liz, look." He worked to sound apologetic. "Last night was a mistake, okay? We both had too much to drink—"

"*I* didn't."

"And because of the reunion there was a lot of nostalgia in the air, and—"

"Oh, just fuck off, Paul." Liz flopped back angrily on the bed.

"What?"

"Don't give me the 'It was a mistake' speech! You knew

what you were getting into when I offered to drive you home! You wanted it as badly as I did!"

Was that true? *Had* he wanted it as badly as she did? He couldn't remember. Post-reunion, the night was one big, sensual blur.

"Fine, you're right," he admitted to placate her. "But it was just sex. Nothing else."

"Are you sure? Maybe it was the beginning of something," she ventured, the hopefulness in her voice making him feel like a total creep.

"Liz." Paul cradled his head in his hands. She wasn't going to let this go.

"I have an idea." She reached out, caressing his bare back with her big toe. "Why don't we have dinner tonight?"

"I can't." Paul stood up abruptly. "I'm at the bar tonight."

"Tomorrow night, then."

"*Liz*, I don't want to have dinner with you, okay?"

Anger flashed in her flinty green eyes. "Oh, I get it. I'm good enough to screw, but not good enough to share a meal with."

"That's bull and you know it."

"Then prove it. Have dinner with me."

"Sometime," he mumbled, hurriedly reaching for his shirt and buttoning it up. Anything to get her off his ass and get the hell out of here. "But not tonight. And not tomorrow night."

"Then when?"

"I don't know when!" He scooped his jacket up off the floor. "Look, I gotta go."

"Fuck and run!" Liz snapped. "Some things never change!"

"You got that right," Paul muttered under his breath. He flung open the bedroom door, hurrying down the immense, winding staircase. Twice his feet nearly went out from under him on the polished marble floor of the foyer. He'd forgotten his socks, but he didn't care. All he wanted was to get out of there in one piece without cracking his skull or running into little Gary with the accusatory eyes. He felt sorry for the kid, having Liz as his mother. But right now, only one thing mattered. Flinging open the front door, he was free.

"Pee—yew! You stink!"

To drive the point home, Tuck held his nose right there at the breakfast table, until Katie's mother leveled him with one of her disapproving stares and he slunk down in his seat, poking listlessly at his pancakes. Katie, dripping with sweat after her five-mile run, knew Tuck had only been telling the truth. She was beyond pungent; she was downright ripe.

"Sorry," she apologized, still breathing heavily.

"I don't know why you have to do that," her mother said, biting into a piece of toast. "Taxing your body that way. Couldn't you just take a nice, brisk walk?"

Katie smiled indulgently. "I could. But running helps clear my head. And it keeps the weight off."

Each time she ran, she thought back to when she first resolved to lose the weight. It was in college, right after she left Didsbury for good. She started a fitness program in tandem with joining Fat Fighters, of which she was now a lifetime member. Back then, she could barely stroll around the block without getting winded, never mind running. But gradually, she was able to do more and more. Now, she ran a minimum of five miles a day, five times a week. Running was her relaxation, the rhythmic pounding of her feet against the pavement hypnotic as any mantra. It was her time to think, daydream, muse. This morning's run had been no exception.

Flying down the silent, dilapidated streets of her childhood, she went over last night's reunion. Her mind kept circling back to Paul van Dorn, sifting through their words for nuance and inflection. Had he been flirting with her when he said *he* wasn't confused about his masculinity? She wasn't sure. Anyway, why should she care?

"Katie, sit down and have some breakfast with us."

"In a minute, Mom."

Stalling for time, she poured herself a glass of cold water, drinking it down slowly to avoid cramps. The breakfast table was laden with toast, sausage, pancakes, eggs—all the foods she loved, all the foods that would make her fat again if she didn't watch it. She didn't want to appear ungracious, but she was going to have to have a chat with her mother about the way she cooked. One year of living in this house again and she'd have to go to a tent maker for her clothing. She had to be vigilant.

She poured herself some coffee and helped herself to some scrambled eggs and a piece of dry toast before sliding into the seat beside Tuck, who held his nose again, shifting his chair slightly away from her. As expected, her mother reacted as if she'd just announced the commencement of a hunger strike.

"That's it? That's all you're having?"

"I just finished a run, Mom. If I eat too much right now, I'll throw up."

Her mother shook her head before turning to Tuck, tapping her fork on his plate like a gavel-wielding judge. "Eat up, mister. Contrary to what your aunt thinks, a good breakfast is *very* important."

Tuck didn't look like he needed much convincing. In fact, he was shoveling food into his mouth so fast Katie was afraid he'd choke.

"Nana, look." He pushed the open newspaper he'd been

glancing at over to Katie's mother, pointing at something on the bottom of the page. "That's what I was telling you about."

Her mother's eyes flicked to the paper before she pushed it back. "We've already discussed this."

Tuck's face fell. "But—"

"I'm sorry, honey. I just can't afford it." She rose to wash dishes.

"What is it?" Katie asked Tuck under her breath.

Tuck furtively slid the paper to Katie. At the bottom of the left-hand page was a boxed announcement about tryout times for Didsbury's Youth Hockey League.

"You play hockey?" Katie whispered, surprised.

Tuck nodded fervently.

"Hmm." Katie skimmed the announcement for the source of her mother's distress, and found it right there on the bottom line in bold: The dues for the year were two hundred fifty dollars. She leaned toward Tuck conspiratorially. "Go blow up some medieval fortress on your computer and I'll talk to Nana about this."

"Really?"

Katie nodded. "Finish your breakfast first, though."

Tuck wolfed down the rest of his food. "Nana, I'm done! Can I go play on the computer?"

"Yes, but only for an hour." Katie's mom turned around to make firm eye contact with her grandson. "Okay?"

"Yes, Nana, love you bye." Grinning, Tuck flew up the stairs to his room.

"Don't think I don't know what you two were hatching up," her mother said. "Just because the tap's running, doesn't mean I'm deaf."

"Mom, I can cover the fee if Tuck really wants to play hockey."

"There's more than the fee involved, Katie. There's equipment."

"I'll cover that, too."

"Made of money now, are we?"

Katie was silent. She knew her mother: The only time she ever resorted to sarcasm was when she felt defensive. It had happened a lot right after her father died and money was especially tight. Her mother must have thought that by offering to cover Tuck's hockey fees, Katie was inferring she wasn't providing well for him.

Removing her hands from the soapy water, her mother wiped them on her apron with a sigh. "I'm sorry I snapped at you. It's just"—her voice cracked a little—"hard."

"What is?" Katie put down her coffee cup. "Talk to me, Mom."

Tears filled her mother's eyes. "I love having Tuck, I really do. But sometimes I don't have the energy."

"But I do." Katie wiped the tear coursing down her mother's cheek with her thumb.

"You have your book to write."

"I can do both. I told you that was one of the reasons I moved back. To help out with Tuck."

"I know, but . . ." her mother glanced uncomfortably out the window. "The hockey is a lot of money. *A lot.*"

"So?"

"Maybe Tuck needs to learn that we can't always get what we want."

Katie laughed bitterly. "I'm sure Tuck already knows that, believe me."

Her mother's eyes found hers. "What if Mina never gets better?" she whispered.

"Mina's going to be fine, Mom." Katie folded her into an embrace. "It's a process. One of the things that's going to help her through is us having faith in her. Right?"

Her mother nodded, sniffling against her chest. "I'm sorry. I'm being silly."

"No, you're not."

"Katie? Tuck's right. You stink to high heaven." They broke apart, laughing.

"So, you'll let me cover Tuck's hockey fees?" Katie pressed.

"Yes," her mother conceded reluctantly. "I just worry, because it's mostly the rich kids in town who play youth hockey. They're the only ones who can afford it. What if Tuck feels out of place?"

"He'll be *fine*," Katie said. "He'll have new equipment like everyone else."

"And when the other boys ask what country club his parents belong to? Where he *lives*?"

Katie swallowed. "He'll handle it, Mom. Kids are remarkably resilient." Personal experience had taught her that much.

"All right." Her mother grabbed a dishrag and began drying a plate. "If he makes the team, and you're willing to cover the costs, then hockey it is for Tuck. But if he gets hurt—"

"Then I'll cover his medical bills, too," Katie teased. Impulsively, she wrapped her arms around her mother once more and gave her a big, sloppy kiss. "Everything's going to be fine. Stop worrying."

Paul might have fled Liz Flaherty's without his socks, but at least he'd left with enough time to shoot back to his own place for a shower and change of clothes. He was surprised he felt anxious about his meeting with the president and vice president of the Youth Hockey League Board of Directors.

He knew both men. Doug Burton, the president, had been

Paul's coach when he was on the Bantam team. VP Charles "Chick" Perry's son Chandler had played hockey with Paul until tenth grade, when a knee injury sidelined him for good. Chick also golfed regularly with Paul's dad.

Paul's decision to coach once he returned to Didsbury had been a no-brainer. Without hockey in his life, he would die. Hockey was who he was. It had shaped everything about him. He'd contemplated coaching on the minor league level, but was afraid it would be too painful to coach men his own age, men who could skate freely without the same kind of fears that Paul lived with. Besides, he wanted to give something back to the community that had championed him his whole life.

He strode through the doors of the Didsbury Country Club, trying to remember the last time he'd been here. It had to be when he'd been drafted by the Blades. His dad had taken him here for scotch and cigars to celebrate. There was lots of back-patting and talk about being a star, the best, the cream of the crop. He remembered his father dragging him from table to table, telling total strangers all his son had achieved. And now . . .

Squaring his shoulders, Paul smiled at the stooped mâitre'd, Kenneth, who'd been here as long as Paul could remember.

"Mr. van Dorn." Kenneth extended a veiny hand for Paul to shake. "It's been too long. How may I help you?"

"I'm here to meet Doug Burton and Chick Perry for lunch."

"Both men have already arrived. I'll show you to the table."

Paul dutifully followed Kenneth through the dining room. Though there appeared to be some businessmen present, the large, sunny room was filled mainly with well-heeled women of different ages in various stages of eating disorders. He scoured the room for his own mother, surprised to find her absent. Whenever someone in the family couldn't locate her, the joke had always been "Check the DCC." Didsbury Country Club, tennis, and various social committees: That was his mother's life.

Kenneth led him outside to the covered patio overlooking the rolling green hills of a Robert Trent Jones–designed golf course. Paul had never "gotten" golf, despite his father's occasional encouragement. Where was the rush? The danger? The *blood*? He knew lots of hockey players played golf to relax, but he wasn't one of them.

"Paul." Doug Burton rose with a warm smile for the boy he'd once called "Baby Gretzky." Paul would have recognized him anywhere: same granite features pocked with small scars, same scary brush cut, though it was now gray. "Good to see you."

"Good to see you, too, Coach Burton."

"Please, call me Doug."

Paul paused, waiting for Chick Perry to struggle out of his chair. A hugely overweight man with a florid face and unruly eyebrows, he nonetheless still managed to project an air of quiet superiority, not surprising considering how much money he was worth. Clasping Paul's forearm, he shook it so hard Paul wondered if he was hoping some change might drop out of his sleeve. "Paul." *Shake shake shake.* "So wonderful"—*hacking cough, wheeze, shake*—"to see you."

"You, too, Mr. Perry," Paul replied carefully, worried for the older man's health. The exertion it had taken him to get out of the chair had been so substantial Paul was afraid the reverse action of sitting back down might be the catalyst for a coronary.

"Please." He hurled himself back down into his chair, gasping. "None of this 'Mr. Perry' crap. From now on it's Chick."

"Chick," Paul repeated, taking his seat. "How is Chandler?"

"He's a big-shot lawyer in Chicago now, with a little boy and a wife with an ass so big you could land the space shuttle on it."

Paul stifled a snort. Talk about the pot calling the kettle black.

"Tell him I say hello," said Paul politely.

"I will, I will." Chick reached for his water glass, chugging down the contents.

"Drink?" Coach Burton offered.

Paul briefly considered the offer, applying the "hair of the dog" theory to his hangover. One or two beers might make him feel more human. Then again, suppose it didn't work? He was still feeling like he'd been dragged behind a chariot, and there was no way he wanted to risk feeling even worse. "Water's fine for me," he said, helping himself to a glass from the large, sweating pitcher in the middle of the table.

Chick pulled a silk handkerchief from his pocket, running it over his gleaming face before turning to Paul. "I just want to say, on behalf of Doug and myself, how sorry we are about what happened to you."

Paul stiffened. "Thank you, sir. I appreciate it."

"To be a successful professional athlete, and then be forced to retire in your prime." He shook his head sadly. "It's a tragedy."

Don't forget the part about my longtime girlfriend dumping me because I was no longer a hockey star. That was really special.

"Your father said you've done a real nice job with Cuffy's," Chick continued.

"I have. Stop by sometime. Drinks'll be on the house."

"I sure will."

Paul fidgeted, anxious to get the ball rolling. He'd come prepared to endure a certain amount of empty pleasantries, but kicking off the conversation by talking about his premature retirement was rapidly sending his mood south. "Have you guys already ordered?"

"I told Kenneth to bring three plates of the catch of the day," boomed Doug. "I hope that's all right."

"Terrific," Paul lied. Fish . . . his stomach heaved. He should have taken Alka-Seltzer before coming.

"So, Paul." Doug's voice was collegial, but there was no mistaking the uneasy glance he shared with Chick. "Chick and I have talked to the other members of the hockey board, and we want to congratulate you. You've been chosen to coach the squirt snowbelt team."

Paul blinked, stunned. His first thought was, *This is a fucking joke, right?* But the longer the silence at the table dragged on, the more he was forced to acknowledge that Chick and Doug were in deadly earnest.

"Now, I know you were hoping to coach the midget travel team," Chick continued in the kind of voice one associated with calming someone unstable, "but that's Coach Doherty's domain. Always has been, always will be."

Coach Doherty? Paul couldn't believe what he was hearing. The guy had to be seventy if he was a day.

"I'm surprised he's still coaching at his age," Paul replied without missing a beat. "I thought he'd like to go out while he was at the top of his game."

Chick chuckled nervously. "I don't think Doherty has any intention of retiring, Paul."

No, he'll probably drop dead on the ice, having stroked out after yelling at some poor kid.

Paul held his tongue, but it was hard. If there was one coach he'd hated when he was growing up, it was Dan Doherty. Doherty was real old-school; not only was he a fer-

vent believer in the "Skill/drill/kill" approach to coaching,
he was also big on humiliating his players if they didn't perform up to his standards. Paul could still hear Doherty's
voice in his head, calling him a "goddamn pussy" in front of
the whole team for the penalty shot he'd missed in a crucial
game against Hartford. The guy was a total SOB, an emotional terrorist. Worse, he swanned around town like he was
some big-time hockey player, when the only thing of note
he'd ever done was back in 1959, when he'd scored the winning goal that won Didsbury High the state championship
that year.

"You seem surprised," Chick observed carefully.

"You could say that."

"It's a matter of paying dues, Paul." Doug Burton's voice
was resolute. "You're new. New guys start at the bottom of
the totem pole."

New? Paul longed to shout. *I played for the fucking New
York Blades!* Instead he forced a polite smile, which both
men returned. The silence at the table resumed. Finally,
Doug broke the ice.

"I sense you're upset, Paul."

"Well," he began calmly, "I thought that since I've actually *played* in the NHL, I might be the logical choice to
coach the midget travel team. As we all know, those kids are
the best. They need the best coach they can get, someone
who's experienced hockey at the highest level." He looked
at both men carefully. "Don't you think a change of blood
after all these years might be good?"

Doug nodded slowly. "Maybe. Eventually. But for now,
Coach Doherty remains the midget travel coach."

Paul clenched his jaw. "I see." He thought of asking if
they'd consider letting him coach the midget home team, but
he didn't want to sound desperate. No, what he wanted was
to coach hungry young athletes who knew the game and

lived for it the way he had! Not spazzy little nine- and ten-year-olds who weren't even allowed to check each other!

"Paul." Doug's voice was cajoling. "It's a matter of paying dues, like we already said. You have to *earn it*, son."

Paul bristled. "You don't think I've paid dues?"

Chick sighed, tenting his sausage-size fingers. "What happened to you was unfortunate. No one denies that. But you can't just waltz back into town and declare yourself sheriff. Understand what I'm saying?"

Doug Burton leaned over, giving Paul a paternal pat on the back. "We need your skill and expertise with the little guys. You can appreciate that, can't you?"

Paul stopped himself from responding lest his foot get permanently lodged in his mouth. The nausea he'd been holding at bay threatened to wreak havoc as his fish dish was placed in front of him. "I appreciate your offer. I need to think about it."

"There are lots of men in this town who would love the chance to coach the squirts," said Doug. "If you're not up to the task, we need to know as soon as possible."

"I'm up to the task," Paul shot back.

"Is that a yes, then?"

"Yes."

Pride, Paul mused to himself the next morning as he jogged down the leafy streets making up the heart of Didsbury's exclusive Ladybarn District, could be a dangerous thing. Had Doug Burton not inferred he was inadequate, chances are he would have suffered through the rest of their uncomfortable lunch, said his farewells, and called the next day to say he wasn't interested. Now look where he was: committed to coaching the squirts. For what? To prove something to his ex-coach? There was something to be said for engaging your brain before opening your mouth. At least he hadn't embarrassed himself and thrown up his fish.

He pushed himself to run faster, warm rivulets of sweat trailing down his face and chest. He might not be able to fly down the ice anymore, but he could still fly down paved streets, though there were times when dizziness suddenly overtook him and he had to slow down or stop altogether.

Running helped him sweat out the bitterness that sometimes threatened to engulf him. When he ran, he wasn't Paul, the promising young hockey god who'd been forced into early retirement, or Paul the neophyte bar owner, or Paul the returning hero. He simply *was*, brain and body working in tandem to drive him ever forward toward an endorphin high that made his disappointment bearable, if only for a short while.

He rounded Locust Drive, with its mock Tudor mansions and well-manicured lawns boasting discreet signs for home security systems, and began his downhill descent on Piping Rock Lane, toward Main Street. The steep, sloping road jarred his knees but he kept on, gritting his teeth. He may not be a Blade anymore, but he was still a warrior, and a warrior pushed through the pain. Not only that, but this warrior was going to produce a squirt team so hot people's heads were going to spin.

Deep in thought, he failed to notice when the light at the corner of Church Street and Main turned red. Running out into the street, he barely had time to register the screeching breaks before he was out cold, darkness dropping down on him as fast as a curtain.

CHAPTER

04

I killed Paul van Dorn.

Teeth clacking like castanets, Katie threw her car into park and lurched out the driver's side door, too preoccupied to close it. One minute she was cruising down Main Street looking for someplace, *anyplace*, that might serve lattes; the next Paul had run into her path and she was smashing down on the brake, bringing the car to a screeching halt.

"Paul?"

He was breathing. Hearing his name, his eyes fluttered open, straining to focus. His face was red from physical exertion. Sweat soaked his T-shirt, gluing it to his muscular upper torso like a second skin. Blood flowed from a cut to his scalp. Katie wondered if he'd been trying to commit suicide. If so, she sure wished he'd picked someone else's car to hurl himself in front of.

"I saw the whole thing!" a young woman pushing a

stroller called breathlessly from the curb. "He wasn't even looking where he was going!"

Katie barely heard; her eyes remained riveted on Paul. He seemed intact, but you never knew. What if he was bleeding internally, his life slowly slipping away, the same way hers would when she was on trial for vehicular manslaughter? Oh God. Tearing off the silk scarf around her neck, she pressed it to his bleeding head. Paul groaned, opening his eyes briefly before closing them again.

"Do you have a cell phone?" Katie called to the woman. The woman nodded. "Could you call an ambulance?"

"No." Paul groaned. "No ambulance."

He was sprawled in the middle of Main Street like a limp rag doll, but that didn't stop him from trying to call the shots, Katie noticed.

"No ambulance," he repeated more forcefully.

By now, a small crowd had gathered on the sidewalk, murmuring, "That's Paul van Dorn!" Thankfully, the observation wasn't followed with, "He was just mowed down by Katie Fisher."

Katie put her face close to his. "Paul?"

"Katie?" He looked up at her woozily. "What are you doing here?"

"That was my bumper you just tried to kiss."

Paul chuckled, then grimaced. Clearly, laughing hurt. "Getting revenge for high school, huh?"

"Actually, I thought you were trying to end it all."

"Believe me, if that was the case there are a lot more pleasant ways to go about it."

"Such as—?"

"A hotel room, two hookers, some downers and a bottle of Jack Daniels."

"Nice to see you've put some thought into it," Katie said

dryly. As he struggled to push himself up on his elbows, she said, "What are you doing? Don't move!"

Paul rolled his eyes. "Katie, listen to me." He gently removed her hand from his head, replacing it with his own. "I don't need an ambulance."

"You don't know that."

"I *do* know that. Believe me, I've had worse knocks than this out on the ice."

"You could be bleeding internally. You could be concussed from hitting your head on the pavement. You don't know."

"Okay, look." Paul continued pressing the scarf to his head. "If it'll make you feel better, you can drive me over to the emergency room, okay? But there's no need to trouble EMS. Agreed?"

Katie mulled this over. He *was* sitting up and talking. Then again, what if she agreed and he died in her car? Would she be liable?

"Katie?"

"Okay, I'll drive you over to the hospital. You'll need stitches to the head, at the very least."

Paul pulled the scarf away and pressed his fingers to the cut on his head. "It's nothing. A scrape." He wiped his bloody fingers on his T-shirt.

"C'mon, macho man, let's get you in the car."

"Well?"

Katie leapt out of her butt-torturing chair the minute Paul reentered the emergency room waiting area. She'd read every outdated issue of *Woman's Day* and had memorized all the top stories on Headline News while she waited for the doctors to release him. It didn't help that the woman sitting next to her kept groaning with a stomachache.

Paul was a sight. Blood smeared his running clothes, and his face remained pale. A small patch of his head had been shaved and covered with a gauze bandage.

"Four stitches," he told her. "No biggie."

Katie felt awful. "That's it? Are you sure?"

He shrugged. "A few bruised ribs."

"No concussion?"

"I'm fine," he replied curtly. He glanced around the emergency room with a shudder. "Let's get out of here."

Katie walked out with him, glad to be free of the hospital's oppressive atmosphere. Should she take his elbow and guide him to the car? He seemed to be walking all right.

Pausing at the curb, Paul peered at the parking lot. "Which car is yours again?"

"The blue Neon." He didn't remember? Was he concussed?

He turned to her, embarrassed. "Would you mind giving me a lift home?"

She led him to her car, rushing to open the passenger door for him.

"It's *stitches*, Katie," Paul said with amusement as he ducked into the passenger seat. "I'm not an invalid."

"I was just trying to be nice," she countered, closing the door. "I wasn't going to let you *jog* home, was I?" Sliding into the driver's seat, she turned on the ignition. "Where to?"

"Dover Street. One-fourteen."

"Oh."

"You seem surprised."

"I am. I guess. I mean—"

"You thought I'd be living in Ladybarn, right?"

Katie nodded. Paul was right. Her natural assumption was that he'd be living in the wealthiest part of town, the part he'd grown up in. Instead, he'd chosen a solidly middle-class neighborhood to call home. She wondered why. As if reading her mind, he said, "I didn't want to run into my folks all the time."

"I see." Throwing the car into drive, she eased out of the parking space and followed the winding, tree-lined road that led out of the hospital grounds. Dover Street . . . Dover Street . . .

"Make the right onto Scudder, turn left down Laurel, follow it all the way to Dempsey, then make the final right onto Dover."

Katie glanced at him. "Did that blow to the head give you psychic powers?"

"No."

"Then how did you know I was trying to figure out how to get there?"

"Your face. You're scowling. You looked pained."

"That's because I'm nervous," Katie admitted, following his first instruction to make the right onto Scudder Road. "I've never driven with a celebrity before."

"Former celebrity. Let's get our terms right." His gaze turned curious. "You weren't nervous on the ride *to* the hospital."

"I was too busy thinking you were going to croak in my car."

Paul laughed loudly. "You would have had to get new seat covers!"

"What, are you kidding me? I would have sold the car intact on eBay. Too bad there are no bloodstains or anything. Think of the value it would have added."

He laughed again. "You're funny," he said, as if it surprised him.

And you're nice, Katie thought, feeling equally surprised.

Paul looked down at her bloody scarf crumpled in his hand. "You have to let me get you a new one."

Katie clucked her tongue dismissively. "Don't worry about it."

"No, I insist."

"Keep it as a souvenir: 'Baby's first pedestrian accident.'"

Paul laughed again. "You're a real wiseass, you know that?"

"I try," said Katie, marveling over the fact she was sitting in a car bantering with Paul van Dorn. Never in a million years could she have imagined this scene, nor how alive it made her feel. "If you don't mind me asking, what were you thinking about so deeply that you jogged out in front of a car?"

Paul slumped in his seat. "Youth hockey. I'm coaching this year."

"And this is bad because—?"

"I'm coaching squirts."

"I don't know what that means."

"Younger boys, nine- and ten-year-olds."

Katie smiled. "Maybe you'll be coaching my nephew, then."

"If he makes the team."

"Right." She hadn't even thought of that. These kids had to try out, and some of them might not make the team, Tuck included. "Why don't you want to coach squirts?"

"It's not that I don't want to," Paul said carefully. "I would just prefer coaching the teenage boys. They're more skilled."

"Which must mean coaching them is more prestigious," Katie observed.

"Well . . . yeah."

"So this is purely an ego issue, then." She turned the car down Laurel Avenue.

"Are you analyzing me, Miss Sociologist?"

"Maybe."

"You still want to interview me for that book?"

Katie's heart jumped. "I would love to. What's your schedule like?"

"Late mornings, early afternoons are best."

"I could take you out to lunch, if you'd like. I hear the curly fries at the Penalty Box are to die for."

"Yeah?" Paul sounded pleased. "Where'd you hear that?"

"My mom. Your bar is the talk of the Episcopal Church."

"Not the clientele I'm seeking but what the hell, I'll take the free PR. You want to do it there, then?"

With you I'd do it anywhere. Katie smiled brightly to cover the sudden surge of desire shooting through her. "Sure. When?"

"How's Friday sound?"

"Sounds good. Should I just meet you there?"

"That makes the most sense. Katie?"

"Yeah?"

"You're going the wrong way down Laurel."

"What?" Katie slowed the car. "You said right."

"Left. It's not a big deal."

No, except she looked like a ditz. She quickly pulled into an empty driveway and turning the car around, drove off in the right direction. She could feel Paul watching her as she concentrated on her driving. The more he looked at her, the more she thought *she* might be the one to die in the car—of a sheer heart attack brought on by acute anxiety and lust. Finally she couldn't take it anymore.

"What?"

Paul shook his head, marveling at her. "I still can't get over how great you look."

Katie colored. Praise made her feel vulnerable. Praise from a man this gorgeous made her feel like she was sitting behind the steering wheel naked.

"Thank you," she managed.

"How did you do it?"

"Diet and exercise. I run, too."

"Yeah?" Paul's eyes lit up. "Maybe we could run together sometime."

"Maybe."

Perhaps she was wrong, but she could have sworn she saw disappointment flit across his face. She was baffled. Why would he want to run with *her*? Maybe that was an ego thing, too. Maybe he thought he could kick former fat girl Katie's ass out on the open road. If so, he was in for a big surprise.

"So," Paul said casually, "do you have a boyfriend?"

Katie clutched the steering wheel hard to avoid driving up onto the sidewalk. "Not right now, no. How about you? Do you have a boyfriend? Oh God—I mean girlfriend."

Paul put his hand on her knee and Katie's foot nearly shot through the floorboard.

"*Relax.* I don't bite." Paul removed his hand. "I used to."

"What? Bite?"

"No, have a girlfriend. She dumped me when I retired."

"Nice."

"Happens all the time." He sounded resigned as he gazed out the window. "Where you living now?"

"Where I've always lived. On Herbert Place. I'm staying with my mother."

"I don't know where Herbert Place is," Paul admitted.

"Over the tracks, close to the printing factory."

He turned back to her, concerned. "Is it safe to run there?"

"Of course," Katie retorted with a frown. "Why wouldn't it be?"

Shrugging, Paul leaned back against the headrest with his eyes closed. They drove the rest of the way in tense silence.

"I'm sorry," he said as they rolled to a stop in front of his house, a modest split-level that Katie thought was pretty nondescript. "I didn't mean to insult you."

Katie switched off the ignition. "It's okay. I can be a little touchy sometimes. I'm sorry, too."

The silence returned, but this time it was tense in a new, different way. Katie took a deep breath. She wanted this to be over. No, what she really wanted was him. She'd settle for a candy bar.

"Friday, then?" Paul reconfirmed.

"Friday."

"Thanks for the ride, Katie," Paul said softly.

He leaned over and kissed her. Soft enough to be sweet, but just enough pressure for it to mean something.

Katie's mind reeled. She'd just been kissed by the boy she used to fantasize about kissing, the same one who used to call her "Bubble Butt" in high school.

"I—I better go. I've got research to do at the library."

"Okay," Paul said easily, opening the car door. "See you Friday, then. Thanks again for everything you've done for me today, especially not killing me."

"My pleasure."

Where is Dunkin' Donuts?

Katie's first impulse after dropping Paul off was to head to the nearest Dunkin' Donuts to drown her confusion in a box of Munchkins and a fresh cup of coffee. Once upon a time, food had been her answer to everything, both good and bad. Get a nearly perfect score on the SATs? Celebrate by eating half a cake. Missing your father? Cram the pain down by devouring a pan of brownies. Katie recognized this impulse for what it was: a way of obscuring the real emotional issue at hand. What was going on between her and Paul van Dorn?

Katie knew sexual tension when she felt it. Granted, she hadn't had tons of experience with men, but she had some, and there had definitely been sexual tension between them in her car. Definitely.

And that kiss . . .

She closed her eyes, wanting to experience it all over again. It was like watching a movie in slow mo; his body leaning toward her, the brief flash of desire in his eyes, the first press of his lips on hers—all real, all able to be conjured at will. But what, if anything, did it *mean*?

She forced herself to go to the library to work, though concentration was hard to come by. Afterward, she decided to go to the local meeting of Fat Fighters. The earlier impulse toward donuts was a tip-off she needed support. That's what the group was there for.

The Didsbury chapter held its weekly meeting in the basement cafeteria of the local Unitarian church. Trying to ignore the faint smell of mildew as she walked down the frayed carpet of the basement steps, Katie came on the scene ubiquitous to every Fat Fighters meeting she'd ever attended: a snaking line of chatting women of all shapes and sizes lined up to weigh in. Taking her place in the line, Katie pulled out her Lifetime member card and waited. It felt like forever before she even crossed the threshold into the cafeteria, where women were stepping on and off scales, their successes or failures dutifully recorded by a Fat Fighters employee. Exultation mingled with desperation depending upon the verdict. Katie watched as one woman preparing to be weighed removed her shoes, socks, sweater, earrings, and wedding band—anything that might lower the number on the scale. It worked: pumping her fist victoriously in the air, she put her clothes and jewelry back on and went to sit with the rest of those who'd been weighed and were waiting for the meeting to begin.

"Psst! Katie!"

Shocked to hear her name, Katie looked out on the sea of folding chairs to her left. There sat Denise Coogan, the transsexual, waving to her.

"I'll save you a seat," Denise mouthed, putting her Gucci bag on the empty chair beside her. Katie smiled and took a few steps closer to the scale. Denise turned to talk to the other woman beside her, a heavy blonde in sweats who seemed to giggle at everything Denise said. She wondered who the other woman was.

Finally it was Katie's turn to weigh in. It always surprised her how nervous the process still made her, even though she'd achieved her goal weight four years ago and had maintained it. Slipping out of her loafers, she handed her card to the woman in charge of weighing in, then climbed onto the scale. The woman nodded approvingly. "Still a lifetime member," she said, handing Katie back her card. "Congratulations."

Katie smiled, hurrying to take her seat beside Denise. "Katie, you know Bitsy Collins, don't you?"

Katie blinked. There was no way the heavy blonde beside Denise could be Bitsy Collins. Bitsy Collins had been so nicknamed in high school because that's what she'd been— itsy bitsy, petite. Not only that, but Bitsy had been one of Katie's primary tormentors. She was a close friend of the dreaded Liz Flaherty. Bitsy and Liz had ruled the school.

"Um . . ."

Bitsy held out a plump hand. "I know, hard to believe it's me."

"That's why you're here," Katie said kindly, hoping she hadn't looked too shocked by Bitsy's appearance.

"I'm trying." Bitsy sighed.

"If I can do it, anyone can do it," Katie assured her. "I didn't see you at the reunion."

"No way was I going to the reunion looking like this."

Katie nodded her head knowingly. She understood that feeling of believing yourself so physically grotesque all you want to do is hide. She wanted to dislike Bitsy the way she still disliked Liz, but she couldn't. She knew the pain Bitsy was in, as well as the courage it took to finally do something about it.

Eventually, everyone was weighed and seated and the group leader, a small, smiling woman named Lolly, strode to the front of the cafeteria. "Hello! My name is Lolly and I lost one hundred and twenty-five pounds on Fat Fighters. Tonight I want to talk about the crazy things some of us have done in the past to try to lose weight. Anyone?"

"I once put myself on a scrambled egg and water diet," one woman said.

Lolly dutifully wrote "Scrambled egg and water" in large, childish scrawl on the portable blackboard behind her.

"I once tried living on coffee, cigarettes and Skittles," volunteered another woman with a pile of knitting in her lap.

Lolly's list grew to include such classics as diet pills, diuretics, laxatives, starvation, hypnotism, pasting "fat" pictures of one's self on the fridge, and various diet plans.

Denise leaned over to Katie. "I used to snort cocaine," she whispered.

"I used to snort cheese doodle dust," Katie whispered back.

Denise laughed loudly, causing several women to turn around and glare. That was one element of Fat Fighters Katie disliked: the sometimes evangelical fervor of some of its members.

A lecture followed where Lolly outlined why Fat Fighters, with its emphasis on portion control and exercise, was the way to go. Katie had heard it all before, but she still felt she needed to be here. It was empowering to know she wasn't the only one who still struggled with food issues.

When the meeting ended, Bitsy leaned over to Katie. "Denise and I are going for coffee at Tabitha's. Wanna come?"

Katie hesitated. Tabitha's was Didsbury's only coffee shop. It served coffee. Plain black coffee, both caf and decaf. And cake. Its lunchtime specials included tuna casserole and sloppy joes. All the waitresses were over sixty and said things like, "What can I do ya for, hon?" No latte, no low-carb chai, no biscotti, no anything.

"Is there a Starbucks nearby?" Katie asked hopefully.

Denise and Bitsy looked at each other and burst out laughing.

"A Starbucks?" Bitsy practically shrieked. "In *Didsbury*?"

"Sorry," said Denise. "Tabitha's is the only game in town."

"You up for it?" asked Bitsy.

Katie nodded. She wasn't totally sure what to make of Bitsy. But after being kissed by Paul van Dorn, she knew a lot could change in ten years. What did she have to lose?

"*I saw the* fear in your eyes when I asked you to join us," Bitsy said to Katie later when the two of them, along with Denise, were safely ensconced in a booth at Tabitha's. Unable to completely resist temptation, the three of them agreed to split a piece of crumb cake, the perfect accompaniment to their plain black coffee.

"I don't blame you," Bitsy continued. "I was a total bitch to you in high school."

"Yes, you were," Katie agreed, nibbling on her cake.

"Well, what goes around comes around," said Bitsy ruefully. "I mean, look at you now."

"You can lose the weight," Katie encouraged.

Denise looked at Bitsy with envy. "She's already dropped ten, the witch."

"That's great," said Katie, meaning it. Psychologically speaking, she knew how important reaching that ten-pound milestone was. "Keep it up."

Bitsy sighed. "I'm trying, but it's hard. Frank is the junk food king. The man never met a Ho Ho he didn't like."

"A boy after my own heart," trilled Denise. She turned to Katie. "You remember Frank, don't you? Frank DiNizio? Played football?"

Katie tried to conjure his face, but all she could see was a pair of grizzly-bear-size shoulders. "Sorry," she apologized. "I don't really remember him."

"He has a flat head like Frankenstein," Bitsy offered helpfully.

Katie coughed to cover a laugh, taken aback by Bitsy's bluntness.

"Do you remember him now?"

"Kind of." The description of his head helped.

"Well, anyway, he *says* he's supportive, but then he brings all this crap into the house."

"A diet saboteur," Denise put in knowingly. "The worst kind of evil."

"Tell him to put all the bad stuff out of sight," Katie advised.

"I think I'll just tell him to keep it at the bar with him." She took a sip of her coffee. "He tends bar nights at the Penalty Box," she explained.

"Really?" Katie's interest was piqued. Here she was with two townies. She had no doubt she could get a world of info on Paul if she wanted, but she had to be subtle. "Does he like it?"

"He says Paul's a better boss than Cuffy was, that's for sure."

Denise shuddered. "Cuffy was an old perv."

"Did you both stay in Didsbury after high school?" Katie asked.

Denise popped her entire portion of crumbcake in her mouth before answering. "I was in Boston for a long time. I came back two years ago after my mom died. She left the house to me."

"That gorgeous Queen Anne up on Maple," Bitsy swooned. Katie had no idea what house she was talking about. Maple was part of the Ladybarn District.

"What do you do?" Katie asked Denise.

"I'm an insurance adjuster. *Very* glamorous."

"And you?" Katie asked Bitsy.

Bitsy smiled proudly. "I'm a stay-at-home mom."

"How old are your kids?" Katie asked.

"I just have one, my son, Christopher. He's nine."

"So's my nephew, Tuck!" said Katie, regretting it immediately. Didsbury was small; everyone had to know what Tuck's circumstances were.

"How's Mina doing?" Denise asked tentatively.

"She's still in rehab. We'll be allowed to see her in a few weeks. Tuck's very excited."

"I think it's great that he's with your mom," said Bitsy. "God knows your sister—" Denise shot her a sharp look and Bitsy clamped her mouth shut. She looked mortified.

"I'm sorry," said Bitsy. "I didn't mean—"

"It's okay," Katie assured her quietly.

"So, what are you doing back in Didsbury?" Denise asked Katie.

Katie told them about her sabbatical from Fallowfield

College to work on her book. Both women looked impressed.

"I knew you were a professor or something," said Denise. "How?"

"The way you dress: kinda LL Beanie. Plus that book bag you've been dragging around."

Katie glanced down at the large canvas tote at her feet. Not only did it serve as her purse, but it also contained her laptop as well as several books and papers. Without it she felt naked.

"Guilty," she said with a smile.

"Are you going to talk to Paul van Dorn for the book?" Bitsy asked.

"I was planning to," Katie said carefully. "Why?"

Bitsy shrugged. "No reason. Frank says he's real moody, that's all."

"I'd be moody, too, if my career blew up in my face before I was even thirty," said Denise.

Moody. Katie filed that one away. She turned to Bitsy. "You must be happy Liz is back in town," she made herself say.

Bitsy made a sour face. "Liz and I fell out years ago."

"Really?"

"She was scandalized when I got pregnant with Christopher and had to—excuse me, chose to—marry Frank. Apparently marrying someone who earns less than three mill a year is bogus, dahling."

"I never liked her," Denise sniffed.

"Me, either," Katie confessed.

Bitsy giggled. "Me, either! But I was so desperate to be popular, I was willing to trail behind her like a puppy dog and do whatever she said." She shook her head. "Pathetic."

"I can't wait to see how long it takes her to lure Paul van Dorn back into her web," said Denise.

"You think?" Katie asked, trying to sound offhanded.

"Oh, please." Denise stole a piece of Katie's cake. "If it has money and a dick that works, Liz is there. I just hope Paul isn't that stupid or depressed."

CHAPTER

05

Katie felt anxious walking into the Penalty Box. For someone who prided herself on holding the attention of a hall full of students, having lunch with an ex-jock should have been a piece of cake. Instead, she felt as if she were going to meet her parole officer.

The place was packed. Katie had never been here when it was Cuffy's, but even she could tell Paul had made the Penalty Box his own: There was hockey memorabilia everywhere, much of it personal. A game of tabletop hockey in the corner was generating loud whoops and shouts from the four businessmen who were playing. Katie recognized two of them; one had graduated the year before she and Paul, the other headed up the insurance company in town. Once again, Didsbury's insularity was brought home to her. In Fallowfield, it was possible to walk down the street or go out to lunch and not see anyone you knew, or even recognized. Not here.

Katie was surprised at the variety of people having lunch; everyone from hard hats to suits to moms with kids in tow.

And in the middle of it all, loving every second of the attention he was being paid, was Paul.

Katie had no doubt Paul loved the hum of conversation in the Penalty Box. It probably reminded him of the sound of the crowd, the background music to so much of his life. Surrounded by tangible signs of his glory days (photos, trophies, jerseys, banners, signed pucks, battered sticks, skates) and a clientele who loved hearing his stories about the NHL, it would be easy for him to forget what had happened. Night after night, he was the main attraction. She was sure he could have turned the tavern into a bona fide sports bar with a mega sound system and multiple TVs, but then the focus would be on the screens . . . not him.

Katie hung back by the door a moment, watching him. He sat perched on a stool at the far end of the bar, surrounded by three young guys who looked to be high school age. One was wearing a New York Blades jersey; another held out a picture for him to autograph. There was no mistaking the pure pleasure on Paul's face as these young men hung on his every word, adoration in their eyes. Discreetly as she could, she pulled out a pen and jotted down. *Ex athletes need to cling to former identity—the importance of remaining in the public eye.* She was just capping the pen when Paul spotted her. Pointing in the direction of an empty booth, he mouthed "Five minutes," then continued talking to the starstruck adolescents.

Katie slid into the small wooden booth and laid out the items she needed for the interview: list of questions, notepad, microcassette recorder. She hadn't been sitting for more than a minute before a waitress swung by with a menu, asking if she wanted anything to drink. "A Diet Coke would be great," said Katie.

She was busy pretending to study her notes when Paul sat down opposite her. "Sorry 'bout the delay," he said. Katie nodded uncertainly in the direction of the bar. "Is that Frank DiNizio?"

"Yeah. Don't you remember him from high school?"

"Not really. But it's nice of you to have kept him on."

"What, are you kidding me?" Paul chortled. "Frank's great at what he does. He's fast, he's amiable—the customers love him. Plus, look at the guy: he's built like a slab of concrete. If you were drunk, would *you* mess with Frank?"

"Good point."

Paul slid a white box across the table toward her.

Katie eyed the box suspiciously. "What's this?"

"Open it and find out."

Katie opened the box. Inside was a beautiful silk scarf, its delicate floral print exactly her taste. "You didn't have to do this!"

"Maybe I wanted to."

Katie felt herself blushing. "Are you flirting with me?"

"Do you want me to be?"

Katie swallowed. "I think it's important we keep this interview strictly professional."

"Absolutely."

"I mean it, Paul." Katie narrowed her eyes. "This isn't a bribe, is it?"

"What do you mean?"

"Give the interviewer a beautiful silk scarf in the hopes she'll go easy on you."

Paul smiled sexily. "You were going to go hard on me?"

"Oh, here's my Coke," Katie said, grateful for the waitress's reappearance.

"Do you know what you want?" Paul asked.

"Hang on." Katie opened the menu and scanned it

quickly, searching for something that was either low cal, healthy, or both. "I'll have the hamburger, no roll, with a small salad with Russian dressing on the side."

"You, boss?" the waitress asked Paul.

"Cheeseburger, coke, and some curly fries."

"You got it."

The waitress trotted off.

"I'm disappointed you didn't order my world-famous curly fries," said Paul.

"I'll just nibble on a few of yours, if that's all right."

"Nibble away."

Her eyes went to the bandaged cut on his head. "How are you feeling?"

"Fine. How 'bout you? Run down any more pedestrians this week?" Paul joked.

"Clipped two old ladies and a mailman."

Paul applauded lightly. "Very good. I think you get bonus points for the old women." He jerked his head in the direction of the large tote bag beside her. "Do you go anywhere without that?"

"What do you mean?"

"It was in your car, and the other day I saw you leaving the library with it."

"It's got my laptop in it. And some sociology texts."

Paul grinned. "Anything fun?"

"No. Not really." She moved her tape recorder to the center of the table.

Paul frowned. "Do we really need that?"

"I do. I'm the world's worst note taker. Besides, I don't want to risk misquoting you."

"Fine." He smacked the table. "Let's do it!"

His enthusiasm was a cover. Katie could feel him tensing as she turned on the tape recorder and once again uncapped her pen. "At the reunion, you were very annoyed when I re-

ferred to you as an 'ex-athlete,'" she began cautiously.
"Maybe you can start by telling me how you feel being an
athlete has shaped your self-image."

Paul chuckled darkly. "Got a few years? No, seriously, I
started playing hockey when I was three . . ."

For the next hour and a half, Katie listened carefully as
Paul answered her questions on everything from the influ-
ence of coaches to the definition of success. He was a good
interviewee: thoughtful, well spoken, with lots of anecdotes
both humorous and poignant she'd be able to use. He was
also much more patient than she: three times their meal was
interrupted by someone wanting an autograph. Katie wanted
to tell them to take a hike, but it didn't seem to bother Paul
at all. In fact, he loved it. Katie made a note of that as well.

"Let's talk about the homoerotic undertones in sports,"
she said.

Paul thrust his head forward as if he hadn't heard right.
"Excuse me?"

"The homoerotic undertones," Katie repeated.

Paul speared a curly fry. "I'm not sure what you're getting at."

"Oh, c'mon," Katie said dubiously. "All that butt slap-
ping and hugging?"

"What about it?"

"You don't think it's a way for you guys to show physical affection for each other in a way that ensures your masculine identity is in no way impugned?"

He leaned back, studying her. "Are you making this stuff
up?"

"No. For your information, Paul, studies show that
there's an erotic basis underlying the fraternal bond in male
groups."

Paul snorted loudly. "I've never heard such a load of crap
in my life."

"You're threatened by it," Kate observed, scribbling on her pad.

"I'm not threatened by it!"

"Then why are you getting so upset?"

"I'm not upset!" Paul insisted. "A sports team is a *family*, Katie. When families are happy about something, they hug each other. End of story."

"So I guess you pat your father's ass when you're happy."

"Oh, Jesus." Paul put his hand to his forehead as if warding off a headache. "Fine. We're all a bunch of macho men who are afraid of being called fags, so we only touch each other affectionately when we're celebrating a victory. Is that what you want to hear?"

"If it's the truth."

"You tell me. You're the one armed with a degree and statistics. I just lived it."

Katie decided to change the subject. "Let's talk about your retirement."

"What about it?" Paul snapped.

Oh, shit, Katie thought. What dark path had she led their conversation down without meaning to? She was going to have to proceed with caution.

"Some other retired pro athletes have told me—"

"Who else have you talked to? Maybe I should have found that out before I agreed to this."

"It doesn't *matter*."

"It does to me."

Katie folded her arms across her chest. "Are you telling me you won't talk to me any further unless you know who else I've interviewed?"

Paul nodded.

"Here," Katie said, riffling furiously through the paperwork in her canvas bag. "Here are my other sources." She practically flung the folder at him.

"Hmm," Paul murmured as he scanned the list.

"As you can see, there are some bigger names there than yours." Katie snatched the folder back and was shoving it back into her bag when she realized what she'd said.

"I'm sorry," she murmured. "I didn't mean—"

"Where were we?" he asked in a tired voice. The anger in his eyes had flamed out. In its stead was melancholy.

"I was about to ask you: I've been told that when an athlete retires, or is cut, it's not uncommon for him to become persona non grata to his former teammates." She took a deep breath. "Have you found that to be true?"

Paul pushed a curly fry around his plate with his fork. "Yes."

"Why do you think that is?"

"Because you're a reminder of what can happen to any of them at any time. They have to cut you off. If they don't, their concentration will suffer and so will their game."

"That seems awfully harsh to me."

"It's just the way it is." He leaned forward, turning off her tape recorder. "You know what? I've had enough of this for today. You've got everything you need, right? From those bigger names?"

"Paul—"

"I'm *done*, Katie." He slipped out of the booth and stood by the table. "Lunch is on me, by the way." Without another word he turned and walked away, disappearing into a back office.

Stunned, Katie slowly packed up her things. Why couldn't she have watched what she said? Because he'd pissed her off, that's why. What was the word Bitsy's husband had used to describe Paul? *Moody.* Tormented was more like it. Clearly he'd yet to come to terms with his past.

He reminded her of so many others she'd interviewed, men who looked in the mirror and thought, "I *was* somebody!"

It was sad.

Paul had assumed the squirt tryouts would be a breeze, the contenders falling into two distinct camps: kids who could play and kids who couldn't. Instead, he spent a large part of the afternoon watching fifty boys of varying talents vie for coveted spots on the team. In doing so, he began to understand why so many coaches were hard-asses: you had to be. If you felt bad for every poor kid who wanted a spot on the roster but couldn't perform, you'd never pull a winning team together. Winning was what it was all about.

He had them go out on the ice in pairs to assess their passing skills; made them shoot pucks at him as he stood in goal. Some kids had good aim; others couldn't put the puck in the net if it was the size of a barn. Gauging their speed on the ice was another big factor. He watched their ability to stay on their feet. Finally, he had them play a mock hockey game to see if, even at this young age, they had a sense of where they should be on the ice. They didn't. Someone would shoot a puck into the corner and they would all go after it, a pack of wolves competing for the wounded rabbit. Still, there were some talented kids, Katie's nephew among them.

He and Katie had briefly made eye contact at the beginning of the tryouts. Since then, though, her eyes had been glued to her nephew, and all Paul's concentration had been on the kids. He hated that he didn't have time to go away and think about assembling his team. It was traditional in Didsbury for the kids to find out the day of tryouts who had made the team. Clutching his clipboard, Paul walked out of the boys' locker room to the arena, where the boys and their parents sat expectantly. A knot began forming in his stomach.

"I want to thank all of you for coming today and trying out. Unfortunately, not everyone can make the team. It was very difficult for me to choose my players, because all of you are talented in your own way." He paused, making sure he made eye contact with all the boys and their parents. The fear he saw in some of the parents' eyes unnerved him. You would have thought they were waiting to hear whether their children were being sentenced to Death Row.

"Okay, then, so, uh, here's who made the team."

He read out the names, his voice getting louder and louder in order to drown out the cursing, tears, and howls of parental protest. Katie's nephew made the team. So did Bitsy DiNizio's son and, unfortunately, Gary Flaherty. It would have made his life a helluva lot easier not to put Gary on the team, but that wouldn't have been fair. The kid was a fast skater, though not the most adept at stick handling. Paul could fix that. Besides, it wasn't his fault Liz was his mother.

"My son was robbed!" one father cried, spittle flecking his beard like a mad dog. "I know where you live, fucker!" he shouted as he barreled toward Paul.

"Hey!" Paul grabbed the man by the arm. "Watch your language!"

"My son deserves to be on the team!" the man shouted.

"Maybe next year," Paul said gently, turning away. The man grabbed Paul by the elbow to turn him back around. Paul shook his arm loose, squared off, and slowly said, "I want everyone who made the team to stay, and everyone who didn't to leave. Is that clear?"

His gaze slowly ranged over the crowd, pausing at Katie. She looked shaken. All the boys were wide-eyed and silent. Paul stood, watched, waited, arms folded in front of his chest. Eventually, those who didn't make the team filed out of the arena with their muttering and weeping parents.

He was left with twenty goggle-eyed boys and their parents. "Sorry you had to see that. Some parents become very emotional when their kids don't make the team." There were nervous titters. "I'm going to keep this brief. The registration fee for the year is two hundred fifty dollars. Our first practice is"— he glanced down at his clipboard, heart sinking—"next Tuesday at six thirty a.m." Groans of displeasure filled the arena.

"These kids are supposed to get up before the crack of dawn, go to practice, and then attend a full day of school?" one mother called out incredulously.

"I don't make the rules, ma'am, nor do I set the practice time." *Not only that, but I managed to live through it, and so will your son, unless he's a totally uncommitted wuss.* "If you've got a problem with it, take it up with the board." Paul smiled at the boys. "I'll have your jerseys ready for you at the next practice, as well as the team handbook. The name of this team has always been the Panthers. That okay with you guys?"

The boys nodded. "Cool," a few murmured.

"Good. That's it, then. Parents, when you fill out the registration form upon leaving, would you please also consider signing up to volunteer? We need all the help we can get. Thanks again, everybody." He smiled broadly at the boys. "See you guys next week!"

"See you, Coach van Dorn!"

"Paul?"

Katie hesitated, wondering if he'd heard her. She'd sent Tuck ahead to grab a place in the registration line for them, then hung back, waiting for the crowd of parents and kids to disperse. Everyone did—except Liz Flaherty, who was obviously wondering what the hell *Katie* would have to talk to Paul about.

Hearing his name, Paul turned. Momentary dismay skidded across his features. Katie cringed. She hoped she wasn't the source of his displeasure.

"Ladies?"

Liz eyed Katie. Katie eyed Liz. "After you," Liz said politely.

"No, after you," said Katie.

"This is private," Liz said pointedly.

"So is this," Katie shot back.

Paul scrubbed his hands over his face. "Will one of you please talk? I've got to get down to the bar."

Liz threw Katie a haughty look. "I'll go first, then, if you don't mind."

"By all means." Katie walked away until she was well out of earshot. She watched Paul and Liz out of the corner of her eye. Paul kept shaking his head "No." Liz went to put her hand on Paul's shoulder, but Paul stepped out of reach. The next thing Katie knew, Liz was stomping toward her.

"All yours," she said with a scowl.

Tentative, Katie made her way back to where Paul now sat on one of the benches. "Lovers' quarrel?" she asked, half fearing the answer.

"In her dreams."

"I'm sorry," they both said at the same time. Then they both burst out laughing.

"That was odd," said Katie, discomfited.

"I'll say. What are *you* sorry about?" Paul asked.

"Upsetting you during the interview. And you?"

"Getting upset during the interview. Sorry I was so testy." He glanced down. "I can be a jerk sometimes."

"I remember."

He cracked a sad smile. "I should probably apologize to you for high school, too."

"Water under the bridge."

"Can I make it up to you?"

"Make what up to me?"

"Years of being a boneheaded jock who made your life hell. Bruising your bumper. Being a crummy interview subject. All of it."

Kate's heart began stammering in her chest. "It depends. If it involves champagne and caviar, maybe. If it involves watching sports, no."

"How about something in the middle, like dinner?"

Katie nodded slowly. "Dinner could be nice."

"What's your pleasure?"

"Anywhere but the Penalty Box."

Paul looked surprised.

"It would be nice to talk to you without the adoring masses," Katie explained.

"Hmm. Well, the Tiv sucks, so that's out."

"Not in the mood for bratwurst?"

"Never." Paul tapped his pen against his clipboard. "How about that French place, Mirabelle, over in Langley?"

"Isn't that place extremely costly?"

Paul just looked at her.

"Right, I forgot, you're loaded." Katie sighed. "Mirabelle it is."

"How 'bout I pick you up around seven tomorrow night?"

"Fine." Katie took his clipboard and pen and wrote down her address and phone number for him. "You need directions?"

"I'm pretty sure I can figure it out."

"Okay, then," Katie said, slightly breathless. "Tomorrow night it is."

CHAPTER

06

"Change of plans."

Katie stared at the picnic basket in Paul's hand. She'd dressed for a night out at a chic French restaurant, making sure to wear the scarf he'd given her. Paul, on the other hand, was more casually dressed: chinos, blue LaCoste shirt, Pumas. He was smiling at her, completely oblivious to her confusion.

"I thought we were going to Mirabelle?"

"I called to make reservations. They've gone out of business. I took the liberty of picking up a few things for us instead." He lifted the basket by way of explanation.

"I wish you'd called me," said Katie, holding the door open so he could come inside.

"I tried. The line's been tied up for hours."

Tuck. On the computer. Time to chat with him about that.

"Well." Katie sighed. "Let me go get changed."

"No," Paul said quickly. "I mean—you look nice. Lovely scarf."

"Thank you. A blind jogger gave it to me."

Paul laughed.

"Seriously, let me—"

"Don't." There was no mistaking the appreciation in his eyes as he looked at her. "I've got a blanket. I promise you won't get dirty."

"Okay," Katie said uncertainly. Embarrassed, she added, "My mother is dying to meet you. Would you mind?"

"I'd love it."

Katie excused herself and went to the kitchen to get her mother. Earlier her mom had been in her usual "home" wear: elastic-waist blue jeans and a turtleneck topped with a fleece. Now, to Katie's astonishment, she was in one of her best church dresses, a tropical-print number that made her look like an escapee from a Jimmy Buffett video.

"Why did you change?" Katie gasped.

"I wanted to make a good impression," her mother replied.

"It's Paul van Dorn, Ma, not Prince Charles."

Her mother shrugged diffidently and with a flounce, started toward the living room, Katie trailing behind.

"Paul." Her mother gracefully extended a hand. "So honored to meet you."

Please God, Katie prayed, *don't let her drop down into a curtsey.*

Paul smiled politely. "Nice to meet you, too, Mrs. Fisher."

Katie couldn't meet his eye; she was too busy staring down at the brown shag carpet, hoping it would open up and swallow her.

"How's your head injury?" Katie's mother continued

chattily. "I hear medical science is doing simply wonderful things for brain damage these days."

Katie lightly cupped Paul's elbow, steering him back toward the door. "We'd really love to stay and chat, Mom, but we have to run. See you later."

"Sorry about that," she said once they were outside.

"What?" Paul asked, getting the car door for her.

"My mother's transformation into a curtseying neurologist. I don't think I've ever heard her use the phrase 'so honored to meet you' in my life."

"There's a first time for everything. Ready?" he asked as he slid into the driver's seat.

"Where are we going?"

"I thought we'd go down to Nesmith's Creek."

"O-okay."

"Not okay?"

"Isn't that where high school kids go to make out?"

"Not anymore. At least, I don't think so." He winked at her mischievously. "Guess we'll find out."

Engine roaring, he backed out of the driveway with a screech of the tires and began racing up the street. Katie had been so preoccupied with getting him out of her mother's house she'd failed to notice what kind of car he had. All she knew was that it seemed to go very fast, very quickly and the seats were low to the ground.

"What kind of car is this?"

"A 1969 Shelby Cobra," Paul said proudly, revving the engine again. "Just bought it."

Katie smiled indulgently. She knew nothing about cars. As long as it had four wheels and got her where she wanted to go, that was all that mattered. Speed and status meant nothing to her.

"So this picnic," she began tentatively. "What have we got in the basket?"

"Wine, of course. Some pâté. Caviar. Fresh mozzarella and roasted peppers. Crackers. Brie. Granny Smith apples. And last but not least, chocolate truffles."

Katie barely heard the specifics, her mind translating the picnic menu into "Fat, fat, and more fat." She tried not to panic. Going off Fat Fighters for one night wasn't going to wreck years of careful dieting, right? Besides, she was starving. She'd been so nervous about tonight she'd barely been able to choke down any food all day.

"How's the book coming?" Paul asked. He was driving so fast Katie swore she could feel the G forces beginning to pin back her flesh.

"Fine. Um, Paul, could you slow down? You're driving a little fast."

He flashed her a confident smile. "Don't worry. I know what I'm doing." He continued, "What did you think of that parent going after at me at tryouts? Nuts, huh?"

"What a lunatic that guy was!"

"You didn't recognize him?"

"No. Should I have?"

"That was Cheech Mahoney's little brother, Des. Used to turn his eyelids inside out for fun?"

Katie sighed. "Now I remember. This town is too small."

"Nothing wrong with that," said Paul, negotiating an extremely sharp curve that had Katie swearing the car had just gone up on two wheels. "These sports parents are nuts."

"Weren't they always?" Katie asked, gripping the door handle, hard.

"Not the way they are now."

"I meant to ask you something about practice." *If we don't die in a fiery wreck first.*

"Mmm?"

Dusk was falling outside, the sky a muted gray streaked with soft bands of pink. Perhaps it was the way the light hit the planes of Paul's face, but all Katie could think as she looked at him was: *This guy is breathtakingly perfect.* It was a disconcerting thought.

"Would you mind if I occasionally attended practice? To observe for the book?"

"No problem," Paul said easily, "but I'd check with Tuck if I were you. He might feel a bit self-conscious with you there."

"Ah. Hadn't thought of that."

"I saw you signed up to be home game penalty box official."

"What?"

Paul chuckled. "Let me rephrase that: I see Tuck signed you up to be home game penalty box official."

"That little—! I know nothing about hockey!"

Paul leaned over, patting her knee. "You'll learn."

Katie had never been to Nesmith's Creek, but she'd always wondered about it, having heard from Mina it was lovely. In high school, it was known as a big make-out spot. She'd often contemplated taking a walk there on a weekend afternoon, but the threat of people sniggering, "There goes Orca" or "Beached whale" as she strolled along the mossy embankment had always kept her away. Now, sitting with her feet tucked up beneath her on a plaid blanket beside Paul van Dorn, she knew it was a place she'd return to, especially the gorgeous weeping willow he'd chosen for their picnic spot. It seemed the perfect place to just relax and let her thoughts drift by.

"What can I get you?" Paul asked, looking pleased with himself as he surveyed the array of foods he'd set out.

"Some Brie on a cracker with a slice of apple would be

nice," said Katie, coughing loudly to cover her rumbling stomach.

"You okay?" Paul looked concerned as he sliced into the Brie.

"Bug flew down my throat," Katie fibbed. She was so hungry her ribs ached. And yet, taking the hors d'oeuvre Paul made for her, she could feel her throat closing up from anxiety. Awful, what nerves could do to the body. She forced herself to take a nibble of the cracker, washing it down with a hearty gulp of wine. The wine seemed to help. Tipping her head back, she drank more.

"You know, this reminds me of one time when the Blades were playing down in Florida . . ." Paul began.

An hour later, Katie realized two things: One, that Paul had spoken almost entirely about the past, and, two, that she was drunk, having downed three glasses of wine very quickly on an empty stomach.

"You haven't eaten very much," Paul pointed out.

"No." Looking at the food now, the last thing Katie felt was ravenous hunger. Instead it brought bile to her throat.

"Are you afraid of getting fat again?" Paul asked bluntly.

Katie turned her head so sharply to look at him the world went reeling. Oh, this was not good. She put down her wineglass, placing both palms on the blanket for support.

"No," she said faintly. "Well, maybe. A little."

"You can always run it off tomorrow." He held out some red peppers and mozzarella to her. "C'mon, I want you to eat a little more."

Katie waved it away, the smell seeping into her nostrils, making her stomach tumble against her will. "I'm fine, Paul, really."

"I bet you know the calorie count of everything."

"Pretty much."

"How many calories is this?" Taking her right hand, he delicately kissed each of her fingertips.

"Zero." Katie breathed, beginning to feel light-headed.

"And this?" Gently cradling her forearm, he placed his lips to the soft underside of her wrist.

"Zero again," Katie answered as mellow heat began whispering its way through her system. She closed her eyes, pummeled by dizziness. Was it him or the wine that made her head swim so? Did it matter?

"How 'bout this?"

Eyes still closed, Katie felt Paul's hand slide around to cup the back of her neck. Then it happened just the way she'd always dreamed it: his mouth on hers, soft, sweet, beguiling. The mellowness in her body seemed to burn off in a rose haze, making way for giddiness as his mouth pressed on, expertly parting her lips. Katie allowed herself to be steered into his embrace. How safe it felt here, sheltered in his warm, strong arms beneath the canopy of the willow tree. How right.

Mouths still enjoined, Paul gently lowered her to the ground, stretching out beside her. Katie felt the world tilt, and tilt again, as nausea shot up the back of her throat. She abruptly opened her eyes.

"You okay?" Paul whispered. The way he was smiling at her, so sweetly and full of concern, sent another volley of desire somersaulting through her.

Katie nodded weakly. She didn't want this to end. She wanted to be taken up in his arms again, where she felt cherished and protected. Perhaps the wooziness would pass if she simply ignored it and focused on him instead. Returning his smile, Katie let her fingers feather down his right cheek, delighted when he snatched her hand from his face and pressed his lips, hard, to her open palm.

"You are so, so lovely," he declared.

I am so, so nauseous. Katie's heart held still as he leaned in to kiss her again, his eyes wickedly blue. She closed her eyes, trying to feel it all at once—the desire, the heat, the longing—but couldn't get past the galloping dizziness that seemed to intensify with each passing second. Snuggling closer to her, Paul wrapped her in his arms. His mouth was making demands now that she struggled to meet. There was danger here, darkness. She knew it. She felt it. She wanted it.

And she would have succumbed to it, were it not for the mad tumbling of her stomach.

"Oh, God." Tearing her mouth from his, Katie rolled away from him and proceeded to throw up on the grass as quietly and daintily as she could. Her head was roaring now, voices of humiliation and shame drowning out the angelic chorus that had heralded desire just moments before. When she was done, she rolled onto her back, covering her face with her hands. "Please take me home."

"Katie, are you all right?" Paul asked anxiously.

"No, I'm not all right!" She peered at him through the screen of her hands. "I just threw up on a first date. Pass me a piece of apple, please. I'm sure my breath is disgusting."

"Only if you take your hands away from your face."

"Fine." She tore her hands from her face but turned her head away, the mere motion sending another round of queasiness juddering through her. *If I throw up again,* she vowed, *I'm going to pull a Virginia Woolf right here in the creek.*

"Here." Paul had come around to where she was facing, putting the apple slice in her hand. Katie's fingers closed around it and she popped it into her mouth. "Better?"

Katie nodded.

"It would be nice if you'd open your eyes," Paul coaxed.

"Too embarrassed."

"Don't be silly, Katie. C'mon."

Katie reluctantly opened her eyes. Paul was sitting Indian-style on the grass, looking worried. "Are you okay? What just happened?"

Katie averted her gaze. "I didn't eat all day because I was so nervous about tonight, and then I sucked down three glasses of wine on an empty stomach, and *voila!* I turned into the fabulous new Tipsy Tillie doll! Just kiss her and she throws up on the grass! Batteries not included!"

"Oh, Katie." He put his hand out but Katie rolled out of reach. "It's okay. Really. But why were you nervous?"

"Because I was seeing *you*," she muttered.

"I'm flattered," Paul replied softly.

"And I'm mortified." She whipped off the scarf around her neck and handed it to him. "Do me a favor, will you? Strangle me."

"Quit hiding behind jokes and talk to me."

"I'm not hiding," Katie insisted, acute embarrassment burning through her at being so transparent. When he didn't take the scarf, she retied it around her neck and rose unsteadily on her feet. "I really need to go home."

"Why don't we try this again?"

"What, a date?" Just shaking her head made her eyeballs feel like loose marbles rolling around in her head. "I don't think so."

"Why the hell not?" The edge of anger in his voice as he hurriedly gathered up their picnic foods and threw them into the basket got her attention. "So you drank on an empty stomach. So you threw up. So big deal."

"I don't know, Paul." She took a few unsteady steps. "I have to think about it."

"What's to think about?" he demanded, slamming the picnic basket shut. "Katie?"

"Paul, I really need you to get me home." The wine was making her temples pound and her stomach was still doing the samba. All she wanted was to crawl between the clean, crisp sheets of her childhood bed.

"Not until you tell me what you're thinking."

"I'm *not* thinking, Paul. I'm drunk. And humiliated. And ashamed. And—"

"I've got the picture." Taking her arm, he slowly walked with her to the car, opening the door for her. "We'll talk about this when you're feeling better." He leaned down, face close to hers. "I'm not letting you off the hook, Fisher. Don't forget it."

Katie just groaned and looked away.

"*Aunt Katie? Why* do you keep popping aspirin?"

Katie looked over at Tuck, anxiously bouncing along the brick path beside her. They were on their way to visit Mina at Windy Gables, the rehab facility. Katie loved the way these places always seemed to have names conjuring up images of serenity: Windy Gables, Seven Oaks. As if all the residents were peaceful, contented folks. She supposed it made sense, though. What else could you call it? Detox Acres? Cold Turkey Meadows?

"Aunt Katie has a headache. It's no big deal."

The last thing she'd wanted to do when she got up that morning with the hangover from hell was drag her ass out of bed, but she'd promised to take Tuck to see Mina, and there was no way she was going to let him down. Besides, she wanted to see Mina, too. It was the first time since her sister had been admitted that she was allowed to have visitors. So here she was, sunglasses keeping the glare out of her eyes, aspirin not working nearly as well as she would have liked. It didn't help her mood when she'd come down to breakfast to find her mother pacing the kitchen floor like an expectant father.

"Well?" she demanded eagerly, following so close be-hind Katie as she went to get coffee that Katie could feel her breath on her neck. "How was your date?"

"It was great!" Katie chirped. "He kissed me and then I threw up in the grass. I was every boy's dream date." When her mother pressed for details, Katie refused to talk about it. She took her coffee back upstairs to her room and hid there until it was time to bring Tuck to see Mina.

"You nervous?" she asked Tuck as they drew closer to the large, ivy covered brick building that once had been the pri-vate home of Didsbury's first banker. The setting was beau-tiful: gently sloping lawns, plenty of trees. It *was* peaceful here.

Tuck barely shook his head.

"It's okay to be nervous, you know," Katie assured him. "I'm nervous, too."

Tuck just shrugged.

Entering the building, they were directed to a large glass conservatory at the back of the mansion called "the lounge," filled with plants and patio furniture. Katie was relieved to see there were already other people there. It made what she and Tuck were about to do feel less awkward somehow.

A minute later, Mina came through the door. She was tinier than Katie had ever seen her, the jeans and T-shirt hanging off her small wiry frame making her look more like an adolescent boy than a grown woman. Her hair was cut pixie short, making her big, long lashed eyes seem even more vulnerable than usual. There was an awkward split second where they all looked at each other. Then Mina broke into a broad smile and ran toward them, arms out-stretched.

Katie watched as she gathered Tuck into her arms, cov-ering him with kisses. Tuck stood rigid, arms at his side, his expression unreadable as he endured his mother's loving onslaught. Katie desperately wished he'd hug Mina back, and almost came right out and said so, but she didn't want to push him to do anything he didn't want to do. Finally, Mina released Tuck from her crushing embrace, riffling his hair.

"I can't believe how big you got, buddy."

Tuck rolled eyes, absently kicking the toe of his sneaker against the glossy teak floor.

"Katie." Mina's eyes teared up as she drew Katie into an embrace, which Katie returned. Katie couldn't believe how fragile her sister felt, the sharp bones of her shoulder blades poking through her T-shirt like a little bird's wings.

"Are they feeding you enough?" Katie asked.

"Figures you'd ask about food," said Mina. It was said with affection, so Katie tried not to take it personally, even though it did smart a little.

Mina glanced around the conservatory. "It's so stuffy in here," she murmured to Tuck and Katie. "Why don't we take a walk outside instead?"

They started out the conservatory door, Tuck running ahead.

"He hates me," Mina lamented as soon as Tuck was far away enough not to hear, pulling a pack of cigarettes and some matches out of her T-shirt pocket.

"He doesn't hate you," Katie soothed. "He's angry at you. And he has every right to be."

"I know, I know," said Mina, lighting up.

"You're allowed to smoke here?"

Mina's laugh rang with disbelief. "Are you kidding me? *Everyone* smokes here. And drinks tons of coffee! It's insane." She inhaled, blowing out a puff of smoke. "Transferring our addictions to something legal, that's what it boils down to."

"How are you doing?" Katie asked tentatively as they veered off the winding brick path, choosing instead to follow Tuck down a large sloping lawn that led to some benches beneath a cluster of magnificent oaks.

"Okay. Not to sound like a cliché, but I'm taking it one step at a time."

Katie nodded. "Listen, do you want some time alone with Tuck? I could get lost for an hour or so, go get some coffee—"

Mina put her hand on Katie's arm, shaking her head. "It's okay. I have to let him come to me. This is fine."

"You sure?"

"I'm sure."

They watched as Tuck ran in loops around the trees, in his own world entirely.

"Remember that feeling?" Mina said wistfully, rubbing her arms.

"Not really," Katie replied dryly.

"Oh, you." Mina sounded just like their mother. "I'm so glad you came." She slipped her free hand into Katie's.

"Me, too."

"Is he doing okay?" Mina asked, eyes still following Tuck. "I mean—*really*?"

Katie squeezed her sister's hand. "He's doing fine. The school year just started and he really likes his teacher. He's playing hockey. Mom thinks he spends too much time on the computer, and I'm starting to agree."

"How *is* mom?" Mina purred.

"Don't start, Mina, okay? Mom really saved your ass."

"Hey, I'm not denying it." Mina took another drag off her cigarette. "There's just a ton of stuff coming out in therapy that makes me realize a lot of the way I am has to do with the family."

"Like?"

Mina glanced away. "You know, Dad's death, that maybe that's what made me act out. It was a way of dealing with the sadness as well as being a pathetic bid to get Mom's attention."

Katie swallowed. "Makes sense."

"Not as effective as cramming a box of Twinkies down my throat but hey, we all have to find what works for us." Before Katie could protest Mina took a step back, admiring her.

"You look great, Katie. Really."

"Thanks."

"Are you still doing—whatsitcalled—Lard Losers?"

"Fat Fighters," Katie corrected. "Yes, I am."

"Still running?"

"Yup."

"Wow," said Mina, impressed. "More power to you. I'd rather listen to Mom sing than exercise." She threw her cigarette down on the ground, stubbing it out with the heel of her Frye boot.

"Unfortunately, some of us *have* to exercise." Which reminded Katie: Even if she still felt crummy when she and Tuck got back to Didsbury, she was going for a run.

"Mom, look!"

Katie and Mina both looked to see Tuck do a series of perfectly executed back flips. Katie applauded while Mina shouted "Way to go, bro!" and lit up another cigarette. They ambled down to where Tuck was still giving his impromptu gymnastics display.

"Want to sit with us?" Mina asked, gesturing toward a bench.

Tuck sprang to his feet. "Boring!"

"I'll give you boring," Mina replied, darting after him. Tuck shrieked and began running from her, laughing. Watching them together, Katie was struck by how Mina seemed more like Tuck's older sibling than his mother, which had always been the case. Perhaps that was part of the problem: Mina didn't really know how to mother Tuck, having been virtually a child herself when she'd had him.

"Oh, God." Mina limped back to where Katie sat, panting. "Maybe I *should* start to exercise. I thought my lungs were going to burst."

Katie looked around. "Where's Tuck?"

"He said he was thirsty. I told him if he went back to the house, they would give him something to drink."

"Will he be okay?"

"No, some ex-junkie or alkie is going to drag him off into the woods," Mina drawled. "Christ, you're worse than Mom."

"I'm just expressing concern."

"He'll be fine, Katie, *okay?*" Mina shook another cigarette out of the pack and lit up. "You worry too much."

Katie thought Mina didn't worry enough, but she kept her mouth shut.

Mina took a long drag off her cigarette. "So, what's new with you?"

"I went on a date with Paul van Dorn last night and narrowly avoided throwing up on him."

"What?"

"You heard me."

"Hockey Paul van Dorn?"

"That's the one."

Mina tapped cigarette ash on to the ground. "I thought he was Mr. NHL superstar."

"He was," said Katie, stealing Mina's cigarette from her and taking a puff. "He had to retire early. Concussion. He bought Cuffy's and redid it. Now it's called the Penalty Box."

"Oh, *man!*" Mina chortled. "What a *loser!*"

Katie bristled. "What do you mean?"

"If you were loaded and had to retire early, would *you*

come back to Didsbury?" Mina shook her head. "Man, oh man. If I had his kind of money I'd get the hell out of that one horse town and never look back. He's pathetic."

Katie didn't know what to say. On a certain level, Mina had just expressed—albeit more cruelly—what she herself had thought. Had Mina just verbalized Katie's reluctance to get too close to Paul? Was she afraid of getting sucked back into the small town she'd worked so hard to escape? "People are different," Katie finally said. "They want different things."

"I guess," said Mina, sounding unconvinced. "But if you ask me, he's a loser."

"Wasn't it great to see your mom?"

Katie glanced over at Tuck, who was resting his head against the passenger side window of the car. The mood was unusually subdued, bordering on the melancholy. Katie wasn't surprised: Mina had wept when they left, promising to call every day now that she was allowed to do so. Katie could tell that Tuck didn't believe her.

"Tuck?"

He twisted his body away from her.

"Honey, talk to me."

"I wish you were my mom," Tuck said sadly.

Tears leaked into the corners of Katie's eyes. "Your mom loves you, Tuck," she said, trying hard to keep her voice from cracking. "Didn't she look great? Can you see how hard she's trying to get better?"

"She stinks like cigarettes."

Katie stifled a laugh. It was true, Mina reeked of tobacco. The whole facility seemed to reek of tobacco. And burnt coffee. "Well, if you want, we can get her some perfume for Christmas. How about that?"

"I guess."

"You know, when your mom was little she was addicted to computer games just the way you are."

Tuck turned to look at her. *"Really?"*

"Oh, yeah. We used to play them at our cousin's house all the time. There was one, *Dark Castle*, that made the sound of squeaking bats. She loved that one."

Tuck laughed with delight. "What else did she play?"

Katie thought. "Well, there was one called *Doom*, where you run around and try to kill things that are after you."

"Cool."

"I think you probably inherited the computer game gene from your mom."

"Did she play hockey, too?" Tuck asked eagerly.

"I'm not sure. She might have. Ask her next time you see her."

"I will." He sank back in his seat, looking pleased. "Aunt Katie?"

"Mmm?"

"Do you think maybe my dad liked computer games, too?"

"He might have," Katie said cautiously.

"Maybe he was a hockey player! Maybe that's why I like it!"

"Maybe it is," Katie agreed. "It's certainly possible."

"Cool," Tuck whispered to himself, rocking in his seat. "Was my dad named Tuck?"

"I don't really know," Katie fibbed. There was no way she was going to tell him he got his name because of Mina's adolescent fixation with the Marshall Tucker Band. *Good thing I didn't have a kid when I was in my teens*, Katie thought. *His name would have been Ring Ding*. Katie wondered if he even knew his full name was Tucker. He'd been called Tuck since birth.

"You know, I meant to ask you something about hockey, Tuck."

"What?" He was practically bouncing in his seat. It didn't take much to make him happy. All you had to do was pay a little attention to him.

"Would you mind if I sat in on a few of your hockey practices? For my book?"

"Sure!" Tuck exclaimed. "You can see how great I am!"

Katie laughed, making a mental note of his masculine self-confidence for her book. "I already know that, sweetie. But it'll be fun to see you on the ice."

CHAPTER

07

I knew she'd be here, Paul thought as Katie slipped into the rink with Tuck. She'd been on his mind. He could understand her being embarrassed. But hemming and hawing about seeing him again seemed way out of proportion to what actually happened. It wasn't like she'd thrown up *on* him, for God's sake.

Juiced on coffee and an early-morning run, he strode into the locker room to meet the boys. They seemed sluggish, not surprising given the early hour. But their faces perked up when he began handing out jerseys. Their excitement over seeing their names printed on a hockey sweater brought him back to his own childhood. He loved the yearly ritual of getting a new sweater. He could still remember slipping on his Blades sweater for the first time, holding his arms aloft in triumph at the press conference that had been called to announce he was going to New York as the league's number one draft pick. It seemed like yesterday.

"Okay, listen up."

Twenty pairs of restless eyes found his. "These first few practices I want us to concentrate on having fun." How small they looked, huddling around the wooden benches in their gear, clutching their miniature sticks as if their lives depended on it. "Who watches hockey on TV?"

Everyone raised his hand.

"Who knows *all* the rules?"

Roughly half the team raised their hands.

"Right." Paul covered his disappointment with an encouraging smile. "I'll start by explaining the basics to you out on the ice. Then we'll warm up, and I'll have you play a game that'll help all of you develop your skating." He made eye contact with each and every one of the boys, a technique he'd learned from his Blades coach, Ty Gallagher. "If there's one saying I want you to remember this season, it's this: There's no *I* in the word *team*. Got it?" The boys nodded, and Paul clapped his hands together loudly. "All right, Panthers, let's hit the ice!"

Fastening the chin strap of his helmet he led the kids out to the ice. His eyes quickly searched to see where Katie was sitting. She was a few rows up from the players' bench, laptop balanced on her knees. Paul gave a small nod of acknowledgment, which she returned.

He slowly began circling the rink, urging the boys to follow suit. He noticed immediately that Tuck Fisher was a good, strong skater. So was Liz's kid, Gary. Eventually he halted, sizing up each boy as he skated past.

"Okay!" Paul blew the whistle around his neck. "We're going to play a game called one foot face-off. Darren Becker and Chuck Wilbraham, I want each of you in goal. The rest of you, I'm going to send you out in two groups of three. When I blow the whistle, I want the first group to play, pushing off only on your left foot as you skate. When I blow the whistle again, I want the next six boys on the ice, but I want them to push off only with their right foot. Any team who skates past their opponents while puck handling gets two points; you'll get one point for each goal scored. We'll keep alternating teams and legs until I say we're done."

He picked six boys at random, sending them out on the ice facing one another three on three. "All right let's go!"

He stepped back and watched. Right away there was trouble. A number of boys forgot they could only use their left leg to push off, while others seemed to think pushing off left meant dragging their right legs behind them like pint-size Quasimodos.

"Stop!" Paul blew the whistle, and the boys halted. "Watch me, okay?" He demonstrated the left leg technique for them, doing the same on the right. "Any clearer?" The boys nodded. "Resume play!"

His eyes strayed to check out Katie, tapping away on her laptop. *What the hell could she be writing?*

Most of practice was taken up with the one foot face-off drill. Twice he had to stop because Tuck was checking. When the team was done practicing, Paul barked, "You guys did great!" He led them in a cool-down skate before sending them to the locker room to get changed for their school day.

He watched from the ice as Katie folded up her laptop. She seemed to be waiting for him. Doffing his helmet, he skated over and went to sit down beside her. "Have book bag, will travel," he joked as he shifted her canvas tote to the floor. "What were you writing?"

"Notes." She lifted her eyes to his. "May I say something about your coaching?"

"It's my first day on the job and you know nothing about hockey," Paul replied, "but sure, be my guest."

"You tell the boys 'Great job!', but your expression says otherwise. You looked pained to be here."

"I *was* pained," Paul tried to joke. "They don't know what the hell they're doing."

"That's why you're here," Katie reminded him. "To teach them. Maybe you could try hiding what you're thinking?"

"Anything else, Madame Sociologist?"

Katie cracked a small smile. "That's all for now, Coach van Dorn."

"Your nephew's got some anger issues," Paul noted, running a hand through his sweaty hair.

"I know." Katie looked distressed. "I guess it's not surprising."

"No." What was surprising was how awkward this exchange felt. "Feeling any better?"

"Much." Katie's face contorted with embarrassment. "I'm so, so sorry."

"Don't sweat it." Paul patted the back of his neck with a towel. "I would like a rain check, though."

Katie squirmed. "Paul—"

"What's the problem, Katie?" He couldn't keep the irritation out of his voice as it reverberated through the cold, empty rink. "What are you so afraid of?"

"I'm not afraid of anything!"

"Then what's the problem?"

Katie hesitated.

"I'm asking you to have dinner with me, not marry me." He couldn't tell if it was the wrong thing to say as Katie stared down at her feet, face turning red. "What?" Paul prodded.

"It depends," she murmured.

"On?"

"Where we go."

He couldn't believe she was issuing *conditions*. Normally he'd say "To hell with you, lady," but Katie was different. "What's your pleasure?" he coaxed. "French? Italian? Chinese?"

Katie didn't look particularly enthused by any of them. Then it dawned on him: It's not the cuisine she's hung up on. It's the calories.

"How 'bout this: I'll make us a healthy, low-fat dinner at my place." Katie looked skeptical and he got defensive. "Some men *do* know how to cook, you know. I happen to be one of them." He was lying through his teeth, but so what? How hard could it be to chuck a piece of meat in the oven and boil some vegetables?

"What's your specialty?" Katie asked.

"That's for me to know and for you to find out. If you think it's too fattening, we can go running for hours afterward to burn it all off."

Katie raised an eyebrow. "Are you mocking me?"

"Totally. So let's say seven, my place, Friday night?" He rose. "Deal?"

"Deal?" Katie scoffed. "Is that how you usually finalize plans for a date?"

"No. As a matter of fact, I usually do this." He glanced around quickly to make sure the rink was empty, then kissed her swiftly on the mouth. When he pulled back, she was smiling. "Deal?"

"Deal," Katie murmured.

"You won't be disappointed," he promised.

"*Leave it to* Anthony to give directions no one can read," Paul muttered to himself, squinting as he tried to decipher the chicken scratch before him. Paul's confidence about cooking for Katie had faded as the week wore on. By Wednesday morning, he was in a blind panic. Unsure of what to do, he called his former teammate and friend

Michael Dante, half owner in a Brooklyn restaurant called Dante's. Michael tried talking Paul off the ledge, assuring him that if he could read, he could cook. But Paul was dubious, so Michael put him on the phone with his brother, Anthony, Dante's head chef. After picking Anthony's brains for half an hour about putting together a meal that was impressive and tasty yet not too high in calories, Anthony had finally roared, "*Idiota!* I'll prepare the damn dinner myself and FedEx it up to you. All you'll have to do is pop things in the oven and sprinkle a little cheese here and there. Think you can handle that, birdbrain?"

Paul was pretty sure he could; that is, until the food actually arrived and he had to decipher Anthony's instructions for each dish. The almond cookies were self-explanatory. He'd figured out the marinated carrot sticks pretty fast; ditto the sea bass baked with artichokes. It was the green beans he was having a hard time with. He called the restaurant.

"Dante's. May I help you?" answered a woman with a very pleasant voice. Anthony's wife, maybe?

"Yes, hi, I need to speak to Anthony. It's an emergency."

"Who should I say is calling, please?"

"Paul van Dorn."

"Hold on."

A few seconds later, Anthony picked up. "Let me guess: the almond cookies are too simple for your sophisticated palate."

"No, everything's great. It's just these beans . . ."

"What about them?" Anthony asked suspiciously. "They were picked fresh, I swear on my mother's grave."

"What am I supposed to DO with them? I can't read your handwriting." He grabbed the foil lid, squinting hard. "The bigger the skull—"

"Butter the skillet! Butter the skillet!"

"Butter the skillet," Paul repeated thoughtfully. "Ah."

"Those concussions leave you retarded or what?"

"It's your handwriting that's the problem, not my brain!"

Anthony heaved a long-suffering sigh. "Butter the skillet, put the heat up to medium, and dump in the beans when the butter starts to foam. When the beans are nice and coated, add the grated cheese—which I packed in there for you because God only knows what kind of *immangiabile* cheese you have up there in the sticks and I only buy from Tony Culotto, the best—toss it all together, throw in a little salt if it needs it, and serve it immediately. *Capisce?*"

"Got it."

"Good luck, brain boy," Anthony said with a chuckle as he hung up the phone.

Butter the skillet. Paul transferred Anthony's dishes to his cookware and disposed of the evidence, burying all the containers in the trash. There was no way Katie could fail to be impressed. The dishes that Anthony—correction, he—had prepared *were* simple yet elegant. There was nothing swimming in a cream sauce that would freak her out.

He checked his watch: ten minutes till game time. He'd made sure to tidy up, but he wasn't sure it mattered. Apart from the bare necessities, most of his life was still packed in boxes scattered around the house. He vowed daily he'd finish unpacking, but somehow, he never got around to it.

He'd picked up some candles to help create atmosphere, and had gotten some fresh flowers, too. His stereo system was set up, so that was a plus. Wine was chilling in the fridge and the table was all set. The only thing left to do was relax and wait for Katie—*and* keep an eye on the food in the kitchen. He looked around. Things looked just a little *too* perfect, so he loaded up the drain board with pots and pans and a bunch of utensils. *Much better.* Now it looked like he'd been playing chef all day.

His doorbell rang at seven on the dot. Paul was glad: One

of the things he'd never gotten used to in Manhattan was the premium placed on being fashionably late. It drove him nuts. When he said seven, he meant seven, not seven-*ish*. One good thing about being back in Didsbury was the absence of all those ish-es.

"Hey." Opening the door, he gave himself permission to drink her in. She was a vision, her long blonde hair shimmering softly in the fading sunlight, her coltish legs swathed in tasteful black trousers. The scarf he'd given her was tossed jauntily over the left shoulder of her maroon turtleneck. She was holding a bottle of wine.

"You look great," Paul murmured, kissing her cheek as he ushered her inside. "I'm beginning to think that scarf is the only one you own."

"It is," Katie admitted.

"Well, it suits you." He took the wine from her. "Why don't you sit down on the couch and I'll go open this."

"Oh, no," Katie replied in a teasing voice. "I want to see the chef at work."

Paul nearly blanched. "Most of the work is done. But sure, come on."

Katie inhaled deeply as he led her into the kitchen. "Smells great. What is it?"

"Well, there's marinated carrot sticks, and for a main dish, there's sea bass baked with artichokes. There's also green beans, but I still have to sauté those."

Katie rested a hip against the counter, watching him uncork the wine. "And you cooked all this yourself?"

"Everything except the almond cookies."

Katie nodded approvingly. "Very, very impressive Mr. van Dorn."

"Thank you," said Paul, not quite meeting her eye. He made a show of checking the oven. "Won't be too much longer. Just remind me I have to get started on the green beans in fifteen minutes or so."

"No problem."

Handing her a glass of wine, he poured some for himself. "Shall we?" he said, guiding her back out to the living room. Katie stopped in the middle of the room, surveying her surroundings.

"Did you just move in?"

Paul ducked his head, embarrassed. "Yeah, about six months ago."

"*Six months ago?* From the look of things, I thought for sure you'd only been here a few weeks."

"It takes me a while to get around to things sometimes," Paul mumbled, easing himself down on the coach.

"The fireplace is nice," she noted. "I always wanted a house with one of those."

She meandered some more among the boxes, peering curiously into those that were open. One box in particular caught her attention; she crouched down to inspect it more closely, only to spring up and back away. "Oh, God."

"What?" Paul shot forward, alarmed. "A mouse?"

"No, our high school yearbook. Please tell me you'll destroy it as soon as I leave."

"We could look at it," Paul suggested.

"Not unless you want to watch me commit seppuku on your living room floor."

"Does that involve high heels and a spangly, push-up bra? If so, I'd love to watch."

"Actually, it involves a sword."

"That could be fun, too," Paul murmured suggestively.

Katie closed the box, making a point of pushing it into a far corner.

"Oh, c'mon," Paul protested. "It can't *all* have been bad."

Katie stared at him.

"Haven't you ever heard the expression 'That which does not kill me, makes me stronger'?"

Katie's eyebrows lifted. "A Nietzsche-quoting jock. I *am* impressed."

"Hey, I made it to one or two philosophy classes when I was an undergrad."

"Just one or two?"

Paul smiled sheepishly. "Well, you know, I had other stuff to do."

"I'll bet." She joined him on the couch.

"Seriously, Katie. You have to give Didsbury a little credit. It made you the woman you are today, right?"

She took a sip of wine. "I guess I never thought of it that way."

"And it's not completely awful. I bet if you try, you can name three things about Didsbury you actually like."

"Easy: you, my mother, and Tuck."

"It can't be people."

Katie sighed. "Fine." She closed her eyes, concentrating. "Okay: it *is* gorgeous here in the spring and summer."

"One."

"Drummond's Fudge Shop—though I can't go in there anymore."

"Two."

"Winterfest."

"And that's three." Paul was waiting with a smile as her eyes sprang open. "See, not completely horrible." He slid an inch closer to her on the couch. "I've always been a big Winterfest fan myself. Maybe we could go together this year."

"Maybe," Katie said faintly.

He chose to ignore the noncommittal nature of her reply, taking a sip of wine instead. "You did eat today, right?"

"*Yes.*"

"Because we don't want you throwing up again, do we?"

Katie looked mortified. "Please promise me you'll never mention that again!"

His hand covered his heart. "I swear I'll never mention you throwing up again."

"Honest?"

"Swear."

"Okay, then." Katie touched her glass to his, eyes twinkling wickedly. *"Deal."*

"Touching glasses is not how I seal deals, Professor."

"Oh, no? Show me, then."

A challenge. A dare. Paul loved those. Eyes fastened on her beautiful face, he carefully peeled her delicate fingers from around the stem of her wineglass, placing it on the floor along with his own. Then he took her in his arms, pressing his lips against hers. Mere contact sent electricity bulleting through his system, but it wasn't long before his head began to swim as he realized it was *she* who deepened the kiss, *she* who made her pleasure known as their tongues sought each other's hungrily. She wanted him just as badly as he wanted her. The realization excited him. He could feel her trembling against him as he tightened his embrace, but rather than soothe, he moved to conquer. Tearing his mouth from hers, he moved his lips to her throat, kissing, nipping. Katie's head fell back with a moan.

"More," she whispered.

Paul crushed his mouth down on hers again. The spice of her perfume, the heady taste of her lips, the soft press of her breasts against his chest all conspired to drive him mad. And yet, in the back of his mind . . . food. He could hear Anthony's voice in his head yelling, "I cooked special for you and you let it burn, you ungrateful 'tard!" It spoiled the mood. Paul pulled back, resting his fevered brow against hers.

"I hate to be a spoilsport," he whispered, "but dinner is going to burn."

Katie sighed. "I know."

"Can we call a time-out?"

"You and your sexy sports talk." Her fingertips traced his cheek. "That's fine."

"Good." Paul couldn't resist a wink as he rose, extending a hand to her. "Just make sure you leave room for dessert."

Katie was proud of herself: not only did she sip her wine slowly throughout dinner, but she actually *ate*, despite a mild case of the tummy wobbles brought on by the certainty that when dinner was through, she and Paul van Dorn were going to *do* it. Desire, hot and sharp, sizzled through her just thinking about it.

"Here, let me help you clear off the table," she said and began gathering dishes.

"You don't have to do that," Paul said immediately.

"I want to."

"No, really," he implored, but Katie was too quick for him. Picking up her plate, she carried it over to the kitchen garbage can, pressing her foot down on the lever that made the lid spring open. That's when she saw it: a sea of crumpled foil containers. Katie turned to Paul. His hands were held up in surrender.

"Guilty."

Katie chuckled as she scraped the remains of her plate into the trash. "You could have told me the truth, you know."

"How, after boasting to you that I could cook?"

"I don't care whether or not you can cook."

"No, but you do care about the calorie count of every morsel you put in your mouth. I wanted to make sure dinner was tasty but not too fattening."

Katie flushed with appreciation. "Thank you." She looked at him curiously. "Where did you order from? Isn't the only take-out place around here Wang's?"

"It's a long story. But the food is from Dante's. In Brooklyn. Remember I told you about my friend Michael?"

Katie nodded. Michael, Michael, Michael. That's all she'd heard about over dinner: Michael and the Blades. Michael and his restaurant. "You talk about Michael an awful lot, you know."

"Yeah?" Paul seemed thoughtful. "Well, he *is* one of my best friends. And he's the only one on the team who keeps in touch."

"You talk about the past a lot, too," Katie continued gently, making another trip out to the dining room to collect more dishes. Paul's eyes darted to hers as she returned to the garbage.

"What's wrong with that? Our past is what makes us who we are."

"It can also stop us from fully living in the present, if we're not careful."

"Is that what you think I'm doing? Living a half life?"

Katie hesitated. "You never talk about the Penalty Box or coaching."

"I just started coaching," Paul pointed out. "There's nothing *to* talk about."

"It's not a criticism, just an observation. Maybe I'm aware of it because I spend so much time doing the opposite: trying to blot out the past."

"Isn't that just as unhealthy?" Paul asked.

"Probably," Katie answered. "I just get the sense that you haven't quite come to terms with things."

He pressed his lips to her forehead. "Let me worry about my head, okay? Your only concern is my heart."

"But the two—"

"Enough." He stilled her with a finger to her lips. "How 'bout this? Why don't you finish up in here, and I'll light a fire in the living room?"

"Sure, leave me to do the dishes."

"Well, it *is* women's work."

"Take that back!" Katie demanded, playfully smacking his arm.

Paul feigned cowering. "I take it back, I take it back." He squeezed her shoulders lightly. "Yes to the fire?"

Katie let her eyes drift shut a moment, imagining the two of them stretched out before dancing firelight.

"Yes," she whispered. Yes to everything.

Paul had just put another Duraflame log on the fire and was sitting back on his heels when Katie entered the living room. She assumed he was waiting to see if he'd need to poke at the flames to get a good roar going. Absorbed in his task, he hadn't heard her come in. Katie took advantage of the opportunity to study him in the firelight. He looked relaxed, his normally watchful gaze almost peaceful, the hard muscles of his thighs straining through his jeans. Katie cleared her throat to make her presence known. Paul glanced up at her over his shoulder, smiling. "So, what do you think?"

"It seems to be going okay." She sat down on the rug before the fire. Paul was still standing, back to her, poking at the rising flames. Katie let her gaze drift to his calves, remembering them from the day she'd bumped him with her car. They were sculpted and firm; an athlete's calves. Her gaze traveled up his back; beneath the black turtleneck she could make out the perfect V formed from his shoulders to his waist. Katie couldn't help noticing how the ribbed material hugged the strong, broad shoulders. Her gaze crept down again; Boxers or briefs? An image flashed in her mind of silk sheets barely covering his naked hips as he lay back against a mountain of pillows, his rock-hard chest bare and inviting. Swallowing, she forced her eyes to the dancing flames.

"The fire's doing well now," she noted lamely.

"Yep," Paul laid down the poker and sat beside her, putting his arm around her. Katie rested her head on his shoulder.

"This is nice."

He tilted her face up to his. "Let's make it even nicer."

Katie closed her eyes. She heard him murmur her name softly as his hand slipped from around her shoulder and he wrapped his arms around her, drawing her into a loving embrace. It was so easy to return his affection and twine her arms around his strong neck, to surrender to the feeling of his mouth slowly clamping down on hers, eager, restless. Delight tripped through her as she became aware of how effortlessly their tongues danced together.

Secure in Paul's embrace, Katie felt as if she were awakening from a long slumber and was now experiencing the glories of the world for the first time. Here was desire, need, unforgettable fire. And here was Paul, flickering candlelight tracing patterns on his strong, handsome face.

"I want you, Katie." He sounded as if he were aching.

"So take me," Katie whispered, her hand reaching up shakily to begin peeling off her turtleneck.

Paul groaned, a low rumble escaping from his chest as he gently took her hand from her shirt, replacing it with his own. Their eyes met and held as he slowly, painstakingly, slid her turtleneck up and over her head, letting it drop to the floor. Paul smiled his approval, his lips just grazing her throat as he quietly reached around to unfasten Katie's bra. Blood was pounding in Katie's ears as that garment, too, fell away, revealing her bare chest. Silently, almost reverently, he bent his head down to kiss the top of each breast before taking a step back and tearing his own shirt off over his head, his eyes once again locked on her face.

"C'mere," he said softly. Katie stepped in to the gap between them and into his embrace. Someone's body felt as if it were alight—hers? His? Both? She couldn't be sure. She watched his face as he languidly closed his eyes, his hands coming up to cup her shoulder blades and anchor her against him.

The sweetness and restraint in Paul's movements was almost too much for Katie to bear. Already excited, she dug her fingers deep into his neck as she pulled him down for a hard kiss, her tongue swirling around his, daring him to return the favor. He did—but not before tightening his grasp around her and using the full force of his body to maneuver them toward the couch, sitting on the edge with Katie standing before him. She shuddered sharply as his hands tantalizingly caressed her sides, her ribcage, the hollow of her stomach—everywhere but where she most wanted him to touch.

"You're torturing me," Katie whispered, her fingers brushing the soft buzz of his hair.

"Well, we can't have that, now, can we?" Paul teased. Katie's breath froze as he leaned forward, his tongue snaking out to taste each hardened nipple. Then, opening his mouth wide, he took as much of her right breast into his mouth as he could before scraping his teeth back and forth across both nipples. Katie felt herself dissolving.

"More?" Paul asked seductively.

Katie nodded fervently, gasping aloud as he latched on to her and suckled hard, a deep whimper rising up from her throat. If he kept up much longer, she was going to come just standing there, the deep throbbing intensity within her abdomen blazing out of control the longer he suckled. She was beginning to feel crazed. She wanted him here, now, in her.

Through sheer force of will, she tore herself from his mouth, looking down at him. Paul gazed at her with desire while Katie hurriedly undid the zipper of her slacks, peeling them down her hips.

"Feeling shy?" Paul taunted as his eyes dipped down to take in the sight of her in her panties. Pulling her roughly to him, he hooked his thumbs over the silky top of her bikini underwear, yanking them down. Katie kicked them aside, a throaty, primitive groan escaping her lips as he pulled her onto his lap, her legs straddling his hips. The pounding of her own heart, the crackling of the fire, Paul's ragged breath—all were making her fevered. She twined her arms tightly around his neck, reveling in the delicious torture he inflicted upon her as his mouth returned to sampling her breasts, one minute biting the nipples, the next soothing them with his tongue.

"I—I want— " Katie gasped.

"Just relax, Professor," Paul soothed, clearly delighting in pleasuring her. Katie moaned softly to herself as his tongue tickled and licked its way up to her earlobe. That alone would have been enough. But Paul gave her more, his nimble fingers reaching down between her legs to stroke her. Katie held her breath, and then he was there, two fingers snaking their way inside her at the precise moment his teeth sank into the soft underside of her throat.

"God!" she cried out.

"That would be me," Paul replied, and they both burst out laughing, though Katie's laughter quickly turned to staccato gasps as his teasing fingers continued to move in and out of her body.

"Paul, please," she begged him. "Please."

"Please what?" Paul growled, fingers quickening their pace.

"Please make love to me," Katie rasped, her head falling back.

For a second, nothing happened. Then she felt the universe tilt as he lifted her up and she was on her back, sprawled on the rug before the fire. Katie panted, waiting, as Paul fumbled with the zipper of his jeans. He was naked now, and she took him in her hand. He was hard, silky in her palm, his whole body going rigid as she slowly stroked him. Now she was the torturer, the one calling the shots. Still holding him in her hand, she brushed the tip of him over her and was rewarded with a feral growl. Close, they were so close, and he was perfectly positioned: one thrust and he would be deep inside her body, the agony of their bodies quenched. Katie's hips began angling up to meet his as she barely rode the tip of him. But instead of plunging deep inside her, he took care of protection, and then came up on his elbows, looking down into her eyes as he lovingly pushed the damp tendrils of her hair off her face.

"This is it," he said, his mouth covering her face in passionate kisses. "No turning back. You sure?"

"I'm sure," Katie whispered feverishly, pulling her knees up as he eased himself into her.

The fit was perfect, tight. Katie's breath came rapidly as he began thrusting slowly, almost dreamily, inside her. "I've fantasized about this from the minute I saw you at the reunion," he said, the huskiness of his voice giving Katie goosebumps. He pushed deeper.

Katie groaned her response as his body continued moving in hers: hard, deep, assured. "This okay?" he rasped, changing the angle of his thrusts so that every one of his strokes was rubbing against her sex. Katie swallowed, barely having time to nod yes before he began quickening the pace, his teeth carving a groove into her shoulder as he bit down. That was it: Katie's head snapped back and an unrestrained scream of pleasure erupted from her lips as he drove her over the edge. When she returned to her senses, she saw his eyes burning in the firelight, the intensity almost too much to bear.

"Hold on," he said, thrusting relentlessly. Katie could feel her own pulse begin to climb back up as Paul started to lose control. She savored the moment, watching as his open mouth drew in great gulps of air. He was close now, she could tell. He pulled her thigh up even higher on his hip, Katie matching his rhythm. At last, he gave one final, frenzied thrust before emptying himself into her.

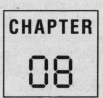

CHAPTER

08

"You okay, Professor?"

Paul's words brought Katie back to herself. Her body might be snuggled against his in front of the roaring fire, but her mind was floating blissfully out in the cosmos. She wondered how long they'd been holding each other, the need for speech superfluous.

Katie brushed her nose against his. "Please don't call me that. It makes me feel like I'm on *Gilligan's Island.*"

Paul laughed. "Who does that make me? The Skipper?"

"Ginger."

"Mmm, kinky."

Katie turned on to her back, eyes following Paul as he rose to fetch an afghan from the couch. The flickering shadows created by the fire played across his rippling muscles. His body was perfect. *And* he was good in bed. Katie couldn't believe her good luck.

Lying beside her, Paul propped himself up on one elbow

while the fingers of his free hand brushed easily over her right hip. He slid down her body, kissing the spot he'd just caressed. "What are these?" he asked innocently.

Katie lifted her head, peering down the length of her body as Paul continued to gaze curiously at the intricate network of pearly white lines crisscrossing her hips.

"Those are stretchmarks," she said quietly, moving to turn away from him. "From when I was fat."

Paul pulled her back toward him, pressing his mouth to the marks and letting his lips linger. "I think they're beautiful."

Katie snorted. "My God, you can sling the bull."

Paul lifted his eyes to hers. "I'm not bullshitting you, Katie. They're hieroglyphics. I read them and I can see where you've been and how hard you've worked to get to where you are now. They're part of you, so they're beautiful." He kissed her right hip again before spreading the afghan over the two of them and settling back down with Katie nestled in his arms.

"This is very romantic." Katie sighed. "But please tell me you have a bed we can repair to after a decent interval of canoodling."

"Of course I have a bed. What do you think I am?"

"With all these unpacked boxes, I thought you might bed down on the couch every night," Katie ribbed.

"I have a bed," Paul repeated, kissing her forehead. "Trust me."

"I could help you unpack, you know."

Slightly, almost imperceptibly, Katie could feel him tense.

"No, that's okay. I don't need help."

"It might be fun."

"I don't think so," Paul said with unmistakable terseness.

He drew her closer, stroking her hair. "Let's just concentrate on us."

"Us," Katie repeated uncertainly. The concept made her feel nervous.

Paul's gaze was questioning as he pulled back so he could look at her. "You don't sound too thrilled."

"No, I'm fine, I mean, I'm thrilled, this was thrilling, look at my thrilled face." She made a silly face, but Paul didn't laugh. It was best to tell the truth. "I just think we should keep it kind of quiet, that's all."

"What the hell for?" Paul scowled. "I'm going out with the smartest and most beautiful woman in Didsbury and I have to keep it a secret?"

"I'm only in Didsbury temporarily. Remember?"

"So?"

Katie sighed with frustration. "People talk, Paul."

"*So?*" he repeated.

"Maybe it's not such a good idea for us to be too obvious, you know? You're Tuck's coach, remember?"

Paul groaned.

"And then there's Liz," Katie brought up tentatively.

"*What?*" Paul bolted upright, staring at her in horror as if she'd just started speaking in tongues. "What does Liz have to do with anything?"

"She wants you, Paul. Everyone knows it."

"*So?*"

"Stop saying 'so'!"

Paul's expression remained incredulous. "You're going to let *Liz Flaherty* dictate what we can and can't do? Are you nuts?"

"She can stir up trouble," Katie muttered. "You know she can." His inability to see the implications of Liz knowing about them irked her. Tugging on his fingers, she pulled him back down beside her. "I just think it's better if we keep this quiet," she said, resting her chin on his shoulder.

Paul thought about it for a moment, then drew back suspiciously. "You sure this isn't about me?"

"You?"

"Yeah. Me. As in the hotshot college professor doesn't want it to get around she's playing footsy with the loser ex-jock."

Katie stared at him. "Is that really how you see yourself?"

Embarrassment flashed across his face. "No, of course not—"

"Then don't talk about yourself that way," Katie said sharply. "And don't talk about *me* that way." She withdrew, feeling a bit wounded. "This has nothing to do with what other people think."

"Except Liz Flaherty."

"I just don't want any trouble, Paul. And I don't want Tuck running into any problems, either."

Paul scrubbed his hands over his face. "You want to be secret fuck buddies? Fine."

"Why are you having such a hard time with this? I thought for sure you'd agree."

"I can see your point with Tuck. But factoring Liz into the equation is insane. So she gets upset that we're together. So big deal."

Together. What, exactly, did being "together" mean? She was leaving at the end of the summer to go back to Fallowfield. "I'm tired," Katie said, nuzzling against his chest. "Let's not talk about this anymore."

"So you decide the subject is closed and that's it?"

"You're 'so'-ing again." She cupped his face with her hand. "You want to open the subject back up?" she said gently. "What more is there to say?"

"I happen to be crazy about you, Katie." The fierceness in his eyes took Katie aback. "If you want to keep this on the QT for a while because of my being Tuck's coach, that's fine. But we're not hiding this forever."

"No, of course not," Katie said, laughing nervously. She appeared to be following along, but her mind was still back at *I'm crazy about you.* Was that the runner-up to "I love you"? He was beginning to remind her of the items on her "Forbidden Foods" list—delicious treats she had to guard against because if she succumbed and had even one, all hell would break loose and she'd backslide completely.

"I'm proud we're together," Paul was saying. "Proud to say you're mine."

"All right, Tarzan, I get the picture," Katie joshed, hoping to bring the intensity of the moment down a notch. "Let's just play it by ear and see how things go. Agreed?"

"Agreed," Paul muttered with gruff reluctance. Katie snuggled deeper in his arms, determined to banish her own doubts. This was nice. This was good. They could sort out the details later.

If ever Katie needed evidence Didsbury was a very small town, it came the next morning as she was leaving Paul's house. No sooner had she walked down the drive than a cheery female voice called out, "Mornin,' Katie!"

Katie halted, peering across the street. Mrs. Greco, the town librarian, was waving at her as she fetched her paper from the mailbox.

"Hi, Mrs. Greco," Katie managed to call back. She could just imagine what the old woman was thinking.

"Beautiful morning, isn't it?"

"Lovely," Katie returned, desperately stabbing her car door with her key.

Slept with Paul van Dorn? she imagined Mrs. Greco calling.

Twice, Katie imagined calling back.

How was it? Mrs. Greco asked as another neighbor came out of her house and stood on the lawn, listening.

Great! Katie replied.

"Have a nice day," the real Mrs. Greco concluded, ducking back into her house.

"You, too," said Katie, sliding into her car. It took every ounce of restraint not to peel out.

Driving back to her mother's house, Katie wondered how soon Mrs. Greco would tell everyone she saw Katie Fisher creeping out of Paul van Dorn's house early Saturday morning. She hadn't really been creeping, but still.

It shouldn't matter, Katie told herself.

But it did.

It wasn't just Liz Flaherty making her life hell that concerned her, or fear it could hurt Tuck. It was coupledom and all the trappings that went with it. She'd worked hard to get the hell out of Didsbury. Getting serious with Paul threatened that.

Still, they'd had a wonderful night and morning together. He was a skillful lover, strong and considerate. And he *did* have a bed: King-size and luxurious. It had been so nice to be able to spread out after sleeping in the single bed of her childhood.

She pulled into her mother's driveway and killed the engine, checking her watch. Nine a.m. Opening the front door to her mother's house, she was greeted by, "OH, THANK GOD!" and the sound of a chair scraping back in the kitchen. Two seconds later her mother appeared in the living room, wild-eyed. She'd been crying. "There you are!" Her mother threw her arms around Katie. "Thank God you're alive!"

"What?" Katie asked, mystified. Out of the corner of her eye, she saw Tuck's head peek around the corner then disappear.

"I was worried sick when you didn't come home last night! If you weren't here by noon I was going to call the police."

Katie grasped her mother gently by the shoulders. "Mom, you knew I was going over to"—she lowered her voice in case little ears were listening—"Paul van Dorn's last night, remember?"

"Yes, of course I know you were at Paul's," her mother replied impatiently. "But I figured you'd be home by midnight! And then as the hours went on and on—"

"I spent the night," Katie blurted.

The living room throbbed with silence.

"You spent the night?" her mother said. "Couldn't you have called to let me know?"

"I didn't think you were going to wait up for me, Mom."

"Of course I was going to wait up for you! You know I don't sleep until all my chickadees are in bed, safe and sound."

Cradling her mother's elbow, Katie steered her toward the couch. "I'm not a chickadee," she reminded her as they sat down. "I'm a grown woman. I don't need to account to you for my actions."

"Who's talking about accountability?" her mother asked. "How about some simple consideration?"

Katie blushed. "I'm sorry. I just assumed you'd know where I was."

"Oh, and why is that?" her mother snapped. "Do you make it a habit of sleeping around?"

Katie took a deep breath, taking her mother's hands between her own.

"Mom, I'm not Mina," she said in a quiet but firm

voice. "I'm not going to disappear for days on end. I'm not going to climb out of my window in the middle of the night. I'm not going to bring home a new guy covered in tattoos every two weeks. You're not going to have to sit by the phone waiting for a call from the police. Okay?"

Her mother looked away.

"I'm sorry I didn't call you," Katie continued, "but I really thought it would be fairly obvious where I was."

Her mother stared hard. "I don't like it. I don't *approve* of it."

"Well, I'm sorry about that, but I'm twenty-eight years old. I'm going to do what I want, whether you like it or not."

Her mother was silent.

"I could get my own place," Katie offered.

Her mother's head whipped around. "No! I love having you here. And it would break Tuck's heart if you left."

"Well, if you want me to stay," said Katie, "you're going to have to get used to the fact that I might be spending some nights with"—her voice dropped again—"Paul."

Her mother looked perplexed. "Why do you keep lowering your voice every time you mention Paul van Dorn?" she boomed.

Katie covered her face with her hands. God help me, she thought, by the time this day is over, my night with Paul will be the lead story on the local news.

"Because. Of. Tuck," Katie said through gritted teeth. "Paul is his coach. I just think it would be awkward for Tuck if he knew, you know—"

"I understand," her mother said quickly as she looked at Katie with hopeful eyes. "Is it serious?"

"Is what serious?"

"You and you-know-who," her mother whispered.

"Define serious," said Katie, straining to look around the

corner to see if Tuck was sitting at the bottom of the stairs listening to every word being said.

"Serious," her mother repeated dreamily, a faraway look coming into her eyes that Katie associated with zombies. "As in—"

"No."

Her mother blinked with surprise. "You don't know what I was going to say!"

"Yes, I do, and the answer is no."

"Yet you're sleeping with him." Her voice was sour with disapproval.

"Yup," said Katie, refusing to be apologetic. "That's the way things work here in the good old twenty-first century."

"I don't like it."

"You've made that very clear," Katie said sweetly, patting her mother's hand. "Now, I'm going to make some coffee. Would you like some?"

"Aunt Katie?"

Katie had no sooner reached the top of the stairs than Tuck came scurrying out of his room, his socks making him slip on the wooden floor. She could tell just by looking at his face that he'd heard at least some of what had been said.

"Yes, sweetie?"

"You're not going to move out, are you?"

Katie looked at him steadily. "Why would you think that?"

Tuck shuffled his stockinged feet.

"You were listening in on me and Nana, huh?"

"No!"

"It's okay," she assured him. "C'mon, let's talk."

Katie led him back to his room, which was surprisingly neat. She'd expected piles of stinky boy clothes, scattered books and CDs, an unmade bed. Instead she found his bed made and everything in its place. She wondered how much of it had to do with her mother's insistence on tidiness, or whether it was a reaction to the chaos of life with Mina. Probably both.

She perched on the end of his bed. "What did you hear?"

Tuck shrugged.

"You're not going to get in trouble, I promise you. Just tell me."

Tuck's eyes met hers uneasily. "I heard you asking Nana if she wanted you to move out and I heard Nana being mad at you because you were at Coach van Dorn's all night."

Shit. The kid had bat hearing.

"Anything else?"

Tuck shrugged again.

"Okay, Tuck. I need you to listen." Katie almost burst out laughing as his eyes opened wide in a pantomime of super attentiveness. "First of all, I'm not moving out until it's time for me to go back to Fallowfield. I only said it because sometimes grownups do things that other grownups don't like, and I thought it might make Nana happier if she didn't have to worry about me."

"Because Nana didn't like you being with Coach all night," Tuck observed.

"Right," Katie answered, heat rushing to her cheeks. This was harder than she thought.

"Is the coach your boyfriend?" Tuck asked hopefully.

"He's—my friend." Was that the right answer? Apparently not, if the dubious look on Tuck's face was any indication.

"A good friend," Katie amended lamely.

"Are you having sex with him?"

Katie's mouth slowly fell open. It took a minute for her to recover herself and try to figure out how to handle the question. She had to keep reminding herself that Tuck had been exposed to situations other children had not. Beneath his innocent demeanor was a very jaded little boy. "That's none of your business," Katie said gently.

"Sorry," Tuck muttered.

"No, it's okay to ask questions. It's just that some things are private, and that's one of them. Which is why it would mean a lot to me if you didn't say anything to anyone about me and your coach."

"But it's cool," Tuck countered with a whine.

"Yes, but it's *private*," Katie reiterated. "The only reason you know is because Nana went a little wacko there." Tuck laughed. "Right?"

Tuck nodded.

"So let's keep this under our hats for now. Not a word to your friends, or anyone on the team, or anyone. Okay?"

"Okay," Tuck said reluctantly. "But."

"But what?"

"Like, maybe you'll fall in love and get married and then you and Coach could adopt me!"

"Tuck." Katie's voice was pained. "You have a mother, remember? And she loves you very much."

Tuck pretended not to hear as he went to his computer.

"Tuck?" Katie wanted to wrap her arms around him tightly and assure him everything was going to be all right. But she knew her nephew would push her away when he was in this mood. He'd play deaf, just like he was doing now.

Katie sighed. "I'm going to go get some work done in my room. If you want to talk any more, just come on in, okay?"

Tuck gave no indication of hearing.

Katie walked out into the hall. It wasn't until she was sitting in front of her own computer that it dawned on her that in some ways, she was no better than Mina. For just as her sister had done so many times, she, too, had just asked Tuck to lie.

"That shit-eating grin on your face can mean only one thing: Either you won the lottery or you bagged your dream girl. Which is it?"

Frank DiNizio's question made Paul chuckle as he slid onto a bar stool at the Penalty Box, sipping his Sam Adams. The place was hopping, which was what he wanted on a Saturday night. He'd called Katie and asked her if she'd like to go to a movie, but she'd begged off, saying she was falling behind on working on her book. Paul wondered if it was the movie, which had already been playing there for several years—or if she just didn't want to risk being seen with him.

"C'mon, bro, spill," Frank urged, pushing a cosmopolitan toward a blowsy, half-drunk woman before giving his full attention to Paul. "What happened?" Frank had been following Paul's pursuit of Katie with curiosity.

Paul's look was sly. "What do you think happened?"

"Whoa!" Frank held up a bear-size palm for Paul to high-five. "Way to go, my man! Way to go!"

"Yeah, well, we'll see."

Frank thrust his giant head forward in disbelief. "Whazzup?"

Paul frowned. "She's being weird about it." He took another sip of beer, scanning the bar. He was always keeping an eye out for trouble, or making sure the staff weren't goofing off.

Frank nodded knowingly. "Wants the ring already, huh?"

"Just the opposite. Doesn't want anyone to know."

Frank's brows collided. "What's up with that?"

"I'm not sure," Paul confessed. "She's worried about

conflict since I coach her nephew. If the kid does really well, which I think he will, I could be accused of favoritism. But beyond that, it doesn't make sense. At least not to me."

"Maybe she's got a steady back in Vermont and she doesn't want word to get out."

"Thanks, Frank." That possibility had never crossed Paul's mind. He entertained the thought for a moment, then cast it aside. Katie didn't strike him as the cheating type.

Frank looked philosophical. "Maybe she's not thrilled about dating, you know—"

"A jock? An ex-jock? A failed jock? A bar owner? A youth hockey coach?"

"Mother o' God, relax, will ya?" Frank shook his head. "I was going to say 'a townie.'"

Townie. Paul hated that word. But that's what he was, wasn't he? He thought back to high school, how he and all his cool jock friends had contempt for all the local "losers" who stuck around town. *They* would never stay in a place so small, boring, provincial. *They* would go out and conquer the universe. And now look at you, Paul said to himself disgustedly. Ten years later and you're right back where you started. Full circle. Failure.

He sighed, downing another mouthful of beer. "Well, whatever her reason for wanting to keep quiet, I'm not going to keep my mouth shut forever."

"Damn straight."

"Any other woman would be proud to be on my arm."

"Damn straight," Frank repeated. His eyes flicked to the doorway. "Speaking of which, here comes one now."

Liz. Paul knew it without even turning around. She'd been stalking him for days, leaving messages on his answering machine, trying to corner him in the parking lot after hockey practice. He should have known she'd eventually turn up at the bar. Maybe he should stop spending so much time here. Just because he owned the place didn't mean he had to be here all the time. He could hire a general manager. But he liked being here. The patrons liked him being here, too. They loved hearing his hockey stories.

"There you *are*." Liz kissed his cheek, wiggling her bottom seductively as she tried to get comfortable on the bar stool beside his. "You've been a very hard man to get hold of." She leaned toward him. "But that's okay," she whispered. "Who wants to hold a man who *isn't* hard?"

Paul could barely look at her. "What do you want, Liz?"

"To talk to you."

"Really."

"Yes." She turned her attention to Frank for a moment. "Hi, Frankie."

"Liz," Frank muttered.

"Can I have a Grey Goose martini?"

"With or without a twist of cyanide?"

Liz turned to Paul. "Your bartender is being rude to me."

"Just get her the drink, Frank," Paul said wearily.

"Whatever you say, boss," Frank said with a salute, waddling off to prepare Liz's drink.

Paul shifted his attention back to Liz. "You wanted to talk?"

"You owe me a dinner," Liz purred.

Paul frowned. "What?"

"You promised to take me out to dinner, lamby, remember? That morning you left my house in such a hurry?"

"Sorry. I've got no memory of that."

Liz's nails dug into his arm. "*I* do."

"Desperation is very unattractive," Paul informed her as he removed her fingers from his forearm. "Hasn't anyone ever told you that?"

"I'm not desperate," Liz huffed. "I'm merely here to collect what was promised me."

"Jesus H," Paul muttered. Was there a bigger pain in the ass on earth than Liz Flaherty? "You want dinner?" Paul was beginning to feel like an animal caught in a steel trap. The only way he'd escape would be to gnaw off one of his own limbs. "Fine." He pointed at one of the booths where a family of four was just leaving. "Go sit there and I'll join you in five minutes."

Liz glanced disdainfully at the booth. "Eating in the Penalty Box is not what I had in mind."

"Take it or leave it." Paul noticed that Frank had edged close to them, doing his damnedest to look preoccupied with the glasses he was drying. *Big head, big ears*, Paul thought. *He's probably listening to every word that's going down. Not that it matters.*

"Paul." Liz's voice was laced with condescension. "Clearly, you're not thinking straight. Do I have to spell it out for you?" She put her mouth to his ear, her voice breathy with need and seduction. "If you take me out for a nice, romantic dinner for two, I promise I will give you the best sex you've ever had in your life."

Paul pulled away with a chuckle. "Actually, Liz, I had the best sex of my life last night." Frank stifled a snort as he went to take someone's order at the other end of the bar. Paul wanted to snort, too. Was it cruel admitting how happy it made him to watch Liz's face fall?

"What?" she hissed. "Who?"

"None of your business." He was dying to tell her. It would be worth it just to see her reaction. But Katie would kill him.

Liz's eyes shone bright with malice. "It's not the former Miss Piggy, is it?"

"Who?"

"You know who. Katie Fisher." She practically spat Katie's name. "I saw you talking to her that day after tryouts."

"Katie's nephew, Tuck, is on the team."

"Mina's little bastard? Yes, I'm aware of that. Unfortunately, Gary and Tuck are becoming fast friends." She took a demure sip of her martini. "So, are you fucking her?"

"No. And even if I was, it's none of your business."

"Well, there's no law saying you can't sleep with two women at the same time, lamby."

"Read my lips, Liz: I don't want to have dinner with you. I don't want to sleep with you. I'm in a relationship with someone else. *Okay?*"

Liz drained her martini glass and rose regally. "You know, I don't like being rejected, Paul."

"Are you beginning to get the message?"

She kissed his nose. "I'll give you one more chance. And then things are going to get nasty."

CHAPTER

09

Katie looked on in envy as Bitsy and Denise split a brownie at Tabitha's. Usually after a Fat Fighters meeting they split dessert into thirds. But not tonight: Katie had put on two pounds. Lolly, who was working the scale, tried to make her feel better by invoking one of Fat Fighters's favorite phrases, "It's only a number." *Really?* Katie longed to shoot back. *Then why are we all here? Clearly some numbers are better than others.* Instead, she kept quiet, resolving to run every day. It was those damned almond cookies she'd had at Paul's. Those, and the veggies drenched in butter and cheese. She was sure of it.

"So, Katie," Bitsy purred, "how long do you intend to keep us in suspense?"

Katie smiled uncertainly. "I don't follow."

"We want details, girl. Is he good in bed or what?"

A sick feeling began in the hollow of Katie's stomach. "Who?"

"Who!" Denise whooped. "P van D, of course!"

Katie felt the power of speech draining away. "I—I—how?" *Mrs. Greco. Bigmouthed old—*

"Paul told Frank and Frank told me," Bitsy explained.

"And then Bitsy told me," Denise added. "In strictest confidence, of course," she added solemnly, crossing her heart.

Katie's temples began to drum. She would kill Paul. She would aim for him with her car and this time, she'd do it right and flatten him like a pancake.

"Well?" Bitsy pressed.

Katie stared down into her coffee. "You can't say anything to anyone." She lifted her eyes to theirs. "I *mean* it."

Bitsy shrugged. "Of course."

"No, I really mean it," Katie repeated fiercely. Her friends exchanged alarmed glances.

"Honey, no offense," Denise said, casually picking the walnuts out of her brownie, "but why on earth would you want to hide that you've bagged the hottest bachelor in Didsbury? If it was me, I'd have a T-shirt made declaring, I'M DOING IT WITH VAN DORN, and wear it everywhere."

"Really, Katie." Bitsy looked perplexed as she sipped her own coffee. "He's *the* catch."

To you townies, Katie caught herself thinking uncharitably. She hated that that was the first thought that flew into her mind, but she couldn't help it. In a tiny pond like Didsbury—actually, Didsbury was more like a puddle—Paul was indeed the biggest fish. But there was an ocean out there, one she'd made a conscious effort to escape to, one she planned on returning to. How could she say that to her friends without insulting them?

Katie sighed heavily. "I don't want problems with Liz. And I don't want it causing any problems for Tuck."

Denise blinked. "I don't follow."

"Paul coaches Tuck and Chris as well as Liz's son, Gary," Bitsy explained. She looked at Katie. "You're afraid Paul might be accused of favoritism if Tuck does well?"

Katie nodded. "Exactly."

"Okay, I get that," said Denise, tipping her walnut shards onto Bitsy's plate. "But to keep it hidden from Liz Flaherty is to deprive the good citizens of Didsbury of a much deserved pleasure." She chugged down some coffee. "I'd sell my firstborn to see Liz's face when she finds out about you and Paul."

"Can you *have* a firstborn?" Bitsy asked uncertainly.

"Let's not get into this," Katie begged.

"Anyway, I hear Liz almost tossed her cookies when she found out Paul was seeing someone," Bitsy confided.

The queasy feeling in Katie's stomach bubbled up again. *"What?"*

"Frank told me Liz was at the Penalty Box last night, sticking her tongue in Paul's ear. He told her he was seeing someone else and to get lost. She was not happy."

Katie scowled.

"Cat fight! Cat fight!" Denise called, clapping her hands.

"Guys, look." Katie was upset but determined to play things down. "It's not really that big a deal, okay? I mean, it's not serious. It's casual."

"Then why did flames just shoot out of your eyes like Godzilla when you heard about Liz?" Denise queried sweetly.

"Flames did not shoot out of my eyes. This relationship—if you can even call it that—is casual. I repeat: casual. Because of Tuck," Katie reiterated. That would be her defense: Protecting Tuck.

"Does Tuck know?" Bitsy asked.

Katie hesitated.

"Katie, if Tuck knows, you're dead in the water," Bitsy

declared. "Little kids cannot keep secrets. Especially juicy little secrets like *that*."

You don't know Tuck, Katie thought. Tuck kept it a secret that his mother often left him alone for days on end with nothing but a loaf of white bread and peanut butter and jelly to eat. Tuck kept quiet about all those mornings he woke to find Mina passed out on the floor in a pool of her own vomit. Tuck could be very discreet if he had to be.

"We'll see," said Katie.

"So, how *is* all that hockey stuff going?" asked Denise, eyeing both Katie and Bitsy with interest.

Bitsy's eyes met Katie's. "You've been at practice. You tell me."

"What has Christopher been saying?" Katie asked.

"That it's fun but hard. He says, and I quote, 'Sometimes coach is mean.'"

"It's true," Katie admitted reluctantly. "Paul seems to forget they're little boys. He pushes a lot. It's transference. He's unable to compete himself, so in order to ensure his own masculine ego stays intact—" She broke off. "What?"

"You're talking like a textbook," Denise pointed out gently.

"Sorry."

"Maybe things will get better once they actually start playing," Bitsy suggested.

"Maybe," Katie agreed. "The first game is, when, next Thursday?"

"Yes, against the Richmond Condors."

"I love these names," Denise cooed. "Panthers, condors—they're so aggressive."

"Of course they are," said Katie. "Their purpose is to conjure masculinity, force and prowess with one word."

"You're doing it again, Professor," Denise teased. "Gettin' all highfalutin' on us."

Katie blushed. " 'Professor' is Paul's nickname for me," she murmured.

"What's your nickname for him?" Bitsy wanted to know.

"I don't really have one."

"Of course. Because it's just casual," Denise deadpanned.

Bitsy's face lit up. "Wouldn't it be great if you and Paul fell madly in love and got married and you stayed here?"

"That would be heaven," Denise concurred. "You're fun to hang with, Katie."

So are you, Katie thought as she looked down at her hands. But staying in Didsbury was the last thing on earth she wanted.

The only other time Katie had visited the Penalty Box, it was the middle of the day in the middle of the week. Entering now on a weeknight, she wasn't sure what to expect. *I should have phoned ahead to find out if Paul was going to be here.* Then she realized: *Of course he is. He lives for the attention.* He certainly wasn't spending his free time settling into his house.

She found the bar packed, mostly with men. Their eyes were glued to a large-screen TV adjacent to the bar. Hockey was on. Katie looked at the score posted on the bottom left-hand corner of the screen: ATL, 2, NYB, 1. NYB . . . New York Blades. Paul had his old team on the box. Talk about masochism.

Slipping off her coat, Katie scanned the room. No sign of Paul, though that didn't necessarily mean he wasn't here. He could be in the men's room. She decided to get herself a drink.

She studied Bitsy's husband as she approached the bar.

Seeing him again, Katie remembered him from high school after all. The only difference was the beginnings of a belly.

"Evening," Frank said pleasantly as Katie sidled up to the bar. "Help you?"

"Um, a Perrier, please."

"That it?"

"Is Paul around?"

Frank's expression turned guarded. "Depends who's asking."

Katie playfully cocked her head. "You have no idea who I am, do you?"

"No, ma'am, I don't." He studied her. Katie loved it when the light finally broke in his eyes. "Katie?"

Katie laughed.

"Holy shit!" Frank exclaimed, pounding his hand on the bar. "You look amazing!"

"Thank you," Katie said, appreciative of the compliment.

"Paul told me you were a knockout now, but I never expected this."

Pride turned to mild displeasure as Katie thought: Yes, Paul tells you lots of things, doesn't he? Well, that's about to change.

"Is he around?" Katie asked again.

"Yeah, he's in the back office right now. I'll have one of the girls go get him. Yo, Izzy!" he called out to a curvaceous brunette putting a basket of nachos down at a nearby table for two. "Go get the boss, will ya?"

Izzy frowned. "He said he didn't want to be disturbed."

"Tell him his girlfriend is here." Frank winked at Katie. "That'll light a fire under his ass."

"Thanks," Katie managed, trying to ignore Izzy as she icily sized Katie up before heading toward the back of the Penalty Box. "Really, I'm not his girlfriend," she longed to call after the jealous girl.

"Here you go." Frank plunked down a Perrier bottle and a glass full of ice in front of Katie. "On the house."

Katie fumbled in her book bag. "No, I insist on paying."

"Don't even think it. Paul would kill me if I let you pay." Frank nodded his head knowingly. "You two are getting along real good, huh?"

"Actually, I've come here to kill him."

Frank laughed uneasily. "He'll just be a minute."

Self-conscious, Katie slid onto a bar stool. She'd never sat *at* a bar before. She wasn't there three seconds before she felt a tap on her shoulder. Turning, she found herself gazing down into the face of a very short, bearded man wearing a Blades jersey and a lascivious smile. The jersey, she noticed, had been autographed by Paul.

"Buy you a drink, gorgeous?"

In your dreams, Rumpelstiltskin. This was why she disliked bars. They were filled with men who were filled with booze who liked to hit on women. "No, thank you," Katie said politely, slipping off the bar stool and heading in the general direction she'd seen the sour-faced Izzy go. Katie didn't care if she wound up in a broom closet; anything would be better than hanging at the bar being hit on by unofficial members of the van Dorn fan club.

"Hey."

She'd nearly reached the back of the room when a door opened and Paul came out of what she assumed was his office, Izzy glowering at her in his wake.

"I'm glad you came down," Paul said happily, putting an arm around her waist and kissing her cheek.

Katie stiffened. "Don't," she whispered.

"Right." Paul frowned, letting his arm drop. "What's up?"

"I need to talk to you. I—"

"Paul van Dorn! You rock, buddy!"

Before Katie could get any more words out, a group of three young men in their early thirties, all wearing Blades jerseys, surrounded them.

"Thanks," said Paul.

"Man, we drove up all the way from Long Island to come here."

"That's great," said Paul. "You guys all set for drinks? Munchies?"

"Screw munchies, dude, I want to know how you managed that deke in game three against Toronto in '04!" said one of the guys.

Paul's face lit up with pleasure. "Well, it went down like this . . ."

Fifteen minutes later, Paul was done telling his story, the three guys from Long Island had had him sign everything from their jerseys to photos to napkins, and Katie was doing a slow burn.

"Sorry about that," Paul apologized.

"No, you're not," Katie said quietly, without any accusation. "You love it."

Paul shrugged easily. "Yeah, I do. That a problem?"

"Only when I need to talk to you."

"Let's go in my office."

Katie had to admit, she did like the feel of his hand on the small of her back as he gently guided her through the door. But when he switched on the light, she gasped, and it wasn't from pleasure. The place was a sty.

"Hang on." Paul cleared the couch of the giant, inflated bottle of tequila and cardboard cutout of some buxom blonde holding a bottle of rum aloft, and offered her a seat. "We get a lot of promo stuff from liquor companies, as you can see."

"Paul, this place looks like a bomb hit it. How do you keep track of anything?"

"Don't worry. I know where everything is."

"Does all this really make you happy?" Katie blurted.

Paul looked baffled as he pushed a box filled with Bacardi key chains out of the way. "What?"

"The bar, youth hockey, Didsbury. Are you happy?"

"Is that what you came to talk about?" Paul asked, scratching absently behind his left ear. "Whether I'm happy?"

"No. But I'm curious."

"It is what it is."

"But is it what you *want*?"

"I can't have what I want, Katie." His voice was brusque.

"I know, but—this—I mean—"

"This is fine." He slid the length of the couch so he was sitting right beside her, and planted a tender kiss on her mouth. "More than fine now that I have you."

Katie's hands knotted in her lap. "That's what I came to talk to you about."

"Not sure I like the sound of that," Paul replied guardedly.

"Paul, why did you tell Frank about us when we specifically agreed we were going to keep things quiet?"

"Frank won't tell anyone."

"Except Bitsy. Who told Denise Coogan."

"Denise." Paul shook his head in wonder. "Man, can you imagine what her shoe size must be?"

"Don't change the subject."

"What was the subject again?"

Katie stared at him.

"It was going to come out eventually, Katie. You know that. I don't see what the big deal is."

"It's—"

"Tuck," he finished for her wryly. "It's all because of Tuck."

"Right."

"You do know that doesn't hold much water, right?" His ice-blue eyes were uncomfortably direct.

Katie glanced away.

"Care to tell me what's really going on here?"

"That *is* what's really going on."

"Fine, whatever you say. But I'm not hiding this relationship forever. It's ridiculous. And insulting. If you don't want me, I know plenty of women who do."

"Like Liz Flaherty?" Katie snapped.

Paul chuckled. "Jealous?"

"Of the she wolf of the SS? Hardly. No, I just happen to know from Bitsy, who heard from *Frank*"—she glared at Paul—"that Liz was here angling for a ride on your joystick."

Paul looked amused. "And that bothers you."

"Of course it bothers me! You—you're—" she was painting herself into a corner.

"I'm what, Katie?" Paul raised a questioning eyebrow. "I'm yours?"

"Yes," Katie muttered.

"Ah. So let me make sure I'm getting this straight: I'm yours, but no one can know I'm yours. Or, no one can know I'm yours until *you* want them to know I'm yours."

"It sounds awful when you put it that way!"

"That's because it is awful, Professor." He put his arm back around her, kissing her hair. "It's awful and mean and cruel."

Katie closed her eyes, trying to fight the greed for him she felt rising in her bones.

"It's for Tuck," she heard herself saying. "I don't want this to aversely affect Tuck. And I don't want to deal with Liz Flaherty."

"Fine," Paul murmured, scraping his teeth against the

soft skin of her throat. "We'll keep this quiet for now. For Tuck."

"And . . . you'll tell Frank . . . to keep his trap shut." Katie moaned.

"Yes."

"And"—her mind began fogging as his teeth nipped at her—"you'll tell Liz to take a hike next time she comes sniffing around for tookie?"

"Yes," Paul swore, eager fingers struggling with the buttons of her blouse. "Now be quiet and let me show my favorite teacher a thing or two."

"*You had sex* with him in his office with a bar full of people on the other side of the door!? That is *so* not you!"

Katie smiled indulgently at Mina's remark, letting it pass. Despite Katie's transformation from duckling to swan, in Mina's mind Katie was forever the reclusive, overweight sister hiding in her room surrounded by books. God forbid Mina face the fact that Katie was, like her, an extremely attractive, sexually active woman.

"Is it serious?" Mina asked, blowing a line of smoke out the side of her mouth.

Katie sighed. She and Tuck had come to Windy Gables on their weekly visit. This time Katie had had to bribe Tuck into coming by promising she'd take him for ice cream after the visit—not that he was making much of an effort to interact with his mother. Thankfully, Mina wasn't forcing it. "Why is that the first thing people want to know?"

"Human curiosity, I guess." Mina's eyes followed Tuck as he ambled far ahead of them, kicking angrily at every pile of leaves he passed. "So, is it?"

"Serious? No," Kate replied emphatically. "I enjoy his

company and the sex is great, but I can't really see it going anywhere."

"Love 'em and leave 'em. That's the Katie Fisher way."

The sarcasm in Mina's voice irritated Katie. "Hardly."

Mina slowed down, carefully perusing Katie's face. "You really like this guy, don't you?"

"Why do you say that?"

"I can tell," Mina replied jauntily. "It's a sister thing. Same way you always knew when I snuck out of the house at night. Speaking of which"—she took a drag on her cigarette, jerking her head in Tuck's direction—"is he behaving himself?"

"Always," Katie said as she glanced fondly at her nephew. "He's a good kid, Mina. You know that."

Mina's mouth twitched. "Not too pleased to see Mommy today, I see."

"Cut him some slack. He's actually been helping Mom turn her sewing room back into a bedroom for you."

Mina jerked to a halt. "What?"

"For when you get out in January. Mom figured—"

"What?" Mina hissed. "That we'd be one, big, happy family?"

"*No*, she figured—and I agree with her by the way—that it might be best for Tuck if you transition by coming home for a few weeks before just uprooting him and moving him somewhere else."

"Oh, this is great. Classic." Mina hurled the butt end of her cigarette to the ground, stamping on it. "How come no one thinks to ask me how I feel about all this? It's just my *life*, that's all."

"I thought you had discussed it with Mom."

"Yeah, right. She comes here to visit and all she does is talk about church." Mina shook her head. "No way can I be under the same roof as Mom. *No way*."

Katie was dumbfounded. "I don't see what the problem is."

"No, of course, you, don't, Miss Goody Two-Shoes."

"Go to hell, Mina! Who do you think chauffeurs your son to school and hockey practice and everywhere in between? Who do you think bought him his hockey gear?"

"No one asked you to!"

"Right. No one asked me to." Katie suddenly felt exhausted. "Can we not do this, please?" Mina had turned her back to Katie and was kicking at the ground, shoulders hunched. "Mina?"

Mina whirled back around to face Katie. "Sorry," she muttered.

Katie gave her a quick hug. "Me, too."

"Can I just say one thing?"

Katie stiffened. "What?"

"There is no way I can go back home, Katie. I swear to God, I'll kill myself."

"You can't do it for Tuck?" Katie implored. "Just for a few weeks?"

"I've already got a place for me and Tuck."

Katie couldn't hide her surprise. "You do?"

"Yeah. Kinda." Mina crouched down, plucking a half-dead dandelion from the ground. "My friend Snake said we could stay with him until I find a place."

"Snake?"

Mina frowned, crushing the dandelion in her palm. "That's right, I forgot; all my friends are lowlife scum."

Katie gave a short laugh. "No offense, Mina, but you have to admit the name *Snake* doesn't inspire images of wholesome living."

Mina almost smiled. "Snake's a good guy. He's been through the program and he knows what I'll be facing. He'll be very good support for me."

And will you be sleeping with him? Or will Tuck have to reacquaint himself with an endless stream of faceless lovers going in and out of your bedroom?

"What does Snake do?" Katie asked politely.

"He's a bouncer. At the Tender Trap."

"Niiiice." The Tender Trap was the topless bar one town over in Summersby.

Mina released the crushed dandelion from her hand. "Don't be so judgmental, Katie, okay?"

"Sorry." Mina was right. For all Katie knew, Snake could very well be Didsbury's own Mr. Rogers. But she doubted it.

"Does Tuck know Snake?"

"No." Mina's mouth pinched. "But I'm sure he'll like him. Snake's got a chopper."

Just like Mr. Rogers! Look at me, Aunt Katie, Uncle Snake is taking me for a ride!

"He'll think that's cool," Katie was forced to admit.

"Exactly." Mina seemed relieved. "See? I know what I'm doing."

They walked on in companionable silence, both watching Tuck. He'd grown bored with kicking leaves and was now walking along with his head thrown back, staring up at the cloudy sky.

"Watch where you're going!" Katie called.

Mina looked at her sharply.

"Sorry. Didn't mean to overstep my bounds."

"Katie." Mina grabbed Katie's arm. "I just had a great idea!"

"What's that?"

"Do you think maybe you could ask your boyfriend if there are any waitressing jobs open at his bar? Snake said he could get me a job dancing at the Trap, but I'd really like to avoid that if I can. And I have waitressed before."

"I'll see what I can do," Katie replied cautiously. "But I'm not promising anything."

"You're the best!" Mina exclaimed, throwing her arms around her sister. "What would I do without you?"

CHAPTER 10

Praise them. The words thundered in Paul's head as he followed his team into the locker room following their 4–2 defeat to the Richmond Condors. One of the coaching manuals he occasionally thumbed through spoke of the importance of pointing out what a team did right before delving into what they did wrong. He would follow that advice, even though the chaos he'd witnessed on the ice had sent his blood pressure through the roof. He had to remind himself they were young and inexperienced. Discipline, skill, and finesse would come in time.

It had better or he'd lose his mind.

"Guys, gather round."

Twenty sweat-drenched, weary little bodies packed in close to him.

"I'm really proud that . . . all of you remembered to wear your cups today." Jesus, was that the only positive thing he could come up with? He had to do better than that. "Some of you worked very hard today. But there are a few things we need to go over, okay?"

The boys nodded tentatively.

"One of the things we need to remember is that we don't all skate to the puck." Paul could feel the muscles in the back of his neck knotting as he recalled the way the whole team would dive into the corners like a pack of coyotes chasing a rabbit. It was pitiful. "Another thing we need to remember is that hockey has rules." He gazed deeply into each and every pair of eyes. "You can't pass over the blue line, remember?" Some of the boys nodded vigorously, including Chuck Wilbraham, who had been one of the worst offenders. "Chuck, if you know the rules, why did you keep passing over the blue line?"

"I forgot," Chuck muttered.

"Your forgetfulness helped us lose," Paul snapped. They shouldn't have lost. He'd drilled them to death, played mock games with them during practice, and fed them an encouraging slogan each week. Entering the rink today, he was brimming with confidence, certain that his boys were golden, solid. Yet the minute they hit the ice, they fell apart. If they didn't get their act together, he would be the laughingstock of the Youth Hockey League.

"Mr. Bitterman." His eyes sought the red-haired boy who was his first-line left winger. "When the puck comes to you, you do not stop moving and wave to your parents, saying, 'Look, I've got the puck!' Got it?"

The boy cast his eyes down.

"Mr. Becker." Paul's voice was stern as he stared into the face of his top goalie. "Getting your gloves tangled up in the goal netting wasn't a good defensive strategy, was it?"

"No, Coach."

"Tell me why."

"Because Richmond scored and I wasn't ready."

"That's one way of looking at it." Paul's left temple twitched. "Another way to look at it is like this: You were caught like a fly in a goddamn spiderweb. People were laughing." Paul began rubbing the base of his neck. The more stupid foul-ups that came to mind, the more upset he found himself becoming.

"Mr. Fisher!"

Tuck met his gaze directly.

"No one likes a puck hog, you got that? You start passing it to your teammates or your behind is going to wear a groove in the players' bench!"

"But—"

"No buts!"

"Yes, Coach," Tuck muttered.

Let's see, did that take care of all the screwups? Nope, wait, there was one more. "Wingers!"

Six pairs of anxious eyes forced themselves to his.

"When you weren't all chasing the puck, you were playing table hockey, skating up and down your zone in a straight line! *Play the ice!*" He shook his head. "Honestly, guys, what the hell happened out there? I'm incredibly disappointed."

"Sorry, Coach," mumbled a lackluster chorus of voices.

"What are we?" Paul demanded, echoing a refrain he started every practice with.

"Warriors?" the boys called out somewhat uncertainly.

"That's right. We're warriors. And what do warriors do?" Again his eyes touched each and every one of them. "They win battles. How? By being ruthless, skilled, and cunning. By always being one step ahead of the enemy. By keeping their wits about them at all times. Are you boys wimps, or are you warriors?"

"Warriors! Warriors!" the boys shouted, regaining some of their fighting spirit.

Paul nodded. "*That's* what I like to hear. See you at practice on Monday."

Katie was so busy working on her book, taking care of Tuck, and trying to keep her relationship with Paul a secret that fall turned into winter without her even noticing. One morning the leaves on the trees were brilliant red and yellow; the next the trees were bare and she was shoveling the driveway after half a foot of snow had dropped out of nowhere. Katie never minded the winter, and now that Winterfest was here, she was actually excited, especially since Tuck had never been.

She and her nephew made their way down to Harkin's Pond where the festival was traditionally held. The pond was frozen solid, peppered with smiling skaters doing lazy laps around the ice. Booths were set up selling everything from hot chocolate to baked goods, while tobogganers flew down the surrounding hills, their delighted screams piercing the late morning air. A curling competition was underway, baffling Katie completely; she couldn't understand the appeal of throwing what appeared to be a lead tea kettle down the ice.

"Hey, you."

Bitsy sidled up to Katie, clutching a cup of hot chocolate in her mittened hands.

"Hey." Despite the carnival atmosphere of the festival, Katie felt on edge. Pleading the Tuck defense, she had made it clear to Paul she was uncomfortable going to the festival with him. He'd been annoyed, but he hadn't pushed the issue. She spotted him across the pond, sitting on a bench talking to some other men as he laced up a pair of skates.

"It's really packed," Bitsy noted.

Katie nodded. She'd heard from her mom that the festival had grown in popularity in recent years. If the swarm of people tramping around in the snow was any indication, her mother wasn't exaggerating.

Tuck tugged on Katie's ski jacket. "Can I find Gary and roast marshmallows with him?"

"Okay," said Katie. "But if you go anywhere else, let me know."

Tuck ran off, leaving the two women alone.

Bitsy blew into her cup. "I can't deal with all this food; I want to stuff my face."

"I know." Katie said. "Back in high school, I used to hit every food booth, but cram it all in my bag to eat later. I was afraid if anyone saw me eating they'd call me a pig."

"That's really sad, Katie."

"I know. But I always loved everything else about the festival: the skaters, the snowman building contest, even being outside. There's nothing like cold, crisp winter air to make you feel alive."

"Speak for yourself." Bitsy took a big gulp of hot chocolate. "Why aren't you with Paul?" Before Katie could answer, Bitsy continued, "Let me guess: if the town finds out about the two of you, life as we know it will come to an end."

"Don't give me a hard time, Bits, okay?"

"There he goes."

At first, Katie thought Bitsy was referring to Tuck. But then she saw her friend's eyes were trained on the ice, where Paul had just started skating. Katie watched him, amazed by the ease with which he breezed past all the recreational skaters. Everyone else present turned to watch him, too. Reading their faces, Katie could see they were all thinking the same thing she was: that skating was as natural to him as breathing.

Katie edged closer to the ice. In all the months they'd

been spending time together, she had never seen Paul looking so blissful. Never. It was if he'd been transported to a different world.

Spotting her, Paul skated over to the edge of the pond. "Care to join me?"

Katie shook her head vehemently. "I can't skate." Her voice dropped to a whisper. "I don't want anyone to know about us, remember? Go back out on the ice."

Paul snorted. "What, I can't even talk to you?"

Katie peered at him. "Shouldn't you be wearing a helmet?"

"I should. But I'm not."

"Is that wise?"

"Probably not. But you know what? It's been years since I've skated on this pond and felt the wind mess up my hair and freeze the tips of my ears. I wanted to experience that again. The freedom."

Katie smiled. "I don't blame you. It sounds wonderful."

"It is. See you at practice Monday," Paul concluded, skating back to the center of the pond. Then he was off, racing up and down, wind tussling his hair just the way he'd described it.

"Again."

Katie watched in disbelief as Paul made the young Panthers sprint from one end of the rink to the other for what had to be the tenth time. She was accustomed to seeing him challenge them at practice, but this went beyond skill building. It was downright sadistic.

"Again."

Her eyes sought out Tuck. Initially one of the more enthusiastic sprinters, he was beginning to lag physically, and was far from the only boy struggling to complete the drill.

They all were. All wore looks of dogged determination, none of them wanting to disappoint their coach.

She looked down at her laptop and began typing. "Sports purports to train young boys to be men," she wrote. "Whether conscious or unconscious, it reinforces gender roles of competition, work, and success—all key components of assumed male superiority. Coaches, who serve as initiators in the patriarchal rite—"

"Again."

Katie's head snapped up. *Not again!* He couldn't be serious! She watched as Chuck Wilbraham, straggling far behind the other boys, slowed to a halt on the ice.

"Move your butt, Wilbraham," Paul called out, "or I'll move it for you."

"But Coach," the little boy said, panting, "I—"

He never finished his sentence as a stream of vomit erupted from his mouth. Horrified, Katie half rose in her seat as Paul blew the whistle around his neck.

"Okay, guys! Enough for today. See you Wednesday!" Paul skated over to Chuck, putting an arm around his shoulders. Katie strained to hear what was being said, but couldn't make it out. All she knew was that the boy was nodding and hanging on every word Paul said. Then he joined his teammates in the locker room.

"Can I speak with you a moment?" Katie's voice rang out across the arena.

"Sure." Paul skated off the ice, doffing his helmet as he joined her a few rows up from the players' bench. "Man, are you a sight for sore eyes," he said, leaning in for a peck to her cheek. Katie jerked away.

"Care to tell me what *that* was all about?"

Paul looked confused. "What?"

"Making little boys sprint the length of the ice till they vomit their guts up."

Wariness crept into Paul's eyes. "It's a drill, Katie. And only one of them puked."

"That's one too many for my taste. I'm sure Chuck's parents will be thrilled when they ask him how practice went and he tells them he threw up because 'Coach' was being a sadist."

"It happens."

"It shouldn't." She studied his face, searching for a sign of remorse, or a look weighing what she said. There wasn't one. "You're punishing them, aren't you?"

Paul narrowed his eyes. "What?"

"You're punishing them," she repeated. "You can't play anymore, so you're living vicariously through them. God forbid they're not the best! It'll reflect badly on you."

Paul rubbed sleep from his eyes. "Have I ever mentioned how much I hate being psychoanalyzed before seven thirty in the goddamn morning?"

"I'm not psychoanalyzing you—"

"Not much! What else would you call telling me how I feel? You think because you have a degree in sociology and talked to a bunch of jocks and ex-jocks for a book that you know how sports works? Don't take this the wrong way, okay? But you don't know dick, Katie."

Heat swam to Katie's cheeks. "I know those boys are only nine and ten years old—not professional athletes, which is what you're treating them like! I know sports is supposed to be fun for them!"

"It *is* fun!"

Katie's laugh sounded more like a growl. "That sure didn't look like fun to me."

"Because it was practice! It builds fortitude. It builds character."

"Character," Katie snorted. "You don't care about character! All you care about is winning!"

Paul looked at her like she was stupid. "What the hell do you think sports is about, sweetheart?"

"Don't sweetheart me." Katie seethed. "You're wrong: it's not what sports is about, it's what it's become! I understand you're trying to inculcate—"

Paul held up a hand. "No big ivory tower words, please."

"Do big words scare you?"

"Of course they do. I'm a dumb ex-jock, remember? Try to stick to one-syllable words so I understand what you're saying, Professor."

Katie ignored him. "You know what this constant pressure to win, win, win does?"

Paul picked at his teeth. "I'm sure you're going to tell me."

"It makes you lose perspective. You forget they're little boys, Paul. You view them as a means to an end, the end being your own success."

"Really." Paul stared at her for a moment. "Why don't you—who has never played a fucking sport in her life, I might add—tell me a little bit more about myself."

Katie backed off. "I'm not trying to criticize you," she said.

"You sure as hell could have fooled me."

"I'm just trying to point out something you're too close to see." She glanced around the arena to make sure they were alone before putting her hand on his thigh. "This is youth hockey, Paul. Not the NHL. Much as you would like to think otherwise, those kids are not vying for the Stanley Cup. Can't you let them have fun? Let yourself have fun?"

Paul pushed her hand away. "See, this is where your ivory tower cluelessness rears its ugly head. You know where the fun of playing sports comes from, Katie? *Winning.*"

Katie shook her head.

"Listen to me," Paul continued sharply. "*It's about winning.* You think those kids lie awake in their beds at night and think, 'Gosh, I hope hockey teaches me about teamwork.' Hell, no! They want to *win*! They want to get out here on the ice and kick the other side's ass! It's always been that way. Yeah, playing a team sport builds camaraderie and all that crap, but those are by-products, not the goal! The goal is to win!"

Katie stared at him. "They're just little boys, Paul," she repeated.

"Little boys who want to *win*. I was one once, remember? I know what I'm talking about here."

"Well," she resumed firmly, "I just think—"

"I've had enough of what you think," Paul retorted. "I'd like it if you didn't come to practice anymore."

Katie stared at him in disbelief. "But—"

"You must have enough material for your stupid book by now."

"It's not stupid!"

"Yeah, fine, whatever." Paul looked weary. "Just don't come to practice anymore, okay? You're a distraction."

"And you're pathetic," Katie muttered beneath her breath.

Paul did a double take. "Excuse me?"

"I said you're pathetic," Katie repeated primly as she snapped her laptop closed. "It's all about you, whether it's coaching youth hockey, or hanging out down at your bar, or even racing down the ice at Winterfest. The great Paul van Dorn, star of the ice." She rose. "I'm glad you've got such a handle on who you once were, Paul. Maybe it's time to figure out who you are now."

CHAPTER

11

Paul had been called many things in his life: prodigy, prick, talented, tragic. "Pathetic" had never made the roster—until now, when Katie lobbed the word at him like a grenade.

He chewed on the word as he went to hunt her down at the Didsbury Library.

Following practice, he'd gone back to his house with the intent of finally unpacking some of his belongings. Their conversation had left him so riled that he'd gone out for an extended run, the best way he could think of to diffuse the angry energy pounding through him. Pushing himself through the winding streets of his neighborhood, Katie's words kept coming back to him again and again: Was he indeed "pathetic," trying to live vicariously through the young boys he was coaching? Was it wrong to want so badly to win?

The more he thought about it, the more irritated he became. Katie's opinions on sports were based on social theory with a smattering of observation thrown in. The woman had never played sports in her life. She had no firsthand knowledge of the intangible rewards sports could bring or the power it held to transform one's life. He needed to make her understand: *That* was what he wanted his boys to experience.

With good coaching, discipline, and hard work, he knew hockey could provide these kids with some of the most rewarding moments of their lives. They could learn how wonderful it was to be working together as a part of a larger "family." Plus they could experience the pleasure of achieving a hard-earned goal. But nothing—nothing—trumped the rush of winning. He didn't just want that for himself; he wanted it for all of them.

She was right about one thing, though: he had worked them too hard at practice. He thought back to his own days in youth hockey, and to the emotional and physical terrorism inflicted on him by hard-asses like Dan Doherty. He didn't want to be like that. He wanted to be tough, but compassionate. To lead by example, not humiliation. It was possible to instill discipline without driving them to the edge. Playing on the Blades under Ty Gallagher had taught him that much. Come Wednesday's practice, he would apologize to them for his behavior.

As for Katie, he couldn't rest until he found out whether she really thought him pathetic. It killed him that the woman he was falling in love with might believe that. Who did she think he was, anyway? No, wait. Who did she expect *him* to be? He was an athlete, for God's sake, not some pipe-sucking, tweed-jacket-wearing egghead professor.

Paul sighed, pushing through the heavy double doors of the library. Sometimes he wondered if her efforts to keep him at arm's length weren't some unconscious form of payback. He'd treated her badly when they were younger; now it was her turn. Or something. He was starting to sound like her now, all analysis and cool rational observation.

He was struck by the silence. He couldn't remember the last time he'd been in the library—any library. It had to be back in eleventh grade, when he was doing research for a history paper on Teddy Roosevelt. If Paul recalled correctly, he'd managed to squeak by with a C. He'd never had to pay much attention to grades. He knew by tenth grade that he'd go pro. Even when he was at Cornell, professors had tacitly looked the other way. What mattered was how he performed on the ice, not in the classroom.

Instinctively, his eyes scanned the room to see if anyone he knew was here. Mrs. Rooney, the squat elementary school nurse everyone called the Dorian Gray of Didsbury, was spread out in the lounge area, thumbing through the most recent issue of *Troutfishing Gazette*. Roger Mendoza and Gus Titus, both retired from the shoe store they used to own together, sat opposite each other at a small table playing chess. Over in "New Books," an older, well-coiffed woman in a peach velour running suit stood with her head cocked sideways, scrutinizing book spines. Paul could hear pages turning, the heat kicking on and off, even the sound of people tapping away at computers— but no human voices. The effect was somewhat eerie.

Mildly unnerved, he approached the octagonal information desk at the center of the hushed, carpeted oasis. Mrs. Greco sat transfixed before a computer, her fingers flying across the keyboard so quickly it sounded like raindrops pounding a tin roof. He hated disturbing her, but if he didn't talk to Katie now, it would eat at him all day.

"Mrs. Greco?"

His busomy, blue rinsed neighbor looked up. "Paul." Her

smile was pleasant as she approached him. "What can I do for you? Are you here to get a library card?"

"No."

Mrs. Greco's smile drooped. Paul realized he should have just lied and said he was here for a card before easing the conversation around to Katie. As it now stood, he was pretty sure Mrs. Greco thought he was an illiterate idiot.

"How can I help you, then?" Her voice was crisp but quiet: the perfect librarian voice, designed not to disturb.

"I was wondering if Katie Fisher was here, by any chance."

"She is indeed," said Mrs. Greco with a lascivious wink. "I noticed her car parked outside your house Thursday night."

"Um . . . yeah." Maybe he *was* an idiot. He had no idea how to respond to her statement, other than thinking it was kind of creepy that Mrs. Greco was so attuned to her neighbors' lives. Then again, this *was* Didsbury, where gossip was the number one pastime. Katie had told him that was one of her main reasons for leaving. He was beginning to see her logic.

Mrs. Greco was staring at him expectantly. *Words, Paul. Use your words.* "Katie and I are kind of seeing each other," he offered.

"I figured," she purred, giving him another wink. Paul felt his stomach tilt: She was old enough to be his grandma. Her innuendo was giving him the heebies.

"So she's here?" he said again.

"Yes," Mrs. Greco replied, pointing toward the back of the library. "The last carrel on the left." She leaned in to him as if imparting a secret. "Thank God she lost all that weight. I always used to say, 'That girl has such a pretty face. If she would just get rid of all that blubber, she'd be a knockout.' And I was right."

Paul forced a smile onto his face. "Thanks for all your help, Mrs. Greco."

"Anytime, Paul."

He made his way to the back of the library, slowing as he approached Katie. Her back was to him, and like Mrs. Greco, she, too, was typing furiously, though the sound was more muted.

Paul stood watching her a moment. Her book bag lay on the floor beside her. Her long blonde hair was tied back in a loose ponytail, her shoulders hunched over the keyboard in a posture of extreme concentration. Unthinking, Paul reached out and touched her hair. Katie shot up out of her seat with a frightened gasp.

"Oh!"

"Sorry! I didn't mean to scare you."

"Scare me? You nearly gave me a heart attack!" Katie barked. Library patrons from surrounding carrels clucked their tongues.

"What are you doing here?" Katie whispered.

"We need to talk," Paul boomed. Katie gestured for him to be quiet. "We need to talk," Paul repeated in a whisper.

"This isn't a good time. I'm trying to work."

"All I need is five minutes."

"All right," Katie said, slowly easing back down into her seat. "Five minutes."

Paul took the chair from a nearby empty carrel and pulled it next to hers.

"Do you really think I'm pathetic?" he demanded, forgetting to whisper.

"Sshhh," someone on the other side of Katie hissed.

"That's what you came here to talk about?" Katie whispered.

"Just answer the question," Paul whispered back.

Her fingers poised on her keyboard, Katie said, "Of course not."

"Then why did you say it?"

"Because I was upset. And you were mean to me."

"Mean to you?!" Paul bellowed.

"Will you shut the hell up, please?" a man growled from three carrels away.

"I was upset," Katie repeated in a fierce whisper. "By the way you pushed the boys around, and then telling me you didn't want me at practice anymore." She looked at him uncertainly. "Did you mean that?"

"What, about practice?"

Katie nodded.

"Yeah, if you don't mind. It really does distract me."

"Okay," Katie agreed unhappily.

Paul drew his chair closer. "Look, I wanted to tell you, you were right about pushing the boys at practice. That was wrong."

"Yes, but can you understand that you were doing it because—"

"Don't psychoanalyze me, Katie," he interrupted sharply. "Not now. Okay?"

"Yeah, don't psychoanalyze him," the growling man echoed.

Paul rubbed his forehead, frustrated. "Can we go somewhere else?" he hissed. "This is ridiculous!"

Katie sighed, shutting down her laptop. "My mother's house is five minutes from here. Do you remember how to get there?" Paul nodded. "Meet me there."

"Your mother isn't going to make me autograph a dish towel or something, is she?"

"As if you'd mind," Katie snorted. "No, my mother is in

Hartford for the day. Some church outing. Park up the street, though. Just in case."

Paul rolled his eyes. "Meet you in five, then."

It felt strange, inviting Paul over to her mother's house when she wasn't around. Traditionally, Mina was the one who brought guys home in the middle of the day. Until now, the only man Katie had ever rendezvoused with covertly at this house was the Lucky Charms leprechaun.

She arrived a minute before Paul did, enough time to unlock the door and peel off her jacket before answering the doorbell.

"Come on in," she told him. "Let me take your coat."

Paul slipped off his shearling jacket and handed it to her before taking off his snow-caked hiking boots. He looked around the room. "This place is really cozy."

"Thanks," said Katie, putting the coats and boots in the coat closet. She wondered if he really meant it, or if "cozy" might be a euphemism for "small." Well, it was small, there was no denying that. Her mother's shelves crammed with knickknacks didn't help, either.

"Your mom collects thimbles," Paul noted as if reading her mind.

"And dolls. And bone china." She glanced at him over her shoulder. "Your mom collect anything?"

"Prescriptions." Paul sat down on the couch, waiting for her.

"Do you want anything to drink? Coffee? Diet Coke?"

Paul waved a hand. "I'm fine." He patted the empty space next to him. "C'mere."

Katie sat down beside him, reminding herself that they'd come here to talk, period. She could *not* let herself think about the obvious opportunity presented by the empty house, or the way the winter sun shining through the picture window was hitting his hair, making him look golden, like Achilles.

"Do you really think I don't know who I am now?" Paul began, putting his arm around her shoulder.

Katie fidgeted. Why had she said that? She had no idea how to answer.

"Katie?"

"I think," she began carefully, "that you're not dealing with who you are now. With *where* you are now."

"How is that any different from you not dealing with who you once *were*?" Paul countered.

"We're talking about you right now, Paul. Not me."

"Fine. So I'm not living in the present." Paul's voice was terse. "What am I doing or not doing that makes you think that?"

"Well, you still haven't unpacked your house, for one." Katie forced her eyes to his. "It's like you're afraid to, because it would mean, I don't know, that you really *do* live in Didsbury. Deep down, I don't think you believe that yet."

Paul's jaw clenched. "Go on."

"The bar: You're so happy when people want you to autograph things, or ask you to tell them stories about your time in the NHL. It's like you need the attention to prove to yourself that you still exist or something. I don't know. It's hard to explain."

Paul frowned. "And with coaching?"

"You're obsessed with winning."

"Newsflash, Professor: all coaches are obsessed with winning." Katie opened her mouth to say something but the look of warning that shot across his face made her hold her tongue. "I don't care what you sociologists say the meaning behind organized sports is. For the athletes and their coaches, it's all about winning.

"I know what it feels like to win, Katie, especially when you've busted your ass to do so. It's the most amazing high in the world. I want the boys on the hockey team to experience that."

"Because you can't anymore?" Katie asked quietly.

"As their coach, I can. And there's nothing wrong with that. That's what you don't see. Of course I want them to do well on the ice! If they win it's proof I'm doing my job well. That's important to me." His gaze turned quizzical. "If you think I'm such an emotional cripple, why the hell did you get involved with me?"

"Well, for one thing, you're cute as a button."

"I want a serious answer here, Katherine."

Katie recoiled. "Don't call me Katherine! No one calls me that except my aunt Lily, and she talks to rocks and plants. Never call me Katherine."

"Katie." He said it with so much tenderness it brought an unexpected rush to her heart. "If I'm such a mess, why go out with me?"

Katie found herself chewing on her left thumb. "Well, because you're smart," she said quietly. "And funny."

"Keep going."

Katie dropped her hand from her mouth. "You egotistical bastard!"

"I said keep going."

"And tender. Sweet." She reached out to lightly touch his cheek. "I like you, Paul. I just wish you liked yourself more. That's all."

Paul looked amused. "You know what your problem is, Fisher?"

"What?"

"You think too goddamn much. Instead of looking at every person and situation and trying to fit it into some kind of context, why don't you just relax and enjoy yourself? You're too rigid."

"Rigid," Katie repeated flatly.

"Yeah."

"Actually, I prefer the word *disciplined*."

"There you go thinking again, Katherine."

Before she could protest he kissed her. Katie hadn't seen it coming and it hit her with full force as yearning overtook her. She could have him here, now, if she wanted. Be a bad girl, like Mina. The thought aroused her even more. She was tired of being good   being rigid. She'd show him. She kissed him back, nipping hard at his lower lip. Paul pulled back in surprise.

"Wanna see my room?" she asked seductively.

"Sure," said Paul, with a smile that set an inferno blazing within her. "Lead on."

Leading Paul by the hand up the carpeted stairs to her bedroom, Katie finally understood why Mina so thoroughly enjoyed being "bad." There was something delicious about knowing you'd be making love in the middle of the morning when the rest of the world was hard at work. Especially doing it here, in this house that wasn't even hers. By the time she steered him down the hallway and into the bedroom of her childhood, the sense of wickedness she was feeling was intoxicating.

"Let's see what we've got here." Paul stood in the middle of her room. Katie watched him take it all in: the white lace curtains; the faded rosebud wallpaper; the narrow single bed where, in high school, her hand often crept below the covers thinking of *him*; the white wicker chair more pleasant to look at than sit on; the desk piled high with research-filled folders and books marked with Post-its. He nodded slowly, smiling. "I can see you here," he mused. "As a kid, I mean."

"You can see a fat girl with a secret stash of Baby Ruths beneath her bed?"

Paul shook his head. "No. I can see you hiding here. Taking refuge."

Katie was struck by the insight. She never gave him enough credit when it came to sensitivity, did she? It was easier to stick a label on him—"unhappily retired ex-athlete"—than to admit what he really was: complicated and compelling.

She joined him at the center of the room, putting her arms around him, a gesture he returned. His solidity was a comfort. He still had the body of an athlete: hard, chiseled, no excess softness anywhere. It amazed her, the pureness of his masculinity, and the fact that he didn't do anything to play it up or enforce it. It was simply who he was. Reaching up to cup his cheek—rough and unshaven—she was rewarded with a shower of fevered kisses to her fingertips, and a hunger in his eyes.

"Now what?" Paul murmured.

"Let's be bauud."

Paul laughed, scooping her up in his arms and carrying her over to the narrow bed. He lay her down softly then stretched out beside her, the two of them facing each other. They had no choice: the bed was too small for them to comfortably lie side by side. How many times had she had this exact fantasy in high school? Only this was better. Back then, reality would intrude and in her mind's eye she'd see him howling in agony because he'd wrenched his back carrying her to the bed. How deep had her self-loathing run, that even her fantasies had been tainted by her weight?

Paul kissed the tip of her nose. "What are you thinking about?"

"If I tell, do you promise not to make fun of me?"

"Cross my heart."

"I used to fantasize about this in high school. About you picking me up and throwing me on the bed and ravaging me."

"Yeah?" Paul propped himself up on one elbow. "Was it good?"

Katie blushed. "Yes."

"What was I wearing?"

She thought, then laughed. "Your hockey uniform. But without the helmet."

Paul, laughed, too, and lay back down. His hands reached up to tenderly cradle her face. "Is that what you want, Professor Fisher? To be ravaged?"

Katie's pulse quickened. His uttering that one simple sentence made her whole body tingle. "Mutual ravaging might be nice," she murmured, bringing her lips almost to his, but not quite. Paul didn't move. Neither did she. The air in the room shimmered with anticipatory tension. Katie could feel it bouncing off the walls. Who would move first to make contact? She closed her eyes, tortured by longing, enjoying each passing second of this little game they seemed to be playing. *Kiss me!* she pleaded with him in her head. But he didn't. Neither moved. Their breath was coming in unison now, mingling. She couldn't tell if it was his heartbeat or her own that was pounding. *Unbearable*, she thought. *This is deliciously, wonderfully, unbearable.*

She opened her eyes to see Paul's eyes boring into hers as if he were able to read her secrets. Their faces were so close she could catalog every small imperfection he had, including the tiny white scar that ran across the bridge of his nose. Heat radiated from his body, wave after sizzling wave wrapping them both in a fevered cocoon. Yet his eyes were what held her. Paul's eyes, daring her to make the first move. Telling her that whatever she started, there was no going back.

Eyes still open, Katie put her mouth softly to his. He had yet to reach for her, or she for him. They lay like this, lips joined, bodies silently but separately communing. Katie moved to part his lips with her tongue. His tongue caught hers, sending shock waves of desire through her body as she let the velvet sweetness of sensation wash over her. *Now*, she thought hungrily. *Now he will draw me into an embrace.*

Instead, he took his tongue from her mouth and began tracing the outline of her lips with its tip. Back and forth he went, slowly, deliberately, sampling first her bottom lip, then her top. Katie wanted to open her mouth to his again, grab his handsome face in her hands and kiss him until he didn't know who the hell he was. But they were playing this wonderful, teasing game, and it was his turn to call the shots. His exploration of her mouth continued, careful, slow, tender, Katie's breath growing more ragged the more he prolonged her exquisite agony.

It was torturing him, too. Katie sensed it in the rigidity of his body mere inches from hers, in the bulge in his jeans that she brazenly decided to reach down and cup. Groaning, Paul halted the sweet game he was playing with her mouth and turned his attentions to her neck, nuzzling there. Katie couldn't stop trembling. She wanted to give more, wanted him to *do* more. So, he thought he could torture her endlessly, did he? Well, two could play at that game.

Cupping him harder, she began rubbing him—slowly, deliberately. He stiffened further, tearing his mouth from her neck to trail his hot, wet tongue down her throat to the opening of her blouse.

Katie waited, panting. Nothing. She stopped moving her hand. Stalemate. It was too much for Paul; his fingers reached for the front of her blouse and simply tore, buttons flying, shirt tails pushed apart so he could undo the front clasp of her bra. He sat up, hurriedly pulling his shirt over his head and flinging it to the bedroom floor before settling back down beside her. Katie looked in his eyes: usually ice blue, the irises seemed to be deepening right before her eyes, desire darkening them. She drew close to him, rubbing her chest against his, reveling in the male/female contrast. Paul groaned, eyes shut. Below the waist, Katie put her hand to him and began rubbing harder, feeling him strain again against the soft denim. If they were still in high school, maybe this was as far as it would go. She'd get him off, he'd get her off, they'd awkwardly dress, and split up to study.

But this wasn't high school.

Hips gently rocking in rhythm with her strokes, Paul drew her to him, lowering his head as he ran his face across her breasts. The friction created by the light grizzle of his beard scrambled Katie's senses. She was hot neon: burning, blinding. Her hand stopped its movements for a moment so she could fully savor the thrilling sensation of roughness as he moved his face back and forth between her breasts. When he took her nipple in his mouth and sucked hard, Katie felt the world crack open.

Her hand returned to his manhood. She tugged his zipper down, fumbling blindly with the hard metal button at the top of his jeans. Impatient, she thrust her hand beneath the waist band of his briefs, eager to grasp him in her palm. He was hard, smooth, pulsing. Waiting for release. She began moving her hand up and down slowly. Paul groaned, and rolling away from her freed himself from the rest of his clothing. Heat thrumming in her lower belly, Katie quickly did the same. When he turned back to her, he was protected and in full arousal. The beauty of him, standing there with the sun streaming through the windows, took Katie's breath away. He *was* Achilles. He *was* golden.

Slowly, deliberately, she drew her feet up, planting them on the bed. Then she let her legs fall open in casual, playful invitation. She had never done this before, acted the wanton seductress in full daylight. She watched as a change came over Paul's face, transforming him from man to devouring beast, his gaze on her so hungry, so greedy, that she shuddered. Teasing, Katie tried to clasp her legs back together, but Paul dropped down on the bed, prying them apart. Grasping her hands and holding them fast above her head, he drove into her full force. Katie screamed, pain and pleasure mingling as they began their frenzied coupling.

He loosened his grip on her hands, and Katie instinctively wrapped her legs around his hips, her nails clawing at him.

"Now" she yelled, her hands beating out her frustration on his back. *"Now!"*

"You make me wild," Paul rasped, teeth tearing at her throat as he increased his tempo. He was pounding in and out of her with such force Katie could feel herself being slammed into a whole other dimension. Pain was pleasure, pleasure pain as he drove into her again and again, their screams mounting as they vaulted from mere mortality to unbound ecstasy. *Yes!* Katie thought, feeling closer to him than she ever had to any human being in her life. This was certainly *not* high school.

CHAPTER

12

"Katie?"

Katie sprang up, clutching the bed sheet to her chest. What the hell was her mother doing home? She was supposed to be away all day with her church ladies! Why was it that Mina could do half the high school football team on her lunch hour and no one was ever the wiser? So much for the good girl being bad. . . . Katie flew across the room, locking her bedroom door just as her mother reached the other side, jiggling the knob.

"Katie? Are you all right?"

"I—I'm sick, Ma." Paul, propped up on one elbow in her narrow bed, was watching her with an amused smile. Katie scowled. This wasn't funny!

"Honey, why is the door locked?"

Katie pressed her eyes shut. She'd have more privacy in a women's prison.

"Katie?" Her mother tried the door again.

"Just a minute, Ma. You woke me up."

She gestured for Paul to get into the closet. He feigned not understanding. Katie shook her fist at him. Taking the hint, Paul swung his legs over the side of the bed and sauntered over to her closet, quietly closing the door behind him.

Katie sprang into action, kicking their clothing under the bed, opening the window a crack to rid the room of the pungent aroma of sex, and giving herself a quick spritz of perfume *down there*. Then she threw on her robe. "Coming, Ma." Putting on what she hoped was a listless expression, she unlocked the door.

"Oh, Katie." Her mother charged inside, eyes brimming with concern. "Just look at you. Pupils dilated, face flushed"—she put her hand to Katie's forehead—"and burning up with a sweaty fever to boot. I'm calling Dr. Vreeland."

"Mom, I'm fine." *Was that Paul laughing?* "What are you doing home so early?" Katie asked loudly. "I thought you were spending the day in Hartford."

"We had to come back. Mrs. Simon had the runs." She smiled at Katie. "You remember Mrs. Simon, don't you? She babysat for you when you were small."

"Sure I remember: she thought a six-year-old would want borscht as an after-school snack. How could I forget?" Wrapping an arm around her mother's shoulders, Katie steered her toward the door. "No offense, Mom, but I really need to lie down." She added a fake cough for good measure.

"I'm sorry to have disturbed you, sweetie. But I heard you moaning—"

"I was having a nightmare."

"My poor baby. How about I make you some tea?"

Katie stalled. "Tea . . . might be . . . nice." She looked around, trapped. Would that be enough time for Paul to climb out the window? It would have to be.

"Good." Her mother seemed happy to be able to pamper her. "Tea it is!"

Smiling wanly, Katie escorted her mother out onto the upstairs landing, watching as she made her way downstairs. As soon as she heard the tap running in the kitchen she dashed back into her room, closing the door.

"The coast is clear," she whispered. She waited. Inch by inch the closet door slowly opened and Paul emerged, swiping at his eyes. Katie was right: he'd been laughing himself silly.

"Nightmare?" he hooted.

"Shut up!" Katie shushed at him. "We don't have much time."

"For what?"

"You to climb out the window."

Paul's jollity faded. *"What?"*

"The window, the window," Katie repeated, gesturing wildly at it as if he might not know what she was referring to. She threw the sash open wide, peering below. "You can shimmy down the trellis."

Paul joined her at the window, surveying the situation. "That trellis doesn't look like it'd support a rosebush, never mind a full grown man."

"Do you enjoy giving the neighborhood a show?"

"What? Oh." Paul covered himself and backed away. "Good catch."

"Mina used to climb down this trellis all the time. You'll be fine," Katie insisted, as she fixed him with a pleading stare. "You don't have a choice."

"Yeah, I do," Paul snorted. "I can put on my clothes, walk downstairs, say hi to your mom, and leave."

"You can't," Katie insisted. "Then she'll *know*."

"Know what? You sleep over my house all the time!"

"She'll know—you know—that we've done it—*here*."

Paul looked perplexed. "Yeah? And?"

"You don't know my mother. It would shatter her if she thought I was being immoral under her roof. I'm the good one, remember?"

"We're all adults, Katie. I'm sure your mother has seen and heard a lot worse."

"That's my point," said Katie, dropping to her knees to pull their crumpled clothing out from under the bed. "I don't want her thinking I'm like Mina."

"She won't think that."

Katie thrust his clothes at him. "Please, Paul. I swear I'll never ask you to do anything like this again. Just please go out the window."

"You need help, you know?" Paul muttered, stepping into his briefs. "Seriously."

Katie nodded fervently. She'd agree to anything he said, as long as he put his clothes on and disappeared before her mother returned. She popped her head out the window again. He could just crawl down the trellis, walk up the street and drive off in his car.

Paul was dressed. "What about my coat?" he asked. "And my boots? You want me to climb down into the snow in my *socks*?"

"I'll bring them to you later today, okay?"

"You owe me, lady." He drew her into his arms. "You realize that, don't you?"

"Yes, yes," Katie said quickly, kissing his nose. "Go! She'll be back any minute!"

"Relax," said Paul, swinging his legs over the windowsill.

"Tea's on the way," Katie's mother called up the stairs.

"Oh, God." Katie wrung her hands. "Go, go. GO!"

One minute Paul was on the windowsill. The next there was the sound of cracking wood, followed by a strangulated scream. Katie thrust her head out the window: the trellis had ripped away from the side of the house. Paul lay beneath it on her mother's snow-covered driveway, writhing in agony as he clutched his left ankle.

"Aahhhhhh! SONAFABITCH! Ahhhhhh!"

"Shit," Katie whispered. She hustled down the stairs and into the kitchen.

Her mother stood there with a steaming cup of tea in her right hand looking astonished. "Katie? Why is Paul van Dorn lying in our driveway screaming?"

So much for those cha cha lessons I was planning on this week."

Katie shot Paul a sidelong glance, unsure if he was kidding or angry. It was hard to tell; his face was screwed up with concentration as he hobbled to her car on the crutches they'd just been forced to rent in the emergency room. His left foot was encased in an air cast. It was badly sprained, but not broken. *Thank God.*

"I don't know what to say," Katie murmured feebly, unlocking the car.

"You do realize this is the second time you're responsible for sending me to the emergency room, don't you?" Paul pointed out as he threw his crutches into the backseat.

"The first time was your own fault," Katie replied, glancing away so he wouldn't see her wincing as he hopped two steps on one leg and maneuvered himself into the passenger seat.

"If your reflexes were faster you wouldn't have hit me," Paul countered sweetly, closing the car door.

Katie smushed her face up against the window. "If you weren't such a retard, you wouldn't have run in front of my car in the first place," she said. She marched over to her side of the car and slid behind the wheel. She'd already put the car into drive and was wheeling out of the hospital parking lot when she noticed Paul grinning at her.

"What?"

"You called me a 'retard,'" he said tenderly. "Does this mean you care?"

"Bite me, van Dorn."

"Again?"

Heat flashed though Katie's body. "You're bad."

"I try."

They drove in silence for a few blocks. Finally Katie burst. "Okay, I'm sorry! It was nuts to make you climb out the window!"

"Ah, the things we do for love," Paul mused.

Katie nearly smashed into the car in front of her. That word. The *L* word, as unexpected as a snowstorm in June. Did he mean it? Or was he just using the expression as a figure of speech? Probably the latter, but what if he meant it? That would be . . . not good. Because if he loved her, he'd expect her to love him back, and while she did, *just a little bit*, she was still leaving. She was outta Tinytown in eight more months and no one was going to interfere with that—

"Can I point something out?" Paul asked, oblivious to the tempest he'd created inside her.

Katie swallowed. "What's that?"

"Well, thanks to the wonders of gravity, your mother found out about our little sexcapade anyway. So my climbing out the window was all for nothing."

"If the trellis hadn't pulled away from the house, she'd be none the wiser."

Paul leveled her with a stare. "Despite my jacket and boots in the coat closet?"

He had a point.

"Maybe I'll sue you," he murmured, gazing out the passenger window.

"Feel free."

He turned back to her. "At least I wasn't naked. If this were a sitcom, I would have been naked."

Katie laughed. "Yeah, and there would have been an old woman outside pruning her flowers who would have fainted."

"I love it when you laugh," Paul confessed. "It's like your whole being lights up. I know that sounds lame, but it's true."

"Thank you," Katie managed, trying to ignore the burning sensation that came to her cheeks. How was it possible for her to bask in his praise, *adore* it even, yet at the same time wish it away?

Paul was right: she needed help.

Bitsy had barely slid into their usual booth at Tabitha's before, "Okay, what happened to Paul?" shot out of her mouth. All of Didsbury knew their local hero had hurt his ankle. Luckily for Katie, no one knew *how*, which was a minor miracle.

Katie clutched her coffee mug. "He twisted it on the ice. Coaching."

Bitsy and Denise exchanged glances.

"Honey, don't ever think of going to Hollywood," said Denise, patting Katie's hand. "You can't act worth a damn."

"*C'mon*," Bitsy whined. "We're your *friends*. Spill it."

Katie sighed. "He was climbing out of my bedroom window and was supposed to shinny down the trellis, but the trellis broke and he plunged to the ground below."

Bitsy stared hard into her drink. "I see."

"Go ahead and laugh. I know you want to."

Bitsy threw back her head and howled.

Katie turned to Denise. "Go on. Don't you want to laugh?"

Denise feigned offense, splaying her manicured, man-sized hands over her heart. "Laugh at another's misfortune? Never. Though I am curious as to why he had to climb out your bedroom window."

"My mother came home."

"So?"

"I didn't want her to know we'd been fooling around," Katie mumbled.

Denise pursed her lips thoughtfully. "Are you saying your mommy doesn't know you've been playing 'Poke the Rutabaga' with Paul?"

Katie reddened. "It's a long story."

"I'll bet it is."

"Actually, Denise, maybe you can help me with something."

"At your service," said Denise, breaking off a piece of brownie.

"Well, after Paul was released from the hospital"—this sent Bitsy into a fresh gale of laughter that no glare from Katie could stop—"I apologized for what happened and he said, 'Oh, the things we do for love.'"

"Uh huh." Denise looked blank.

"Well, do you think he meant it?" Katie asked. "Or do you think it was just a figure of speech?"

Denise looked confused. "Why are you asking me?"

"Well, you used to be a man."

"A man trapped in a woman's body," Denise pointed out emphatically. "There's a difference."

"Yes, I *know*, but you used to have to *pretend* to be a man, didn't you? Fake the feelings of a man?"

"Uh huh," Denise replied carefully.

"So tell me: As a former man trapped in a woman's body who had to pretend for years to *feel* like a man, do you think he meant it, or do you think he was being glib?"

"I truly wish I had a tape recorder." Bitsy sighed.

Denise picked up another piece of brownie and popped it in her mouth, chewing daintily. "As a former man trapped in a woman's body, it is my considered opinion that he meant it."

Katie's face fell. "Really?"

"Yes. Men have a hard time expressing their feelings. That was his roundabout way of telling you how he felt without taking the risk of saying the actual words and being rejected."

Katie slumped in her seat.

"Don't you agree?" Denise asked Bitsy.

"As a woman who has loved a man who has always been a man and continues to expand into an ever bigger man, I'd have to agree with you," said Bitsy. Her gaze traveled to Katie. "I think he's in love with you."

"What should I do?" Katie asked her friends.

Bitsy arched an eyebrow. "Return the sentiment?"

"I can't," Katie groaned. "I mean I can, but if I do it'll be a big fat mess and I just don't have time for it. I have a book to write." *And I'm leaving.*

"Writing and love are mutually exclusive?" Denise questioned. "That's a new one on me."

Katie pressed the heels of her palms into her eyes. "You don't understand."

"Obviously," Bitsy drawled. "Want to know what I *really* think?"

"No."

"I'm going to tell you anyway: I think you're being a moron."

Katie pulled her hands from her eyes. "You do?"

Bitsy nodded.

"You?" Katie asked Denise.

"Total moron."

Bitsy looked concerned. "What the hell are you so afraid of, hon?"

"Nothing. Everything. Oh, give me a piece of that damn brownie before I start sucking on my own toes. I'm starving!" Katie grabbed a piece of the brownie and crammed it in her mouth, washing it down with a shot of coffee.

"Better?" Bitsy soothed.

Katie nodded.

"Good. Now stop being a twit and just have fun with Paul. What have you got to lose?"

CHAPTER 13

"Oh, man! Did you see my shot from the blue line? Did you!"

Katie shot her nephew an amused glance as they made their way to the local ice cream shop to celebrate the Panthers' victory against the Polecats.

"Of course I did," she assured him. Though Paul had spent the first two periods of the game trying to play everyone, by the third it was clear he was trying to win at any cost, putting his best players on the ice as much as possible. That included Tuck. Katie was in a quandary. If she brought it up to Paul, he'd probably bite her head off. But if she kept quiet, wasn't that being complicit?

"Did you see my deke in the second period?" Tuck continued animatedly.

Katie nodded. She had never seen Tuck this happy in her life. The kid was practically jumping out of his seat with excitement and pride.

"The coach used me a lot," Tuck boasted.

"Yes, he did," Katie agreed, wondering if the ice cream parlor had fat-free yogurt. She hadn't had time to run that morning, though she planned on doing so when she and Tuck got back to the house.

"I know why," Tuck replied, his voice laden with significance.

Katie smiled at him proudly. "So do I; you're a great player."

"Duh! But it's something else, too." He turned to look out the window, suppressing a little smile.

"Oh, and what's that?" Katie asked. "And P.S., don't ever 'duh' me again."

"I think," Tuck said as he turned back to her, "that he might be my father."

Oh, shit. Katie contemplated stopping the car right there. She could barely look at Tuck, whose radiant face shone with the certain knowledge he was right. *He really believes it.* How was she going to let him down gently? "Tuck," she said carefully, "Coach van Dorn is not your father."

"You don't know," Tuck insisted.

"Yes, I do. Coach van Dorn had been out of Didsbury for many years when you were born."

"So? He could have come back for a visit and slept with Mom."

Katie was momentarily dumbstruck. Sometimes she wanted to kill Mina.

"That's very doubtful, hon." Katie reached over to give Tuck's knee a squeeze. "I know it's fun to think someone cool like Coach van Dorn might be your dad, and that might be the reason he's giving you so much ice time, but if he was your dad, your mom would have told you that a long time ago. Okay?"

Tuck pushed her hand away and returned to staring out

the window. "You're just upset because Coach is *your* boyfriend now and you can't handle the fact he might have fucked Mom."

Trembling, Katie eased the car to the curb. "Two things," she said tersely.

Tuck wouldn't look at her.

"Number one: If you ever talk to me like that again, you can find someone else to take you to hockey practice and games. Number two: If you *ever* talk about your mother like that again, your days playing hockey are done. *Got it?*"

Tuck remained silent.

"*Got it?*" Katie repeated loudly.

"Yes!" Tuck yelled back, slumping in the front seat.

Katie eased back into traffic. "Look, I know how hard it is to grow up without a dad. It sucks."

Tuck continued his silent treatment.

"Tuck?" Katie prodded.

"I don't want any stupid ice cream," Tuck muttered.

Katie could feel a vein in her forehead fluttering. "Fine. We'll head home."

Turning the car around, Katie was deeply shaken by Tuck's behavior. He was usually such a good kid, so easy-going and well-behaved. But every once in a while, he'd mouth off. Katie supposed all kids had their moments, but it bothered her that Tuck was only nine and using words like *fuck* so freely, especially in connection with his own mother. Did all nine-year-olds talk like this? She felt out of touch.

"You still talking to me?" she asked.

"I guess." He paused. "It *is* possible, you know."

Katie's hands tightened around the steering wheel. "Tuck."

"Oh, I almost forgot," Tuck said brightly, changing subjects completely. "Gary Flaherty invited me to sleep over his house tonight. Can I?"

The request brought Katie up short. Just because she disliked Liz was no reason to dislike her son. Gary and Tuck did seem to get along well. In fact, Tuck had taken to referring to Gary as his best friend. "Let's see what Nana says. If it's okay with her, then you can go."

Katie had never been to Windy Gables except on Sunday afternoons, and was frankly surprised to find she was allowed to visit on a Friday night. After being checked to make sure she wasn't smuggling any drugs or alcohol inside, the attendant at the front desk buzzed for Mina. She appeared from around the corner, looking casual in an oversized sweater and jeans. She seemed genuinely happy to see Katie.

"Geez," Mina said, lightly taking Katie's arm as they walked down the hall, "don't you have anything better to do on a Friday night than hang out here?"

"Not really."

"What about your hockey boyfriend?"

"I'll see him tomorrow night."

"Can't take him two nights in a row, huh? I hear that."

Katie had never thought of it that way, but she supposed Mina was right. Paul insisted on being at his bar on Friday night, and though he always asked Katie to join him, she never agreed. She simply wasn't a bar person. Besides, he spent the whole night playing happy host. He didn't need her there.

Katie had never been in Mina's room before; she'd only met her sister in the lounge. She was surprised to find a very simple but tastefully decorated room with two twin beds. Mina hopped onto the bed closest to the window, sitting cross-legged opposite the most intimidating-looking man Katie had ever seen in her life.

He was at least six foot two, with a shiny bald head and a long, scraggling moustache. Tight black jeans hugged his massive thighs, while a black leather vest covered his bare chest, revealing bulging biceps covered in tattoos. He had a skull tattooed on top of his left hand and spitting cobra tattooed atop the right.

"This is Snake," Mina said, picking up the deck of playing cards in front of her.

Katie graciously extended her hand, trying to remember all that Mina had told her about him. She knew he was clean and sober and rode a motorcycle. Oh, and he had an apartment and was willing to put Mina and Tuck up until they found a place of their own. An image flashed in her mind of Snake dropping Tuck off at school on his motorcycle. She made it disappear.

"Pleased to meet you," said Snake. His voice reminded Katie of nails tearing down sandpaper. Snake was obviously a smoker.

"You, too." Katie edged closer to the bed. "What are you guys playing?"

"Rummy," said Mina, dealing the cards. "Snake's too dumb to play poker."

Snake chortled darkly. "Yeah, right."

Katie sat down. "Mina? Do you think I could talk to you for a minute?"

"Anything you have to say to me you can say in front of Snake."

Snake nodded sagely, exchanging a three of clubs for an ace of hearts.

"Okay." Katie puffed up her cheeks, blowing out her breath. "It's about Tuck. He's convinced Paul van Dorn is his father."

Mina snorted. "I wish!"

"Who the fuck is Tuck? Rummy!" called Snake, throwing down his cards.

"You can't have rummy that quickly!" Mina frowned. "You cheated!" She gathered up the cards. "Tuck is my son. I've told you a million times."

Snake narrowed his eyes. "You never told me you had a fucking kid."

"Yes, I did," Mina countered angrily. "Remember? When you said I could crash with you when I got out, and I said it wouldn't only be me, it would be me *and* my son, and you said that was cool?"

Snake grunted. "I guess I forgot."

Mina screwed up her eyes. "You doin' H again?"

"No, I'm not doin' H," Snake replied, looking offended. "I just got a lot on my mind right now. The kid's cool, the kid's cool. As long as he doesn't get in the way."

A look passed between Snake and Mina that made Katie uneasy. *Get in the way of what?* she wondered. Their screwing? Their setting up a crystal meth lab in the kitchen? Katie hated thinking that way but Snake didn't exactly inspire confidence.

"You in?" Mina asked Katie, holding up the deck of cards.

"No, I'm fine. You two play, I'll just babble."

Snake chuckled. "She's funny, your sister."

Katie threw Snake a look. "I'm *in* the room, you know."

"Gotcha."

"Snake?" she ventured. "What's your real name?"

"Snake," he answered gruffly.

"You expect me to believe your mother named you Snake?"

"I named myself Snake when I was reborn into the brotherhood of the highway," Snake replied solemnly, the look in his dark eyes letting Katie know this line of questioning was going no further. "That's all that matters."

"Gotcha," Katie answered. Reborn into the brotherhood of the highway? Yeah, this guy was a *great* role model for Tuck.

"So, what's up with Tuck?" Mina asked, dealing the cards.

"He's doing really well on the hockey team," Katie began. "Paul's been putting him on the ice a lot."

"Hockey's for pussies," Snake muttered.

Katie bristled. "Oh, really?"

"Yes, ma'am."

"Name a sport you think isn't for pussies," Katie challenged. *Rolling midgets? Crushing beer cans against your forehead?*

Snake thought. "Bowhunting. Sports ain't macho unless something dies."

Katie found herself dumbstruck for the second time in one day.

"I'm glad he's having fun," said Mina, furrowing her brows as she decided which card to put down in place of the one she'd just picked up.

"He is, but today in the car, he told me he thought Paul was putting him on the ice a lot because he was his father."

"Poor little fucker," said Snake.

Katie took a deep breath, trying to ignore him.

Mina seemed distracted. "So—what do you want me to do about it?"

"Well, when he's here with me on Sunday, maybe you can set him straight."

"Katie, I can't just bring it up out of nowhere," Mina said.

"Why not?"

"Because it's weird! If he asks me who his dad is, then I'll tell him. But I'm not just gonna, you know, bring it up."

"Do you know who his dad is?" Katie blurted.

"Not exactly," Mina said, watching Snake intently as he perused his cards. "It doesn't really matter."

"It does to Tuck," Katie pointed out. "What have you told him in the past when he's asked?"

"Not to ask again," said Mina. She and Snake laughed.

Katie blinked. *You're a bad mother,* she thought. *You're a bad, shitty mother and you don't deserve a kid like Tuck.* "Don't you think he deserves a better answer than that?" she said quietly.

"Who are you, Mother Theresa?" Mina snapped. Snake guffawed loudly, prompting Mina to grin. She obviously enjoyed having an audience.

"No," Katie said. "I just—"

"—want what's best for him," Mina mimicked. "Look, I'm his mother, I'll handle the situation as I see fit. Got it?"

"Got it," Katie bit out.

Her tone must have gotten to Mina. Mina's face softened, and she put down her cards. "I'm sorry. I don't mean to be such a cranky bitch."

"It's okay."

"No, it's not." She rubbed her arms anxiously. "It's just really hard, Katie. Figuring out what to tell him and what not to tell him. If I say I don't know who his dad is, I look like a total slut. If I tell him who I think his dad might be, then he might grow up and track these guys down."

"And that's bad?"

"Yeah, it's bad," Mina spat out. "One of 'em's married with three kids." She looked at Katie sheepishly. "I was always looking for that daddy figure, I guess."

"It's better he don't know anything," opined Snake.

"Who asked you?" Mina sneered.

"I'm just sayin' it won't kill him not to know. I never knew who my old man was and I turned out fine."

An image of Tuck ten years on began coalescing in Katie's imagination: he was covered in tattoos, flying up and down Didsbury's hills on a jerryrigged chopper, his name changed to 'Cuda.

"Yeah, you turned out great," Mina jeered affectionately. She touched Katie's arm. "I'll do what I can if the topic comes up," Mina promised her. "Okay?"

Katie sighed in capitulation. "Okay."

Fourteen-seventeen Tittenhurst Drive. That was the address Katie was looking for as she crawled the affluent streets of the Ladybarn neighborhood in her ear, looking for Liz Flaherty's house. Weybridge, Cavendish, Claremont— even the street names conjured images of wealth. Back in high school, when Katie was restless and couldn't sleep, she would sometimes imagine these leafy silent streets, dreaming about how wonderful it must be to live in one of these grand houses, with their built-in pools and lush English gardens and security systems. She assumed everyone who lived here led a charmed, golden life, free from the pain and suffering of plain existence. It wasn't until years later she realized wealth was no protection from dysfunction or misfortune. Every family had skeletons and heartache.

Rounding Tittenhurst, she slowed her pace even more. A police cruiser going in the opposite direction slowed as it passed her, the officer behind the wheel blatantly staring her down. Did he think she was casing the neighborhood? The thought amused Katie immensely.

She finally found the house, a huge mock Tudor mansion boasting a small koi-filled pond and a tennis court. In the drive sat a sky gray Mercedes. Beside it, a red Dodge truck that Katie recognized as belonging to Lane, Gary's nanny. It was Lane who usually drove Gary to and from hockey practice. She seemed nice.

Katie parked her humble Neon behind the Mercedes and sat a moment, engine running. Would it be rude to just honk the horn for Tuck to come out? She wasn't sure she could deal with Liz Flaherty on an empty stomach. It was ten a.m. Liz probably wasn't even up yet. Katie killed the engine and headed up the front walk. Her usual Saturday morning attire consisted of yoga pants and a T-shirt, but not today; on the off-chance she might encounter Liz, she wore chinos, a sweater and a touch of makeup. She remembered something her mother had said years ago: Women don't dress for men. They dress for other women. *Boy,* thought Katie, *was she ever right about that.*

Katie rang the doorbell, praying Lane would answer. Her hopes were dashed when the ornately, carved wooden door opened to reveal Liz in tennis whites.

"Katie." Her voice was like dry ice. "Come in. I was just on my way over to the country club. Do you play?"

"What, tennis?" Katie asked, stepping over the threshold. "No."

"Pity. It's a wonderful game. Invigoratingly competitive."

"I'll take your word for it," said Katie, gazing around the massive marble foyer that was bigger than her mother's house. She tried not to gawk or feel envy. It was truly a magnificent home.

"Is Tuck ready?" she asked politely.

"The boys should be down in a moment," Liz replied, an unpleasant smile frozen on her frosted pink lips. Katie couldn't escape the feeling she was being sized up. From the moment she'd stepped into the house, Liz's eyes had swept her from head to toe several times, assessing, perusing. She knew Liz did that to everyone, but the intensity and dis-pleasure of Liz's gaze made this feel more personally intrusive somehow. Katie glanced away.

"Did Tuck behave?" she asked, focusing on the gorgeous spiral staircase.

"A perfect angel," Liz assured her. "Although someone does need to teach him the proper way to eat soup. He tends to slurp."

Katie grit her teeth. She was not going to take the bait.

"How's your book coming?" Liz asked.

"Fine," she replied, surprised Liz was able to retain a fact about someone other than herself in her head.

"About athletes, isn't it?" Liz's tone was pointed.

"About how team sports shape male identity."

"Not exactly bestseller material."

Ignoring the barb, Katie looked up at the ceiling, then at the artwork in gilt frames lining the walls. "This house is really beautiful," she made herself say, hoping the change of topic would help.

"Well, it helps to marry a rich man." Liz regarded Katie. "That *is* one of the reasons you're sleeping with Paul van Dorn, isn't it?"

Katie stared at Liz. *"Excuse me?"*

"Oh, c'mon," Liz purred as if they were the oldest and dearest of confidants. "I know all about you and Paul."

How?! Then it came to her: Tuck.

"Honestly," Liz continued, picking up her tennis racket and swinging it as if hitting an imaginary ball, "there are other ways to ensure your nephew gets lots of ice time besides screwing his coach."

"How dare you?" Katie hissed.

Liz leveled her with a shrewd stare. "I could say the same to you."

Katie's hand shot out to stop Liz's racket in mid-swing.

"I'm not in the mood for games, Liz. Speak plainly or shut up."

Liz's mouth curled into a sneer. "You think he's all yours, don't you?"

"What are you talking about? I don't understand."

Liz clucked her tongue. "No, of course you don't." Carefully placing her racket against the wall, she sauntered over to a Chippendale sideboard, returning with a rolled-up pair of socks. "Will you please return these to Paul? He left them here."

Katie's chest constricted. "You're a liar, Liz."

"Check with Gary," she replied, smiling sweetly as she retrieved her racket and headed out the door. "Sorry. Gotta run. Don't want to be late for my game. Enjoy the rest of your day, Katie. I'm sure you can find your way out."

CHAPTER
14

Katie wolfed down another bite of her chocolate donut as she stared forlornly out the windshield of her car. Leaving Liz's, she dropped Tuck off at home and drove directly to the nearest Dunkin' Donuts, where she ordered a large coffee and a dozen donuts to go. Still in the parking lot, she had worked her way through two jellies and one Bavarian crème before diving into the chocolate. She washed down another big bite with a shot of hot coffee. She didn't care if this was a bad way to cope and she didn't care if she got fat again. The donut was delicious and the taste of sugar and fat as it filled her belly made her feel so much better. At least for now.

Liz's bombshell had knocked her for a loop. The minute Katie got Tuck in the car she'd wanted to interrogate him, demanding to know if he'd told Gary about her and Paul. But she was so heartsick and upset she knew she'd make a

mess of things. Better to wait until she was thinking clearly
to find out how the cat had slipped out of the bag.

She didn't know what to think or believe. So what if Liz
handed her a pair of socks, claiming they were Paul's? Any
idiot with socks could do that. It was Liz's chilling, "Check
with Gary" that clinched it. For Liz to even *say* that . . . Katie
smashed the rest of the donut into her mouth. Was it really
possible Liz's nine-year-old son could vouch for Paul's having spent the night—maybe many nights—at Liz's? Katie
lay her forehead on the steering wheel. "I knew I should
never have come back to this stupid town! I knew it!"

Her hand crept back to the open box of donuts beside her.
Lifting her head, she went to take a bite of a sugar-glazed
she'd pulled out, then stopped herself. Stuffing her face was
only masking the pain, not solving it. She needed to deal
with the real issue. She closed the box and stashed it on the
backseat, intending to bring it home. Her mother and Tuck
would be delighted.

She felt better, if only for a minute. The real issue was
Paul. Was he cheating on her? Salty tears trickled down the
back of her throat. Crying meant she cared and she hated
that. She didn't want to care. She didn't want to *hurt*.

She had to talk to Tuck *and* Paul and find out what was
going on. Paul would deny sleeping with Liz. Tuck would
deny telling Gary. But Tuck was a terrible liar. All Katie had
to do was stare at him, maybe speak sternly, and he'd cough
up a confession. In that regard he was more like her than
Mina.

"*Tuck? Can I* come in?"

Katie knocked softly at Tuck's bedroom door, which he'd
started to lock. Katie understood completely: It was the only
way to get any privacy, and it drove her mother crazy.

"Come on in," Tuck grumbled, unlocking the door.

Katie was surprised to see a book in his hand. Usually his butt was glued to the chair in front of his computer.

"What are you reading?"

"*Harry Potter*. Gary let me borrow it."

Katie nodded approvingly. Liz might be an intimate of Lucifer, but Gary was a nice kid. He was exposing Tuck to new things, which was good. So much of Tuck's life up until now had been about deprivation.

"Do you like it?"

Tuck shrugged. "It's pretty good."

"Mind if I sit down?"

Tuck shrugged again, pushing a pile of dirty clothing off a nearby chair and onto the floor. An aroma arose, that of sweat and dirt and mischief. Katie was glad to see his room was a bit untidy. It meant he finally felt at home. "Am I in trouble or something?" he asked nervously.

Katie sat. "Why would you think that?"

"I dunno." Tuck perched on the edge of his bed, bouncing anxiously. "Usually people only come to my room when it's something serious or something."

"That's not true. Nana comes to your room all the time to give you your clean laundry and change your sheets."

Tuck frowned. "I don't mean that."

"I know you don't." Katie glanced around. "Did you have fun at Gary's?"

Tuck nodded. "He's got a maid. And a nanny. And his own TV!"

"Wow! So, what did you guys do?"

"Watched TV. Oh, and he's got this really cool computer game where you can play hockey against Wayne Gretzky and Mark Messier!"

"Wow!" Katie enthused again. "That sounds like fun."

"It was."

Katie's hands curled around the arms of the chair. "Speaking of hockey, did you tell Gary about me and the coach?" Alarm flashed in Tuck's eyes. "It's okay if you did," Katie assured him quickly. "I just need to know."

Tuck stopped bouncing. "Do you promise you won't get mad at me?"

"I promise."

"Do you swear on a stack of bibles you won't get mad?"

"Yes," Katie replied patiently. "Now tell me."

Tuck gulped and began babbling. "We were playing the hockey game on the computer and talking about hockey and the team and Gary said he'd seen the coach naked and I said no way and he said yeah the coach had slept over his house and I said well big deal the coach is going out with my aunt and he said no way and I said yes way but it's a secret."

"I see."

"Are you mad at me?" Tuck asked, sounding scared.

"Of course not." Katie struggled to regain her breath. "I just need to know if you boys said anything to Gary's mother."

Tuck looked down at his swinging feet.

"Tuck?"

He wouldn't look at her, choosing to recite to the floor instead. "We went down for dinner and Gary's mother was there and Gary said tell your cool secret and I said no and he got mad so *he* told her and then she started asking all these questions and stuff."

Katie felt a burning behind her eyes. "What kind of questions?"

"Just, you know, if you and the coach were in love and if you ever slept over his house and stuff like that."

"And what did you say?" Katie managed.

"That you slept over sometimes but I didn't know if you

were in love." Tuck looked up at her, the color draining from his face. "Am I in trouble?"

Katie sat down beside him on the bed. "Honey, I've already told you, *no*."

"I didn't mean to tell, Aunt Katie, it just kinda came out."

Katie put her arm around him, surprised when he didn't rebuff her. "I know, sweetie. Don't worry about it."

"Mrs. Flaherty was really nosy," Tuck said defensively.

"Yes, it sounds like she was."

Tuck looked confused. "So is the coach going out with you *and* Mrs. Flaherty?"

"I don't know, honey." Katie's voice cracked with pain and she sought to cover it with a well placed cough. "But it's nothing you need to worry about, okay?" She smoothed a stray lock of Tuck's hair. "Go back to *Harry Potter*."

Paul knew something was wrong the minute Katie walked into his house. First, she didn't notice he'd started unpacking; he'd had to point out the artwork now gracing his walls. Second, she was monosyllabic. That wasn't like his beloved professor *at all*: Katie liked her syllables, the more the better. He knew he'd have to ask the question every man dreads: "Is everything okay?"

"Are you sleeping with Liz Flaherty?"

Paul frowned. *Where the hell had that come from?* "Why would you think that?"

"Oh, gee, I don't know." Katie reached into her book bag and took out a pair of black socks. She put one sock on each of her hands. "Hello, Mr. Sock," she had her right hand say to her left in a cartoon voice. "Where do *you* come from?"

"Why, I belong to Paul van Dorn," her left hand replied. "I've been at Liz Flaherty's house!"

"Hey, me, too!" her right hand exclaimed. "Liz said we

should be returned to Paul, so she asked Katie to do it, since Tuck spilled the beans and now Liz knows *allllll* about them!"

"Why were Paul's socks at Liz's?" Katie's left hand asked wonderingly.

"Gosh!" her right hand squealed. "That's just what Katie wants to know!"

Katie tore the socks off her hands and threw them down on the table. Paul stared at them. They were his, all right. The socks he'd forgotten the morning after the reunion, when he was scrambling to get away from Liz before she locked him up like one of Bluebeard's brides. *God. Damn. Son. Of. A. BITCH.*

"Are they yours or not?"

Paul slipped a sock on to his right hand and lifted his eyes to hers. "They are," he had his hand say to her quietly, "but it's not what you think."

"You don't want to know what I think!"

Paul jumped up, hobbling as fast as he could on his one good leg so he could beat her to the front door. "You're not leaving," he declared, blocking her way. His ankle throbbed with pain but he ignored it. He'd dealt with worse.

"You're supposed to be on crutches," Katie said. "And take that stupid sock off your hand."

Paul peeled the sock off his hand and threw it to the floor. "Screw the crutches. Talk to me."

Katie began tapping her foot impatiently. "Out of my way, Tiny Tim."

"Not until you hear me out."

Katie clucked her tongue. "Fine."

"I slept with Liz the night of the reunion. I was drunk off my ass and believe me, I regretted it in the morning. I was in such a rush to get the hell out of there I left my socks."

Katie frowned. "Oh, really."

"Yeah, *really*."

Katie looked dubious. "You expect me to believe she's been hanging on to your socks for months?"

"She has! Why, I don't know. You really think I'd two-time you with Liz?"

"She's never gotten you out of her system!" Katie became teary. "Never. Maybe you feel the same way—"

Paul shook his head. "You're the one I can't get out of my system, Professor." He reached out, gently cradling Katie's cheek in his right hand. "I would never cheat on you," he said softly. "I love you."

Katie slowly backed out of reach. "Don't say that," she whispered.

"Why the hell not?" Something broke free inside him. "It's the truth! I love you!"

Katie's hands flew to her ears.

Paul pulled them away. "What the hell is your *problem*?"

"You don't understand," Katie insisted.

"Yeah, I do!" Confidence pumped through him, brought on by a sudden clarity of vision. "You love me, too, but it scares the living hell out of you! Why else would you be so upset about Liz if you didn't feel anything for me?"

"I'm *fond* of you," Katie mumbled, hanging her head. "I'm not in love with you."

"I guess we're free to go out with other people, then."

Katie's head shot up.

"Ah-ha!"

"That wasn't fair!" Katie stamped her foot. "You— you're confusing me."

"There's nothing confusing about this at all."

"I still can't believe Liz would hang on to your socks," Katie said suspiciously.

Paul snorted. "Look what Monica Lewinsky held on to! Who the hell knows why people do these things?"

Katie turned away from him.

"I love you," Paul murmured.

"Stop saying that!" Katie cried.

"Because—?"

"It complicates things." She turned back to him. "It throws a monkey wrench in the works." Her voice dropped. "It confuses me."

"So you keep saying. I don't see what's so confusing about love."

"This isn't what I saw for myself," Katie revealed with a quiver in her voice. "I had my life all mapped out." She threw a hand up in the air dramatically. "And then this!"

"What's 'this'?" Paul asked, imitating her gesture.

"You."

Paul couldn't resist a self-satisfied smile. "I'm flattered."

"Mucking up someone's well laid plans is nothing to be proud of, van Dorn."

"I've got news for you: Sometimes, what we have planned for our lives and what fate actually has in store for us are two different things."

"Well, I don't accept that," Katie replied obstinately, "and neither do you. If you did, you wouldn't be so obsessed with still winning. You would *let it go.* You wouldn't have resigned yourself to your fate and crawled back to Didsbury."

She shouldn't have said it, and they both knew it.

"Is that what you think?" Paul asked politely. "That my career blew up in my face and because I couldn't think of anything better to do, I came back to Didsbury?"

Katie hesitated. "Yes."

"I see." Paul rubbed his chin. "This town did a lot for you, you know. Whether you want to admit it or not."

"We're not talking about me. We're talking about you."

"Right, where were we? Oh yeah: Me crawling back to

Didsbury. What a loser, huh?" He hobbled over to the side
of the couch, where his crutches rested. Placing them under
his arms, he propelled himself to the front door, opening it
wide. "I think you should go now."

"Paul." Katie's voice turned appeasing. "We need to talk
about how Liz's knowing is going to impact Tuck. You
know she's going to tell anyone who listens."

"You know what, Katie? Right now I don't give a shit
about Tuck or Liz."

Katie knit her hands together nervously. "You're mad."

"Yeah, I'm mad. 'This isn't what I saw for myself,'" he
repeated. "What the hell does that mean?"

"I—"

"I'm not good enough for you? You're a hot-shot academic and it's beneath you to fall in love with a jock?"

"That's exactly it, Paul." There was sadness in her voice.
"You're *not* a jock. Not anymore. You're a bar owner."

"Fine, I'm a bar owner. Is there something wrong with
that?"

"Not if it's what you really want to do."

"I've told you before: I *can't* do what I really want to do.
So I'm doing this instead. And if that doesn't meet with your
approval, you can kiss my townie ass!"

Katie's mouth fell open.

"You're a snob, Katie. I'm glad you set such high standards for yourself. I understand that. It's admirable. But I'm
sick to death of trying to live up to them."

Collecting her coat, Katie lingered at the door. "I guess
I'll see you at the Panthers game Monday afternoon."

Paul nodded curtly. "We'll talk."

Katie returned his nod and started down the front walk
toward her car. Paul watched her go, waiting until she was
out of sight before closing the front door. Then, with all the

force he could muster with his good leg, he kicked his goddamn sock out of the way.

"Hit me again."

Paul was drunk, but not so drunk he couldn't interpret the
disapproving look crossing Frank DiNizio's face as he
poured Paul another shot of Wild Turkey.

"This is it," Frank announced. "You're officially cut off."

"I own the bar."

"That's nice. You're still cut off."

Paul muttered a few choice words under his breath and
threw back the whiskey, relishing the taste of fire as it slid
down his throat. After asking Katie to leave, he didn't know
what the hell to do with himself, so he'd come down to the
Penalty Box. He hated being morose, but he couldn't help
replaying their evening in his head. How had things deteri-
orated so quickly? And who was to blame?

Liz, that's who.

He was still trying to wrap his mind around her hanging
on to his socks. He imagined her curled up with them at
night, or running them over her body, and shuddered. What
the hell was wrong with her? She'd had countless opportu-
nities to give them back to him, yet she hadn't, probably because she'd been lying in wait for an opportunity just like
this one to wreck his life. Fucking Liz.

He wished he hadn't asked Katie to leave. Now he wasn't
sure where they stood. They should have continued talking,
hashed everything out. But her denying her feelings made
him angry. Did she think it was easy for him to say he loved
her? He'd been carrying it around inside for weeks, not saying anything for fear of upsetting the delicate balance of
their relationship. He'd finally come clean and where had it

gotten him? A seat at the end of the bar, drowning his sorrows in booze and self-pity.

She pissed him off! He was sick to death of trying to meet her approval. Yeah, he was flattered she thought him capable of more, but things were what they were. No use crying over spilt milk and all that crap. He was back in Didsbury and if she didn't like it or approve, well, *hasta la vista baby*!

He banged his shot glass on the bar. "One more, Frank! C'mon!"

Frank shook his head. "I already told you."

"One more or you're fired," Paul threatened, half smiling. Maybe he'd do it, just to remind Frank who was in charge here.

Frank sighed. "Why don't you just go home, boss, okay? I can call you a cab."

"I don't want a fuckin' cab and I own the fuckin' bar so you'll do what I say!" Paul bellowed. Heads turned. "What?" Paul jeered at them. "You've never seen someone drunk before?" He slid off his bar stool and picking up his crutches, propelled himself to the middle of the bar. "Do you know who I am?" He looked around. "Do any of you have any fuckin' idea *who I am*?"

"Yeah, you're an asshole," someone called out.

Paul twisted around wildly. "Who said that? Who? I'll kick your ass!" The room fell silent save for the jukebox pumping out AC/DC's "Highway to Hell." Talk about apropos. "So! Is anyone gonna answer my question?"

"You're Paul van Dorn," a woman called out from one of booths along the wall.

Paul raised a crutch in her direction. "That's right! I'm Paul fuckin' van Dorn and I own this bar! Paul fuckin' van Dorn, first-round draft pick for the New York Blades! Have any of you losers ever played in the NHL? Huh? Any of you losers ever win the Con Smythe?! Any of you ever skate the Stanley Cup?!"

"Boss." Frank gripped his forearm and began steering him toward the back office. "That's enough."

Paul felt everyone's eyes on him as Frank dragged him through the room. Losers! He signed autographs for them whenever they wanted and told the same stories over and over just to make them happy, and what did he get in return? Stares! Of confusion. Of amusement. Of *pity*.

"Fuck all of you!" he cried. "At least I *was* someone once! At least—"

Frank clamped his hand over Paul's mouth as he pulled Paul over the office threshold, kicking the door shut behind them. "Sit," he commanded, releasing Paul with a small shove. Paul felt dizzy, weaving on his crutches. Frank scowled. "Sit or I'll make you sit."

Paul did what he was told, sinking down onto the junk-covered couch. He was hit with an unexpected wave of exhaustion and his head suddenly felt as if it were stuffed with cotton, his tongue thick. The urge to close his eyes and fall asleep was strong.

"What the hell was that all about?" Frank demanded.

"Do you think I'm pathetic?" Paul blurted. Even though Katie had denied meaning it, the charge had lodged in the back of his mind ever since.

"In general, no. But tonight? Fuckin' A."

Paul grunted, glancing around his office through drooping lids. The place was a mess, promo items littering his desk and the floor, old hockey gear he couldn't bear to part with stacked in the far corner. What else had she said? Oh, yeah. Nothing wrong with being a bar owner, if that's what he wanted to do. But it wasn't.

"Go away," Paul muttered, waving Frank away. "I'm going to crash here, just leave me."

"You sure?"

"I'm sure. Tell everyone out there I'm sorry, and that drinks for the rest of the night are on me. Okay?"

Frank patted his shoulder. "You got it, Paul."

Frank left, quietly closing the door behind him. Paul's eyes strayed to the hockey gear in the corner; from the shoulder pads that had protected him from slashes, to the skates he'd been wearing when Ulf Torkelson brought him down for the last time. Clearing the couch of junk, Paul curled up in a ball, pulling the ratty old afghan draped over an arm of the couch close around him.

Then he did something he hadn't done since the neurologist told him he couldn't play hockey anymore. He wept.

CHAPTER

15

In high school, Katie had trained herself to tune out the whispers and snide remarks that followed her everywhere. It was a skill she thought she'd retained, until she entered the rink for the Panthers' game against the Cornwall Bob-o-Links. Hostile glares guided her to her seat, accompanied by low whispers and the occasional snicker. She did her best to quell the anxiety rippling through her as she took her seat beside Bitsy, but it was hard. It felt like all the Panther parents were giving her dirty looks.

"Hey, hon." Bitsy sounded cautious as she handed Katie a mug full of coffee from her ever present thermos. "How was your weekend?"

"Shitty." Katie stiffened as two women, both mothers of boys on Tuck's team, turned around to stare at her, their faces smug with condemnation. "Someone want to tell me what's going on here?" Katie asked, though she had a pretty good idea.

Bitsy hesitated. "Liz has been—saying things."

"Like—?"

Bitsy and her husband shared an uneasy glance. "She's saying the reason Tuck is getting so much ice time is because you're sleeping with Paul. She's passed around a petition to get Paul fired."

Katie put her head in her hands. "Great."

"I guess Tuck told Gary?" Bitsy asked.

Katie nodded forlornly.

"I told you kids that age can't keep a secret."

"You were right," Katie conceded as she lifted her head to look around. "Where is Liz?"

"Last I saw she was outside the ladies' room, trying to get people to sign her petition."

Katie moved to get up but Bitsy's hand stayed her. "Don't. That's exactly what she wants."

"But she's smearing me!" Katie protested as two more parents pinned her with a disapproving stare. Katie stared back until they broke eye contact.

"Let her," Bitsy counseled. "Believe me."

Katie settled back in her seat. A cold sweat was beginning to break out on her chest and back. The same thing used to happen in high school when kids would make fun of her. Then, as now, her principal tormentor was Liz Flaherty. Maybe you could never fully escape your past. Katie sipped her coffee, trying to maintain her dignity as the whispering swelled to murmuring. "They believe Liz," she said to Bitsy, straining to keep the incredulity out of her voice.

"Can you blame them?" Bitsy asked carefully.

Katie looked at her. "No, I can't," she said after a moment. "If my kid wasn't being played, I'd be pissed, too." Heartsick, she scoured the ice for Tuck, who was warming up with the team. She watched him circle the ice alone—

once, twice, three times. Was it her imagination, or were the other boys being standoffish toward him?

Frank held out his Doritos to her. Katie hesitated, then thrust her hand in the bag. Screw it. A handful of Dorritos wouldn't kill her.

"You probably don't want to know this, but Paul got totally shitfaced at the Penalty Box Saturday night," Frank confided between bouts of chewing. "Basically insulted everyone there."

"You're right," Katie said through a mouthful of Doritos, "I don't want to know."

Bitsy looked confused. "I thought you were seeing Paul Saturday night."

"I was. I did." Misery shot through her. "We argued. About Liz and other stuff."

"Well, you did a number on his head," Frank continued. "I mean, he was—"

Bitsy elbowed him. She looked at Katie in disbelief. "You fought about *Liz*?"

Katie nodded. She told Bitsy and Frank the tale of the socks, asking their opinion.

"Liz is totally capable of holding on to socks for months," Bitsy declared.

"Women are screwy," was Frank's pronouncement.

"So, you don't think he's slept with her since the night of the reunion?"

Bitsy looked shocked. "Paul? *No way*. He's totally smitten with you."

Katie groaned. This was not what she wanted to hear, though she knew it was true. She'd spent all of Sunday thinking about Saturday night, trying to sort out her feelings and determine whether she was a snob. There was only one way to find out.

"Do you think I'm a snob?" she asked Bitsy.

"No!"

Katie held her breath. "What if I told you that I'd rather have knitting needles shoved in my eyes than live in Didsbury for good? That the day I left to go to college I vowed I would *never* come back here, except to visit? That every time I open the paper and see the utter lack of cultural life I want to hop into my car and go back to Fallowfield immediately? Would you think I was a snob then?"

Bitsy considered this. "Yes."

Katie's shoulders sank. "I thought so."

"Is that true?" Bitsy sounded wounded. "Do you really hate being back here?"

"Of course not." Katie chose her words carefully. "It's just a little too slow for me, you know?"

"Did Paul ask you to stay?"

"No."

"Then why did he accuse you of being a snob?"

Katie wiped Dorito crumbs from her mouth. "*He* thinks *I* think he should have done more with his life after hockey."

"And do you?"

"Yes." Katie felt like a snob admitting it. "But only because he seems so damn unhappy!" She leaned over to Frank. "Aren't I right? Doesn't he seem unhappy?"

Frank chewed thoughtfully. "He was Saturday night, I'll admit that."

"I don't think he's really dealt with his past."

Bitsy looked at her like she was naïve. "Who has?" she asked.

Gutless. That's the best word Katie could come up with for Liz's absence during the Panthers' game. Liz had come to the arena, disseminated her poison, and left.

As for Paul, Katie couldn't decide whether he didn't care,

or if he was simply oblivious to the tide of ill will flowing both their ways during the game. Just as he'd done the week before, he was evenhanded the first two periods, in some cases playing kids who'd barely logged any ice time previously. But when the Bob-o-Links deked their way into a one-point lead, Paul broke out his secret weapon: Tuck. It pained Katie to watch her nephew fly down the ice, knowing that most of the parents there believed his prominence had to do with *her*. And the way Tuck smiled in adoration at Paul . . . Katie could see that every time Paul tapped him to play, Tuck viewed it as further proof Paul was his father. She needed Paul to break him of that notion, and fast. And she needed to disabuse Paul of a few notions himself.

She waited until the game was over and the players and their parents had left before approaching him. Paul always waited until every child had been picked up before leaving. Today he was sitting with Darren Becker, whose parents never watched him play. Katie felt for the kid: Every time he hit the ice his eyes combed the stands, hoping in vain to see his mother or father there. "Do you want me to try calling your mom again?" she heard Paul ask him gently.

Darren shook his head. "No. She said she's on her way. She probably got tied up in traffic or something."

"If it's a problem for your mom to get here, I can drive you home," Paul offered.

The boy's face lit up. Getting a ride home from the coach carried cache. He looked about to accept Paul's offer when his mother hustled into the rink, briefcase in one hand, cell phone in the other. "Sorry I'm late," she said breathlessly. "I'm on the phone with a client." She snapped her fingers at her son impatiently. "Ready?"

Darren nodded, collecting his backpack and equipment. "See you at practice tomorrow, Coach," he called over his shoulder at Paul.

"Good game, Darren," Paul called after him.

Katie could tell from Paul's frown of displeasure that he was thinking the same thing she was about Darren's parents.

"It's nice of you to wait," she observed.

Paul shook his head. "You think I should say something to his folks? It's really bad for his morale."

"I think anything you say to the parents right now wouldn't be taken seriously," said Katie, sitting down beside him.

"Why's that?" Paul asked, his eyes following the zamboni now smoothing the ice. There were circles under his brilliant blue eyes, and his pallor was gray.

"You're not going to like this," Katie warned him.

"Love the sound of that." Paul loosened his tie. "Before we get into the fun stuff, I want to apologize for Saturday night. Asking you to leave like that was a little abrupt."

"Not really. We both needed time to think." She studied his face. "You look exhausted."

"I am. Haven't been able to sleep."

"Me neither." She drew a deep breath. "We need to talk."

"The words every man wants to hear." His eyes locked with hers. "Shoot."

Katie drew her coat tight around her, less from the cold blasting through the rink than from needing a sense security. "It's Liz," she began on an exhalation of breath. "She's telling everyone the reason you use Tuck so much is because we're sleeping together. She's circulating a petition to have you removed as coach."

"Screw her," Paul scoffed. "It'll never happen." His tone was offhand, but his expression said otherwise. Anger smoldered in his eyes and his jaw was clenched so tightly Katie kept imagining his teeth cracking.

"Whether it happens or not isn't the point. I spent the entire game getting dirty looks from parents."

"Screw them, too."

"No, Paul. That's not the right attitude. They have a right to be upset. You're not being fair." She swallowed. "This is doing damage to *Tuck*." When he said nothing, she pressed on. "You have to stop playing him so much. It's not fair to the other kids, and it's not fair to him. He's nursing a fantasy that you're his father. Did you know that?"

Paul looked taken aback. "No."

"Well, he is. And the more ice time you give him, the worse it's going to get. So please, stop."

"Fine, I'll stop. And we'll lose."

He reached out, stroking her hair. Katie closed her eyes a moment, relishing the sensation. "Don't distract me," she commanded quietly. "I'm not done."

Paul's hand dropped. "Of course you're not."

The wisecrack hurt. "What does that mean?"

"You're going to tell me we have to break up for Tuck's sake. That he'll never catch a fair break if we don't." Katie could feel her face beginning to turn red. "Right?"

"Paul—"

"Don't interrupt, I'm not done yet. Then you'll remind me you're going back to Fallowfield in the fall, as if no couple in the history of the world has ever endured a long-distance relationship. I'll point this out to you, and you'll squirm and stutter and say it has nothing to do with that. You'll claim it has to do with me not fitting into your vision of things. Then you'll say I'm trapped in the past and you can't be with someone like that." His gaze was hard. "Did I nail it, or what?"

Katie's voice trembled. "It's not that cut and dried."

"No, it's not. Because I left out the most important part of the equation."

"What's that?" Katie asked uneasily, rocking in place to keep warm. The temperature in the rink seemed to have dropped twenty degrees in the past thirty seconds. Or maybe it was just the humiliation of being so accurately parodied.

"You love me, and you can't deal with it. I'm not the only one with a problem reconciling the past and the present. You've got one, too, but you're too damn intellectual to see it, never mind admit it."

"That's not true," Katie whispered fiercely.

"Sure it is." Paul stood up, draping his sports jacket over his right shoulder. "You're afraid of your past and, according to you, I revel in mine. Look, it's okay. I understand. I'm now an underachieving townie. You're a high-powered professor scaling the heights of the ivory tower. We had a little fun between the sheets, and now you want out before the really tough questions start getting asked. It's cool."

Katie could barely find her voice. "I never meant—it's not—"

"We're done, Katie." He smiled at her sadly. "There, I said it. Now you don't have to stress over letting the ex-jock bar owner down easy."

"I don't view you that way!" Katie protested. "I don't —"

"We could go round and round on this," Paul cut in wearily. "But let's not. It's been great. I love you. I'm sad it didn't work out, but that was your call, not mine. I'll make sure Tuck doesn't have any hassles. Thanks for letting me know about Liz's big mouth. Maybe while you're still in town we could meet for the occasional cup of coffee and talk. I know Didsbury doesn't have a Starbucks, but I'm sure we could find *some* place that would satisfy your sophisticated tastes." His eyes darkened, filling with pain. "I always enjoyed talking to you, Katie." He leaned over, planting a soft, lingering kiss on her forehead. "Good luck with your book."

• • •

Katie lay on the narrow, lumpy bed of her childhood, staring at the water stain shaped like a sheep on the ceiling. Normally, the smell of her mother's pot roast wafting beneath the bedroom door would have set her stomach grumbling in anticipation. Tonight it made her queasy.

Her mind had been blank as she watched Paul leaving the rink. She went to collect Tuck, who loved playing the video games in the rink's lobby. In a daze, they'd come straight home, Tuck's raving about ice time going in one ear and out the other. She didn't have the energy to respond or refute; all she cared about was getting to her mother's house as quickly as possible and hiding in her room.

How many times had she lay here like this as a teenager, crying lonely tears? She wittled away hours visualizing herself thin and successful, plotting her escape from this town that felt like a prison. And now here she was ten years later, doing the same thing. The only difference was, she *was* thin and successful. Did she actually owe that to Didsbury, the way Paul claimed? She wasn't sure. But the yearning for escape--especially now—remained as strong as ever.

She was supposed to break up with Paul. His actions had shocked her, not because she hated having the tables turned, but because he had so perfectly anticipated everything she was planning to say. Was she that transparent? Or had her reservations become a broken record he could recite verbatim? She suspected it was a bit of both.

"Katie?"

She took a deep breath. "Yes, Mom?"

"Dinner will be ready in a few minutes."

Katie hesitated. "I'm not really hungry tonight. Thanks." She could practically see her mother's puzzled face on the other side of the door as she tried to figure out the appropriate response.

"Can I come in a minute, honey?"

"Sure," Katie made herself say.

Her mother entered and perched beside Katie on the bed, taking her hand. As a little girl, Katie had always loved her mother's long, delicate fingers, thinking her hands so elegant. She still thought so, though time was beginning to mottle the skin. It was hard watching her mom age.

"What's going on?" her mother asked gently.

"Nothing. I'm just tired, that's all."

Her mother smoothed her brow. "You sure that's all?"

"Yes." Katie felt her heart cracking. She squeezed her eyes shut, trying to stave off tears. It didn't work; a teardrop worked its way out of the corner of her right eye, heading toward her ear.

"Talk to me, Katie."

"It's nothing," Katie tried to say dismissively, but the words lodged in her throat, coming out like a croak. What was *happening* to her? She wanted to wail, to put her head in her mother's lap and weep over how mean and dumb boys were. It was an adolescent rite of passage she'd heard about but had never experienced. Until now.

"It's Paul," she sobbed. "We broke up."

"Oh, Katie." Her mother sounded upset. "What happened?"

"I don't know," Katie sniffed. "Actually, I do. I fucked up."

"Language, dear," her mother tut-tutted.

"Fuck, fuck, fuck!" Katie chanted defiantly. "If I want to say it, I'll say it!"

"You're right, honey. You 'fuck' away all you want."

Katie lifted her head, catching her mother's eye. They both began laughing before Katie dissolved back into tears. "See, this is why I didn't want to get involved! Because I *knew* it would end badly and I knew I'd wind up in pain and

I worked so hard to get my life in order!" She curled onto her side, hiccupping with sobs.

"You can't avoid pain, honey," her mother pointed out tenderly as she stroked Katie's hair. "However you fu— messed things up with Paul, I'm sure you can fix them."

"That's the thing. I don't know if I want to." She flopped onto her stomach with a howl, burying her face in her pillow. "I don't know what I want!"

"You'll figure it out," her mother soothed. "I know you will. You always do."

Katie raised her tear-stained face. She hated her mother's unswerving faith in her. It felt like pressure. "What if I don't?"

"You will."

"But what if I *don't?*"

Her mother sighed. "I guess I'll just stop loving you."

"Thanks for your help."

"What do you want me to say, sweetheart?" Her mother sounded bemused. "If it's meant to be, it'll be. But first, you really *do* have to figure out what you want."

CHAPTER

16

Big. Brass. Balls. That's the only explanation Paul could come up with for Liz Flaherty breezing through the door of the Penalty Box, looking like she owned the place. As if to confirm he wasn't hallucinating, Paul glanced at Frank, whose shocked expression mirrored his own.

"She's got some pair on her, that one," Frank noted with the faintest hint of admiration in his voice.

"My thoughts exactly."

Paul's guts churned as he watched Liz approach. You ruined my fucking life, he wanted to yell. You and your goddamn sock trick! He wished he could shake her until her teeth rattled in her head. He knew Liz was only partially to blame, but still. It felt good to have a target for his rage. The loss of Katie had left a hole inside him he needed to fill. Anger seemed as good a choice as any.

"Paul." Liz looked surprised when she leaned in to give

him a kiss on the cheek and he stepped out of reach. "Oh, now, don't be that way, lamby."

So, that was how it was going to be: Liz playing cutesy, him warding her off. Who had the energy for this shit? Seriously. But what was his choice? Not playing along would prolong the torture. And since he wanted her the hell out of there, he gave in.

"What do you want, Liz?"

Her gaze was seductive. "Do you mean in general, or to drink?"

"To *drink*."

"My usual," she said coolly, looking at Frank. "A Grey Goose martini." She turned back to Paul. "He's so dumb."

For a split second, the sour look that streaked across her face made her look ugly. *What did I ever see in her?* Paul wondered. She'd always been a bitch. *Yeah, but a popular one.* A pretty, vivacious, popular bitch who bent over backward—sometimes literally—to please him in high school. Disgust for his adolescent self filled him.

"How's your petition going?" he couldn't resist asking.

"Pretty well." Her expression was serious as she took a long, slow sip of her drink. "I'd watch it if I were you."

Paul chuckled meanly. "Back at ya, baby."

Liz did a small double take. "Meaning—?"

"If I find out you're spreading any more lies about me and Katie Fisher, you're going to be sorry."

Liz looked amused. "What are you going to do, Paul? Bore me to death with one of your NHL stories?"

"I mean it, Liz. Leave Katie alone."

"I didn't do anything!"

"Right. Except spread it around that she was the reason Tuck was getting so much ice time, not to mention giving her a pair of socks I left at your house *months* ago."

"Was she upset?" Liz batted her eyes innocently. "I *so* didn't mean to upset her. Truly."

"You didn't. We had a good laugh over what a mess you are."

Maybe he was imagining it, but he could have swore Liz gave the slightest of flinches. Good. He wanted her to flinch, to feel guilty. Perhaps then she'd leave him the hell alone once and for all.

"See, this is what I don't get," Paul continued, sliding onto the stool next to hers. "What did you think would happen? You'd give Katie the socks and she'd think we were still sleeping together and we'd break up and what—? You and I would get together?"

"Maybe," Liz said. "After you had a chance to come to your senses."

"I came to my senses the morning after the reunion, Liz. That's what you don't seem to get. No offense, but you're pathetic."

Liz chortled. "Look who the hell's talking!"

"Do you think insulting me is going to make me want you?"

For the first time in a long time, Liz looked vulnerable. "You know I don't mean it," she said miserably.

"I don't care if you mean it or not. Just leave me alone, okay?"

"This isn't over, Paul." There was a brittle determination in her voice he knew only too well.

"Yeah, it is." Paul's voice was firm as he removed her drink from her hand. "Leave."

"What!"

"You heard me. As of today, you are banned from the Penalty Box."

"You can't do that!"

"Yes, I can. Cross the threshold again and I'll have you arrested for soliciting."

"I hate you!" Liz hissed.

"Glad to hear it." Paul patted her shoulder as he slid off the bar stool and sauntered away. "Have a good one."

"*Mom, I want* you to meet Snake."

Katie held her breath as her mother stepped forward to stiffly shake hands with the tattooed giant who had just conveyed her daughter home from rehab on a chopper. You had to hand it to Mina; she sure knew how to stop conversation. The frozen smile on her mother's face was painful for Katie to see.

"Nice to meet you, Mr. Snake," said her mother.

Mina stifled a snort and Katie cut her with her eyes. Couldn't Mina at least give her a little credit for trying? Apparently not, if the smirk plastered to her sister's pretty face was any indication. How Katie longed to slap it off!

"Snake's putting me and Tuck up till we find our own place," Mina continued.

Katie's mother looked confused. "But—"

"I know you prepped the sewing room for me, Ma," said Mina, catching Katie's eye, "but really, it's better this way."

"Oh," said Katie's mother, looking crestfallen.

"You could have let her know before now," Katie pointed out under her breath.

"Mind your own business," Mina muttered, craning her neck as she tried to peer into the kitchen. "So, where's my son?"

Katie went to the bottom of the stairs. "Tuck!" she called up, surprised to find herself blindsided by tears. She brushed them away. "Your mom's here!"

The day she and her mother thought might never come

had indeed arrived: Mina was out of rehab and was taking Tuck away to live with her and Snake. Melancholy had hung over the house for the better part of a week, much of it generated by Tuck, who protested to anyone who would listen that the last thing he wanted to do was go live with his mother. Katie tried everything she could to soothe him, from promising she'd still attend all his hockey games to equipping him with his own cell phone so he could call her whenever he wanted. Yet nothing seemed to calm the storm raging inside her nephew, who grew more agitated the closer it drew to Mina's release date. Now that it was here, Katie wasn't surprised he'd taken to hiding in his room. If she thought she could get away with it, she'd do the same thing.

"Tuck!" Katie shouted again. "Your mom's here!"

The bedroom door flew open. "I'm not deaf!" Tuck shouted down the stairs. Katie turned back to the adults, chastened.

"I believe he'll be joining us in just a moment," she said.

Tuck's heavy, reluctant tread on the steps echoed in the hall. He appeared in the living room unsmiling, arms stiff at his sides as if he were a robot.

"There's my baby," Mina cooed, flying to him and folding him into an embrace. If it bothered her that Tuck did nothing to return the gesture, she didn't show it. Instead, she broke contact and wheeled him around so he was facing Snake. "Tuck, this is Snake. We're going to live with him till we find our own place."

Katie felt sick. She couldn't believe this was the first time Tuck and Snake were meeting. You didn't do that to a kid, just thrust someone on them like that! She looked down as her tears tried to return. She lifted her head to see Snake stepping forward, extending his hand.

"Pleased to meet ya, little guy."

Katie had to give him credit; he was trying. The same

couldn't be said for Tuck, who refused to shake his hand and returned the friendly gesture by rolling his eyes. Mina cuffed him in the head. "Where the hell are your manners?"

"It's cool," Snake cut in quickly, shooting Mina a questioning glance. "Little guy's a bit overwhelmed. I can dig that." He tried another tack: "Wanna check out my chopper?"

"No," Tuck replied contemptuously.

"Speaking of Snake's chopper," Katie interjected, "how are you planning to get all Tuck's stuff over to the new place?"

Mina draped an arm over Katie's shoulder. "This is where you come in."

"I'll bet."

"I figured we could use your car, sis," said Mina. *You should have asked,* Katie thought angrily, but held her tongue. She wanted everything to go smoothly for Tuck's sake. If that meant biting back her anger and loading up her car with his stuff, she would do it.

"Where do you live, son?" Katie's mother politely inquired of Snake. Katie loved the fact her mother was calling Snake "son." Snake was forty if he was a day.

"You know those apartments down by Tully's Basin?" Snake replied. Katie's mother nodded uneasily. "That's where I hang my hat, ma'am."

Katie's mother smiled brightly, a smile Katie knew was designed to cover rising panic. Everyone in Didsbury knew about the apartments by Tully's Basin; they were notorious for crime, drug busts, and general mayhem. "Oh, how nice," her mother twittered. "And what did you say you do for a living?"

"I'm a first grade teacher at St. Mary's Catholic School."

"Well, I—I guess—things really did change in the Church after Vatican II."

Snake guffawed. "Just fuckin' witcha! I'm not a teacher. I'm a bouncer. At the Tender Trap."

Katie's mother looked more confused than ever.

"Let it go, Ma," Katie advised.

"Can I finish packing?" Tuck asked sulkily.

"Sure," Katie and Mina replied at the same time. Mina shot Katie a dirty look. "Sorry," Katie mouthed. "We'll be up in a few minutes to get you," Mina finished.

Looking relieved, Tuck flew up the stairs, crashing the bedroom door closed behind him.

"He's a little upset," Katie observed.

Mina's face was hard as she rifled in the pocket of her parka for her cigarettes. "Yeah, well, he better get over it, and fast."

"Hey." Snake's voice was filled with consternation. "Cut the kid some slack, will ya, Mina? This is a lot of shit for him to process."

Katie looked upon Snake with newfound admiration. Maybe he wasn't a homicidal maniac after all. "I wrote out all the stuff you need to know about Tuck's schedule," she said.

Mina waved her hand in the air dismissively as she lit up. "Tuck can tell me himself. I don't need *instructions*."

"Dear, could you not smoke?" Katie's mother asked.

"I could, but I am."

"Mina, Mom asked you not to smoke," Katie snapped. She was sick of Mina terrorizing their mother. It had always been that way, Mina doing and saying what she wanted because their mother was too afraid of what would happen otherwise. It was time for it to stop. "It's *her* house," Katie continued. "You should do what she asks."

"Why, so I can be a boring goody goody like you?"

Katie glowered. "Put out the goddamn cigarette, Mina."

"Girls." Their mother was wringing her hands.

"Your sister's right," said Snake, plucking the cigarette from between Mina's lips. "You should show a little respect."

"Fine," Mina said brusquely. Katie could see from the flash of pink to her cheeks that Snake had embarrassed her. "Sorry, Ma." She turned to Katie with a sneer. "Happy?"

"Very."

"Who wants pie?" Katie's mother squeaked.

Snake's face lit up. "I would love a piece of pie, Mrs. Fisher."

"We don't have time for pie, Snake!" Mina said. "I have a ton of shit to unpack and I'm sure Tuck does, too."

"Actually, Tuck has very little to unpack," Katie said dryly. She turned to Snake, who was disappointed at being denied pie. "Do you know how to hook up a computer?"

"I'm sure I can figure it out, and if I can't, I'll just get you on the horn."

"Please do. It's his prized possession." She shot Mina a look: *You sell it, you die.*

"We'll work it out," said Snake. "Hell, the kid himself can probably do it."

"Thank you," said Katie.

"No problemo."

"Enough chitchat, we gotta roll." Mina zipped her jacket. Katie's mother began to sniffle and excused herself to go into the kitchen. "Shit," Mina grumbled.

"Give her a break," Katie replied. She knew she was sounding like a broken record but she couldn't help it. "She's been taking care of him for close to a year! She's allowed to miss him."

"Amen," said Snake.

"Thank you," said Katie. She was beginning to like this guy. "I think we should load Tuck's stuff in my car and then we'll follow you and Snake," she continued.

Mina looked contrite. "I appreciate it, Katie, really."

"You should." Mina could be so goddamn maddening. Combative one minute, genuinely grateful the next. "Mind if I fetch Tuck?"

Mina shrugged. "Knock yourself out."

Katie climbed the steps as though she was ascending to the guillotine. She knew it would hurt when Tuck left; she just hadn't anticipated *how much*. The threat of loss made each step feel as if she were mired in quicksand. If she could drive Tuck to Tully's Basin without breaking down completely it would be a miracle.

"Tuck?" Katie knocked softly at the door, receiving no answer. She knocked again, louder this time. "Tuck?" Still no reply. She leaned her forehead wearily against the door. *It's going to be okay, buddy, I swear.* She knocked again. This time, when she got no answer, she plunged inside, fully expecting to find Tuck stretched out on his bed, feigning deafness in that way only children can. Instead she was met by a cold blast of air from the open window across the room, curtains flapping violently in the winter wind.

Tuck was gone.

Paul's heart sank as the doorbell rang. It had to be a fan. When he'd first returned to Didsbury, he'd assumed anyone wanting to meet him would simply come to the bar. He'd assumed wrong; fans regularly showed up on his doorstep, a phenomena he found incredibly unnerving. In Manhattan, at least there had been a doorman in the lobby of his building. Here, any nutcase could just show up. Thank God he'd had brains enough to get an unlisted phone number.

He hit the mute button on the remote; he didn't want whoever was on the other side of the door to hear the TV. He glanced at the screen, at the image of Michael Dante handing him the Stanley Cup, and just for a moment, the room seemed to brighten. He had taken to watching footage of old Blades games, especially the one that had earned them their most recent Cup. That had been the greatest night of his life; he'd scored two goals, including the game winner. He'd never skated better.

The doorbell rang again. Paul groaned, ignoring it, concentrating instead on the images on the screen. Every time he watched it, he relived those heady feelings of triumph, the exhilaration of knowing your team was the best in the whole goddamn world. He'd felt immortal. Invincible. If an angel had sidled up to him that night and whispered in his ear that in less than a year and a half, his career would be dead, he would have laughed his head off.

The bell rang again. *Goddammit.* Paul put the DVD on hold, freezing an image of himself holding the Stanley Cup aloft on the screen before storming over to the front door. Clearly this person wasn't going to take no for answer. He knew he looked like crap—he had bed head, stubble grizzled his face and chin, and the sweats he was wearing had seen better days—but he didn't care. That's what they got for ambushing him in his lair on a Saturday morning.

"Coming!" he barked as the impatient SOB on the other side of the door rang the bell *again*. Michael Dante had recently told him a story of someone showing up at his Brooklyn brownstone claiming to be the Angel of Death. "You're a little early," Michael had said. "Could you come back in, say, fifty years?" He closed the door in the guy's face and that was that. The lesson being: Always try to keep your cool.

Paul unbolted the locks and swung the door open, expecting to confront a starry-eyed Blades fan laden with paraphernalia for him to sign. Instead he found Tuck Fisher.

"Tuck?" His first thought: *Something's happened to Katie.* "Everything okay?"

"No." The boy was on the verge of tears. "Can I come in?"

Paul only hesitated a beat. The kid was upset. No way could he turn him away. "Come on in." He ushered Tuck inside. "Have a seat."

Tuck made a beeline for the couch, folding his hands between his knees as he sat down. "I'm sorry," he said tearfully. "I didn't know where else to go."

"It's okay," Paul assured him, growing more alarmed. Whatever was happening, it wasn't good. "Can I get you something to drink?"

"Sure," Tuck said uncertainly.

"Let me go see what I have. Sit tight."

Paul went into the kitchen, scouring his refrigerator for something a kid might like. Red Bull was out, and so was the Guinness. "You like Gatorade?" he called out to the living room.

"Sure."

"You got it." He grabbed the plastic bottle from the fridge and brought it out to the boy. "Here you go."

"Thanks." Tuck twisted the bottle open and gulped, wiping the excess on the back of his sleeve. His eyes were drawn to the TV. "Whatcha watching?"

Paul felt embarrassed by the image of himself frozen on the screen. "Old games."

Tuck twisted toward him. "You got knocked in the head a lot, right?"

Paul grimaced. "Right."

"So you had to quit?"

"Yup." Paul took a seat on the other end of the couch. "So, what's up?"

"I ran away," Tuck admitted quietly.

Great. "How come?"

Tuck's eyes strayed back to the screen. Paul could tell he was straining not to cry. He remembered what it was like to be that age, caught between pure, unself-conscious childhood and adolescence; wanting to be perceived as mature, yet still wanting to cry and be comforted when you were hurt.

"It's okay," Paul coaxed. "Whatever you tell me stays right here in this room."

Tuck's eyes clouded with suspicion. "You swear?"

"I swear," Paul scoffed, feigning indignation. "I'm your coach, right? I'm not gonna let you down."

"I guess," Tuck muttered.

"So, what's going on? Why did you run away?"

Tuck picked at a hole in his jeans. "Because I don't want to live with my mom. She got out of rehab today and came to pick me up and I don't wanna go. I wanna keep living with Nana and Aunt Katie."

"Gotcha." How much should Paul let on he knew? He knew all about the situation from Katie. But he didn't want to tip his hand by saying or doing anything that would let Tuck know they'd talked about him. "How come you don't want to live with your mom?"

The hole in Tuck's jeans became bigger. "She's kinda messed up."

"But she's been in rehab, right?" Paul tried. "Maybe she's better now."

Tuck frowned. "Doubt it."

"People deserve second chances, don't they?"

Tuck said nothing, concentrating on the growing tear in his pants.

"I'm sure she loves you and she's been working hard to get her sh—act together."

Tuck jerked his head up, grinning. "You were gonna say 'shit.'"

"Yeah, I was. Let's get back to your mother. Doesn't she deserve another shot?"

"She showed up with some guy named Snake!" Tuck said indignantly. "And we're gonna live with him down in *Tully's Basin!*"

"What's wrong with that?" Paul asked, even though he knew the answer.

"I won't even be able to catch the bus from there!"

"I'm sure you will."

"My mom doesn't have a job!"

"She'll get one." Tuck's expression was so cynical it took Paul aback. "I'm looking for a new waitress," he heard himself say, which was true. Izzy couldn't keep orders straight; he'd had to let her go. "Does she have any waitressing experience?"

"I think so," Tuck said eagerly.

"Tell her to stop by the bar and talk to me, okay?"

Paul was glad to be able to help, though his motives weren't exactly pure: If he helped Mina out, maybe he'd score some brownie points with Katie. Maybe she'd come to see him as a compassionate, loser bar owner instead of just a plain loser bar owner. He'd take what he could get.

"This is a nice house," said Tuck, glancing around. "Kinda boring, though."

"I'm still putting it together. Don't try to change the subject. We're talking about your mom."

The momentarily lightness in Tuck's face drained away, replaced by a look of mulish determination. "I still don't wanna live with her."

Paul sighed, scratching the stubble on his left cheek. "I'm not sure you have a choice, pal."

Tuck turned shy. "Can I live here?" he asked in a small voice.

"Tuck."

"Are you my dad?" Tuck blurted.

The desperation in his eyes was like a stake puncturing Paul's heart. He made sure his voice was firm but gentle. "I'm not your father."

Tuck deflated. "Are you sure?"

"Yes."

"Because my mom has screwed lots of guys—"

"Tuck." Paul's voice was sterner this time. "I swear to you, I am not your father."

Tuck's eyes began watering. "Then why were you using me on the ice so much?"

"You know why. We talked about it at practice. Because you're a great hockey player and I wanted you guys to experience winning."

"Maybe I inherited my hockey skills from you," Tuck continued stubbornly. "Maybe—"

"Tuck, listen to me!" The sharpness in Paul's voice shocked both of them. Paul wasn't sure it was the best way to deal with this, but it was the only way he knew how. He hoped it wouldn't mess the kid up further. "I'm not your dad. Okay? I'm not. Though I have to tell you, if I had a kid, I'd want him to be just like you."

Tuck hung his head, defeated. "Can I live here anyway?" he whispered, raising his glistening eyes to Paul. "I'd be quiet. I'd keep my room neat. I'd even clean the house for you if you wanted."

"Tuck." Paul looked at the boy. "You and I both know you can't."

Tuck turned away.

"However." Tuck looked back at him, hopeful. "Any time you need to talk, you can come to me. Okay? It doesn't matter if it's the middle of the day or the middle of the night. If you need to talk, you call me."

"But I don't have your phone number."

Paul drew him in a playful head lock. "Obviously, I'm going to give it to you, you knucklehead!" He released him. "But if you give it out to anyone on the team, you are dead."

"I won't," Tuck swore solemnly.

"Good." *Now what?* "I guess I should run you home."

"Can't I just stay here a little while longer?" Tuck pleaded.

"Fine." Paul passed Tuck his phone. "But I want you to call your mother and let her know where you are."

"*I'm gonna beat* his ass," Mina seethed when Katie returned downstairs to announce that Tuck had shinnied down the drainpipe outside his bedroom window and taken off.

"Maybe that's why he ran away," Katie suggested.

"Maybe you should—"

"Ladies." Snake's voice was a growl. "We got a serious problem here, okay? Let's focus on that."

"I guess we should call the cops," Mina said.

"That might not be necessary," Katie said carefully. "I have a feeling I might know where he is."

"Oh? Where?" Mina demanded.

"He's either at his best friend, Gary's, or else he's at Paul's."

"Paul's!" Mina squawked. "*Your* Paul?"

"He's not my Paul anymore, but yeah, that Paul."

"Why the hell would he be there?" Katie threw Mina a piercing look, relieved when recognition finally broke in Mina's eyes. "Oh, shit. I can't believe this." She turned to Snake. "Guess we better go get him."

"I think I should get him," Katie countered.

Mina snorted in disbelief.

"Think about it, Mina. He ran away because he doesn't want to move in with you." She folded her arms across her chest. "I think you and Snake should go over to the apartment, and I'll load Tuck's stuff up in the car and then go find him and bring him over to the apartment."

"She's got a point, babe," Snake said to Mina.

Mina's eyes churned with resentment. "And what if he's not with either of them? What then?"

"Then I'll call you and we'll figure out what to do next." Katie looked at both Snake and Mina. "Okay?"

"Sounds like a plan to me," said Snake, scratching the tattoo on his left shoulder.

Katie looked at her sister apprehensively. "Mina?"

Mina threw her hands up. "Fine. Aunt Katie can go rescue Tuck and look like the big hero. *What. Ever.*"

She stormed outside, leaving Katie staring into Snake's troubled eyes.

"She's not feelin' so good," Snake offered.

Katie reached for her coat and keys. "Who is?"

Katie went to Gary Flaherty's first rather than heading straight for Paul's. She spent the ride over trying to imagine the thought process of a nine-year-old boy: *If I were running away, where would I go? Answer: My best friend's house.* But Tuck wasn't there, and thankfully, neither was Liz. Lane, Gary's nanny, was distressed to hear Katie had "misplaced" her nephew, but she promised not to say anything to Gary for fear of alarming him.

Katie's heart battered against her ribs all the way over to Paul's. What if Tuck wasn't there? She knew he'd been hoarding his allowance for months. What if he'd gone to the train station and was bound for Manhattan? Images unfolded before Katie's eyes of Tuck wandering Times Square, overwhelmed and afraid. . . . Tuck's face on the back of a milk carton . . . Tuck, one of myriad nameless faces on some CNN special on runaways . . . She tried pushing them away, but it was difficult. Growing up with Mina had trained Katie to always expect the worst.

She pulled into Paul's driveway with a screech, coming

closer than she would have liked to rear-ending his beloved Cobra. At least he was home. Whether Tuck was there was another story.

Before she even had a chance to ring the doorbell, the front door swung open and she was face-to-face with Paul, looking like he'd been run over a truck. Katie peered at him questioningly. There was no need for words as Paul gave a small shake of the head. Tuck was inside.

"Hey, buddy." Katie made sure she sounded affable as she greeted her nephew, who sat transfixed in front of the TV watching a hockey game. Katie smiled indulgently. Then she realized it was an old game that prominently featured Paul. Paul hit the remote and the screen went dark.

"Hey!" Tuck protested.

"Hey yourself," said Katie.

"I just called Mom," Tuck said sheepishly. "Nana said she'd already left for the apartment." He could barely look Katie in the eye. "Am I in trouble?"

Paul and Katie exchanged sad glances. "Not with me you're not. Your mother might be another story." Katie approached her nephew carefully, as if he was a cat up a tree she didn't want to startle or distress. "Shinnied down the drainpipe, huh?"

Tuck shrugged. "I guess."

"You guess! Either that or you're magic and can fly. Which is it?"

Tuck looked timid. "Shinnied."

"You're lucky you didn't fall and break your neck."

"Yeah, or your ankle," Paul put in dryly. He picked up Tuck's empty Gatorade bottle. "If you need me, I'll be showering."

Katie glanced up at him gratefully. "Thanks."

"No problem," said Paul, disappearing down the hall to his bedroom. The image of him showering flooded Katie's body with unexpected desire, embarrassing her. Here her family was in crisis and what was she thinking about? Clear water cascading down Paul's chiseled body. She needed help.

Katie turned to Tuck. "We need to go," she said softly.

"I don't want to." He turned away from her, muffling a sob.

"I know, baby," Katie whispered, beginning to cry herself. "And believe me, I wish you didn't have to. But your mom has worked so hard, getting better for you. You owe her a second chance."

Tuck turned back to her, throwing his arms around her neck. "But what if she messes up again?" he wailed. "What if it's the same as before?"

"It won't be," Katie promised, holding him tight. How frail he felt in her arms. She wasn't sure she'd ever been allowed to hug him this tightly. She didn't want to let him go.

"But what if it is?" Tuck lamented.

"Then you call me, and I come pick you up, and you and me and Nana figure out what to do."

Tuck whimpered, clutching tighter. This wasn't what he wanted to hear.

"What about that Snake dude?" he hiccupped into Katie's neck.

Katie broke their embrace, smiling as she looked down into Tuck's eyes. "I know he looks kind of scary, but I think he might be okay. And you're only there temporarily," she reminded him. "Until you and your mom get your own place."

"Yeah right," Tuck jeered, wiping away the trail of snot dripping from his nose.

"Here, a tissue might work better." Katie reached into her purse for a Kleenex. She handed it to Tuck, who honked like a goose as he blew into it. "Nice one."

Tuck half giggled, half hiccupped. "You'll still come to my games?"

"You know I will."

Tuck nodded. Sadness swept his face. "The coach isn't my father," he said glumly.

Katie's throat felt tight. "I know that, honey."

"But he said I could call him if I needed to. And he said he might give Mom a waitressing job."

"He's a good guy," Katie agreed, moved by Paul's generosity.

"Maybe you guys will get married and then you won't go back to that college."

Now was not the time or place to tell Tuck things were done between her and Paul. The kid had enough on his plate. One more melodrama would do his head in.

"Right?" Tuck persisted.

"Right," Katie whispered, tossling his hair. "Are you ready to go?"

"I need to thank the coach."

"Let's wait for him, then."

Out of curiousity, Katie turned the TV back on, commanding the DVD to pick up where it left off. The screen sprang to life and there was Paul, tearing down the ice faster than she'd ever seen a hockey player skate, the puck ripping off his stick into the net as if it were the easiest thing in the world. The roar of the crowd was deafening. Even now, watching it on TV, Katie was gripped by a sense of what it must have been like to be there: the excitement, the adrenaline rush. Paul's face lit up with a huge smile as he pumped his fist in the air and was swarmed by his teammates. A number of them were unabashedly crying.

"That was one helluva night."

Katie looked up guiltily to see Paul watching her and

Tuck. His hair glistened wet from the shower, his blue terry robe knotted tight at his waist.

"I'm sorry," Katie stammered. "We didn't know how long you'd be."

"Not a problem."

Katie turned off the TV, nudging Tuck in Paul's direction. "You wanted to say something to the coach?"

"Sorry for interrupting your day," Tuck mumbled.

"You didn't," Paul assured him. "I'm glad I could help." Over Tuck's head, his eyes sought Katie's. "Everything okay?"

"Everything's fine."

"So, I'll see you at practice Monday morning?" Paul said to Tuck.

Tuck looked momentarily panicked. "Aunt Katie? Mom doesn't have a car."

"Don't worry," Katie soothed. "If you need me to bring you to practice, I will. It's not a problem. Just call me." Katie gave him a reassuring smile. "It's not a bother, hon. *Okay?*"

"Okay." Tuck seemed mollified. He stuck his hand out awkwardly for Paul to shake. "Thanks, Coach."

"You're welcome," said Paul.

"Thanks, Aunt Katie." He ran to Katie and wrapped his arms around her waist.

Katie closed her eyes, resting her chin on the top of Tuck's head. "You're very, very welcome."

When she opened them, she saw Paul watching them, something akin to longing in his expression. Unable to handle it, she turned away.

"Katie?"

She turned back.

"Can I talk to you a minute?"

"Sure." Katie pointed Tuck in the direction of the door. "Go wait for me in the car, okay? I'll be along in a minute."

"'Kay," said Tuck, leaving Paul and Katie alone.

"What's up?" Katie asked. She hated admitting it, but being alone with Paul was unnerving, and not only because she knew every inch of that naked body beneath the bathrobe. She was in turmoil, part of her hoping he'd apologize for abruptly dumping her, part of her angry at him for doing it, part of her relieved. She'd once read somewhere that the ability to hold conflicting emotions was a sign of emotional intelligence. If so she was a genius.

"I wanted to let you know I straightened Tuck out on the paternity issue."

Katie put a hand to her chest, relieved. "Thank you."

"Look," Paul said, running a hand through his wet hair, "I told Tuck to tell his mom to come down to the Penalty Box to find out about a waitressing job. We need someone fast, and if she can do it, I'd love to help her out. Tell her to stop by tomorrow morning."

"I will. I'll bring her myself if I have to. That's really nice of you, Paul. Seriously."

"No problem."

Silence fell. Katie was familiar with its tenor, the silence of two people with unfinished business who didn't know what else to say to each other. She jangled the keys she'd extracted from her purse.

"I guess that's that, then."

Paul nodded.

"I'll see you around. If not at the Penalty Box tomorrow, then at Tuck's game."

"Yup," Paul said, studying his bare feet.

He looked back up at her. What was going through his mind that could make him look so lost? Was he sad for himself? Tuck? *Them?* If she asked, would he tell her? Would it be what she wanted to hear? Katie swallowed. "I have to go. Tuck's waiting in the car."

Paul nodded, showing her to the door.

"Drive safe," he called after her as she made her way down the drive. Katie noticed the living room curtains across the street fluttering. Mrs. Greco. She waved and stepped into the car. It was time for both her and Tuck to begin the next phase of their lives.

CHAPTER

18

"*How do we* kill her?" Bitsy whispered to Katie.

Lolly, the Fat Fighters's leader, had come to tonight's meeting with two Tam-o-Shanter–clad, felt puppets named McFatty and McSkinny who spoke to each other in Scottish accents about making smart food choices.

"You dinnae want to eat that fish and chips, lass, d'ya ken?"

"Och, I'll have a wee helping of veggies. And a dram of sparklin' mineral water."

When the puppet talk turned to the caloric hazards of haggis, Denise excused herself to go to the bathroom, never returning. Katie and Bitsy found her waiting for them at their usual booth at Tabitha's. "We could stuff some oat cakes down her throat," Denise suggested, shaking her head as if to disperse the memory of what they'd endured.

"Death by bagpipes might be an option," Katie added, fighting to keep her eyes open. Tuck's departure had left her completely exhausted. Time felt bent. The day before, she hadn't known what to do with herself. She was so used to taking Tuck to see Mina on Sunday that the prospect of a day with no plans made her nervous. Eager to escape her mother's crying jags, she'd gone running until her limbs felt liquid, then came home and collapsed into a nap. Bad idea. The nap played havoc with her body clock, and she spent that night tossing and turning. When she finally did fall sleep, she dreamed Snake talked Tuck into getting two crossed hockey sticks tattooed on his forearm. She woke with a start and couldn't fall back asleep.

"Katie, I need to ask you something." Bitsy's train of thought was derailed by the waitress walking by with a freshly baked chocolate cake. "Yummm."

"A slice of that is at least six or seven hundred wee calories," Denise said with a burr, admonishing Bitsy with a light slap to the wrist. "You'd have to spend an entire weekend on the treadmill to work that baby off."

"I ken, lass," Bitsy joked back, her eyes glazed with desire.

"Bitsy, dinnae," Katie warned. "You're only twelve pounds from your goal weight. Remember," she added in Lolly's voice, "thin tastes better."

"Than what?" Bitsy asked. The waitress now stood by their table. "The usual for me," Bitsy told her. "Black coffee and—?" She looked at the other two. "What are we splitting tonight?"

"A slice of apple pie," Denise announced.

"Oh, good," said Bitsy as the waitress walked away. "That's got fruit in it. It can't be all bad."

Katie stifled a yawn. "What did you want to ask me, Bits?" If it wasn't so rude she'd rest her head on the table.

"You know how I'm a member of the youth hockey booster club, right?"

Katie nodded.

"We were trying to think of some ways to raise money apart from the usual car washes and candy drives. And we came up with a brilliant idea: a charity auction. We could auction off dinners at restaurants, quilts, a massage, and," she lowered her voice, "a date with Paul van Dorn." Bitsy looked uneasy. "What do you think?"

Katie pushed out her lower lip nonchalantly and shrugged. "Sounds fine."

"You don't mind sharing him for a night?" Bitsy asked. "It *is* for a good cause."

Bitsy and Denise knew nothing about her and Paul calling it quits. Now she'd have to tell them. "Paul and I broke up."

Denise gasped as if she'd just witnessed a shooting. "What *happened?*"

"It wasn't working," said Katie, surprised at the small stab of pain she felt talking about it.

Bitsy looked skeptical. "It wasn't about staying in Didsbury, was it?"

"What do you mean?"

"You didn't dump him because he's a townie, did you?"

"No. He dumped me."

"He did?" Denise squawked with indignation. "That sonofabitch!"

"It's okay," Katie assured her friends. "The timing was off, you know? And we both have a lot of stuff we need to work out."

Bitsy frowned. "What soap did you get those lines from?"

"I'm serious," Katie pleaded in self-defense. She knew the explanation sounded lame, but it was the best she could come up with without going into detail and making her friends feel bad for where they chose to live. It wasn't that she disliked Didsbury. In fact, she had come to regard it affectionately, a place where time standing still was a positive for everyone but her. She was frightened of the compromise she could imagine herself making for love if she and Paul had kept seeing each other. Better that it was over.

"Does Liz know?" Denise asked.

"Not yet. I'm sure she'll find out." Katie hadn't even thought about Liz.

"Oh, Katie, I'm so sorry," said Bitsy sympathetically. "I was hoping—" She broke off. "Well, you know."

"Guess it wasn't meant to be," said Denise. She winked at Katie. "So can I have his number?"

Bitsy clucked her tongue. "No wonder you look so exhausted. You're in mourning."

"For Tuck, not for Paul," Katie quickly pointed out. She filled her friends in on the Tuck situation. Both agreed Tully's Basin was not the most desirable address.

Denise looked uneasy. "Isn't that where that single mother and her three kids were machete'd in their sleep a few years ago?"

Katie stared across the table. "Thanks for sharing, Denise."

"They were bludgeoned, not machete'd," Bitsy corrected. She turned to Katie. "Tuck'll be fine. He's got you, he's got hockey, he's got friends, he's got your mom. Who knows? Maybe Mina's really got it together this time."

Katie wolfed down her portion of pie. "I hope so."

Paul knew Mina was Katie's sister the minute she strolled through the door of the bar. They both had the same delicate features and intelligent, watchful eyes that seemed to absorb everything at a glance. But their main similarity was their attitude: Both carried themselves with aplomb. With Katie, it was learned behavior, even an act. Mina looked like she was born to it.

"Paul?"

He nodded with a friendly smile as this sparrow of a woman approached the bar. "Mina?"

She seemed taken aback. "How did you know who I was?"

"You look like Katie."

Mina's lips pressed into a hard line. "Hardly. I'm much smaller."

"In stature. But you have the same eyes and same features."

Mina ignored this. "I hear you're looking for a waitress?"

"I am. One who's also got experience as a cocktail server. That you?"

Mina laughed, the deep throaty rattle of a lifelong smoker. "Oh, yeah. I worked at Topanga's for years."

Paul nodded, impressed. Everyone knew Topanga's, a roadhouse right outside Didsbury. As a child, Paul was always enthralled by the fleet of shining choppers lined up outside, and the bizarre ceramic heifer on the roof that symbolized—what? The minute he turned eighteen he made a pilgrimage to the bar. He lasted all of five minutes. Conversation had stopped dead the minute he and his preppie friends in their Oxford shirts and chinos walked through the door. Not wanting to go home with a pool cue through his head, he'd left promptly. If Mina could handle the crowd at Topanga's, working at the Penalty Box would be a piece of cake.

"Why did you leave Topanga's?" Paul asked.

"Rehab," Mina said with a challenge in her eyes that dared him to judge her.

"And you're clean and sober now?"

"As a whistle."

"Can you work Friday and Saturday nights?"

"Yup."

"Any days?"

"As long as it doesn't interfere with my kid's schedule."

Finally, some common ground. "Tuck's a great kid."

Mina snorted. "He thinks the sun shines out of *your* ass, that's for sure."

Paul smiled uncomfortably. If he did hire her, he'd have to make it clear he was her boss, and she really needed to show a little respect.

"Will we see you at some hockey games?"

"Yeah, I guess," said Mina flatly. "Hey, listen, I'm sorry about that thing yesterday, Tuck bugging you and all."

"It was fine," Paul assured her. "Like I said, he's a great kid." He glanced at the clipboard on the bar. "All right, let me ask you some other stuff before we make it official." He ran through the gamut of necessary questions: What kind of cash register did you work with before? How would you handle drunk customers? What would you do if another server asked you to give a free drink to a friend? How would you get to work? Mina gave all the right answers, so Paul hired her. That she was good looking was an added bonus—not only to the bar, but to her personally. The more tips she made, the better able she could provide for Tuck. Paul wanted the kid to have as easy a time of it as possible.

Paul tapped his pen against the clipboard. "Any questions?"

"Yeah. What do I have to wear?"

"Jeans are fine. I'll give you a Penalty Box T-shirt when you come in on Thursday to train."

Mina's mouth twisted into a lascivious smirk. "Nice and tight, I suppose."

"This is a business, Mina. I want to make money and so do you."

"Hey, I've got no problem showing off the twins, believe me."

Paul was no prude, but her bluntness had pink creeping up his neck. "Anything else?" he murmured.

"Yeah. Why'd you dump my sister?"

The question was completely inappropriate, of course, but there was such unexpected protectiveness in Mina's voice he felt compelled to answer.

"I dumped her before she could dump me. I wanted to avoid humiliation."

"So it was better to humiliate her instead?"

Was she really humiliated? Paul longed to ask. Does she miss me? Does she think it was a big fat mistake? Here was Katie's sister right in front of him; if he wanted, he could ply her with questions and get answers that only she was privy to, perhaps.

"I'm sorry if your sister felt humiliated," Paul said politely.

"Actually, I have no idea if she did," Mina admitted. "I'm just assuming. You know Katie—total control freak. Her head must have popped off when you took the reins." Mina assessed him. "Not that your relationship would have worked, anyway."

"Oh yeah?" Paul replied with some irritation. "Why's that?"

"Don't take this wrong, okay? But I can't see Katie settling down with—"

"A townie?"

"Well, yeah." Mina was looking at Paul not as if he were her new employer, but some pitiful specimen. "I mean, why the hell did you come back here? There's *nothing* going on. If I had your kind of money, this is the last place I would've wanted to end up. But that's just me," she concluded with surprising humility.

"Yes, it is." Mina and Katie were more alike than Paul initially suspected. Mina was just more brutal in her phrasing.

"Though I think the hockey stuff you do is really nice." Mina gathered herself up to leave. "Thursday, then?"

"Actually, Tuck has a game tomorrow afternoon, so I'll see you there."

"Right."

It bothered Paul that Mina sounded as if she knew nothing about it.

"Well," she continued, suddenly bashful as she eyed her scuffed Frye boots, "thanks. You know." She lifted her eyes. "For giving me a chance and everything. A lot of people wouldn't."

"You're very welcome."

After she departed, the harshness of her words kept ringing in his head. *This is the last place I would've wanted to end up.* Paul glanced around at the memorabilia-draped walls of his bar. Was this really where he wanted to be?

"*Mom, you have* to stop crying." Katie prided herself on being compassionate, but even she was growing weary of her mother's tears, sniffles, and heavy sighs. It was like turning on the radio and always hearing the same song. "You're acting like Tuck is dead!"

"He may as well be for all I get to see him."

"It's been less than a week! I'm sure he and Mina are readjusting to each other. And he's got school. If you want to see him so badly, come with me to his hockey game tomorrow."

Her mother brightened a bit. "There's an idea."

"Or call Mina. I'm sure you two could work out a time you could stop over and see how they're getting on." Of course, that was a bold-faced lie, but Katie was all for fibbing if it helped alleviate her mother's whimpering.

Her mother shook her head vehemently. "I can't go *there*."

"What do you mean, 'there'?"

"You know. Tully's Basin."

"Mom."

"What if someone slashes my tires? Or robs me?"

"Or throws you to the ground and injects you with heroin and you become a hopeless junkie who has to turn tricks to support your habit *and* maintain your costly AARP membership?"

Her mother scowled. "You're not funny, Katie."

"And you're not rational. I know Tully's Basin can be iffy, so if you want, I'll go with you. Just make sure you *call* first. I don't want Mina squawking that we're checking up on her or that we don't think she can handle things."

This seemed to appease her mother even as it filled Katie with a mounting sense of panic. She really didn't have time to accompany her mother to Mina's; she was falling further and further behind in the writing of her book. Her brain simply refused to buckle down. Thoughts of organizing material were constantly replaced by thoughts of Paul. Or Tuck. Or even Snake. She'd be damned if she'd ask for an extension, though. She'd lost weight and transformed her life via willpower, and if she had to draw on the same internal resources to meet her deadline, she would. So what if it meant she'd have no life over the summer? Work was her life, anyway.

"I almost forgot; this came for you." Her mother handed her an oversize, cream-colored envelope with Katie's name and address written out in calligraphic script, postmarked "Fallowfield." Katie tore it open anxiously, deflating when she saw what it was.

"One of your colleagues getting married?" her mother asked.

"Yes. My friend Jo Laurie. Next month."

Katie stared at the invitation in disbelief. Jo, a fellow sociology professor, had been having a discreet affair with one of her graduate students despite a ten-year age difference. Katie had met the young Romeo a few times—he was only a few years younger than she was—but she hadn't been impressed. He wasn't nearly as smart as her friend, and he seemed to take great pleasure in belittling Jo, a trait Katie couldn't stand. Jo had to be pregnant; that was the only reason Katie could come up with for such hasty nuptials. Years before, Jo had been through an ugly divorce and an even uglier tenure battle. If this guy truly made her happy, Katie would keep her trap shut and wish her friend the best.

Even so, the idea of a wedding dampened Katie's already soggy spirits. She'd gone solo to enough weddings to know they were really affairs designed for couples. Whomever she was seated with would spend the evening either trying to fix her up with their second cousin's nephew's neighbor, or else trying to conceal their pity for the academic old maid. She'd be urged to try to catch the bride's bouquet. Colleagues' husbands, pressed by their wives, would politely ask her to dance. She slid the invitation back into its envelope.

"Are you going?" her mother asked curiously.

"If I can find a date." Katie smiled as a thought struck her. "How do you think Tuck would look in a tuxedo?"

CHAPTER
19

Katie had vowed she'd never again set foot in Tivoli Gardens again after her high school reunion. Yet here she was in the tacky schnitzel palace, collecting the ten-dollar entrance fees for the Youth Hockey Auction. The booster club had spent well over a month pulling the charity event together. Denise agreed to be auctioneer, and when Bitsy asked Katie to volunteer, she couldn't turn her down. She wasn't happy about working the door, however. Every parent of a child on Tuck's team seemed to give her a dirty look as they handed over their money. Perhaps she should have worn a sandwich board screaming I'M NOT SEEING PAUL VAN DORN ANYMORE.

The Rhineland banquet room was filling rapidly, testament to the booster club's hard work and the importance of youth hockey to the small, close-knit community. Originally the auction was going to be held in the high school gym, but Bitsy was convinced people wanted "bang for their buck."

"Hi, Aunt Katie!"

Tuck trotted up to the banquet room door, Snake in tow. For a split second Katie wondered where Mina was, but then she remembered: logging hours at the Penalty Box. As far as she knew, her sister's waitressing gig was working out fine. Mina didn't say much about it and neither did Paul—not that Katie talked to him much these days.

"How much ya soakin' us for?" Snake grumbled good-naturedly while Tuck raced into the banquet room to secure good seats.

"Ten apiece."

Snake whistled through his teeth. "Highway robbery." He handed Katie a twenty. "I hope there's some decent stuff to bid on."

"Lots," Katie assured him.

"Like—?"

"A homemade quilt, a massage, guitar lessons, a free one-hour legal consultation with Didsbury's top attorney, dinner at the Country Club, pies—you name it." She omitted mentioning the autographed hockey stick Paul had donated, as well the Blades jersey adorned with autographs from the current roster. She doubted Snake would be interested.

Snake stroked his moustache thoughtfully. "That legal consultation could come in handy after last night." Katie pursed her lips in disapproval, prompting Snake to guffaw. "You've got no sense of humor, Sister Katie."

Katie blushed. "Sorry." Snake started into the banquet room, but paused when Katie called him back. "Thanks for all your help with Tuck."

"Hey, I dig the little fucker, what can I say?" His language made Katie wince, but the sentiment behind it was genuine, and that was all that mattered. She thought back to the first time she met Snake, his concern that Tuck might somehow be "in the way" when Mina moved in. Her fears about him had vanished. In fact, Katie got the uneasy feeling that Snake was more attentive to her nephew than Mina was.

Snake departed, leaving Katie to face a long line of people wanting to get in the door. At the end of the line stood Paul.

"Hey," he said when he finally advanced to the front.

"Hey yourself," Katie replied, feeling self-conscious.

Paul's expression was playful. "Do I still have to pay even though I'm one of the items being auctioned off?"

"I'm afraid so."

Paul guided a ten dollar bill into her palm, his hand lingering a split second longer than it should have. Katie swallowed, putting the money in the cash box. "You're the big-ticket item of the night, you know."

Paul looked uncomfortable. "How sad is that?"

"I think it's sweet you agreed to do it."

"Really?" Paul sounded bemused. "Even though you and I both know that Liz Flaherty will outbid everyone and I'll have to spend a night in horny divorcee hell?"

Paul was right, of course. Liz would take out a second mortgage on her house if it meant bagging a date with Paul. "It's for a good cause," Katie reminded him, though picturing them together irritated her.

"I suppose."

She waited for him to saunter inside but he didn't, even though the line forming behind him was beginning to back up. Instead, he moved off to the side so the next person could pay his entrance fee, remaining close enough to chat with her.

"How's the book coming?"

"Terribly," Katie confessed, returning Ambrose Wilbraham's stony glare as he and his wife smirked at her and Paul. She was tempted to ask Paul to go inside. His standing with her would fuel more rumors in this gossip-driven town. But then she thought, too bad. People are allowed to talk to each other and if these putzes want to think we're still an item, let them.

"How could your book be going terribly? You interviewed so many fascinating people."

Katie shot him a sideways look, catching the mischievous look in his eyes. "Are you speaking of yourself?"

"Myself and others." He took a step closer to her, near enough for her to inhale his scent. This time, she seriously wished he would go away. She had enough to worry about without his pheromones jumbling her senses.

Katie smiled wryly. "Nice to see your ego's intact."

"Something has to be. After dating you, I'm lucky I'm not in a permanent body cast."

"That can be arranged." The air was beginning to feel charged. A few more barbs and they'd cross over the line to flirting. Time to change the subject. "How's my sister doing?"

"Okay," Paul replied slowly.

"You don't sound so sure."

"No, I'm sure." He edged toward the doorway. "I guess I better get inside."

"Need to change into your thong for the grand finale?"

"You wish."

Actually, she did. She checked him out: Jeans, adidas, gray ribbed turtleneck. One of the outfits he looked best in. The shirt made his eyes look crystalline and sexy in a lycanthropic sort of way that hit her low in the belly every time. Eager for distraction, Katie pretended to organize bills in the cash box. "I think you'll bring in a lot of money for the organization," she told him when she finally had the courage to look at him without drooling.

Paul's expression was tentative. "Maybe I'll see you afterward."

"Maybe."

Katie knew Snake would offer the highest bid for one of Tabitha's delicious lemon meringue pies; she remembered how disappointed he'd been when he didn't have time for a slice of her mother's cake the day they fetched Tuck. She herself had bid on—and won—a full body massage with Sage Dragonwagon, the most sought after massage therapist in town, probably because she was the only one.

The massage was all Katie intended to bid on. That is, until Paul stepped out on stage, triggering a chorus of female wolf whistles and catcalls.

Katie felt a thundering begin in her head. She knew it was nuts. She knew it was asking for trouble. But there was no way in hell she was going to let Liz Flaherty win this one.

"Ladies, please!" Denise implored, fanning herself as if the sight of Paul might make her faint. "Control yourselves!" Paul looked like he wanted to burrow beneath the floorboards. It was painfully obvious he hadn't expected such a lusty response. Denise sauntered over to him, draping an arm around his shoulder.

"Hello, Paul," she cooed in to her mike.

Paul winked and the women in the crowd went wild.

"There are some ladies in this room willing to spend big bucks to see your hockey stick," Denise continued. The crowd roared. "Do you promise to show the winner a good time?"

Paul smiled shyly. "I'll try." Embarassment began to give way to amusement as he got into the spirit of things. "I might need some hands-on instruction, though. It's been a long time since I've put one in the net."

The crowd roared. Paul's face turned red, but he was laughing. He sat down on the throne provided for him, while Denise held up a hand. "Everyone, quiet, please." The place settled down. "Now, you know the rules: Paul here goes to the highest bidder, and there's no cap. Ladies, are you ready?"

Katie could feel her nerves snapping. Beside her, Bitsy was rocking anxiously on the edge of her seat.

"Bidding begins at fifty dollars, commencing now!" Denise announced.

"Seventy-five!"

"Eighty!"

"Elghty-five!"

"One hundred!"

Goggle-eyed, Katie sat listening to the chorus of voices vying for a night with her ex. The numbers kept climbing thanks to Liz Flaherty. Everytime someone threw a number out, Liz would immediately raise the bid. When the number reached one twenty, Katie jumped in.

"One fifty!" she shouted, sounding like a mad prophet in the wilderness.

Heads turned. Female heads with narrowed eyes and pressed lips. She knew what they were thinking: Why does she want him? She already has him. She already *had* him. What the hell is going on here? An icy voice broke the stillness.

"One eighty!" Liz Flaherty shot back.

"Two hundred!" Katie countered. She heard gasps. Murmurs. Even a few titters. She didn't care. She was a woman possessed. No one would sway her from her course.

Liz turned and smiled at her. "Three hundred."

Katie smiled back. "Three fifty."

"Are you crazy?" Bitsy hissed, ceasing her nervous rocking just long enough to embed her nails in Katie's left arm. "This is like Monopoly money to her! She'll bankrupt you!"

"We'll see." She directed her attention back to Denise, careful not to make eye contact with Paul, who had to be wondering what was going on.

The room fell into a hush as everyone held their breath, waiting to see what, if anything would happen next. Liz popped a breath mint, chasing it with a bored sigh. "Five hundred."

"Six hundred," Katie spat out.

The rest of the bidding unfolded like a fevered dream, fuzzy around the edges, with everyone's voice, including Katie's own, seeming to be coming from far, far away. Katie wasn't sure at what point the numbers she called out ceased to be real, becoming instead mere sounds being shaped by her mouth without her brain's permission. It felt like she and Liz were singing a duo, the point and counterpoint of their voices the backdrop to a melody only they could hear. Higher and higher the numbers rose, and with them, Katie's pulse. By the time Liz called out "Nine hundred," Katie was in real fear of a heart attack.

Bitsy covered her face with her hands. "Stop," she begged.

"Soon," Katie promised, breathing hard. Everyone in the room was staring at her, waiting. She thought she might faint.

"Nine fifty," Katie called. For the first time since the bidding began, she looked at Paul. The sheer befuddlement on his face almost made her laugh out loud. He was staring at her like she was nuts. Which, come to think of it, she probably was. Wasn't obsession a form of insanity? Well, she was completely *obsessed* with not letting Liz win. Rationality had packed up and left town.

"We've got ninety fifty," Denise announced nervously. Katie looked at her friend; her expression, too, said, "Are you out of your *mind*?" Denise swallowed. "Is that the final bid?"

"Nine seventy," Liz called out. She jerked around to flash Katie a look of extreme exasperation. Obviously she hadn't expected having to bid this high on her "lamby."

"Nine eighty," Katie countered sharply.

"Oh my God," Bitsy moaned. "As soon as this is over I'm bundling you into the car and taking you to the psychiatric hospital."

"Didsbury doesn't have a psychiatric hospital."

"Then I'm building one and locking you in there until you come to your senses."

"Sshh," said Katie, eyes locked on Liz. Her opponent hesitated a second. Maybe it was over.

"Nine ninety," Liz countered wearily.

"One thousand," was Katie's cheerful answer. The room gave a collective gasp. Katie's heart was about to slam out of her chest as she waited for Liz to counter. She felt delirious. *I could do this all night!* she thought giddily. But Liz offered no counter bid. Instead, she picked up her coat and purse and began walking, very slowly, toward Katie.

"I hope you have health insurance," Bitsy breathed.

The roar of Katie's heartbeat in her own ears was deafening. Here it comes, she thought. Showdown at the Didsbury Corral. For one split second, she thought Liz was going to put her purse down and wallop her. But she didn't. She just looked at Katie with pity.

"You're not a stupid woman, but let me give you a little piece of financial advice: There's no man on earth worth four digits of your own money," Liz drawled, throwing a nasty look over her shoulder at Paul for good measure. "You want him? You got him." She turned her gaze to her son, who was slumped down in his seat beside Tuck, trying to be invisible. "Gary, get your things. We're leaving."

With that, Liz walked out of the ballroom.

A mood of disappointment seemed to steal into the room; people had been hoping for a catfight.

Swallowing gratefully, Katie turned back to the stage. The sweat was pouring off Denise, who looked ashen. "We have, um, one thousand dollars," Denise said in a dazed voice, guzzling down a large glass of ice water. "Anyone else?" The room was still as a tomb. "That's it, then! A date with Paul van Dorn, sold to Katie Fisher for the bargain price of one thousand dollars!"

"I want to thank all of you for coming and for making this night a success," Denise continued from the stage over the sound of raucous applause, but Katie barely heard her as she sank back in her chair, exhausted.

What the hell did I just do?

She reached out in front of her for a glass of water, not surprised to notice her hand shaking.

"You want to tell me what that was all about?" Bitsy demanded, sounding more like an irate parent than a friend.

Katie held up a hand, indicating she would explain once she was done drinking. She felt like she was coming down off some narcotic. Whereas minutes before she was running on pure adrenaline, now her brain felt muzzy, her thinking clouded. She felt like she could nod off to sleep right here, right now.

Katie put her water down. Bitsy grabbed her arm, giving it a little shake. "You just paid one thousand dollars for a date with a man who dumped you! Wouldn't it have been easier to pick up the phone and say 'Let's talk about this over coffee'?"

"It wasn't about that," Katie insisted. "It was about not letting Liz win."

"Oh boy, you sure showed her," Bitsy said sarcastically.

"Aunt Katie!" Tuck, who had been sitting with Gary Flaherty and Snake at a table across the banquet room, hurtled toward her. "That was awesome!"

Katie smiled at him. "Was it?"

"I told Gary you were rich and maybe now he'll believe me!"

"Honey, I'm not rich."

"Just deranged," Bitsy put in.

"Yo, Gottrocks." Snake cruised over to the table. "Wait'll I tell Mina you paid a thousand dollars for a night out with the guy she calls 'That shithead.' She's gonna pee herself laughing."

"She calls Paul a 'shithead'?" Katie asked angrily.

"Of course she does. He's her boss."

"The shithead is on his way over here, dear," Bitsy noted. Katie looked up: Paul had hopped off the stage and was striding toward her.

"One grand," Bitsy tut-tutted as Paul approached. "I sure hope he's worth it."

Paul and Katie agreed to go somewhere to talk. But they only made it as far as Paul's car before he opened fire.

"You wanted me? You got me, all one thousand dollars' worth," Paul said dryly, turning the key in the ignition. The car purred to life. "The question is, why?"

"I wanted to give something back to the community."

"My ass."

Katie glared at him in the dark, leaning forward to turn the heat on. His car and his house: always so damn cold. Had to be all those years on the ice.

"I needed a date for a wedding."

"*So?* You couldn't call some brainiac friend with ten degrees hanging on his wall and bring him?"

"It's my money," Katie insisted stubbornly. "I can do what I want." She watched his face twist with displeasure.

"You're really going to make me go to a wedding?"

"Yup. In Fallowfield. One of my colleagues is marrying one of her grad students."

"In Fallowfield?' Paul repeated, voice rising in disgust. "You're going to drag me to some wedding filled with *professors*?"

Katie stared him down. "I just paid one thousand dollars for you. If I wanted to drag you to a party filled with Liberace impersonators, you'd have to do it."

"I'm not going to have to wear a monkey suit, am I?" Katie continued staring at him. "I *hate* tuxedos."

"Too bad."

"I repeat: Couldn't you get one of your colleagues to go with you or something?"

Katie let her gaze drift out to the parking lot. "Believe it or not, most of my male colleagues are either married, or boring as sin."

"Really?" Paul mocked. "I thought everything—and everyone—was better in a college town."

"That's a low blow."

"Just calling it like I see it." Paul yawned. "I'm not going anywhere until you tell me the real reason for the bid."

"You'll laugh at me."

"Probably. Tell me anyway."

Katie slunk low in the bucket seat. "I wanted to kick Liz's ass and things got out of hand."

Paul's eyes gleamed with amusement in the dark. "You didn't think the bidding would go that high, did you?"

"No," Katie muttered.

"Yet you just kept on going. What the hell were you thinking?"

"I don't know. It was like being possessed! Once I

started, I swear, I just couldn't stop, it was like—like—this total adrenaline rush and it just took over. . . ."

"Promise me you'll never set foot in a casino, okay?"

"Oh, God." The full import of what she'd done was beginning to hit her.

"Well, at least I know how you really feel about me."

"What?"

"C'mon, Katie." Paul chuckled as he leaned forward to turn down the heat a notch. "Admit it: The reason you bid so high is because you care."

"It was about Liz," Katie insisted. "Not you."

"No, it was about Liz not *having* me," Paul corrected. "There's a difference."

"What's your point?" Katie practically snarled.

"You're in love with me."

Katie threw him a horrified look. "You're an egomaniac!"

"It's the only explanation that makes sense."

"I told you: It was like I was gripped with some kind of fever. Now that I've come out of it, I can't believe what I've done."

"You'll never admit it, will you? You'll never deal with what you're *really* feeling."

"Look who's talking," Katie chortled.

"Proof we're a perfect match."

"If we're so perfect, why did you dump me?" Katie snapped.

"For Tuck's sake," Paul mocked. "It was all about protecting Tuck, remember?"

"Watch it. You're skating on thin ice."

"I wish." He zipped up his bomber jacket. "When's this damn wedding?"

"In two weeks. We'll have to stay overnight."

"Great. I'll assume the cost of that is covered in the one thousand."

"Of course," Katie said weakly. "Um, Paul?"

"Mmm?"

"I need to ask you a favor."

"A bigger favor than forcing me to accompany you to some ivory tower, politically correct nuptials? I bet the bride and groom are going to pass a talking stick back and forth as they say their vows. . . ."

"Yes, a bigger favor than that."

"Hit me. It can't get any worse."

"Can I borrow a thousand dollars?"

CHAPTER

20

"*I lend you* a thousand bucks to pay for a date with *my-self*. I let you talk me into wearing a damn tuxedo. The least you could do is hold my hand."

Paul smiled triumphantly as Katie accommodated him, taking his hand as they entered the reception. He'd never admit it, but half the reason he wanted physical contact was that he was so nervous he could puke. During the wedding ceremony he hadn't had to worry about interacting with any of Katie's colleagues. But the reception was different. He'd be seated at a table with ten brainiacs and their spouses. He could already picture their reaction when he told them he was an ex–hockey player: They'd nod politely and check for lobotomy scars. At least if anyone asked where he went to college, he could say Cornell. No need to mention he hadn't graduated.

What he'd seen of Fallowfield impressed him. It re-minded him of Ithaca, a small diverse college town surrounded by rolling countryside. Before checking into the hotel, Katie had driven him past her house. He could see she missed it as she slowed the car down, gazing wistfully at the small, brightly painted Victorian. He could picture her on the porch's battered wicker furniture, curled up in one of the chairs reading, or typing away on her laptop. He could imagine her jogging the hilly, leafy streets, or nipping into Starbucks, shelling out four bucks for one of those over-priced coffee drinks she always bitched about not being able to find in Didsbury. He had to admit that Fallowfield did seem a bit more on the ball, culturally.

They'd taken a quick driving tour around the campus, too. Katie pointed out to him the building where she taught. Again he sensed the pull it held for her. It was a squat, industrial looking building, probably built in the '50s, but Katie gazed on it like it was a Greek temple. Was there any place back in the Didsbury that made him feel that way? There wasn't.

Both the ceremony and reception were being held at the Pierpont Hotel, the swankiest in Fallowfield. Katie booked rooms for them so they could crawl upstairs after the reception. Paul told her in no uncertain terms he planned to stay an hour at the reception, max. After that she was on her own. When Katie protested, he reminded her of the loan. That shut her up.

"Oh, hell," Katie muttered, stopping at a large table at the entry to the hotel's banquet room to pick up their place cards. "We're at a table with Margie Schooley and Pietro Rice." Her eyes continued scanning the table. "The rest of the people are okay."

Paul's anxiety surged. "What's their deal?"

"Margie is a stuffy old cow whom I know voted against hiring me, and Pietro is one of those annoying people who never makes eye contact when talking to you. He's always looking around the room, looking for someone more interesting."

"Sounds like a jerk."

"He is. But everyone else we're sitting with is pretty nice."

Paul put on his most charming smile as Katie led them to their table. He was proud to be her escort; in turn, he could tell she was enjoying having him on her arm. Heads swiveled as they walked in. He knew he was the best-looking man in the room, and Katie knew it, too. He could feel her enjoying the others' envy, a sentiment he shared since Katie was, without a doubt, the best-looking woman there. Paul wondered if she knew. Probably not.

"Hello, everyone," Katie greeted her colleagues. "I want you all to meet my friend Paul van Dorn."

A tall, owlish looking man stuck his head forward. "No need to introduce a Con Smythe winner."

Paul smiled apprehensively.

"I'm a huge Blades fan!" The man pulled out the empty chair next to him. "Sit down, Paul, I'd love to talk to you."

Paul glanced at Katie, who gave a small shrug. Maybe the night wouldn't be so bad after all.

The owlish man's name was Duffy Webster, and he was the husband of one of Katie's colleagues. Duffy had played hockey in his day for Harvard, prompting a discussion of playing hockey in the Ivy's. Paul was surprised to discover he liked this guy. There was another guy at the table, too, Tom Corday, a professor on the brink of retirement. All he had to hear was that Paul owned a bar and he was glued to Paul's side. Running a bar was Tom's post-retirement dream. As the booze flowed and conversation became more relaxed, Paul was forced to admit to himself he was having a pretty good time.

Still, it couldn't be denied some people were jerks. Margery Schooley, a manatee in green brocade, stared at him like he was the missing link. As Katie had predicted, Pietro Rice feigned interest in speaking with him, but his eyes restlessly roamed the room. But Paul really liked Tom and Duffy who were down to earth guys—no bullshit, no pretensions. He'd come expecting to be surrounded by bookish snobs who prided themselves on thinking deep thoughts and endlessly discussing topics of profound importance. Instead he found some regular people.

"Can I talk to you a minute?" Katie stood hovering by his shoulder.

"Sure." Paul put down his beer. "Excuse me a moment," he said to Duffy, with whom he'd been discussing the fantastic run of the 1980s Edmonton Oilers.

Katie led him out to the dance floor. Her face was flushed.

"You drunk?" Paul asked.

"Are you? You said you were going to leave after an hour. Two and a half have passed."

"Really?" Paul was shocked. He'd been having a good time.

"Yes." Katie put her left hand on his shoulder, clasping his right with hers. They began shuffling around the dance floor. "I brought you to the wedding so I'd have some company! Instead you've spent the whole night talking to everyone else!"

"I'm sorry," Paul murmured, though he really wasn't.

"I want to leave after this dance," Katie whispered. "I'm exhausted and yes, I'm a little tipsy."

"Good champagne," Paul said. He was feeling a bit mellow himself.

Katie sighed, relaxing in his arms. "It was a beautiful ceremony, wasn't it?"

"I could have done without 'Here Comes the Bride' being played on the didgeridoo, but to each his own." He glanced over at the newly married couple, who sat staring deeply into each other's eyes. No one else in the room existed for them. He turned his attention back to Katie. "Just in case I forgot to tell you earlier, you look gorgeous tonight."

Katie blushed. "You did forget. Thank you."

He nodded, drawing her closer. Her soft ivory skin, her scent like a hidden garden . . . what a jerk he'd been to blow it all up. But there was no going back. If he hadn't been the one to end things, *she* would have. Better to be the dumper than the dumpee.

He'd enjoyed watching her at the reception. She was in her element. He got a kick out of how animated she became when she and Duffy's wife began comparing notes on the books they were each writing, and she seemed so happy to be asked by other profs about her research. Paul overheard her saying she missed being in the classroom. The realization that she was really leaving Didsbury at the end of the summer—and that she was glad of it—hit him. Hard as it was to admit, Katie belonged here.

"So, Margery Schooley?" he asked, impulsively dipping Katie as if they were natural born dancers. "Don't you think someone should tell her she has a beard?"

Katie giggled. "You're evil. And don't dip me again unless you want me to throw up on you."

"Haven't you done that already?"

"I didn't throw up *on* you. I threw up near you. There's a difference."

"And why did you throw up? Because you drank on an empty stomach, just like tonight."

Katie stiffened in his arms. "I ate."

"Two pigs in a blanket aren't a meal, Katie. Don't think I didn't see you pushing your dinner around your plate, trying to make it look like you were eating when you weren't."

"I'm putting on weight, Paul."

"You're nuts." Feeling invincible, he nestled his mouth against her ear. "You look perfect. Good enough to eat." Katie gave a small gasp. "Why don't we go upstairs?" he suggested huskily. "You go up first. I'll follow." Again she stiffened in his arms, but Paul knew she was girding herself against her own desire. He waited. Finally Katie looked up at him, yearning in her eyes.

"Deal."

Five minutes passed. Ten. Fifteen. Sitting on the bed in her hotel room, Katie was fuming. Had Paul changed his mind and stood her up? If so, he could walk home to Connecticut tomorrow.

She slipped out of her heels, massaging her stockinged feet. Things had gone better than expected. She'd been certain Paul was going to be a pill at the reception, her punishment for dragging him there in the first place. Instead he'd become fast friends with Duffy Webster and Tom Corday. It felt strange seeing him mingle so easily with her friends. Yet there was something comforting about it, too, the possibility that the two worlds she currently inhabited could overlap. Thanks to Paul, she'd learned a few things, too. She had no idea Tom dreamed about owning a bar after retiring, or that geeky Duffy had once played hockey.

It felt good to be back in Fallowfield, the familiar faces and surroundings a comfort. She was looking forward to returning for good, though the thought of leaving Tuck filled her with a profound sadness. And, though she'd never admit it to Paul, she *had* arrived at a newfound appreciation for her hometown. It was charming, quaint, and filled with wonderful people. Even the people who'd hurt her in the past no longer held any power over her. If anything, there were times she wanted to go up to them and say, "Thanks for treating me badly. You made me stronger."

Her thoughts were interrupted by a quiet knock on the door before Paul slipped inside.

"Lose your way?" she quipped, a small thrill shimmering through her as he made a point of putting the "Do Not Disturb" sign on the door before locking it. She was nuts to agree to this; it would only confuse an already muddy situation.

"No." Paul tore his bowtie from around his neck and tossed it onto a nearby chair, along with his tuxedo jacket. "There. Now I can breath." He kicked off his shoes and walked toward her. "I was saying my good-byes and I got hooked into another conversation with Tom Corday. He's going to come down to Didsbury in the fall to check out the Penalty Box."

Katie's mouth fell open. "You're kidding."

"Nope. He wants to see what it's like, get a feel for owning a bar."

"I can't believe he's really thinking of retiring and running a bar. He's such a wonderful teacher."

"Well, he says he's bored off his ass and ready for a change. Did you know he never wanted to be an academic? His parents pushed him."

"Really?" Katie felt a spark of envy that Tom had revealed this to Paul, but had never mentioned it to her, despite all the time they'd spent talking at various faculty functions and parties. "People are full of surprises."

"Yes, they are." Paul sat down beside her on the bed, taking her hand. "So."

"Before we start, I want to establish a few rules."

"Oooh, stop, you're making me hot."

"I'm serious," Katie huffed, rising to shed her pantyhose.

"You're also a major mood killer," Paul noted as he lay down, "but go ahead."

Pantyhose a memory, Katie stretched out beside him. "Just because I'm going to sleep with you doesn't mean we're back together."

"Of course not," Paul scoffed, unbuttoning his shirt. "I mean, that's ridiculous. It's the most intimate act two people can share! Why should it *mean* anything?"

"Stop mocking me, Paul, or you can go back to your own hotel room right now."

He touched her cheek lightly. "I'm sorry, Professor. Continue."

"We're both tipsy, so this doesn't really count as a real, you know, encounter."

"Imaginary drunken encounter," Paul said solemnly, tossing his shirt to the floor. "Got it. Continue."

The sight of his sculptured torso straining against his white undershirt derailed Katie, but only for a moment. "I think it's possible for two people to have sex, wonderful sex, sex for sex sake, and just leave it at that. I also think—"

"Katie?"

"Yes?"

"Shut the hell up and let me kiss you, okay?"

Katie blinked. "Okay."

His undershirt flew to the floor and then he was on her, the familiar weight of his body atop hers a pleasant surprise. She hadn't realized how much she missed this, his solidity. Desire coiled low in her belly, radiating as strongly as the first time they had ever made physical contact. Katie marveled over how it was possible to be intimate with the terrain of another's body, yet discover it anew each time for what it truly was: magic.

Paul sighed heavily. "I suppose you want me to kiss you."

"I suppose you want me to beg you."

"That usually comes later."

Katie nipped his lower lip. "Snot."

"Witch."

His lips brushed hers slowly. Once . . . twice . . . three times, each time lingering a little more than the time before.

"I bet you think you're torturing me," Katie murmured as her body stirred to life.

"I bet you like it."

"I bet you're right."

He kissed her hard then, a kiss screaming ownership, if not outright dominance. Katie willed herself to relax, though every nerve in her body was pulled tighter than a drum. She wanted to enjoy this, knowing it was the last time.

"You taste great," Paul murmured, reaching down to caress the silk covering her body. Katie held her breath, losing herself in the tenderness of his touch. How could he be so demanding with his mouth, yet so gentle with his hands?

Before she could answer her own question, Paul's hand slipped quietly beneath her dress, his palm running slowly up and down the length of her thighs. Katie could tell their firm smoothness excited him. He began hardening against her.

Katie stiffened instinctively as his hand neared the top of her panties, then relaxed. Paul was in no rush. He toyed with the flesh beneath the waistband, his fingertips feathering against her soft skin. Katie sighed, transported. His touch was magic, revealing her to herself, loosening all self-imposed restraints until she was liquid in his hands. By the time his hands slid up her body to tease her breasts, she was limp, a flower pummeled by gentle spring rain. Her body curved upward to meet his touch.

"I bet you want to take my dress off," Katie whispered.

"I bet you want me to," Paul countered, kissing her neck.

"I bet you're right," Katie said again, breath catching in her throat.

The alcohol had burned off her inhibitions, making her feel sexy in a way she hadn't before. Small, animal groans of pleasure bubbled from her lips as Paul slowly undressed her. Katie delighted in the pleasure she saw in his eyes as he carefully removed her garments one by one, laying her back against the bed with such sweet care that when he was done, she was surprised to find tears in her eyes. Through half closed eyes, she watched as he undressed himself. There was no hurry in his movements; only self-confidence, a trait she found infinitely sexy. Sinewy as a cat, she snuggled up to him as he climbed back atop the bed, delighted when he rolled her over onto her back, playfully pinning her.

"Now what?" he asked in a voice rough with need.

Katie closed her eyes. "This was all your idea. Whatever you want is fine with me."

There was silence—delicious, suspense-filled silence. Then Paul's hands began exploring, a caress here, a squeeze there. One minute his touch lingered, played; the next his hands moved on, bringing her fully to life in parts of her body she hadn't known could be erogenous. Tension was building deep within her: exquisite, finely tuned. A brush of fingertips in the right place and she would explode. One lusty bite at her plumped nipple and the heat of her own body would consume her.

Paul's command of her senses overwhelmed her, coupled as it was with such sweetness. She could tell he viewed her body as his territory, from the soft swell of her breasts to her hipbones. His possessiveness ought to have set her questioning. Instead she allowed herself to be shaped by it, a shell worn smooth and bright by the rise and fall of their mutual pleasure. Her body was the sea, and he was swimming in her, his whispering of her name beguiling as the ocean breeze.

Katie was floating now, sensation after sensation lapping at her as joy sang through her body, gorgeous as the first rays of sunshine after the long, gray winter months. She gasped as his teeth scraped over one hip, then another, sending the pulsebeat between her legs rocketing. Paul laughed wickedly as his tongue ran the length of her body, pausing only to gently part her knees. Katie wanted to beg him to stop, to wait so she could prolong the moment. But the moment his mouth found her sex, she knew it was useless to struggle. He had barely begun playing with her before pleasure dragged her under, senses drowning in one, long crashing wave.

Slowly she returned to herself. Her trembling ceased. Her breath stuttered its way back to normal. It was Paul whose breathing was ragged now, Paul whose hard body shuddered with needed release. Snaking his way up her body, he levered himself over her, his kisses demanding and frantic as Katie clung to him, desire renewing itself within her.

"Look at me."

His voice was hoarse, his command simple. Katie raised her eyes to his eyes, thrilled by the hunger she saw reflected there. They were twins, one mirroring the other. Their gaze held until Katie was forced to look away, the naked intimacy of the moment too much for her to take. It was then that he donned a condom and slipped inside her, the movement of his body slow and sure. Katie wrapped herself tighter around him. Higher and higher they lifted, two souls ascending above stormy clouds, until finally, unexpectedly, his teeth clamped down on the soft flesh of her throat, and they soared together over the edge.

"That was nice."

Paul propped himself up on his elbow and stared at Katie, who as usual was hogging the covers. "Just 'nice'?"

"Why is 'nice' never good enough for men? Why do men always need to hear 'That was the greatest sex I ever had in my life'?"

"Why do women always need to ask, 'Do I look fat in this?' It's the same thing: insecurity."

"I suppose." Katie squinted at the alarm clock on the nightstand. "It's late."

"We can sleep in," Paul murmured, stroking her hair. In his opinion, the sex had been more than "nice"--it had been phenomenal. It always was. "Thanks for that no-strings-attached, rollicking good time."

Katie narrowed her eyes. "You're mocking again."

"I'm not." He laid back down, their noses close enough to touch. "So, when are you moving back to Fallowfield?" he asked curiously.

The question seemed to take her by surprise. "Beginning of August, I guess." She paused. "I don't think I can get back into my house until August first. Why?"

"Just curious." He didn't want to tell her he wished she was staying. Or, at the very least, he wished he had the surety about life she did. Up until tonight, he thought he had. But seeing her in her element brought home to him the fractured sense of self he was carrying around inside him.

"Won't you miss Bitsy and Denise?"

"Of course I will." Her voice was brisk, a smokescreen he knew was designed to keep emotion at bay. "But they can visit me, and it's not like I *never* come to Didsbury. I'll be back for Thanksgiving, I'm sure."

"It's a bitch of a drive," Paul observed.

"Sure is."

"How does Tuck feel about your going back?"

"Why did you have to bring that up?" Katie sounded pained as she rolled over onto her back.

"I'm sorry. I didn't mean to upset you."

"It's okay, it's just"—she began to get teary—"I'm going to miss Tuck a lot."

"I know you will." Paul tenderly swiped at her eyes. "But he'll be fine."

"As long as my sister keeps it together." Katie looked at him. "Do you swear Mina's doing okay at work?"

"She's doing fine," Paul soothed, which was basically the truth. He *had* noticed her tendency to flirt hard with the male customers, but lots of cocktail waitresses did that; it was a way of maximizing tips. Mina also bristled when it came to taking directions. She'd obey, albeit begrudgingly, making it clear she felt she was doing you a favor. Paul could have done without the attitude, but he knew she was trying to remake her life, so he was cutting her lots of slack. But not forever.

"I can't thank you enough for hiring her," Katie whispered. "It really means a lot to me."

Enough for you to admit you still care? Paul wondered. He was tempted to ask the question aloud, but he didn't want to push things. They'd had a nice weekend at the wedding, much better than he'd expected. They'd made love; they were still friends. Shouldn't that be enough?

Katie yawned. "I'm sleepy."

"Me, too." He hunkered down beside her. "I *can* stay the night, can't I?"

"As long as you don't make that noise."

"What noise?"

"The one that sounds like a whale breathing through his blowhole."

Paul drew back, offended. "I don't make that noise!"

"You *do*," Katie insisted in a voice Paul swore was tinged with tenderness. "But I know you don't do it on purpose."

"Blowhole," Paul muttered to himself as he turned out the light. "No woman's ever told me *that* before."

"Maybe they didn't want to hurt your feelings. I didn't."

"Oh, but it's all right to tell me now since we're broken up?"

"Well . . . yes."

"Good-night, Katie."

"Good-night, Paul." He turned over on his side, dragging the covers with him. "Blowhole . . ."

CHAPTER
21

"So, did you miss me?"

Paul's grin faded as he caught Frank's grim expression as he entered the Penalty Box. "First tell me how your weekend was," said Frank. "Then we'll talk about mine."

"My weekend was good," Paul said. "Better than I expected."

"Yeah?" Frank looked surprised. "Anything interesting happen?"

"A gentleman doesn't tell."

"You used to bash teeth out on the ice for a living. Since when are you a gentleman?"

Paul laughed. "You're right. No, it was good, you know? Fun."

"You guys back together?"

"Nah. We're better as friends, if that makes any sense."

"Sure. What with her leaving and all."

"Exactly." Paul found it comforting Frank viewed the situation the same way he did. It meant he hadn't been crazy to end things. "Now, tell me about the weekend."

Frank came out from behind the bar to park his butt on a stool. "We did great both nights."

Paul joined him. "So, what's the problem?"

"The problem is, the clientele was a little different than usual, and I'm afraid we could lose the locals if the trend continues."

"Explain."

"I don't know what to say without sounding like, you know, a judgmental prick or something."

"Just spill it, for Chrissakes."

"Look, I know you hired Katie's sister as a favor to her to help her get back on her feet. And she's a good cocktail waitress."

Paul's guts began to curdle. "But—?"

"Both nights the bar was filled with bikers. Friends of Mina's. These guys were loud, bro. And obnoxious. Two of them nearly came to blows at the pool table. A couple of others got so shitfaced and sloppy I had to throw them out. They threatened to come back next week and 'mess my face up.' Not what I wanna hear, okay?"

"Shit. Did they at least pay for their drinks?"

"See, that's the thing: They were ordering so many, so fast, I'm pretty sure Mina let some of the tab slide. To my mind, things did not compute when I cashed out at the end of the evening. I always keep a running guesstimate in my head of what the night's grand total will be, and I'm usually in the ball park. This weekend the numbers were way lower than I thought they'd be. I'm telling you, we should use the cash-and-carry system with *tickets*."

Paul frowned. He preferred the simple cash-and-carry system. Foregoing tickets was cheaper, and you didn't have to wrap your head around accounting. There was just one drawback: This verbal system depended completely upon the honesty of employees.

He looked at Frank. "What do you think I should do? You've been in this business a helluva lot longer than I have."

Frank shrugged. "It's a tough call. She's good at what she does."

"Except she might be giving free drinks to friends we don't want in here."

"Right."

"*Shit*," Paul repeated. "Any chance one of the other girls might be messing up?"

"We never had this problem till you hired Katie's sister," Frank pointed out bluntly. "Look, I know it's sticky. We've got no solid proof here. And these guys are, for the most part, paying customers. I think we have to just play it by ear for now. If they come in next week and cause trouble, we'll throw them out, and you can have a heart-to-heart with Mina. Make sense?"

"Yeah." Paul sighed. "Thanks for telling me, Frank. Did I miss any other fun?"

"Doug Burton and Chick Perry stopped by."

"What did they want?"

"To talk to you. They said to call 'em, because it's important."

"Yeah, yeah, yeah," Paul muttered. "I'll call them."

Once again, Paul found himself at the Didsbury Country Club. The only time he ever set foot in the place was when he was summoned by Doug Burton and Chick Perry.

"Gentlemen."

Paul was pleasantly surprised to find them sitting on opposite sides of the table this time, an inversion of their usual

seating arrangement. He politely shook both their hands before sitting down.

"I hear you stopped by the Penalty Box this weekend," he
said.

"We did," said Doug, sipping a beer. "We were very impressed with the décor."

"Less so with the clientele," said Chick.

Doug frowned with disapproval. "You never told us it
was a biker bar, Paul."

"It's not."

"Well, it certainly looked like it the night we were there."

"An aberration. Some gang was passing through town
and stopped." Chick had already taken the liberty of pouring
Paul a glass of water, and he reached for it gratefully, taking
a sip. "So, what's up?"

"Something very serious has occurred."

The gravity in Doug Burton's voice alarmed Paul, who
began wracking his brains, trying to figure out how he might
have screwed up in the past few months. He'd thought
things were going really well. Apparently not.

"It's Dan Doherty," Doug continued with a sad sigh.
"He's got cancer."

"That's too bad," said Paul, meaning it. Doherty might be
the biggest bastard on bandy legs, but he would never wish
illness on the guy.

"He's too sick to coach. The league would like you to
take over and coach his team for the rest of the season."

Paul sat back, stunned. The midget travel team. The team
he'd lobbied to coach at the beginning of the season, a team
with real players with real skill who breathed and ate hockey
as he once had.

"What do you say, Paul?" said Chick, loosening the tie
cutting off the circulation at his corpulent neck.

"Doesn't Dan have an assistant?" Paul asked suspiciously.

"He does. Tommy Lambert. But he's not quite up to the task."

"Who would take over my squirt team?"

"We haven't figured that out yet, but what the hell does it matter?" Doug chuckled. "They're a joke."

"Actually, they're playing very well these days."

"I'm sure they are, son. But at that level of play, who gives a shit?"

They do, Paul thought angrily. Doug leaned forward, staring Paul right in the eye. "Here's your shot, Paul. Doherty's not likely to be back. The midget team is eleven and one. With you as their coach we're sure they'll at least make it to the state semifinals, if not win the championship. How 'bout it?"

How 'bout it indeed. With Doug and Chick staring at him as if the fate of the world hung in the balance, Paul could barely think straight. A chance to coach real players . . . a shot at a championship . . . no Dan Doherty . . . it seemed too good to be true. Be careful what you wish for, his mother used to caution, or you just might get it. Shit.

"I need to think about this."

Doug and Chick exchanged puzzled glances. "I can't believe you're not jumping on this," said Doug.

"Normally, I would. But there are a couple of other things I need to consider." His fingers lightly drummed the tabletop. "When do you need an answer by?"

"Friday, the latest," said Doug.

"I can give you an answer by Wednesday. Why don't you stop by the Penalty Box around lunchtime?"

"Will do," said Doug.

•   •   •

Two minutes until the game with the Winchester Barracudas and no sign of Tuck Fisher. *Goddamn Mina*, Paul thought angrily. He'd already checked with Katie to see if she knew what was up; as far as she knew, Mina was bringing him to the game. Katie's face fell when Paul told her Tuck had failed to show at practice that morning. "Maybe he's sick today," Katie offered weakly.

"Then he—or his parent—is supposed to call me," Paul pointed out. He could tell from Katie's expression she didn't believe Tuck was sick.

Warm-up complete, Paul hustled his team back into the locker room.

"Okay, guys." He clapped his hands together twice to get their attention. "Who can tell me this week's motto?" Every week he gave them a new motto, something to think about and strive for. Hands sprung up in the air like weeds.

"Wilbraham?"

"Your attitude determines your altitude."

Paul nodded approvingly. "And what does it mean?" Hands stretched higher. "Becker?"

"It means if you have confidence, you can go far," the boy said quietly.

"That's right. I know you guys have probably heard some things about the Barracudas: that they play dirty, that they've got big goony guys playing defense. I want you to put it out of your heads. You're better players, and you're better sportsmen. If you believe we can rise above their dirty tricks and win because of our talent, we will."

"Yeah!" the boys cheered. Paul was surprised to find himself believing his own words. He knew the Barracudas' coach: he was an SOB, renowned for calling time-outs and encouraging cheap shots. Initially Paul was certain his boys would get creamed. But then he watched them at practice that morning, noting how far they had come, and pride swelled within him.

Tuck's absence disturbed him. He'd been back with his mother for less than two months and already the kid's life was becoming erratic. It wasn't good. Plus, on a purely selfish level, he could have used Tuck here for this game.

"Coach?"

Gary Flaherty's voice overtook the one in his head. "Hmm?"

"You okay? You're just, like, staring into space."

Paul shook himself out. "I'm fine. You guys ready to go out there and kick Barracuda butt?"

"Ycah!"

"Let's get 'em."

Paul was in torment as he watched his team being pummeled by the Barracudas, his mind continually flashing to a vision of himself coaching the midget travel team. He knew Doug Burton was right: Paul had seen them play, and were he to take over the team, he had no doubt they could blast their way past every other team in the finals and win the div championship. He'd taste glory again, basking in the respect of players who knew what the game was all about. He'd be able to make a *new* name for himself.

"Coach?"

He turned from the ice to see Tuck walking behind the bench, a hangdog expression on his face.

"Tuck. Glad you could make it," Paul said sincerely.

The other players slid down the bench, making room so Tuck could sit down.

"We missed you at practice this morning, buddy."

Tuck just swallowed, eyes straying to the ice.

"Where were you?" Paul asked gently.

Tuck licked his lips nervously, still avoiding eye contact. "There was a problem with the car."

Paul knew Mina didn't have a car. Maybe he meant a problem with that Serpent guy's motorcycle. Paul crouched down so he was eye level with the boy. "Remember what we talked about at my house?" he said in a low voice. "That if you need a ride to practice, you could call me or your aunt?"

Tuck nodded absently.

"Why didn't you?"

Tuck shrugged, tightlipped. Obviously he wasn't going to talk about what was going on.

Paul rose with a sigh. "You know I can't let you play today, right? You missed practice."

"I know," Tuck said in a small voice. The hunger in his eyes was painful for Paul to see. The kid was dying to be out on the ice. It was probably the only place he felt free, the only place where he could escape his problems for a few hours. Paul understood completely.

"How did you get here?" Paul asked.

Tuck squirmed uncomfortably on the bench. "Mom gave me cab fare."

"And how are you supposed to get home?"

Tuck finally tore his gaze from the ice. Paul could tell it was taking every ounce of his strength to keep it together. "She said Aunt Katie would take me home."

And what if Aunt Katie wasn't here? Paul wanted to ask, but didn't. It wasn't fair to grill the child about the sins of the parent. Now he had two things to chat with Mina about.

"I'm sure Katie will be glad to take you home," Paul assured him with a pat to the shoulder. "You'll be our good luck mascot today, okay, buddy?"

•   •   •

Katie decided to take Tuck out for an ice cream after the game. It would cheer him up after not being able to play and having to witness his team go down in flames 7–1 to the Barracudas.

It would also give her a chance to try to find out what was going on at home.

"How's that hot fudge sundae?" Katie asked as Tuck devoured his ice cream. His ravenous appetite struck her as amusing until it dawned on her that maybe he was shoveling food down because he was wasn't being fed enough at home. A lump formed in her throat as she cautioned herself against jumping to conclusions.

"It's good," Tuck warbled through a mouthful of ice cream.

Figuring Tuck might be self-conscious if he was the only one eating, Katie ordered a fat-free vanilla yogurt. She took a few spoonfuls, studying him.

"You seem awfully hungry."

Tuck just nodded, shoveling more ice cream into his mouth.

"How come you were late to the game?"

Tuck expression turned guarded. "Mom thought she'd be able to take me but then she couldn't so then she called me a cab."

Katie poked at her yogurt. "Why didn't you call me? I could have picked you up."

Tuck said nothing.

"Coach van Dorn says you missed practice this morning. That's not like you."

Tuck wiped at his mouth. "Mom was out late and I didn't want to wake her up."

"I see." Katie's heart pounded in her chest. If Mina walked through the door of the ice cream parlor right now,

Katie would jump on her like a wild animal. "You could have called me," she reminded Tuck.

Tuck glanced away. "Mom said we shouldn't bother other people. She said no one wants to hear our problems."

"I'm not 'other people' Tuck. I'm your aunt, and I'd be glad to take you. Why didn't you just use the cell phone I gave you?"

"Don't know where it is," Tuck said very quietly.

The pressure in Katie's chest increased. "Don't know where it is, or Mom took it to use herself?"

Tuck's eyes dropped down to the table. *Son of a bitch.* Mina was dead. That's all there was to it.

Tuck finished his sundae with a flourish. "That was great!"

"Want another?"

Tuck's eyes bulged out of his head. "Really?"

"Sure. This is a special occasion, what the hell."

Katie ordered another ice cream sundae for Tuck. He looked so happy you would have thought she'd given the kid a million dollars. "I hope you don't get a stomachache," Katie worried aloud.

"I won't," Tuck said confidently. "Once, at Gary's, we ate two whole bags of Chip-a-roos and we didn't even puke!"

"Amazing," Katie agreed. Her yogurt was fast collapsing into a white puddle. She took two more mouthfuls, trying to convince herself it tasted as mouthwatering as the concoction her nephew was digging into. The temptation to order some ice cream for herself was overwhelming. *I'm under stress,* she reasoned. *It'll soothe me. I can run an extra mile tomorrow.* But she held fast. If she gave in to the ice cream, she was likely to go on a bender. Considering her jeans felt a little snugger these days than she would have liked, she forced herself to be content with the yogurt.

"How's school going?"

"Good."

"Are you getting all your homework done?"

Tuck nodded.

"Computer working okay?"

"Yeah. Except Snake is always throwing me off so he can look at porn."

"Really." Katie pushed her yogurt away. "I'll have to talk to him about that."

Alarm sprang into Tuck's eyes. "No, don't! I promised not to tell anyone. He said Mom would cut off his balls and feed them to wild dogs if she knew."

Katie shifted uncomfortably. "So, Mom and Snake are kinda going out?"

"Kinda. They fight sometimes. Mom says 'You don't fuckin' own me' and then Snake says 'Fine then find your own fucking place to live you freeloading bitch' and takes off on his motorcycle but then he always comes back and they make up."

"Well, that's good," Katie managed. "Nana misses you, you know," she continued. "She's hoping you can come over soon."

"Mom said she'd rather chop off her left tit than ever go over there," Tuck mumbled forlornly.

Katie opened her mouth to admonish him about his language then caught herself. Mina was the one with the foul mouth, not him. Tuck was just repeating his mother's charming vernacular. Her mind chilled as she recalled what Tuck was like right after Mina had gone into rehab and he'd moved in with her mother. Every other word out of his mouth was a curse. It had taken months to break him of the habit. And now look where he was: right back at square one.

"Tuck, I'm going to ask you something, and if you don't want to talk about it right now, I understand."

Tuck's expression was leery as he peered at her over the rim of his sundae.

"Is everything okay at home?"

"What do you mean?"

Katie brought her hands down into her lap so her nephew wouldn't see how hard she was twisting them. "I mean, is Mom okay? Is she taking care of business—you know, making dinner, washing your clothes and stuff?"

"Snake cooks dinner."

"Whatever. I just want to make sure you're okay, honey."

"I'm okay," said Tuck. He swallowed. "But I would like to see Nana."

"How about I pick you up on Sunday and bring you over to Nana's house and we can all hang out? I bet Nana would make hamburgers for you, if you wanted."

"That would rock!" Tuck perked up a moment. Then his face fell. "I better check with Mom," he said.

"I'm sure Mom will be fine with it," Katie said firmly. "If you want, I'll talk to her about it. That, and hockey practice. I'll arrange to bring you to practice and games, just like before."

Panic streaked across Tuck's face. "But Mom said—"

"You let me handle your mom."

CHAPTER 22

"*GIVE ME A* MINUTE, WILL YA?"

Katie rolled her eyes as she waited for Mina to unlock the door. She'd been ringing the doorbell for at least ten minutes. Mina had never been a morning person, but then again, it wasn't really morning. It was noon.

The door finally opened. Mina stood there in a rumpled, bright red kimono, last night's mascara ringing her eyes.

"Katie." Mina's mouth puckered. "Don't you believe in calling first?"

"I did. You never pick up your damn phone."

"Come in. I guess."

Katie followed her sister inside and was immediately assaulted by the smell of stale cigarettes. They were everywhere: overflowing ashtrays, floating in lipstick-stained glasses, stubbed out in half-eaten pieces of cold pizza lying in an open box on the dusty coffee table. Katie's stomach tumbled. The place was a sty. Katie knew lots of people were relaxed about cleaning. But this was more than mere untidiness. This bordered on squalor.

Mina folded her arms across her chest. "What's up?"

"It's about Tuck."

"Of course it is."

"Can I sit down?"

Mina gestured toward the battered red couch, its frayed cushions covered in piles of dirty laundry. Katie gingerly cleared away the tangled mess of clothing and sat down. Mina remained standing.

"Is this about giving him cab fare to get to the game? Because if it is, I don't wanna hear it."

"Yes, it is," Katie said fiercely. "It's about that and him missing practice yesterday morning, too. He wasn't allowed to play, Mina."

Mina shrugged. "So? He'll play next time."

"That's not the *point*," Katie snapped. "When you came home, you promised to make sure he made it to hockey. You let him down. Paul van Dorn called me this morning. He said Tuck wasn't at practice again this morning."

"He'll live."

"Hockey's important to Tuck! If he keeps missing practice he'll get thrown off the team! Don't you give a shit?"

"Let me tell you something," Mina drawled, eyes scanning the room for an open pack of cigarettes. She found one atop the TV and lit up. "I'm busting my ass, okay? Not only am I working for your asshole of a boyfriend—"

"He's not my boyfriend—"

"But I'm also waitressing two nights a week at the Tender Trap. By the time I get home, I'm exhausted. But you wouldn't know about that, would you? You've never had to work a shit job in your life."

Katie stared at her. "I'm not going to apologize for my life, Mina. I've worked damn hard to get where I am."

Mina took a long puff off her cigarette. "And I'm working hard now!"

"You still have an obligation to your son! I told you when you got out of rehab that I would gladly continue taking him to practice and to his hockey games!"

"And I told you that I'm his mother and I don't need your damn help!"

"Then start acting like it."

Mina chuckled softly as she blew a stream of smoke out the left side of her mouth. "You never change, do you? Thinking you're better than everyone else. Going around telling everyone else what to do with their life."

"This is about *Tuck*, Mina! Not me! Not you! Tuck!"

"Tuck is fine," Mina insisted.

"Is he? Where's his cell phone?"

Mina absently scratched her nose. "I don't know what you're talking about."

"Don't bullshit me. I know you took his cell phone. And if you punish him for telling me, I will send Social Services over here so fast your head will spin."

"They come around anyway," Mina sneered. "Part of checking up on me and my re-integration into society, blah blah blah."

"Good. I'm glad." Katie thrust her hand out. "Give me the phone, Mina."

"What for?"

"Because I'm paying for Tuck to have it, not you. If you're going to use it, then I want it back."

"Fine," Mina huffed. "I'll give it back to him, even though I need it more. Who the hell ever heard of a nine-year-old kid with a cell phone?"

"Welcome to the twenty-first century. They all have them."

"Yeah, well, I don't want him turning into a spoiled brat."

"I doubt that will happen," Katie said dryly.

Mina took a final puff of her cigarette and tossed it into a half empty glass of Coke, where it snuffed out with a hiss. "You done?"

"Not until we resolve the issue of Tuck making it to hockey practice and games."

Mina scrubbed her hands over her face. "You're a huge pain in my ass, you know that?"

"I try."

"You want to take him to practice and his stupid games? Fine, be my guest. He loves you better, anyway."

"Maybe if you took some interest in his life, he'd love you, too," Katie noted softly. Though Mina sounded like a petulant child, Katie saw it for what it was: insecurity. Vulnerability.

"I don't have a car," Mina pointed out sharply.

"Well, I do, so let me help."

"Saint Katherine to the rescue."

Katie ignored her. "I could swing by here before games and pick you up, too, if you wanted. Then we could watch him play together. Afterward I could drop the two of you back here."

"Maybe," Mina muttered. "Let me think about it."

Katie rose slowly, the movement causing the faint aroma of stale laundry to waft to her nose. "We're agreed, then? I can pick him up for practice early in the morning? Take him to games if he needs me to?"

Mina shrugged. "I guess."

"And the phone?"

"He can have it back."

"What did you need it for, anyway?"

"Things. What does anyone need one for?" She frowned. "That it?"

"One more thing." Katie paid no heed to the annoyance

on Mina's face. "Mom would like to see Tuck. Would you mind if I picked him up on Sunday and brought him over there?"

Mina's mouth curled into a slow smile. "Even better: why not have him sleep over there Saturday night?"

"I guess we could do that." Katie tried not to bristle. It was obvious Mina wanted Tuck out of the way and was thrilled to be able to shift responsibility for him onto someone else. Katie tried framing it positively, telling herself it would be good for Tuck. "Let me check with Mom."

Mina snorted. "Like she's gonna say no."

"You could come, too. For Sunday dinner. Wouldn't have to arrive too early."

Mina mimed putting a gun to her left temple and pulling the trigger. "No, thanks."

Katie sighed. "I don't know what your problem is."

"Not everyone is a freak like you who likes hanging out with their mother."

"I don't like hanging out with her," Katie protested. "I just don't *hate* her."

"Whatever."

Katie changed the subject. "How's work going?"

"It's okay. They're just jobs, you know?"

"And Snake?"

"That asshole," Mina groused.

"And you're managing to keep straight and all that?" Katie asked delicately.

"No," Mina flared, "I'm shooting up three times a day and downing two bottles of Wild Turkey before bed every night."

It's possible, Katie thought. If there was one thing she'd learned from Mina's previous bouts with booze and pills, it was what skilled liars addicts were.

"I'm not prying, Mina, I just—"

"I know: you're just watching out for me. And I appreciate that, believe me." Katie was stunned when her sister
came over to hug her. Mina's emotions seemed to turn on a
dime. "Everything's going to be fine. Just have a little patience, all right? I'm still finding my sea legs."

"I know." Katie kissed the side of her sister's cheek.
"And I love you. And I want so much for things to be good
for you and Tuck."

"They will be. Just chill out."

Katie vowed to try.

"How's this?"

Paul ushered Doug Burton and Chick Perry to a cozy
table for four toward the back of the Penalty Box. He'd contemplated seating them in a booth, but there was no way
Chick would be able to slide in and out comfortably, and he
didn't wish to humiliate the man. Chick eyed Paul gratefully
as the three of them sat down at the table. A waitress appeared within seconds to fill their water glasses and give
them menus.

Doug nodded his head approvingly. "Fast service."

Paul smiled. "We try."

Inviting them to the Penalty Box at lunchtime was a
smart move. He felt less guarded here; it was his turf, not
theirs. The food was good, the service superior. The place
was also packed with business people on their lunch hour,
not a biker in sight.

Doug glanced around admiringly. "You do a good
lunchtime business during the week?"

Paul nodded. "We draw from a lot of downtown busi-
nesses, as you can see."

Doug's eyes lit on Paul's old Blades jersey, hanging in a
glass case on the wall above one of the booths. "You a

masochist or what?" he joshed. "If I were you, I'd bust into tears every time I walked past it."

Paul's eyes went to his jersey. "It's part of my history, and it's part of what draws people to the bar," he said. He'd never admit that there were times a lump formed in his throat when he looked at it. There were also times he wanted to take an ax to the case, liberate the jersey, and set it on fire. He was beginning to understand how oppressive your own history could be.

Chick rubbed his pudgy hands together eagerly. "What do you recommend?"

"Well, the curly fries are legendary," Paul boasted, "and we do a mean cheeseburger."

Both men closed their menus. "Sounds good to me," said Doug. He eyed Chick. "You?" Chick nodded.

Orders placed and drinks delivered, the three men engaged in small talk. When the food finally arrived, Paul felt ready to get down to business.

"I've made my decision about taking over the midget travel team." Both Doug and Chick listened intently, mouths chewing furiously.

"I'm going to pass."

Chick choked, lapsing into a coughing fit. "Sorry," he rasped.

"You okay?" Paul asked.

Chick nodded.

Doug's expression was grave as he regarded Paul. "Are you sure you've thought this through?"

"Totally. I'm sticking with the squirts until the end of their season." Paul sipped his beer. "If you're still in need of a coach for the midget travel team next fall, we can talk then. But I'm staying put."

Doug did nothing to hide his displeasure. "Mind if I ask why?"

"Of course not. I think it sends the wrong message to my kids if I bail mid-season. I've worked hard at building a relationship with them—at building *them* up—and I don't want to jeopardize that."

Doug chuckled. "That's very noble, Paul, but I think you're forgetting the big picture here. You take over Dan's position, you've got a shot at winning."

"Winning isn't everything."

He never thought those words would come out of his mouth, but there they were. He never thought he'd believe such a statement, either. But he did. He'd agonized over his decision, knowing what Doug said was right: If he took over the midget team, he might get a shot at being in the spotlight again. But the more he thought about it, the more uneasy he felt about ditching the squirts. He'd worked hard to build up their confidence and camaraderie. Sure, half of them still didn't know what they were doing on the ice, but what did it matter? They were having fun. They were learning skills and values they'd carry forward into adulthood. They believed in him. If he bailed on them, they would think he never cared. They would think *they* didn't matter.

And then there was Tuck.

Every time he leaned toward taking the coaching position with the midgets, Tuck would steal into his mind. He could picture the look of disappointment and pain on the boy's face. Paul was one of the few adults Tuck trusted not to let him down. Paul didn't want to betray that, not with all the kid had been through. Tuck needed Paul, and at this point in his life, Paul needed to be needed. He'd stay with the team to the end of their season, whether they ranked first or last.

Doug carefully wiped his mouth with his napkin. "I must say I'm surprised."

Paul nodded. "I understand that."

"Surprised and disappointed," Doug continued tersely. "I

don't think you realize the opportunity you're passing up. You coaching the midgets would have been magic."

"Then why didn't you make me their coach at the beginning of the season?" Paul challenged.

Doug narrowed his eyes. "Dan wasn't sick then. It's all about paying dues, remember?"

"Then I'll gladly pay mine and stay with my boys."

Paul tried to avoid Frank's eyes as he watched the parade of bikers swagger through the door of the Penalty Box. The usual clientele had filled the bar in the early part of the evening: young families wanting to take their kids out for a burger, groups of single guys gathering around the bar to watch hockey on TV. Couples drifted in for a drink or munchies around ten or so to round off an evening out. But when eleven o'clock hit, everything changed.

Paul heard them before he saw them. He was busy talking about his days with the Blades with a bunch of guys from the local community college who had deliberately sought him out, when he heard the roar of choppers outside. He paused, hoping they might just be passing through. But one by one, they began pulling up in front of the bar, their conversation raucous as they cut the engines. His eyes shot to Mina. She was at the bar filling an order, but he could tell she heard it, too. She looked happy.

Paul counted twelve of them. Bearded, hulking, and tattooed, they cast a menacing eye at the other patrons as they made a beeline for Mina. The mood in the bar changed immediately from collegial to anxious.

"Excuse me," Paul said to the college kids. He approached the gang, who were standing in the middle of the floor surveying the place.

"Hey, guys," said Paul. "Can I help you?"

"I don't know. Can you?" jeered a burly biker with a graying Fu Manchu moustache. He laughed. "Man, I crack myself up."

"I'm Paul, I own the bar." He glanced behind him. "There are some tables toward the back I can put together for you if you want. But I'd appreciate it if you kept the noise down, okay? This is a family place."

Fu Manchu glared at him. "Excuse me, but I thought we were living in a free fucking country."

Paul dug in his heels. "You are. But I own the bar, and I make the rules. If you don't like 'em, you can leave. It's real simple." He made eye contact with each and every one of them. "By the way, did one of you threaten to rearrange my bartender's face last week? 'Cause if you did, you can get the fuck out of here right now."

Speaking to them in their own vernacular got through to them. A few of the bikers grunted, shuffling their weight. They seemed uncertain what to do.

"You want those two tables in the back or what?" Paul snapped.

"Sure," said Fu Manchu. "And five pitchers of Bud to start."

"I'll have one of the waitresses bring them over as soon as we set up the table."

"Not one of the waitresses," Fu murmured lasciviously. "Mina."

Paul's teeth set on edge. "Whatever."

He pushed the two tables together, and gave the beer order to Mina. The bikers were loud and their language was peppered with obscenities anyone in the bar could hear. But Paul's main problem was Mina. Every chance she got, she was hanging around the table, bullshitting with her friends and neglecting other customers. When it was time for her break, Paul called her into his office.

"Tell your friends to leave," he said.

Mina scowled. "What? Why?"

"Because it's interfering with your ability to do your job. They're distracting you. You're neglecting other paying customers."

"No, I'm not."

"Mina, I've been watching you since they came in, okay? You're spending more time yukking it up with them than you should be. Not only that, but Frank tells me the bar tally isn't quite adding up. He keeps a running tab in his head."

"So?" Mina scoffed. "What does that have to do with me?"

"I would hate to think you're giving your buddies free pitchers of beer. Because if I find out you are, you're history."

"I would never do that," Mina said hotly as her face turned fire red.

"Look," Paul continued, "You know I ask all my employees not to have their friends and family hang out here."

"You never told me that."

"It's in the employee handbook. Did you bother to read it?"

"Yes," Mina spat.

"Good. Then you know what I'm talking about. I want you to go back out there and ask your friends to leave. Blame me. Tell them I'm being a hard-ass and you'll lose your job if they don't go."

Mina's gaze mocked him. "Aren't you afraid one of them will get mad and mess you up?"

Paul laughed. "*No.* I played in the NHL, remember? I've fought guys who make those losers look like choir boys. Now I've got a question for you: Aren't you afraid of losing your job? Because you should be."

"Are you threatening me?"

"Yes. I'm your boss, not some schmuck who hangs out here for kicks breathing down your neck, though I know you like to think of me that way. It's time you showed a little respect."

"I'm respectful," Mina said with a sneer.

"Yeah? Well, it's news to me. Go tell your friends to leave."

"You know, you're a snob. Just like Katie."

"Really? And you're basing that on?"

"You just want them out of here because you think they're bad news. You take one look at them and you think 'trouble.' But in reality, they're sweeties."

"I don't give a shit if they're on the verge of being canonized," Paul returned angrily. "They're scaring my regular customers and getting in the way of you doing your job. Get them out of here or you're toast."

"Fine." Mina frowned. "I'll tell them to leave and I'll go be the perky little waitress with the great tits who waits on all the other boring jerks in the bar. Happy?"

Paul bit his tongue. *You know, I hired you as a favor to your sister, and I could just as easily fire you because your attitude sucks.* "Very happy," he replied. "Are *you* happy I'm letting you keep your job?"

Mina said nothing as she stormed out of the office. Five minutes later, the bar was clear of bikers, though they did make a big show of leaving, muttering about "pussy bar owners" and kicking the occasional chair on the way out. Paul was glad to see them go. He wasn't sure he was glad Mina was staying.

CHAPTER

23

Paul always found the end of the hockey season bitter-sweet. The Panthers were down to the last game of the regular season. If they won, they'd make it into the playoffs by the skin of their teeth. If they lost, the season was over.

Spring had snuck up on Didsbury. One minute, people were complaining about digging out from yet another snow-fall; the next, purple and yellow crocuses were bursting through the moist earth, heralding a return to sun and warmer days ahead. Last spring, Paul had formally announced his retirement. He was finalizing the deal to take over Cuffy's and turn it into the Penalty Box. He'd sold his apartment in Manhattan and had bought the house in town.

Now he wondered, *had he chosen the right path?*

He looked around at the anxious little faces in the locker room as they prepared for what could be their final foray of the year on ice. A smile crept to his face; he was proud of them. Sean Bennett, who'd started the season barely able to skate, was now one of the best backward skaters on the team. Back-up goalie Tommy Tataglia used to scream when the team shot pucks at him during drills; now he was one of toughest little SOBs in the squirt division. Finally, there was Tuck, stoic as ever as he laced up his skates, the boy Paul knew had to be saddest about the season ending.

Hockey had kept Tuck focused and gave him something positive to pour his energy into. Paul assumed things weren't as good at home as they could be. Mina had started showing up late for work, and calling in sick far too often for Paul's liking. If it wasn't for Katie, Paul doubted Tuck would ever make it to practice or games.

Katie. Every time he saw her he felt battered and bruised. She was so beautiful. No one made him laugh the way she did. She was looking very tired these days. He'd heard through the Didsbury grapevine that she was coming down to the wire with her book deadline. He knew she'd make it. If there was one thing you could say about Katie, she was disciplined.

The locker room had fallen unnaturally quiet, a phenomena Paul knew well from his days as a player. An outsider would never understand the depth of this brooding stillness, brought on by a unique blend of fear and anticipation.

"Listen up, guys." Paul's eyes swept over his players. He still found it to be the most effective tool in his coaching arsenal. "I know you're nervous. If we win, we go on to the playoffs. And if we lose, this is our last game.

"You busted your butts and gave the game your all. You were all there for your teammates through thick and thin. I can't tell you how proud I am to have been your coach." He began choking up and took a deep, steadying breath. He clapped his hands together twice, breaking the spell. "Now let's go kick some Stingray ass!"

•   •   •

As it happened, the Stingrays kicked the Panthers' ass 4–1, but not for lack of trying on the Panthers' part. Everyone played his heart out, and despite the increasing gap in the score as the game wore on, team morale was good. The boys knew they'd worked hard all year, and Paul could see they genuinely believed he was proud of them.

"You guys were awesome out there," Paul commended as they straggled back into the locker room, sweaty and exhausted.

"We blew," muttered Gary Flaherty.

"No, you didn't. You guys really hustled. Someone has to lose, and unfortunately, today it was us. Here, maybe this will cheer you up." He reached into a large cardboard box on the floor behind him and began pulling out New York Blades jerseys, tossing one to each of them. An appreciative murmur rose up in the locker room as each boy tore off his Panthers jersey, donning the pro jersey instead.

"What do you guys think?"

"Awesome!"

"Cool!"

"I'm never taking mine off!"

Paul chuckled. They looked like a pack of ragamuffins, the sleeves of the jerseys falling far beneath their fingertips, the hem brushing their knees. He'd toyed with the idea of getting them child-size jerseys, but these kids sprouted up so fast they'd likely outgrow them in a year. "I know they're kind of big on you right now, but you'll fill them out sooner than you think, believe me."

"Coach?" Tuck's voice was tentative.

"Yeah?"

"I know that, um, you were really bummed when you couldn't play hockey anymore and stuff, but we're all glad you wound up back here, you know?"

The boys nodded. Paul felt his eyes burning.

"Me, too," he said.

Six weeks later, Paul strolled into the Penalty Box on a busy Saturday night and got the shock of his life: There, sitting at the end of the bar nursing a Coke and reading the latest issue of *X-Men*, was Tuck.

Paul's gaze shot to Frank, whose shrug said "Don't ask me." The place was packed with hockey fans watching a playoff between Philly and Dallas on the big-screen TV.

Paul went to his office and tossed his denim jacket over the arm of the couch before returning to the bar to look for Mina. She was busy taking orders from a pack of paunchy middle-aged men in hockey jerseys. Two were staring at her chest, the other three ogling her ass. Offensive as it was, Paul knew she'd get big tips from them.

"I need to talk to you a minute," Paul said when Mina approached the bar to place her order with Frank.

"Talk away."

"Not here. In private. In my office."

Mina clucked her tongue. "Boss, in case you haven't noticed, it's a little crowded tonight."

"In my office. Two minutes. I mean it."

Paul returned to his office, gorge rising. First he'd deal with Mina, then he'd deal with Tuck. The office was more of a sty than ever, with bar and restaurant supplies now vying for space with the promo items. But he had no choice; the basement was tiny and though he was ashamed to admit it, he still hadn't moved some of Cuffy's stuff out of there. As a result, the staff were forced to hustle in and out of his office.

Waiting for Mina, he poured himself a glass of water

from the cooler and threw three aspirin down his throat to ward off the encroaching tension behind his eyes.

Mina stuck her head around the door. "What's up?"

"Come in. Close the door behind you."

"Ooh, serious." Mina did as she was told, standing with a smirk on her face and hands on her hips in a posture of complete inconvenience that was the final straw.

"This *is* serious. You're fired."

That wiped the smirk off Mina's face. "But—why?"

"Why?" Paul echoed incredulously. "You're never on time. You call in sick at least once every two weeks. And now you've brought Tuck with you to work!"

"He's not in the way."

"It's a bar, Mina. Kids don't belong in bars! What part of that don't you get?"

"What the fuck was I supposed to do?" Mina yelled. "I couldn't find a sitter."

"Bullshit. You—"

The door flew open, revealing another waitress, Daphne, looking mortified at having interrupted. "I, um, Frank needs some swizzle sticks."

"Swizzle sticks," Paul muttered to himself, glancing at the wall of unmarked boxes to his left.

"Top left," Daphne offered helpfully.

"Right," Paul muttered. He reached for the box and handed it to her. "Close the door behind you, will you, please, Daph?"

"Sure, boss." She gave Mina a sympathetic look on her way out the door.

Paul turned back to Mina. "Now, where were we? Oh, yeah, you were claiming you couldn't find a sitter for Tuck. What about Katie?"

"She does have a life, you know," Mina snapped.

"Your mother?"

"I don't like him hanging out over there. She feeds him too much."

At least the kid's getting some nutrition, Paul thought.

"Look," Mina huffed, panic rising in her eyes as she folded her arms across her chest, "I fucked up, all right? I'm sorry. I won't bring my kid here again. I swear."

"No, you won't. Because you're fired."

"Boss." Mina's bravado was gone, replaced by a voice shaky with desperation. "I said I'm sorry. I promise I won't be late anymore. I really, really need this job."

"I'm sorry, Mina, but that's not my problem. You're a good waitress—when you bother showing up. I'm sure you'll be able to find something else."

Paul hated being such a hard-ass, but he had no choice. If she wasn't Katie's sister, he would have given her her walking papers long before now. It wasn't fair to the rest of the staff to keep cutting her slack. She needed to learn that actions had consequences.

To his surprise—and horror—Mina began weeping. "Can I at least finish out tonight? I could use the tips."

"Of course," said Paul. He pulled a tissue from the box on the edge of his desk and handed it to her. "Stay in here as long as you like to get yourself together."

Mina turned on him. "I can't believe you're doing this! You're such a prick!"

"Right. I'm a prick." Paul pushed past her. If he stayed one more minute things would really get ugly. "I'm taking your son over to your mother's house."

A zombie. That's what Katie felt like sprawled on the couch, watching TV with her mom. She was so close to finishing her book she could taste it. It was the first thing she thought of when she woke in the morning, and the last thing to go through her mind before she closed her eyes at night. She'd spent hours working on it today, writing, revising, changing words, shifting paragraphs, reading aloud to herself to see if the writing flowed. She felt like she'd run a marathon.

The doorbell rang, startling her to full consciousness.

"Who on earth could that be?" her mother wondered aloud.

"Probably someone selling Girl Scout cookies to torment me," Katie replied grumpily. She hauled herself up off the couch and plodded over to the door. She was unprepared for the sight of Tuck and Paul standing together on the doorstep.

"Hi, Aunt Katie," Tuck said almost sheepishly, breezing right past her to join his grandmother in the living room. Katie looked questioningly at Paul.

"What's going on?" she asked in a low voice.

"Mina brought him to the bar," Paul replied quietly.

"Why didn't she call me?" Katie hissed. "I would have watched him."

"That's something you need to discuss with her."

"Paul?" Katie's mother joined them at the door. "Come in, come in, please."

Paul hesitated, then stepped over the threshold.

"Have you eaten?" Katie asked Tuck.

"I had some peanuts at the bar," Tuck said happily.

"You want a hamburger, sweetheart?" Katie's mother cooed. "I'll make you one of my jumbo bacon burgers."

"Yes!" Tuck punched his fist in the air triumphantly, following his grandmother into the kitchen.

Katie looked to Paul. "I'm so sorry about this."

"It's not your fault." He sounded discouraged.

"What's up?" Katie asked. She and Paul may not have gone out for all that long, but she still felt she knew this man. She knew when he was troubled, and she knew when he was in pain. Tonight he was both.

Paul was staring at her mother's doll-packed curio cabinet. "Look, I don't know how to say this."

"Then I'll say it for you," Katie said softly. "You fired her."

"Yeah." Paul looked grateful she'd taken the words out of his mouth. "I'm really, really sorry, Professor, but—"

"Hey." Katie tugged on the sleeve of his shirt. "You don't need to apologize. You were more than generous giving her a job in the first place. It was up to her to make a go of it."

Paul glanced uneasily in the direction of the kitchen. "I know, but I worry about Tuck."

"You did the right thing bringing him here, Paul."

Paul frowned. "I don't think your sister was very happy."

"She never is."

"I promise I'll give her a good reference if she needs one. She's a good waitress, she just . . ." He shook his head, looking for the right words. ". . . seems resentful that she has to *work*, if that makes any sense."

"It does. Mina has always thought the world owed her something. Why, I'm not sure."

"I hope your mother doesn't hate me for this," Paul said. He laughed glumly. "I also hope Cobra doesn't come and break both my arms."

"Snake," Katie corrected. "I wouldn't worry about him. He's a pretty decent guy. Sometimes I like him better than Mina."

They shared a bittersweet moment of laughter before awkward silence descended. It dawned on Katie that she'd taken his ubiquitousness for granted. In just a few months, she'd be back in Fallowfield, where every little thing Paul van Dorn said and did wasn't written in the paper or dissected over burnt coffee at Tabitha's. She would miss him. He'd become part of the fabric of her life.

"I guess I should get going," said Paul.

"You sure you don't want something to eat?" Katie offered. "If I know my mother, she'll be making enough burgers to feed an army."

"I should really get back to the bar, keep an eye on things." He smiled sadly. "Sorry again about your sister."

"Again, you have nothing to be sorry for."

"See you, Tuck!" Paul shouted so they'd hear him in the kitchen. "See you, Mrs. Fisher!"

"Bye, Paul," both Tuck and his grandmother called.

Paul leaned over and kissed Katie on the cheek, a move both unexpected and thrilling. A fraternal kiss, nothing that could be misconstrued.

"Drive safely," Katie told him as he walked out to his car.

"Will do," he called back.

Katie stood watching in the doorway as he backed out of her driveway at lightning speed. Then he was gone, leaving her to brood over the mess both she and her sister seemed to have made of things.

Restless, Paul decided not to head back to the bar right away, but to cruise around Didsbury and try to clear his head.

Firing Mina had left him rattled. *Was* he being a prick, depriving a single mother of an income? Katie didn't think so. Truth was, he was relieved to be rid of Mina. Her attitude and unreliability blew him away. If he'd ever talked to any of his coaches the way Mina had talked to him, his hockey career would have been even shorter than it had been.

He wasn't driving anywhere in particular, just driving. But every road held a memory—one of the hazards, he supposed, of returning to the town you grew up in. He pulled up in front of his own house, cutting the headlights but keeping the engine running. What, if anything, did the outside of the house convey about the man who lived inside? Nothing. It was completely nondescript, devoid of any personality. He kept staring, trying to picture himself in it five, ten, thirty years from now. Tried picturing himself living here with a wife and family. He couldn't. Shit, he couldn't even picture himself here with a dog. He couldn't see himself here in the future, and he didn't really see himself here now.

He switched the headlights on again and drove back to Main Street, following the old trolley tracks that still ran down the center of the road. Saturday night and the only place hopping was the Penalty Box. He parked behind the bar and killed the engine, trying to imagine himself growing old in this town. He'd turn into Dan Doherty.

Ambling back into the Penalty Box, he stopped to say hi to the regulars before taking his usual seat at the end of the bar, the same one that had been occupied by Tuck earlier. Mina had pulled herself back together and was hustling back and forth delivering drinks, but that didn't stop her from flashing him a dirty look. Paul ignored it. He opened his mouth to tell Frank to pour him a Boddington's, but his bartender was one step ahead of him, plunking a beer down in front of him before moving away to tend to another customer. Paul stared uneasily at the dark brown draught before lifting it to his lips.

Was he that predictable?

The middle-aged men who earlier in the evening had been ogling Mina approached him, wanting autographs and NHL war stories. Paul obliged, but even while he was speaking there was another conversation going on in his head: What if the fans stopped coming? Would he still want to be here, night after night, if there were no autographs to sign, no glory days to talk about? Would he really be happy being "just" a bar owner who coached youth hockey on the side?

"Gentlemen, can you excuse me a moment?" Paul slid off his bar stool, clutching his beer. "I just remembered something I need to take care of."

The men were gracious, clearing a path so he could depart. No need for them to know what needed taking care of was his mental health. He had to get out of the bar. Now. He felt the way he did when he realized he'd never play pro hockey again: boxed-in, panicky, in need of escape.

He ducked into the back office, quietly closing the door behind him. He remained there, eyes closed, trying to get his inner bearings. He was ravenously hungry. He'd leave, grab a bite to eat, go home, think.

Grateful for something to do, he swiped his denim jacket from where he'd tossed it on the couch earlier in the evening and put it on. It felt strangely light. He looked down: the left front pocket was empty. His wallet was gone.

CHAPTER
24

"My sister didn't steal your wallet."

Katie's words were clipped as she glared at Paul over her iced tea. She didn't know what to make of it when her cell phone rang in the middle of the afternoon and it was Paul, asking her to meet him at Tabitha's. Her heart had swooned a bit—maybe another session of no-strings-attached sex?— before shifting into anxiety mode. Though she hated the interruption to her writing schedule, she agreed to meet him and hustled over from the library, only to be confronted with this.

Paul brooded over his coffee. "I'm telling you, Katie. I left Mina alone in my office when I took Tuck to your mom's. When I got back, the wallet was gone. Frank says no one went in the office between the time I left the bar and the time I came back."

"Are you sure you brought your wallet with you? Maybe you left it another coat."

"I've torn my house apart. I've torn my car apart. I've torn the bar apart. I'm a conscientious guy. I *know* I walked into the Penalty Box with my wallet last night."

"How?"

"Because I remember stopping at the ATM to withdraw five hundred dollars and putting it in my wallet before going to the bar."

Katie crinkled her nose. "What did you need five hundred dollars for?"

"I withdraw five hundred dollars every week."

"For what? I couldn't spend five hundred dollars a week here if I tried."

"We're getting off the subject. I'm sure your sister took my wallet."

"Did you confront her?" Katie asked angrily.

"Not directly."

"What does that mean?"

"At the end of the night I assembled the whole staff and told them I couldn't find my wallet. I asked that if any of them found it to please return it to me, and there would be no questions asked."

"And?"

"What do you think? No one came forward."

"It's been less than twenty-four hours. For all you know, you could go to the bar tonight and it could be sitting there on a table. Or one of your employees could stop by your house today and pop it in the mailbox. Just because no one came forward doesn't mean someone is guilty, especially my sister."

Paul's hand reached across the table. "I know this is hard for you."

"Damn right it's hard for me," Katie replied, gently removing her hand from under his. "Mina's messed up but she would never do that, Paul. Believe me. She's not that stupid."

"She was stupid enough to invite her biker friends to the bar and to bring Tuck to work with her! She's stupid enough to get herself fired. How do you know she didn't take my wallet as a way of saying 'Fuck you' for letting her go?"

"She's not that dumb," Katie repeated staunchly.

"That's what you want to believe."

"I don't understand what all this has to do with me." Katie didn't want to deal with this. All she wanted was to finish her book, go back to Fallowfield, and resume her life.

"I need you to talk to her, Katie. The wallet's got all my credit cards in it, as well as some stuff of great sentimental value. Ask her if she has it. Tell her she won't get in trouble if she does. She can even keep the goddamn money if she wants, I don't care."

"What am I supposed to say? 'Mina, did you steal Paul's wallet? You're his prime suspect because you're such a skank.' "

"She's the prime suspect because she's the only one who had access to it," Paul countered tersely.

"*And* because you think she's a thieving ex-addict."

Paul began kneading the back of his neck. "Katie, I know your sister took the wallet, okay? Now are you going to help me or not?"

Katie rose, throwing two dollars down on the table to cover her tab. "No, I'm not. My sister didn't take that wallet. If you want to accuse her of theft, you're going to have to do it yourself."

Katie's conversation with Paul ruined her concentration for the rest of the day. Leaving Tabitha's, she'd headed back to the library, intent on burying herself in work. Unfortunately, her brain refused to cooperate. She'd write a sentence, then drift off into the stratosphere, imagining a confrontation with Mina. Write another sentence, and imagine Paul showing up at her mother's front door, begging forgiveness after finding his wallet under a pile of junk in his office. When it became clear she wasn't going to get any writing done, she came home, helped her mother start dinner, and then went out for a run to clear her mind. She could always work for a few hours after supper if she needed to.

Did you do it, Mina? Did you?

The thought hounded Katie as she wrapped up her evening run. She truly believed her sister wouldn't be that obvious or that dumb, but you never knew. And Paul! She couldn't believe he wanted *her* to go to her sister to get the wallet back—not that Mina took it. Katie found it hard to believe that Frank could tend bar on a busy Saturday night *and* keep track of whomever might be going in and out of Paul's office. No way. Mina was being blamed because of her past. It wasn't fair.

Calmer now, she jogged back to her mother's house intending to shower before sitting down to dinner. Her mother was parked in her usual spot on the couch, face buried in the paper as she waited for dinner to be done.

"Hi, Mom." Katie was breathing hard as she moved past her toward the kitchen.

"You don't smell very good," her mother observed.

"Neither do you," Katie teased, mopping dripping sweat from her brow.

Her mother's eyes peeked at her over the top of the paper. "You watch it, girlie."

Katie smiled, hearing the affection in her mom's voice. She was in the middle of pouring herself a tall glass of water when the phone rang.

"Want me to get that?" she yelled. She was always very

respectful of being a guest in her mother's house, not automatically picking the phone up without checking first. "Yes, please," her mother called back.

Katie wiped her sweaty palms off on her shorts, then picked up the phone.

"Katie? It's Snake." He sounded upset.

"Snake," Katie replied. "What's up?"

"I thought you and your mom should know that, uh, an ambulance just took Mina to the hospital."

Katie squeezed her eyes shut.

"It looks like she OD'ed or something."

"Tuck?" That's all Katie could manage. Any more and she'd start screaming.

Snake blew out a long, long breath. "Poor little fucker's the one who found her. I was in the shower."

"I'll be right there."

"Hold up, hold up. I can run him over there on my bike if you want."

"No!" Katie pressed her burning forehead to the wall. "I mean, thank you, but I think it would be better if I came to get him. Tell him to sit tight, okay? I'll be there as soon as I can."

"You want me to put together an overnight bag for him?" Snake offered.

"That would be great," Katie managed. "Thankyouforcalling," she blurted in a rush, hanging up the phone.

"Who was on the phone, dear?" her mother asked as she entered the kitchen.

"Snake," Katie replied faintly. "I have to run over and get Tuck. Mina's not feeling well." If she told her mother what happened, she'd want to come with her and it would be a circus. Better to wait until she had a clearer picture of the situation. How could Mina put her mother through this again? And Tuck . . .

"I'll be back soon, Mom," Katie promised, grabbing her car keys from their usual spot on the sideboard in the living room.

"Don't you want to shower first?" her mother called after her as she bolted out the front door. "You're awfully sweaty."

"Tuck's not going to care, Mom." *Believe me.*

Katie arrived to find the door to the apartment unlocked. Snake was sitting on the ratty couch. He rose anxiously as she entered.

"I got here as soon as I could," said Katie.

Snake looked grim. "I appreciate that."

"Where's Tuck?"

"In his room. Doesn't want to come out."

"Do you have any idea what happened?"

"Like I said, I was in the shower. Tuck came running in and said he'd found Mina passed out here in the living room, and couldn't wake her up." Snake grimaced. "I jumped out of the shower and tried to slap her awake but it was no go, so I called the paramedics. She was looking kinda blue by the time they got here."

Katie gasped as if punched. That's what it felt like, actually. As if someone had landed a solid blow to her gut, the shock of it stealing her breath away.

"Were you—was she—doing drugs again? Drinking?"

Snake's eyes flashed with resentment. "I'm clean as a whistle. Your sister . . ." He glanced away.

"What?" Katie pressed sharply.

"A few times I thought I smelled booze on her breath, but she denied it. As for the drugs, I don't know, but I kinda think yes. You'd have to drink a helluva lot to pass out cold like that. I think she must have combined stuff."

"How could she afford it?" Katie wondered out loud.

"Yeah, that was something else I wanted to talk to you about. I found this in our bedroom." He handed Katie a worn black leather wallet. "Belongs to your boyfriend," Snake said. "She must have lifted it at work."

Katie stared down at the wallet in her hand. If Mina was there right now, she'd strike her. She would. She'd rain blows down upon her screaming, *Why! Why! Why! Why can't you get your act together, why?* She felt humiliated for defending her sister to Paul. She opened up the wallet. The five hundred dollars Paul said he'd withdrawn from the bank was gone. Katie closed the wallet.

"There's no money," she said quietly.

"Look, if you don't mind, I'm gonna shoot down to the hospital and see what's going on," said Snake. He looked almost shy as he lifted a small green backpack up off the floor. "For Mina," he explained. "I thought she might need a nightie, some toothpaste, you know . . ."

Katie stifled tears. "I'm really glad she has you."

"Yeah, I'm a pretty awesome dude," Snake agreed dryly. "C'mere." He grabbed Katie into a big bear hug. "Everything's gonna be fine, big sister. Don't you worry."

"I wish I had your optimism, Snake."

He released her from their embrace. "Worry about the shit you can control, and let the big guy upstairs take care of the rest. That's my motto." He swung the backpack up onto his massive shoulder. "See you at the hospital."

"Tuck?"

Katie knew she sounded tentative as she poked her head in the door of her nephew's bedroom. She couldn't imagine what he was thinking or feeling. Tuck was sitting in front of his computer at a small card table set up across the room. He appeared not to hear her, though Katie was pretty sure he had. She crept closer, listening to the sound of rapid gunfire coming from the computer.

"What are you playing?" she asked loudly.

"Grand Theft Auto," Tuck replied, his eyes never wavering from the screen.

How the hell had he gotten hold of that? Merchants weren't supposed to sell it to kids because it was excessively violent. Mina must have bought it for him. A fresh wave of resentment washed over Katie. "Honey, shut down the computer. We're going to Nana's."

Tuck ignored her.

"Tuck?"

"Let me just finish."

"No. Turn off the computer now."

Muttering under his breath, Tuck did what he was told. Katie put a hand on his shoulder and he knocked it off angrily.

"Honey, I know how upset you must be right now."

"No, you don't," Tuck snapped.

Katie swallowed. "You're right. I don't."

It was the right thing to say. Tuck's eyes began watering. "I hate her!"

Let him rage, Katie told herself. If anyone had a right to, it was him.

"I hope she dies!"

Katie remained silent and moved to his bed where a small suitcase sat packed. Katie peeked inside. Snake had done a good job: there was underwear, socks, pajamas, and at least a week's worth of clothing. Katie closed the suitcase.

"Want me to unhook the computer?" she offered gently. "We can bring it back with us to Nana's."

"If Mom dies, can I live with you?" Tuck pleaded.

"She's not going to die, Tuck."

Tuck looked surly. "You're not a doctor."

"You're right again," Katie conceded. "But I'd like to think she won't."

"Well, I don't care if she does."

Katie glanced around the room. "Is there anything else you want to take besides your computer?"

Tuck just looked at the floor.

"We can come back tomorrow for the rest of your stuff if you want," Katie continued.

"I never want to come back here again."

"Then you don't have to. I'll come back and get your things. How's that?"

"Good." He kicked at the floor before looking up at Katie. "Can we leave now?"

Paul entered the Penalty Box hoping to find his wallet lying on a table just as Katie predicted. Instead he found Frank wiping down the bar with a frown plastered across his puss.

"What's up with you?"

"Not only did she take your wallet, but I think she absconded with a bottle of Jack," said Frank.

Paul hadn't said anything to Frank about suspecting Mina, but he could tell Frank knew what he was thinking when he'd gathered the staff and told them his wallet was missing.

"Yeah?"

"Yeah. I was doing an inventory check before you got here. We're short one bottle of Jack."

"Great."

"No luck with the wallet?"

Paul frowned. "I called all the credit card companies just in case."

"Pain in the ass."

"No shit. I'm going to have to replace my driver's license, my Social Security card . . ." Paul shook his head despondently. "There were pictures in there, too. Stuff I can't replace.".

"It sucks." Frank pulled a bottle of Evian out from under the bar and tossed it to Paul. "I'm glad you fired her, though."

"Are you? She was a good waitress."

"She was a friggin' thief. We never came up short until she started working here."

Paul glanced around the bar. Pretty soon the place would start filling up. "I called Randi to work tonight. She's not as good as Mina, but she'll do until we hire someone else." He turned back to his friend. "I can help out, too."

Frank chortled. "I'd pay good money to see you serving drinks."

"I'm not above hard work," Paul replied defensively.

Frank looked thoughtful. "Actually, the customers will probably love it."

"You're probably right."

Both turned upon hearing the bar door open. Paul could barely contain his surprise when he saw it was Katie walking toward him. She'd looked tired earlier in the day when he'd seen her at Tabitha's. Now she looked downright haggard. Her eyes were red rimmed and puffy.

"Hey," Paul said gently as he approached her. "What brings you here?"

"What do you think?" Katie was having difficulty meeting his eye.

"Frank?" Paul called. "Katie and I have something we need to talk about in the back. If anyone calls, can you take it?"

"Sure thing."

Paul wished Frank's gaze didn't convey quite so much pity as he watched them head toward the back of the Penalty Box. Paul knew Katie: She'd suspect they had been talking about her sister and it would make her furious, though right now, Paul couldn't imagine her mustering up that much emotion. She looked completely drained, walking like a woman in a trance.

He guided her into the office where they had once made love, and closed the door. It had barely swung shut before Katie reached into her book bag and pulled out his wallet.

"Here," she said quietly, handing it to him. "I owe you an apology. Don't bother to look inside. The money's gone. Everything else seems intact."

"Katie, sit down." Paul put the wallet in his back pocket and steered her toward the couch, surprised when she offered no resistance.

"What happened?" he asked, sitting beside her. "You obviously talked to her."

"Actually, I didn't." Katie's voice was bitter. "Snake called me. Mina's in the hospital. She overdosed on something. They took her away in an ambulance."

"Holy shit." Paul searched Katie's face. "Are you okay? How's Tuck?"

"Tuck is a very angry little boy, and I don't blame him. She's done nothing but make a big fat mess of his life." Katie looked away. "I'm sorry." Her voice cracked. "I haven't had a very good day."

"I can imagine." Paul touched her cheek. "Anything I can do?"

"Make my sister better?" She covered her face with her hands. "I'm sorry," she apologized again as she began crying.

"No need to apologize." He drew her into his arms. "Let it out, Katie. It's okay."

"How could she do this?" Katie sobbed. "Doesn't she realize what it does to Tuck? She could lose him—not that she
cares! You were right all along: she's a fuck-up. I'm sorry I
asked you to give her a job."

"You didn't," Paul reminded her. "I offered. Remember?"

Katie lifted her head, wiping her running nose on the
back of her sleeve. "You only offered because she was my
sister. If it was anyone else with her history, you never
would have hired her."

"We needed the help. And I wanted to show you what a
great guy I was."

Katie's eyes began watering anew. "Me and my family . . . I bet from now on you'll run far and fast whenever
you see one of *us* coming."

"Never." Paul gently urged her head down to rest on his
shoulder. It felt wonderful holding her in his arms again,
though he wished the circumstances were different. Still, he
was glad to be of help, even if the gesture was simple as offering comfort. "Everything's going to be fine."

Katie lifted her head. "Do you know I hate when people
say that? Snake said the same thing and I thought, 'You
don't *know* that.'"

"We're just trying to be helpful."

"I know that," Katie said quickly. Paul got the sense she
was afraid he'd think she was being critical. "It's just such a
platitude."

"There you go throwing around those big SAT words
again." He squinted hard. "I thought a platitude was some
type of marine animal."

"Very funny. I know you're an ass, but you're not an
idiot."

"God, I love when you say nice things to me."

He watched her expression slowly change as it dawned

on her that he was holding her in his arms, the two of them playfully teasing one another just like old times. She looked embarrassed. "I've bothered you long enough," said Katie, standing up.

"You weren't bothering me at all."

"I should have stopped by the ATM," she continued, more to herself than to him. "I'll bring down five hundred dollars for you tomorrow. Is that okay?"

"You do *not* need to replace the money your sister stole."

"It's the right thing to do," Katie insisted.

"Let it go, Katie. It's not your responsibility."

Katie shrugged and edged toward the door. "I should get going."

"Are you okay to drive?"

"I'm fine," she assured him. "Honestly."

"If you need any help with Tuck, just let me know."

Katie swallowed. "Thank you."

"It's not a problem." Paul moved to open the door, if only to give himself something to do. He longed to take her back into her arms and hold her until she *believed* that everything was going to be all right. He hated seeing her in pain. If there was anything positive in this situation at all, it was that Tuck was back under his grandmother's roof. That, and the knowledge of how strong Katie was. She'd bounce back from this. They all would.

"I'll talk to you soon," Katie murmured. She walked through the door then stopped abruptly, turning around.

"Paul?"

"Mmm?"

"You—you really are a great guy," she said haltingly. But before he could reply, she was already walking away.

CHAPTER 25

How many times would Mina screw up before the family stopped picking up the pieces for her? *But isn't that what families are supposed to do—be there for one another?* Katie wondered. When did compassion and concern cross the line from helping to enabling? Katie's mother was beside herself with fear and worry. She refused to accept Mina had relapsed, claiming her younger daughter had "been lured into temptation by that caveman on a motor scooter."

It was Katie alone who dealt with the doctors and social worker. She made it clear that Child Protective Services did *not* need to place Tuck in foster care, since he had a home with his grandmother. She stressed it repeatedly, worried it wouldn't sink in. The social worker looked annoyed, but Katie didn't care. She'd heard too many stories of kids being shunted off to strangers when in fact there *were* family members willing and able to take care of them. Tuck was *not* going to be a casualty of the system.

Mina had OD'ed on a combo of alcohol and painkillers. She'd had her stomach pumped and had come frighteningly close to dying. When the doctor asked Katie whether she thought the overdose could have been a suicide attempt, it felt as though the floor was giving way. Such a notion never occurred to her. She herself had dealt with depression and despair, but she had never, *never* contemplated suicide. That Mina might have deliberately harmed herself . . .

Katie visited the hospital, and found Mina in her room, in the bed closest to the window, an IV spiked in the vein of her wiry right arm. She looked pale and weak, her dark hair matted with sweat as she lay propped up against a wall of pillows, drowsing in and out of sleep. Hearing Katie enter, Mina's eyes fluttered open. But when she saw who it was, she turned her head away.

"Hey," Katie said gently. She pulled the one chair in the room close to Mina's bedside. "How are you feeling?"

"Better." Mina's face remained averted. "You must hate me."

"I don't hate you. I just want to understand what happened."

"I fucked up," said Mina bitterly.

"Were you trying to kill yourself?"

Mina slowly turned her head back to Katie. "No. How could you even think that?"

"The doctors asked me. I didn't know what to say."

Mina sighed. "Yeah, they asked me, too. I told them that if I'd wanted to check out I would have blown my brains out. Something quick, you know? None of this namby-pamby trying to slip into a coma bullshit."

Katie blinked. Did her sister think she was being witty? "You could have died, Mina. They told you that, right?"

Mina mumbled something unintelligible.

"Don't you give a damn?" Katie asked, voice rising.

"Of course I do. But I didn't, so let's not talk about it anymore, okay?"

Katie shook her head vehemently. "Oh, no, we're talking about this, whether you like it or not. You owe me an explanation. Me and everyone else—especially Tuck."

Mina seemed to shrink against the pillows. "I told you: I fucked up."

"How long have you been fucking up?"

Mina's legs fidgeted beneath the flimsy white hospital blanket. "I've been drinking since I got out of rehab," she quietly informed the ceiling.

"Why?"

Mina looked at her like she was an idiot. "Because I'm an addict, Katie. That's what we do."

"But *why*, when you'd just gone through rehab? I thought you were trying to build a new life for you and Tuck?"

"Because I'm weak," she whispered. "I just wanted the pain to end."

"What pain?"

"The pain of everything: messing things up with Tuck, messing up my whole fucking life—even Dad's death. You know, I once had a counselor tell me that the reason I was so promiscuous, especially with older men, was because I was looking for the male attention that disappeared when Dad died."

"Tuck found you passed out. Did you know that?"

"Snake told me." Mina's eyes shone with remorse. "I never meant for that to happen."

"Obviously."

Mina's gaze drifted out the window. Katie knew it wasn't the scenery drawing her attention, since the room looked out on an intricate series of heating ducts. She couldn't look at Katie. "Tuck hates me, doesn't he?"

"Right now, yes."

"I don't blame him," Mina said forlornly. "I hate myself."

Katie was glad her sister couldn't see the look of disgust on her face. She'd heard it all before: I'm weak, I fucked up, I hate myself—the addict's litany of self-loathing and re-crimination, designed to illicit sympathy from the listener. The problem was, it usually worked. But not this time. If it took every ounce of strength Katie had, she was determined to harden her heart against her sister for her sister's own sake.

"You need a new spiel, Mina," Katie said. "This one's getting old."

"Fuck you."

Katie's chair scraped against the floor as she stood up. "I'm going to go."

"Don't!" Mina begged, whipping her head around to look at Katie. "I didn't mean to be a bitch! Honest. Please stay, Katie. Please."

Katie sat back down. "Why did you take Paul's wallet?"

"I was angry he fired me," Mina admitted sheepishly. "I wanted to punish him."

"He could press charges. You realize that, right?"

Mina looked queasy.

"But he's not going to. Because he's a nice guy."

"I guess if I ever see him again, I should apologize."

"That might be nice. You can apologize to me, too, while you're at it. Paul came to me and told me you took his wallet. Know what I did? I defended you. I told him he was ac-cusing you because of your past and that you would never do that."

Mina's eyes began filling with tears. "I'm so sorry, Katie. Really."

"I have to tell you, Mina: I love you, but right now I don't like you."

"I need help, Katie."

Katie snorted. "Ya think?"

"No, listen to me," Mina snuffled. "I need help with Tuck."

"Go on," Katie said guardedly.

Mina pushed herself up so she was sitting fully. "I was talking to Snake this morning, and he was telling me about the rehab facility he went to, up in Massachusetts. It's a yearlong, residential program." She grabbed a handful of blanket, nervously bunching it up in her hand. "Snake said he'd help me pay for it."

"That's great."

"I was wondering: Would you be willing to take Tuck for the year?" Mina began talking quickly. "He adores you, Katie, and he's really upset you're going back to Vermont. I know Mom can put a roof over his head and all that, but she doesn't relate to him the way you do. Please?"

This was not what Katie had expected to hear.

"Katie?" Mina said hopefully. "Please?"

Katie was stunned. "I'll need to think about this."

"Of course." Mina grabbed a tissue from the nightstand and blew her nose. "I would feel so much better knowing he's with you, Katie. Seriously."

Katie barely heard as her mind went into overdrive. What would she have to do legally? Assume custody? Or could she just take Tuck with her? She'd have to arrange to have his school records sent. That was no big deal. Which bedroom would she give him? What about hockey? Were there youth hockey teams in Vermont? There had to be. Her academic schedule was pretty flexible. That was good. What—

"Katie?"

"I'm sorry. I was just thinking."

Mina looked apologetic. "It's a lot to think about, I know."

Reality decided to make a cameo appearance. "What if

he doesn't want to come with me, Mina? He's got friends here. He's very involved in hockey."

Mina looked disappointed. "Then I guess he'll stay with Mom."

"Have you talked to Mom about this?"

Mina nodded shyly. "She said it would be Tuck's decision. That of course he could live with her again if that's what he chose. She loves him"—Mina began choking up—"and she would love to have him." She covered her face with her hands. "I'm so ashamed, Katie, I ruin everyone's lives—"

"Stop it," Katie commanded. "If you're that ashamed, *do* something about it." She rose, leaning over to kiss her sister on the forehead. "Let me think about all this and get back to you, okay?"

"Where are you going?" Mina called after her as Katie started out of the room.

"Where do you think?" Katie replied. "To talk to Tuck."

Old habits die hard, or at the very least, are likely to resurface in times of stress. Leaving the hospital, Katie proceeded directly to Tabitha's, where she ordered a slice of pound cake and a cup of coffee into which she poured three heaping teaspoons of sugar. Her emotions were so jumbled she didn't even care. What was an extra pound on the scale compared with the ramifications of bringing Tuck back to Fallowfield with her?

Her mother was waiting for her at home. The two of them sat at the kitchen table talking about Mina, Tuck, and money. Katie's mom had agreed to contribute toward Mina's recovery program, believing her youngest daughter deserved another chance. Deep down, beneath the layers of anger and pain, so did Katie. She didn't want to believe her sister was a hopeless case. Both agreed the decision of who to live with should be Tuck's. There were pros and cons to his living in either place. Katie was grateful she felt no pressure from her mother. Through it all, Tuck remained upstairs on his computer.

Katie felt an awful sense of déjà vu as she climbed the steps to talk to him. How many times had she done the same thing, always with the same purpose: to discuss something serious. She knocked loudly so Tuck would hear her over the electronic din of exploding automobiles and gunfire.

"Yeah?" he called.

"It's Aunt Katie. Can I come in?"

"Yeah."

She was shocked by the bedroom's starkness. No books, no posters, no sports equipment. Most of Tuck's belongings were still at Snake's.

"What's up?" Katie asked.

Tuck shrugged.

"Look, I need to talk to you."

Wariness crept into Tuck's eyes.

"Your mom is going back into rehab."

"So?"

"This time it's a yearlong program."

"Big deal. I guess I'll be back here."

"If you want." Katie watched him carefully. "Or, you could come live with me."

Tuck affected nonchalance, his eyes remaining fixed on the computer. "Yeah?"

"Yeah. But you need to think about it. It would mean leaving your friends behind, and starting at a new school, and finding a new hockey team to play on."

Tuck's nonchalance evaporated. "I don't care!"

"Tuck, I really want you to think about this. It's a very big decision."

"You don't want me to come," Tuck accused.

"Honey, I do," Katie said tenderly, reaching out to smooth his hair, surprised when he let her. "I just don't want you to jump into a decision and then later regret it."

"I won't."

"Take a day to think it over. If you still feel the same way tomorrow, we'll start making arrangements to move you to Vermont with me. Okay?"

"Okay."

She patted his shoulder. "Go back to your mayhem."

Katie knew Tuck. Impatient as his mother, there was no way he'd wait a full twenty-four hours before making his decision. When he left the house later that afternoon, Katie knew he was walking around town, trying to imagine what it would be like not to be there. He said nothing of his foray during dinner, but later that night, when Katie was up in her room revising the final chapters of her book, he appeared in her doorway.

"Aunt Katie?"

"Mmm?"

"Can I ask you some questions?"

"Of course." She was glad of the break. Her eyes were starting to cross from all that reading and writing and rereading and rewriting.

"If I move to Vermont with you, can Gary come visit?"

"Of course."

"And we'll come back here and visit sometimes?"

"Don't I come back here to visit you and Nana?"

"Can we visit Coach van Dorn when we're here?"

Katie hesitated. "Of course." She hadn't thought of that, but if it was important to Tuck, she'd do it.

"Could I see Snake sometimes?"

Who would ever have thought Tuck would grow fond of Snake? "Of course, honey. You can see anyone you want."

"But I don't have to see Mom, right?"

"Not if you don't want to, no. But if you change your mind, then we'll figure it out."

Tuck nodded, mulling it all over. How small and serious he looked standing there, a little boy with the weight of the world on his shoulders. He looked at her shyly. "I want to live with you."

A lump began forming in Katie's throat. "You're sure?"

Tuck nodded.

"I'm glad," Katie told him, trying not to cry. "I think it will be great."

"Me, too." The serious look in Tuck's eyes was gone, replaced by an expression of sheer relief, even happiness. It was a look Katie had seen on his face all too rarely. The emotion of the moment seemed too much for Tuck as he backed out of the doorway. "I love you, Aunt Katie," he mumbled.

Katie let her tears fall. "I love you, too, honey," she whispered fiercely.

The rest of the spring and summer passed in a blur. Soon it was time for Katie and Tuck to return to Fallowfield so she could get him enrolled in school and prepare herself for re-immersion into academia. She was excited, not only about returning to her own home and the classroom, but about creating a life for herself and Tuck. She knew it would be hard at first, but Katie never shied from a challenge—except one.

She was touched when Paul called to ask her and Tuck to come down to the Penalty Box for lunch so he could say good-bye. As he'd promised, he'd kept in touch with Tuck once the school year ended, taking him out for the occasional ice cream or movie. Of all the people Tuck was leaving behind, Katie knew it was Paul he'd miss most.

"What do you think you'll have?" Katie asked Tuck as she locked up her car and they began walking toward Paul's bar. "The curly fries are awesome."

"Maybe a cheeseburger."

"Those are good, too."

She held open the Penalty Box door to allow Tuck inside first. The place was dark. Had she jotted down the wrong date?

"SURPRISE!" a chorus of voices rang out as the lights flicked on.

There stood Paul, her mother, Gary, Snake, Frank and Bitsy, and Denise beneath a banner that read GOOD LUCK, KATIE AND TUCK! WE'LL MISS YOU! Tuck looked up at Katie, awestruck. "Awesome!" he exclaimed, running over to join Gary. The two immediately took off to play table hockey. Astonished, Katie approached her family and friends.

"You had no idea, did you?" her mother crowed.

"None at all," Katie admitted. Her eyes traveled to Paul. "Was this your idea?"

Paul nodded. He tilted his head in Tuck's direction. "I wanted to make it special for him."

Katie shook her head in amazement. "You are something else."

"About time you realized it," he ribbed, his gaze holding hers. Katie forced her eyes away. He made her feel vulnerable and transparent, like he could read every thought in her head. She didn't want him to know she was remembering the first time their eyes met at the reunion and she'd been swamped with uninvited desire. Nor did she want him to know the memory of him moving inside her was imprinted in every cell of her body, causing her to flush anew. Yet she couldn't escape the feeling he *did* know. How else to explain the uncomfortable cough he gave to put end an end to the moment?

"Listen up, everyone!" Paul bellowed, even though there were only eleven people there. Katie smiled in amusement. He was acting like he was in a locker room addressing a gaggle of kids. "Drinks are on the house! The staff is in the kitchen, so order whatever you want for lunch! Just make sure you leave room for cake! I'm going to put some music on."

Katie watched him walk away, his confident swagger turning her on more than she cared to admit.

"He has a beautiful ass," Denise rhapsodized, sidling up on Katie's right. "Don't you miss it?"

"Sometimes," Katie admitted.

Bitsy sidled up on Katie's left. "He still loves you."

Katie ignored her.

Denise looked forlorn as she ordered a Diet Coke from Frank, who had happily assumed his rightful place behind the bar. "I can't believe you're really leaving. Fat Fighters won't be the same without you."

Katie was surprised to find herself getting choked up. Returning to Didsbury for her sabbatical year, she never imagined she'd make new friends. Yet here she was, saddened by the prospect of not hanging out at Tabitha's every week with Bitsy and Denise.

"You guys can always visit me, you know."

"You can visit us, too," Bitsy reminded her. "Unless you still find Didsbury too suffocating to ever return to."

"You know I don't feel that way anymore, Bits."

"Good," said Bitsy, looking relieved. "Now aren't you glad you went to the reunion last fall?"

The question stopped Katie in her tracks. She'd never really paused to think about the chain of events the reunion had set off. If she'd skipped it, she'd never have met Denise, who would have never introduced her to Bitsy at Fat Fight-ers. She never would have arrived at an appreciation of her past. And then there was Paul.

She glanced around the bar, looking for him. Predictable as ever, he stood watching Tuck and Gary play table hockey. He appeared to be coaching them.

"Can you guys excuse me?" she asked her friends. "I need to talk to Paul a minute."

She ignored the knowing look that passed between Bitsy and Denise. "Have fun," Denise trilled.

Walking over to Paul, Katie passed her mother on the way: She was talking to Snake about Mina. Katie was glad Paul invited Snake, whom she realized she now considered family.

Katie tapped her former lover on the shoulder. "Got a minute?"

Paul turned, smiling. "For you? Always."

They moved away from the table hockey game. "What's up?" Paul asked.

Katie gestured at the friends and family gathered. "I can't tell you how much this means to me. And Tuck. Look at him." They both eyed the boy, who was completely en-tranced with the game he was playing, a semi-delirious grin plastered to his face. "He's so happy."

"He deserves it." Paul seemed subdued. "I hear you're off tomorrow."

Katie nodded.

"All packed?"

"Of course I am. Remember who you're talking to here."

Paul chuckled. "I forgot how anal retentive you are."

"Nothing wrong with being organized," Katie insisted.

"Make sure you don't run down any more pedestrians, okay?"

"Hey, if someone *runs out in front of my car*, that's their problem, not mine."

Paul responded with the faintest of smiles. Katie could feel her defenses beginning to crack. The longer she stood here like this with him, teasing, flirting, reminiscing, the harder it would be to say good-bye—not just to him, but to everyone.

"I should mingle," said Katie.

"I guess it's your duty as guest of honor."

"Thank you again, Paul," Katie said, heartfelt. "For this, for everything."

"Not a problem. How about a friendly hug for old times' sake?"

"Of course." Katie stepped into the loose embrace of his arms.

"You'll keep in touch, right?" he murmured into her hair.

Katie swallowed. "You know we will." His eyes, his scent, the warmth of his hard body—it was too much. Katie broke contact.

"Take care of yourself, Paul."

Paul smiled sadly. "You, too, Professor."

CHAPTER

26

"This place is great."

Paul nodded, unsure how to react to Tom Corday's pronouncement as he showed him around the Penalty Box, explaining its inner workings. When they'd met at the wedding in Fallowfield earlier in the year, Paul assumed Katie's colleague was being polite when he said he'd like to come down to Didsbury and pick his brains. Yet here he was, hanging on Paul's every word as if owning a bar was the most exciting profession in the world.

"What type of promos do you do?" Tom asked.

Paul noticed his guest couldn't stop running his hand back and forth across the smooth oak of the bar as if stroking a beloved pet.

"Pretty much the usual," Paul answered. "On St. Patrick's Day we did the whole green beer thing, complete with an Irish sing-along. Since it's Halloween next week, we'll probably hold a contest for best costume. We also sponsored a local softball team this summer, which was fun."

Tom looked intrigued. "How does that benefit the bar?"

"They all come in here to drink after the game," Paul explained with a grin.

"Ah."

"You should really talk to my bartender, Frank DiNizio. He's the real heart and soul of the place. Been here for years."

Tom glanced longingly around the Penalty Box for the umpteenth time. "You must be so proud of this place. I'd love to own a bar like this."

Paul smiled, covering his discomfort. He'd bought the Penalty Box because it was a sound financial investment, and because he hadn't known what the hell to do with himself after retiring. Owning a bar seemed as good a choice as any. Tom's unabashed enthusiasm reminded him how little he'd thought things out after his career blew up; how desperate he was to do something—*anything*—with the void he perceived his life to be.

He gave Tom a clap on the back. "Who knows? Maybe some day you *will* own a bar like this."

"You selling?" Tom ribbed.

Paul chuckled. "If I do, you'll be the first to know, I promise."

"Well," Tom sighed, sliding off his bar stool, "I suppose I should head back. Fallowfield is a bit of a drive."

"How's Katie?" Paul asked casually. The question had been on the tip of his tongue all day. Bitsy said she was doing well, but Paul wanted confirmation from someone who saw her regularly.

"She's hanging in there," Tom said after a careful pause. "Seems a little stressed. I don't think she realized what she was getting herself into when she took custody of her nephew. He seems like a great kid, but she's got a very heavy academic schedule, so between that and taking care of him, she's on the go nonstop. But you know Katie; she prides herself on being able to juggle it all."

"Sounds like Katie, all right," Paul agreed. He could picture her bustling here and there, her book bag permanently slung over right shoulder. "Any idea when her book will be out?"

"Next May, I think. I'm not sure. She's very excited about that." Tom looked at him curiously. "You two aren't in touch?"

"Not really."

"Well, I won't pry," said Tom, jangling his keys in his pocket, "but for what it's worth, she did tell me to say hello to you when I saw you."

"Tell her I say hi, too. Tell her—"

He wanted to say more, but stopped.

Katie sat on her porch wrapped in a fleece blanket, hands gripping a steaming mug of sugar-free hot cocoa. Though the October nights had grown chilly, she still liked to come out here to unwind after Tuck went to bed, looking up at the stars or listening to the wind cut through the trees.

Arriving back in town two months ago, she'd had a hard time imagining herself and Tuck settling into a "normal" life, if such a thing existed. Yet here they were, their days busy yet relatively predictable, which was what Tuck needed: routine and stability. He'd had little problem making friends at his new school, and had joined a youth hockey team, proving himself one of the more skilled players.

He seemed well adjusted and happy, which was more than Katie could say for herself.

She enjoyed being back in the classroom, and it was nice to be able to buy a skim chai latte whenever she felt like it, or go see a foreign film, or listen to live music if the mood struck her. But she missed Didsbury. She missed her mother, with whom she'd formed an actual adult bond. She missed Bitsy and Denise. She spoke with both of them on the phone, but it wasn't the same. There was something about hanging out at Tabitha's, analyzing each other's problems and laughing themselves silly over a plain old cup of joe, that no phone call or email could replace.

And she missed Paul.

Sometimes she caught herself playing "What if."

What if she hadn't held him at arm's length? What if she had allowed herself to succumb to the unknown and see where it led? Would they still be together? Or would she be exactly where she was right now: busy but alone, wondering about the man she drove away because she was too afraid to color outside the lines?

She sighed, sipping her cocoa. She wondered if Paul was at the bar right now, entertaining patrons with salty tales of the NHL. She'd heard from Bitsy that he wasn't coaching youth hockey this year, which surprised her. She couldn't imagine him foregoing that kind of hands-on connection with the sport he loved so much. Maybe he was holding out for a coaching position with the AHL team in Hartford.

She closed her eyes a moment, conjuring his face in her mind as she sent her thoughts to him across the silent miles. *I'm sorry I made you feel bad about yourself and your decision to return to Didsbury. I hope you find happiness in whatever you do. If I had it to do all over again, I wouldn't have been so skittish, so scared, so—anal retentive! I would have taken the leap of faith.*

She wrapped her blanket tighter around her, imagining her words being carried to him on the wind. Silly, she knew. But she couldn't help it.

•　•　•

"*Your turn to* get the door."

Katie gave Tuck a frosty look even though she knew he was right. All night long the bell had been ringing as little ghouls and goblins collected their Halloween booty. Tuck and his friends had gone out trick-or-treating after school, wanting first dibs on whatever candy there was to be had. That was fine with Katie, who hadn't wanted him running around at night, possibly getting into trouble.

"I'll pay you if you get the door," Katie begged.

Tuck hugged the bowl of popcorn on his lap tight and kept his eyes glued to the TV. "No way. You said that last time. Your turn."

Katie sighed, hoisting herself off the couch. It was close to nine. Wasn't that late to still be out trick-or-treating? She picked up the bowl of Halloween candy resting on the coffee table. There wasn't much left. *Too bad*, she thought. *You snooze, you lose.*

Opening the door, she was disheartened to see a large kid standing there in a hockey jersey and a goalie mask, holding a pillow case in one hand and a bloodied hockey stick in the other.

"Trick or treat," croaked a gravelly voice.

Katie frowned. She disliked teenage trick-or-treaters. They deprived smaller kids of candy. It wasn't right.

"Let me guess," she said blandly as she tossed a small bag of M&Ms into the pillowcase. "You're supposed to be Jason."

"No."

"Whatever." Katie closed the door. She was halfway back to the couch when the doorbell rang again. She hadn't noticed any other kids walking up the front path to her house, which meant the only one who could possibly be ringing the bell again was Jason. Annoyed, she turned heel and flung the door open.

"*Yes?*"

"I've decided I don't like this treat. I'd rather play a trick."

Katie froze. The voice was different. Familiar. This time she noticed what was printed across the front of the hockey jersey. It was the Blades' logo.

"*Paul?*"

He laughed delightedly as he removed the goalie mask.

"Oh my God!" Katie leaned against the doorframe for support.

"Can I come in?"

Katie pulled herself together. "Yes, of course."

Quaking inside, she led him into the living room. Tuck's screams of delight when he saw who it was threatened to shatter the windows.

"Coach van Dorn!" Tuck leapt up from the couch, throwing his arms around Paul. "What are you doing here?"

"What does it look like I'm doing?" Paul said, dropping his mask, pillowcase and hockey stick so he could embrace the boy back. "I'm trick-or-treating."

Tuck frowned. "You didn't come here for that."

"You're right. I didn't." His gaze fastened on Katie.

Katie flushed. "Can I get you anything to drink?"

"I'm fine." Paul eyed the couch. "Mind if I sit?"

"Feel free."

Tuck leaped on to the couch beside him, barely able to contain himself. "Coach, guess what? I'm first-line center for my new hockey team and they're not as good as the Panthers but it's fun and guess what? I'm taking a computer class and I was a hockey player for Halloween too and got tons of stuff do you want some Starbursts?"

"I would love some Starbursts in a little while," Paul

said, shooting Katie a sidelong look. "But right now, I'd like to talk to your aunt alone for a few minutes, if that's okay with you."

"Totally okay," Tuck declared, bolting off the couch. He turned to Katie. "Can I play on the computer?"

"Go ahead," said Katie, who usually limited his computer time. "But only because this is a special occasion."

"Cool!" Tuck exclaimed, disappearing up the stairs.

Katie turned to Paul. "You do realize he'll probably hover on the landing and listen to every word we say."

"That's okay." Paul nodded with approval as he glanced around the living room. "Very nice. You have good taste." His eyes slid to hers. "I think I'll like living here."

"Excuse me?"

Paul reached for her hand, holding it tight. The gesture felt pure, preordained. Katie held her breath. "I had an epiphany," Paul continued.

"Big SAT word."

"You bet." His eyes were guileless, filled with such raw emotion Katie almost flinched. "I don't want to own a bar in Didsbury the rest of my life."

"I see." Katie's chest began to knot. "Do you know what you want to do?"

He raised his hand to caress her cheek. "Not yet," he confessed softly. "But whatever it is, I want to do it with you. As long as I have you in my future, I don't need to live in the past."

"Paul," she whispered.

"I haven't sold the bar, but I've left it in Frank's hands for now. I have more than enough money to live on while I figure out what I *really* want to do. In the meantime, I thought that maybe—if it's okay with you—I could help you out with Tuck."

"Okay?" Katie repeated incredulously, choking back

tears of joy. She took his face in her hands. "It's more than okay. Ever since I left Didsbury I've been kicking myself for what an uptight jerk I was with you. You had every right to dump me. I was holding back, using Tuck as an excuse because I was afraid if I let myself go, I would fall in love and somehow get sucked back into living in the place I always associated with pain." She touched her forehead to his as her tears began to fall. "But I don't feel that way anymore. Now, when I think of Didsbury, I think of you, and my mom, and all the laughs I had with Bitsy and Denise. I think about all the things you said about how it shaped me."

"But you still don't want to live there."

"No."

"Well, that works out perfectly, then, because neither do I."

Katie raised her eyes to his. "You know what I want?"

"Tell me."

"I want to look in your eyes and let you take my breath away, and the next minute want to kill you because you've left the toilet seat up. I want to reach across my bed and feel you there, solid, real, *mine*. I love you."

"I love you, too, Katie."

"Hooray!" Tuck came flying down the stairs. He couldn't stop moving, hopping excitedly from foot to foot as he grinned at both of them.

"I thought you were playing on your computer," Katie noted.

"I was," Tuck insisted, "but I had to go to the bathroom and I heard you talking."

"I see." Katie suppressed a laugh. "I guess you heard that Coach van Dorn is moving in with us."

Tuck nodded fervently. "Maybe you can coach my hockey team," he said to Paul. "Coach Talbert is a dick."

"Tuck," Katie scolded. "Don't say 'dick.'"

Tuck's mouth fell open in protest as he pointed at Paul. "He does! He said it in the locker room last year! I remember!"

Katie shot Paul a look of disbelief.

"That's true, I did," Paul admitted carefully, "but I probably shouldn't have."

"You know what I think?" said Katie, rising from the couch. "I think we need a group hug."

Both Tuck and Paul groaned.

"Oh, c'mon," Katie chided.

Tuck said something under his breath and Paul rolled his eyes. But Katie paid no attention, gathering them in a bone-crushing embrace of love and hope. For now, they were a family.